CW00523753

95/250

The Fete of Douglas Blouse

Matthew F. Zimmer

ISBN 978-1-914408-71-7

Printed in Great Britain by
Biddles Books Limited, King's Lynn, Norfolk

For Sam

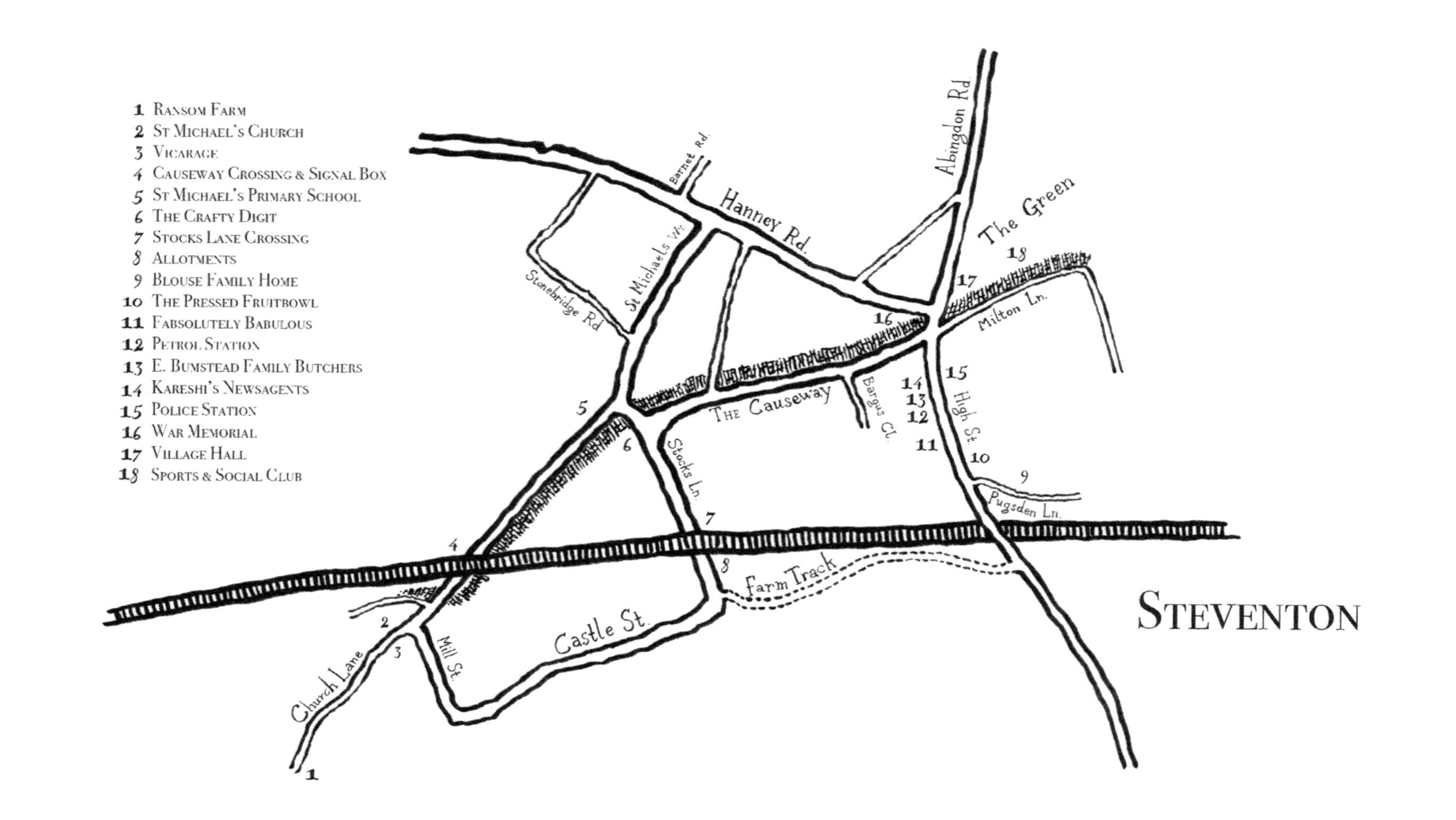
Steventon
1 Ransom Farm
2 St Michael's Church
3 Vicarage
4 Causeway Crossing & Signal Box
5 St Michael's Primary School
6 The Crafty Digit
7 Stocks Lane Crossing
8 Allotments
9 Blouse Family Home
10 The Pressed Fruitbowl
11 Fabsolutely Babulous
12 Petrol Station
13 E. Bumstead Family Butchers
14 Kareshi's Newsagents
15 Police Station
16 War Memorial
17 Village Hall
18 Sports & Social Club
Abingdon Rd
Barnet Rd.
Hanney Rd.
The Green
Stonebridge Rd
St Michaels Wy.
Milton Ln.
The Causeway
Bargus Cl.
High St.
Stocks Ln.
Pugsden Ln.
Farm Track
Castle St.
Mill St.
Church Lane

PROLOGUE

October 1987

'I am God,' the man in the dark overalls messianically proclaimed, striding out of the causeway's dark tunnel of horse chestnut trees and onto the pavement next to the war memorial. Looking at the man, with his arms held out in a Christ-like pose after once again bringing light to the world, Douglas Blouse, standing with his father on the opposite side of the road, almost believed him.

The man claiming to be God and wearing an enormous grin stood on the High Street of the village of Steventon, which after nearly four nights spent in complete darkness was once again bathed in the familiar and reassuring artificial orange glow of the streetlights overhead. In their homes, people were turning their television sets back on to their favourite programmes, electric kettles were bubbling and boiling in the kitchen, school uniforms were being hastily washed, dried and ironed and the candles that had been illuminating those same homes for the past few nights were, with a palpable sense of relief, finally being extinguished.

It turned out that God, real name Mike, actually worked for the electricity board, and after the winds came seemingly out of nowhere on the night of Thursday 15 October 1987, God, along with many others who shared his profession, had been an extremely busy man. The whole of the south-east of England had been pretty much without power since the storm arrived, wreaking unprecedented damage and swathing a path of destruction across the south of England. In the bubble of their little village, power lines had been damaged, trees had been uprooted, roof tiles had been blown off and dustbins rolled in the streets, spewing their contents and sending litter swirling into the air.

Douglas Blouse was glad that the storm hadn't come the week before, otherwise they would have missed his dad appearing on *Bullseye.* It seemed that almost everyone in the village had seen him on telly, and they had all congratulated him on how well he'd done. Now, even God himself offered his warm congratulations, and the caravan was due to arrive next week. Douglas thought that whoever had been on last night's episode must have been pretty disappointed after the power cut.

Douglas hadn't watched television now since Thursday night, just as the winds had really started picking up. When he woke up on Friday morning, the TV didn't work. Nothing did, in their house or anyone else's for that matter. Nearly four whole days now without television or music. He would be sure to switch it on when he got home tonight though, if mum hadn't done so already. He had school in the morning but he didn't care, he wanted to watch something, anything, just to know it was all right again. And listen to music. Maybe both at the same time just to make up for it.

They'd been given the Friday off following the storm; it looked as if everyone had, including the adults. It was like a snow day, only this time it was branches, tiles and rubbish that covered the streets and hampered people's progress to either work or school.

For Douglas the weekend had been fun, wandering around the village looking at all the damage and destruction the storm had brought; climbing on parts of fallen trees on the village green that only a few days ago he'd been gazing up at; looking from the railway bridge down onto the tracks at all the workmen trying to clear the fallen branches and debris that littered the railway, in an attempt to get the trains running back to normal. Douglas had thought how dangerous it must be for the workmen on the railway; but also kind of fun.

It had all made for good entertainment and a welcome distraction, but he had to go back into school this morning to start the new week. Then tomorrow, and then the next day, and the next day, and so it would go on. Forever, it seemed.

Secondary school, big school, had started for him in September, and he was not enjoying it one bit. He'd never felt so out of his depth. It wasn't like at primary school. Primary was small and everyone knew everyone, even if they weren't necessarily friends. Plus he couldn't make his own way to school any more. Now, instead of the short walk down the causeway, he was having to catch the bus (the shelter of which had been blown away by the storm on Thursday night) to make the daunting four-mile journey into town with the other children, some of whom attended his new school, some of whom didn't; some of whom were his age, some older, a lot older; and bigger, much bigger. Dad had assured him that everything was going to be OK with school, and that he shouldn't worry, and Douglas believed him. Why shouldn't he?

Douglas now stood with his dad in the restored illumination of the High Street. The storm had passed and a calm had been re-established in their village; a sense of normality had returned. Maybe it would all be OK after all. Douglas tried to put any thoughts of school, or bus rides or bigger kids, out of his mind. He looked up at his dad, still chatting affably with electricity board God, blissfully unaware that in just two weeks from now his father would be gone, and a new storm would be on the horizon. One that would build in intensity over the next six years; six long and painful years. And it would be one that would once again bring devastation to their village.

PART 1

August 1993

1 *Thursday, August 12*

The caravan had arrived on schedule a week after the great storm of 1987, two weeks after Bertie Blouse had been on *Bullseye*. Had it had been delivered the week before, the storm would have ripped it apart. Maybe for Douglas, that would have been for the best. His dad hadn't been around when it was delivered; he had gone by that point. Douglas didn't know why. He also didn't know whether his dad would be coming back. Instead he had been replaced by a six-berth Marauder 500.

It was in the darkened confines of that caravan, now two months shy of its six-year anniversary, that Douglas Blouse threw his darts, a skill inherited from his father; perhaps the only hereditary talent his father had passed on. He certainly hadn't inherited his dad's social skills, or his womanising abilities. Far from it. Though capable of wild displays of extrovert behaviour, he was often an awkward young man who had become more reclusive as he progressed through his teens, choosing to spend more of his time in the caravan listening to heavy metal cassettes, watching borrowed pornographic and horror videos and playing darts, which, in the small hours of a sticky August night, he continued to do.

The board was positioned just over seven feet away, hanging from a screw attached to a cupboard door above the banquette seating. The meagre orange light cast by the outside street light filtered through the shabby net curtains, barely strong enough to illuminate either the board or the tatty photograph that was pinned to it.

His aim was beginning to let him down, but each tungsten-tipped arrow still hit the face of the man in the picture: the man that once upon a time he had called dad. The picture was pierced with the prick marks of a thousand darts, the face now beyond recognition. The round red dot of the bullseye showed through from behind the man's forehead like an over-sized Hindu Bindi.

Douglas didn't know exactly when the electricity to the house, and therefore also to the caravan, had gone off; and, unlike after the storm back in '87 when that bloke who said he was God had restored the power to the village, he didn't know when, or even if, it would be coming back on. For unlike back in '87, it wasn't the whole of the south-east of England that was without power, or even the whole of the village for that matter. It was just them. This caravan, and the bungalow on whose driveway it was parked.

A lengthy white extension cord snaked out from the bungalow's faded brass letterbox, winding its way into the caravan through an open window, all of which were open. The days had been hot lately, and the nights were muggy. The caravan's gloomy interior was stuffy and uncomfortable; something that did little to improve Douglas's mood.

The extension cable was of no use any more, thus rendering the numerous appliances overloading it surplus to requirements. Douglas had manically unplugged them all and posted the useless extension cable back through the letterbox, giving a short, frenzied pull on the door handle as he did so.

The house was locked.

The small petrol generator he sometimes used as a back-up on occasions such as this had run out of juice about three hours ago. Poor timing indeed, given he was right in the middle of *Night of the Giving Head*, the zombie-themed porno film he had borrowed some time ago now from his friend Peter Glass. Still, he didn't have to worry about returning it, or any of the other pirate tapes he had littered around the caravan, back to their rightful owner, because Peter was dead, and his fat, alcoholic dad, Graham, video bootlegger and ex darts partner of his own father, wouldn't be venturing out to retrieve them. He barely ever left his armchair.

Douglas thought about syphoning some petrol out of the decaying Ford Orion parked next to the caravan, if there was any left in it. Doubtful, considering how many times it had been done previously. The family car hadn't moved in years, and what petrol had been left in the tank had been steadily exanguinated or evaporated over that time. The last time it had belched fumes from its sawn off exhaust pipe was when Peter had shown Douglas how to hotwire it.

Shame about the generator though, Douglas thought; the zombie-themed porno was just getting to the good bit as well. The hordes of horny undead were banging away at the poorly executed attempts at DIY on the isolated house's doors and windows, carried out by its increasingly terrified semi-naked occupants, and it was just a matter of time before they broke in and had themselves some fun. He'd seen it plenty of times before, but that was beside the point. *Night of the Giving Head* was a classic in Douglas's eyes, second only to its sequel, *Return of the Giving Head* (a very similar offering, only this time set in a hospital).

Not that there was much chance of watching either now though, he thought, kicking a cupboard in frustration, the stifling heat of the caravan enveloping him like a blanket of oppressive humidity. His black jeans felt like they were grafted to his legs, his *Number of the Beast* T-shirt clung to his back. He kicked the cupboard again, this time making a hole in it.

The amusing memory of the porn film had deserted him, just like everyone else had. He continued to pace, throwing darts into the gloomy orange darkness. He emitted a jagged, tittery laugh as he threw the arrows. He could feel the anger rising in his stomach as he looked at the man (what was left of him anyway) in the photograph, as his darts became increasingly wayward.

He was alone, and for the first time he really felt it: dad gone six years and now mum too; the one person he'd always had to rely on had left him as well.

He had hit rock bottom.

Outside, in the still of the night, he heard a train. The sound momentarily energised him, and he thought he might go down to the railway. That was always fun. A good rush and a welcome distraction from how he was feeling.

Rock bottom.

He threw another dart as the two words rolled around in his head like Chinese stress balls, an idea forming in his over-heated brain. He threw the last of the three darts, leaving the three arrows grouped satisfactorily together in what was left of his dad's nose. He reached into one of the cupboards above the small table that in the caravan's promotional brochure described itself as 'the Dining Area', and grabbed at a sheaf of papers. He smiled, looking at the identical black and white image printed on each page; the strange tittering laugh again escaped him as he thought back to that day in the newsagent's when he had been chased out of there by Mr Kareshi, who had wasted no time in going over the road and reporting him to the police, who had subsequently paid them a visit, mum defending him as she always did. But she wouldn't any more. Now he was on his own.

Fuckin' old bill, Douglas thought, shaking his head and wiping the slick sheen of sweat from his brow.

He slapped the wodge of papers down on the caravan's dining table, a disturbing smile forming on his lips and a plan now firmly taking shape in his mind. He searched around the messy confines of the caravan for a carrier bag, eventually finding a blue and white striped one, ironically from the newsagent's, in a drawer. He put the papers in it, exited the caravan and stepped into the muggy night of the outside world. He looked over at the dark dormant bungalow, a place that once upon a time, though it was unbelievable to him now, had been their family home. He turned away from it, not caring if he ever saw it again.

He started to walk up the lane, but turned back, as if suddenly remembering something very important. He re-entered the caravan, picked up the meat cleaver lying on the side next to the television, picked it up and slammed it into the dartboard. Flakes of dry, crusty blood fell from the cleaver's dull, hefty blade, the tiny flakes descending in the orange glow of the caravan's gloomy interior like a shaken snow globe. The board wobbled precariously, pitched forward with the weight of the cleaver and fell to the ground. Douglas emitted a loud hyena-like laugh, bordering on hysteria, turned and exited the caravan, slamming the door as loudly as he could behind him, hoping to wake up the neighbours. He laughed again, and again, and decided that he would head for the railway. It was only a stone's throw away, after all.

2 *Friday*

Butch Ransom delicately pushed the last six inches of pink material under the glinting steel foot of the sewing machine. Beneath the desk, his foot tentatively exerted pressure on the grey plastic pedal, maintaining a smooth and steady tempo. If he had been driving a car, it would have been moving at a consistent ten miles an hour, such was the sheep farmer's hard- learned caution.

When he'd first plugged it in six weeks ago, he'd operated the pedal as if he was ram-raiding an off-licence, the material speeding under his rampant foot in a tangled mess that left Butch in abject frustration at what then seemed to be an impossible task. He had come a long way since that day.

He smiled to himself, not quite believing his achievements. The eyes behind the wire-rimmed spectacles perched on the end of his nose shone in the evening sun, as he gleefully watched pink silk unite with white lace. The sewing machine's small light bulb burned like a miniature sun, illuminating the glistening sheen of sweat that coated the farmer's naked upper torso. Beads of sweat dripped from his forehead, down his nose and into his lap, pattering in dark blue droplets on to his cut-off denim shorts.

He fed the last of the material through the machine, took his foot off the pedal, drew the cotton out from the bobbin and cut the slack on the machine's hooked incisor. He picked up the silk garment and tied off the cotton in a neat knot, snipping the straggly piece of left-over thread. He threw it down onto the desk with a delicate but heart-felt enthusiasm, turned off the taunting light of the sewing machine, punched two proud fists into the air, and in his thick Kiwi accent righteously proclaimed, 'Fuckin' stitch that, ya bastard!'

Finn, his faithful sheepdog dozing in the basket behind him, looked up to see what had caused his master to break the almost three hours of solid silence.

Butch straightened up in his small black office chair, emitting a lengthy groan as he did so, having been bent over the sewing machine nearly every night for the past four weeks. He planted his feet firmly on the carpet and pushed himself away from it, happily putting distance between himself and the once alien contraption that had at first tormented him, then goaded him, then at last became compliant, before finally becoming his subordinate as he honed his mastery of the machine.

His faded All Blacks rugby shirt hung on the back of his chair. He turned, perched his glasses on his head and wiped the sweat from his brow with one of its sleeves. With a desperate enthusiasm Butch rolled over to the corner of the room and switched the tower fan back on, groaning in pleasure as the breeze fluttered over the chiselled contours of his upper body. The heat wave they had all been experiencing lately seemed to come to life the day he started work on his new creation, as if to taunt him, and he would forever associate the creation of this dress with the oppressive sweatshop-like conditions of his unforgiving back bedroom. He figured he must have lost a few pounds in the process. All good though, as far as he was concerned. A leaner, meaner physique would do quite nicely for the already well chiselled Kiwi.

Looking proudly at the shimmering pink dress in the fading light of the summer evening, Butch Ransom was happy with his work; and even happier that he hadn't thrown the machine at the wall on day one. He couldn't wait to see Barbara down at the village hall later, to tell her the good news.

He checked his watch: just gone half seven. 'Shit,' he said, not knowing once again where the time had gone. 'Gotta go, boy,' he said to the dozing dog.

Like a prisoner exuberant in his liberation, Butch leapt up from the office chair, grabbing the rugby shirt off its back. He left the fan on and the window open in the hope that by the time he got back, the place wouldn't feel like such a sweatbox. Finn followed him lazily as he exited the room and headed downstairs, the sheepdog's feet gently padding behind him as he descended. He picked up his white vest from off the bannister and struggled to pull it on over his sweaty upper torso. After tying his shirt around his waist, he grabbed his keys and made for the front door.

'Keep an eye on the place,' he said, winking at Finn as he went out.

Butch headed down the side of the house to where his bike stood; he checked the tyre pressure of both wheels, pushing his thumb down on the warm dusty rubber. Satisfied, he clipped on a red back light to the frame and wheeled the bike to the front garden gate. The meeting wouldn't take that long, he hoped. Usual pre-fete business to discuss, but after everything that had happened in the village yesterday, there could well be a little bit more added drama than usual. So he took his lights just in case.

He left his shirt tied round his waist, relishing the modest cool of the evening against his bare arms and legs. His legs had become increasingly exposed over recent weeks, following numerous shortenings to his cut-offs due to the exponential increase in temperature. These denims were now dangerously short; almost Daisy Dukes. Butch was in good shape for a man just past forty: you had to be to do his type of work, and he took pride in maintaining his physique. Plus the women loved it. Butch hoped there'd be a few down at the meeting later, to justify his minimalist wardrobe selection.

Heading away from his picturesque farm standing on Steventon's south-western edge, home to himself, his dog Finn and just over a hundred sheep, Butch built up steady speed on his mountain bike, the chain squeaking and the gears clattering as he increased his effort, youthfully jumping the speed bumps that ran across the faded grey tarmac of the road.

He passed the church on his left as he came into the village. Slowing slightly and standing up on his pedals, Butch craned his neck to get a better view of the damage inflicted on the old building's rear stained glass window. In the fading light of early evening, Butch could still just about make out the hole that seemed to have caught our Lord and Saviour squarely in the groin.

The Causeway came into view on his right. The ancient raised walkway was a true historical feature of the village, serving as its mile-long cobbled spine, dissecting the full length of the village from the church in the south-west to the far end of the village green in the north-east. Butch cycled parallel to the luscious green canopy of horse chestnuts that lined its length. It felt as if the big lung-like trees were breathing sweet cool oxygen directly onto his muscular frame.

As he approached the railway line, Butch was glad to see that the tall red and white barriers of the level crossing were in their raised position, and the red eyes of the warning lights that stood either side of the road were dark and inactive. All was quiet. Unlike yesterday, he thought, recalling the drama of the previous day.

Butch crested the modest incline that took him up and over the railway, theatrically blowing kisses at his friend Dan Fowler up in the signal box. Fowler waved back, at first not realising who it was. When he saw it was Butch, his hand immediately curled around an invisible penis, which he then began to shake vigorously. Like the church, the signal box had suffered similar damage, as Fowler's DIY cardboard window attested to.

Butch pressed on, still running parallel with the causeway, approaching the give-way junction, with Saint Michael's School on his left and The Crafty Digit pub, unusually quiet for this time on a Friday night, on his right.

Butch veered right, the causeway now on his left. The smell of the dense green foliage, mixed with the smell of fried food and warm beer coming from the pub, were intoxicating, and Butch inhaled it all deep into his lungs as he pedalled on towards the village hall in the quiet stillness of the summer evening.

The peace and quiet was not to last for much longer, however, as if someone was slowly turning a volume control up, the voices of four men looming in front grew louder. The raucous sound of one man in particular pierced the stillness of the night, sounding more like the incessant cawing of the crows that could often be heard in the trees beside him. A murder of crows, that was the collective term for a group of crows, wasn't it? Cool term that, Butch thought. What did you call this lot then? Butch thought he knew. A bunch of piss heads, that's what.

They were in fact Morris dancers, though they were in civilian clothes this evening. Butch was on first-name terms with them all, as he was with most people in the village. He could make out the doddery outline of Colin Blunsden, the man accounting for about eighty per cent of the noise currently being made by the group. He could see Colin reaching for some much-needed stability as he slipped on the kerb, nearly going arse over head, close to taking lead dancer Terence Russell, and the blue washing bag that Terence was carrying with him. Beside them were fellow dancers Bob Dobson and Gerry Hayman. As Butch drew closer, he could hear Terence and Colin squabbling. He hung back, grinning, stealthily listening to their exchange.

'Colin, please, try and get a hold of yourself,' Terence said, almost pleadingly, shaking his head. 'You were meant to be giving it a rest today, remember? What's everyone going to think when they see you turning up like this? And more importantly, what will they think of us? It's a big day for us tomorrow, remember? Home town show? Or have you forgotten that as well in your booze-addled brain? Your drinking's got worse, I'm telling you. That money isn't going to last forever, you know.'

'It's my money and I'll do what I want with it, all right?' Blunsden answered back, teetering on the edge of the curb again. 'You're going on like a bleddy old woman, Terence. I need a drink to calm me nerves after what that little Blouse bastard done to my shed. And all my boys he smashed all to bollocks. They never hurt nobody, Terence. The bleddy bastard vandal!' he spat.

'Evening, chaps!' Butch said, breaking cover and swerving towards the ambling foursome, making Colin jump in the process. 'Lovely evening for it.'

'Well well well, if it isn't the man who caught The Ripper!' Terence said.

'What can I say? Right place, right time. Someone's got to be around to save the day, eh? I trust we are all well and looking forward to tomorrow?'

'Ohh absolutely, Butch,' Terence beamed. 'Me and the boys have been practising hard for this one.' He lowered his tone, drawing Butch a little closer. 'Just got to try and keep certain members of the team away from the bar, if you know what I mean,' he said, cocking a thumb towards Colin and his trusty drinking companion Bob Dobson ambling beside him. 'Been letting the side down a bit lately, haven't they, Gerry,? Terence said, addressing the tanned middle-aged man walking beside him.

'They have a bit, chief, yeah. You expect a bit more professionalism, don't you? Especially for a performance like tomorrow. I mean, it's a big occasion tomorrow, isn't it? I know I'm excited.'

'And you can shut up n'all, Gerry, you big bleddy teacher's pet,' Colin said. 'You only been with us for five minutes, and suddenly you think you're a bleddy big shot. You're an apple polisher, that's all you are.'

'Colin, you could do a lot worse than take a leaf out of Gerry's book,' Terence said. 'He may be new but at least he shows some enthusiasm, a bit of drive and passion, which is more than can be said for you two at the moment. I don't have to go dragging him out of the pub every practice now, do I?'

'Bleddy teacher's pet,' Colin mumbled. 'Probably can't handle his drink anyway.'

'These two been liquidising their assets again, have they?' Butch said, shaking his head at Colin and Bob. 'Naughty, naughty.'

'You can shut up n'all, ya big sod,' Colin mumbled derisively.

'That redundancy money will be the death of them two, Butch, I'm sure of it. Ever since that brewery let them go, I can hardly keep them out of the Digit.' Terence once again lowered his voice to a conspiratorial tone. 'I still don't think it's quite sunk in with Bob there. He's hardly said a word since they gave him the bullet. Over two months now, barely said a word. "Pint", that's about all I've heard him say. Thank God he can still dance, that's all I can say, at least he hasn't been robbed of that,' Terence said. 'It's just like he's in shock or something. I think that job meant a lot more to him than we might've thought.'

'He's happy enough,' Colin said boisterously, overhearing the conversation. 'Gives us a bit of time to enjoy the finer things in life, dunnit, Bob?' he said, patting him repeatedly on the back. Bob just stared blankly back at him as they carried on walking towards the hall.

'Bloody 'ell, Butch,' Colin said, 'you shorrem shorrs bleddy shorrtnuff!'

Everybody except Bob Dobson burst out laughing at Colin's slurred attempt.

'I beg your pardon, Colin? Perhaps we can have that again in English,' Butch said.

'Your bleddy shorts,' he said, 'you'll 'ave a bollock fall out if you ain't careful.'

Butch grinned. 'You wish, ya dirty pervert. Anyway I'll see you all down there,' Butch said. He pedalled back on himself, rounding in on the awesome foursome. He raised his arm on approach, as if preparing to deliver an under-arm tennis serve. With perfect timing Colin Blunsden again stumbled from the path. 'And no more drinking, you naughty boy!' Butch said, as the flat of his hand connected with the elderly dancer's backside.

'Bleddy aussie twat!' he yelled in high pitched tones, clutching at his buttocks as Butch disappeared into the distance.

'How many times do I have to tell you, Col!?' Ransom called out over his shoulder, his voice loud and strong in the stillness of the early evening ... 'I'm a bloody Kiwi!'

Butch pressed on, crossing the High Street and veering into the village hall car park, taking in the landscape of the large village green as he dismounted. The vibrancy of the grass was subdued by dusk's failing light. In complete contrast to how it would look tomorrow, the green was eerily quiet.

Wheeling his bike towards the side wall of the village hall, Butch made a quick inventory of the vehicles in the car park, his attention chiefly drawn to the large three-wheeled trike belonging to Reverend Hilda Bowen parked between a very flash-looking red and white Honda Fireblade and the luminously striped Police Ford Transit van belonging to Sergeant Frisk.

As he leant his bike up against the wall, locking it to one of three metallic bike rings, he heard the trill of a bell and the call of a familiar voice.

'Coooeeeeh!' The voice said, getting closer. 'Good evening, my lovely leaping New Zealand lamb!'

Smiling as he pocketed his bike key, and unable to prevent the pride he felt for his textile achievements bursting forth, Butch gleefully responded, beaming at his sewing guru. 'Guess what I finished, Barb?'

'You did it? Finished?' Barbara Rix said, surprised. 'Ohh sweetheart, I am glad. I knew you could do it, my love. I knew you wouldn't give up on it, really well done,' she said, dismounting her bike and giving Butch a short sharp embrace. 'I told you you'd get the hang of it in the end, didn't I?' she said, with genuine pleasure. 'Oh, I can't wait to see it.'

Ransom's smile remained. 'Oh you will, Barb, my sweet, you will,' he said. 'Did they come and replace your window yet?' he asked, changing the subject to a far less celebratory topic.

'Yes ... eventually, but not until this afternoon!' she said, with more than a hint of displeasure marring her usual chirpy nature. 'Not yesterday afternoon like they first thought, or this morning at the latest like they promised,' she said, shaking her head of short auburn hair. 'Still, at least it's all done now. And the new one really does look lovely, and it's double-glazed,' she said with enthusiastic reassurance, 'so it's a lot stronger and harder to break. I just need to get the shop sign printed on the inside of it and it will be as good as new,' she beamed.

'Fabsolutely Babulous!' Butch said, at the same time congratulating her on her new window, and quoting the quirky name of Barbara Rix's wool and fabrics shop.

'Thank you again for all your help yesterday, Butch,' she said, leaning her own push bike up against the wall. 'It was really lovely of you to help me. Let's just hope that things can settle down a bit now.'

'Wouldn't bet on it, Barb,' Butch replied robustly, nodding towards the collection of vehicles parked up outside the hall. 'But we'll see, eh. Stivvy's most wanted is safely under lock and key.'

'Thanks to you,' she said.

'Right place, right time,' Butch said. 'Be interesting what they've got to say about young Douglas's recent behaviour tonight though, eh? Pushed his luck a little too far this time, I'd say. I mean, smashing a few windows is one thing, but what he did to Daisy and then Hilda's dog, well, that's another level, eh? No wonder they're out in force tonight. I shouldn't think Petra and the good reverend are going to be feeling in a very merciful mood after what Douglas put them through. And the strong arm of the law in attendance,' Butch said, nodding towards the police van. 'I think that shows they must be taking it pretty seriously.' Butch smiled and clapped his hands, rubbing them together. 'So it should make for a good show, eh?' he said.

Barbara Rix did not return his smile, only shook her head in dismay. 'I don't think it's something to celebrate, Butch,' she said, picking up a textile bag from her bike's front basket. 'And still no sign of mum?'

'Not that I know of,' Butch said. 'All quiet at Chez Blouse.'

Barbara rifled through her bag, frowning. 'Bugger my old bags, I've forgotten my lock!' she said, immediately raising her hand to her mouth in a belated attempt at self-censorship.

'Well I have buggered a few old bags in my time, Barb,' Butch said breezily, 'but I'll be damned if I'm going to start doing it in the car park.'

Barbara slapped him playfully on the arm. 'I'm telling Hilda about that one,' she said.

'I bet she's come out with far worse than that herself over the past couple of days,' Butch said, raising his eyebrows. 'I bet she even dropped the C word a couple of times during all yesterday's excitement,' Butch said. Barbara's eyes widened in shock at Ransom's suggestions.

'Butch, don't you dare say that word in my presence.'

'Cuuu ... Cuuu ...Cuuuuuu' ... he teased, causing Barbara to whack him on the arm again with her bag.

'Butch ... I'm warning you,' she said slowly.

'Cuuuuumon. Let's get inside,' he said winking and smiling cheekily. 'I'll lock your bike up to mine.'

From his elevated position seated at the long table on the village hall's stage, Sergeant Alan Frisk, wearing his police uniform of blue short-sleeved shirt, black trousers and black tie, watched Butch Ransom and Barbara Rix enter the bustling hall arm in arm. He would eventually be joined by Reverend Bowen and fellow police officer, dog handler Sergeant Laurie Knox. The pair were currently in conversation off to his left, so at the moment it was only himself and Steventon's formidable head parish councillor, Petra Carr, at the table.

Frisk detected an audible swoon and turning of heads from some of the females in attendance as Butch entered the hall with Barbara. Frisk gave them both a smile and a nod from the stage as the pair made their way through the centre aisle of chairs and took their seats on the hall's left-hand side.

Along with a glass of water to his right and an improvised name plaque in front of him, Sergeant Frisk had before him a collection of five crumpled pieces of A4 paper, each showing the same offensive black and white image of a photocopied rear end; the owner of which, Frisk now knew for sure, was Douglas Blouse. The pieces of paper were integral to tonight's meeting, and the five large chunks of railway ballast that had each been wrapped in the paper also took their place on the table, sitting before the police officer like a small Viking burial mound.

To Frisk's left sat Petra Carr, head of Steventon parish council, an individual whom Sargeant Frisk knew only too well. Her constant demands on his time, combined with her condescending attitude, was a continual source of nuisance to Frisk. Almost always consumed with matters of total self-interest, Carr treated him like her own one-man police force, and after yesterday's incident involving Douglas and her daughter Daisy, this approach had gone into overdrive. Mercifully at the moment she was concerning herself with the makeshift name plaques that sat in front of the four members of tonight's panel. She turned over the piece of card in her hand, reversing the DIY plaque to reveal part of the Toblerone logo that made up the underside of the card.

'I mean, how unprofessional can one get, Alan?' she said. 'I mean, look at this. The annual general meeting for the Steventon village fete, attended by respected law enforcement professionals, the head of the parish council and church leaders, and what does that lazy woman come up with? Mis-spelt names scribbled on the back of a chocolate wrapper. And that was supposed to be a raffle prize! She can jolly well pay for that herself. Honestly, Edna Glass's standards really have dropped. I'm beginning to think that she couldn't give two hoots about any of this, you know. I don't think it's too much to ask, do you?'

Frisk gave a non-committal grunt, trying to avoid engaging with Petra. He thought that the packaging worked quite well, although he didn't say so, and he was quite surprised Edna had not chosen to write something rude or insulting on his, given their own personal history. He let the moment pass however, intending to keep chitchat down to a minimum with the parish council's illustrious leader until the meeting was underway. His shirt was sticking to his back, and his black trousers were hot and itchy, and badly in need of a wash.

'And where is Edna now, I wonder?' she continued to herself, surveying the growing crowd, arms folded. 'Oh, she's no doubt over at that bar, a drink in one hand and a cigarette in the other, chatting up whichever Tom, Dick or Harry comes close enough.'

'The bar she's working behind, that you insisted she open,' Frisk said, instantly regretting his comment.

'Yes, Alan, and why is that, hmm? Do you think that maybe we might need something to steady our nerves a little after what that dog-napping pervert put us through yesterday? Honestly, you were there, you've seen what he did to Hilda, what he tried to do to my poor Daisy. The boy is deranged,

Alan, and tonight he is going to get what he jolly well deserves, you mark my words.'

Sergeant Frisk had tuned out from Petra Carr's self-centred monologue, his focus was on the black and white image in front of him. The infamous backside that every train driver working on the Great Western Railway line was now wearily familiar with. He thought of all the times he'd had to go round to knock on the door of Alice Blouse over the years, to tell her the same old story, give her the same warnings. Douglas never listened. Despite all the safety videos he had shown them at primary school, warning them of the dangers of the railway. Thinking back, Frisk believed that all it did was encourage him. So now Douglas was sitting in a police cell, facing the consequences of his actions, alone. His punishment was soon to be made public, and guaranteed to overshadow all other points of order concerning tomorrow's fete listed on the itemised agenda, also on the table in front of him.

Alan Frisk looked at his own name plaque, mulling over the confectionery logo on its underside, trying not to think about how hungry he was. He did a quick mental inventory in his head of the contents of the fridge, scratching the burgeoning brown stubble that sprouted from his chin, though some white ones were beginning to sprout through, he'd recently noticed. He was left disappointed by his culinary prospects. He'd already eaten the lasagne ready meals Jenny had left for him. Other than pushing a couple of buttons on the microwave, he was not great at feeding himself. He could just about manage if required, it's just he'd never had to. Now she had gone away for the weekend to visit her sister, mad auntie Pam, as he called her, who was 'unwell', as his wife labelled her sister's ongoing mental health issues.

He'd been annoyed by Jenny's decision to go, and they'd had a bit of a row. She knew what his job was like, the shift patterns and the inconsistencies of him being around. But that was what it was like when you married a policeman, and she knew that. After much to-ing and fro-ing, Jenny had phoned her mum and it was agreed that they would look after their nine-year-old daughter Katy until her return, hopefully sometime on Sunday. Hopefully.

As for the here and now, well, he just had to get on with it. His focus shifted back to the hall, and the continued murmurings that filled it. Off to his left, in the wings of the small stage, still deep in conversation, were Reverend Hilda Bowen and police dog handler Sergeant Laurie Knox. Reverend Bowen, all in black, stood facing away from the crowd, her face in the shadow of the drawn curtain. Frisk detected Petra making eyes at them, as if intimating that she would like them both to come and take their places at the table. As the wall clock hit one minute to eight, Carr began flapping her hands at Knox and Bowen, indicating in her own inimitable way that she wanted them to come and take their seats.

Keeping her head bowed and walking behind Sergeant Knox, the pair made their way towards the table, Knox chivalrously holding the seat out for Reverend Bowen, her black leather waistcoat adorned with the colours of her Christian motorcycle group hung on the back of her chair. Knox took his seat beside her.

The village hall was now almost full and the murmurings continued even after Petra Carr had limply brought down her wooden gavel three times on the table. Frisk had seen this piece of theatre many times at previous meetings. Never one to miss out on displays of self-centred superiority, Petra Carr often brought her wooden gavel with her. Always one to make sure people knew exactly who was in charge, even if the execution looked more like that of a substitute teacher trying to control a bottom set of unruly school boys. The crowd barely noticed and the mumbling continued as she raised the gavel once again, but it was not the sound of the hammer coming down that brought the crowd to a hush, but that of the village hall's side doors unceremoniously clattering open, and the vociferous sound of Steventon's Morris men, led by Colin Blunsden's crow-like cawing, filling the silence that had momentarily descended on the hall.

Sergeant Frisk had a little smile to himself while Petra Carr looked on contemptuously at the drunken theatrics of the tardy quartet who appeared to be completely oblivious to the many eyes upon them as they ambled into the meeting.

'GENTLEMEN, GENTLEMEN, PLEASE!' Petra squawked, banging her gavel repeatedly on the table, this time finally bringing her to the attention of all present.

Keeping her head low but noting the behaviour of the elderly dancers below her, Reverend Bowen began to slowly shake her head, and Frisk could just about hear her. 'Dear God,' she quietly said to herself, 'Forgive them, for they know not what they do, where they are or what the bloody hell is going on.' Knox, seated beside her, smirked at the comment. Something she did not return.

Petra Carr, now focused entirely on the unsightly disturbance before her, continued her bitter tirade. 'Gentlemen!' she said, 'And I use that term extremely loosely. This meeting was scheduled for eight o'clock sharp. Everyone else got here in plenty of time for its commencement. Myself, Sergeants Knox and Frisk and Reverend Bowen have been here since seven thirty in preparation for tonight's proceedings. And yet here you are, ambling in, disrupting my meeting after the agreed start time, and clearly in no fit state to make any meaningful contribution.'

It was in actual fact only two minutes past eight, and Petra's assessment was a little heavy-handed on the four Morris men, as it was only the loud-mouthed ramblings of Colin Blunsden that were really bringing the group into disrepute. Terence Russell, attempting to act as peace maker in all the hullabaloo, looked rather embarrassed, turning his face up towards the four members of the panel, like the defendant in a trial. He quietened his boys down, flapping his arm at the unruly Blunsden.

'I'm sorry, Petra,' the flustered Terence Russell began. 'It's just, well, the boys are a bit excited about tomorrow, you know. It's special, isn't it, this time of year, playing for a home crowd, and what with practice going so good, well they're all on a bit of a high,' he said, looking down at the floor, 'and, well, I suppose we just lost track of time a little, I'm sorry.'

Or in Colin's case, the last ten years, Sergeant Frisk thought to himself.

'And we ... we think,' Terence Russell went on, cocking a thumb at the dishevelled Blunsden, 'we think Colin here might have had a bit of a toilet accident.'

There was a collective groan from the hall, which soon turned to laughter as Blunsden sluggishly spun round to face the crowd, red-faced and embarrassed, before turning back to face his lead dancer.

'I haven't shit, Terence, you bleddy big-mouthed sod!' he squealed. 'I said I THOUGHT I shit when Butch smacked me on the arse,' Blunsden said, looking around the crowded hall, as if trying to single out the figure of the strapping sheep farmer. 'The big aussie twat,' he continued.

'All right, gents, let's just move it along, shall we,' Sergeant Frisk interjected, rubbing the bridge of his nose, trying to get things back on an even keel. 'Just go and try and find somewhere to sit, will you. Why don't you go over the back there and just stay out of trouble will you ... Look after him, Terence, yes?' Frisk said to the lead dancer.

'Right oh, Sergeant,' he replied courteously. 'Sorry again to be of any disturbance. Come on, lads,' he said to his trailing trio. 'Over here, come on.'

The four men filed past the stage, reminding Sergeant Frisk of the Beatles' Abbey Road album cover, although he didn't remember George Harrison sticking two fingers up in that particular image in the same way that Colin Blunsden did towards the startled Petra Carr as he brought up the rear of the tardy quartet.

'You revolting little man,' she spat as the four men continued on, walking down the side of the hall and, to Frisk's horror, towards the alcoved bar.

Colin Blunsden put a hand on Bob Dobson's shoulder in front of him. 'Actually, Bob, I think I might've shit,' Blunsden casually revealed, a lot louder than clearly intended, but remaining completely oblivious to the sniggering of the meeting's attendees, Butch Ransom included, who slouched in his chair hiding behind Barbara Rix as the Morris men walked past.

Petra Carr did her best to regain her composure, taking a deep breath before retaking her seat. She raised the gavel, looking around at the crowd whose eyes were at last all on her. Forlornly she placed the gavel down beside her glass of water, which she took a sip from.

'Well,' she said, 'now that that ... unpleasantness is behind us, maybe we can continue in some semblance of order. Heaven knows, we've got enough to get through tonight. Also I'm sure that there will be a lot of questions you might have for myself or for the other members of the panel, but if we could please keep those until the end of the meeting I would be most grateful.'

The hall was now in complete silence, save for some distant murmurings emanating from the bar. Petra continued, 'I am sure by now that all of you here are aware in some way or another of the disturbing events that have occurred in our peaceful village over the past couple of days. As you can see by the two members of the Thames Valley police force that make up the panel tonight, this behaviour has not gone unnoticed, nor shall it go UNPUNISHED,' she said, raising her voice. Frisk smiled a little at Petra's attempts to sound tough. 'I wish to address the issue as a matter of utmost importance,' she said, 'and have made it number one priority on tonight's agenda. Ladies and gentlemen, I wish to address the recent actions of one Douglas Blouse.'

There came a sound of murmuring from the hall.

Hearing the name herself, Reverend Bowen, at the end of the panel, took in a deep, audible breath. Her shoulders rose as she slowly lifted her head to face the audience. Once again there was a collective gasp, this time not in amusement or ridicule, but in horror. Horror at the bright red welts that criss-crossed the vicar's face.

4 ...Yesterday

Daisy Carr walked down the grubby stairs of the number 32 double-decker bus feeling pretty damn pleased with herself, and she had good reason, as the piece of paper smouldering in her bag with the three A stars printed on it would attest to.

Stepping off the bus onto the High Street, absent-mindedly forgetting to thank the driver, she was hit by the relentless heat. Her white sleeveless top was sticking to her after the clammy bus journey and she had tied her long blonde hair back to keep it from irritably swishing in her face. She would let it down and wash it later in a nice cool shower. With her exams finally out the way, she could at last really let her hair down.

As she stood on the High Street overwhelmed by thirst, she thought that a visit to Mr Kareshi's newsagent was in order. She contemplated buying a bottle of wine, but decided against it. Mr Kareshi sometimes reported back to her mum if she had been buying alcohol, even though she was now legally able to do so. It could wait. She knew there was one chilling in the fridge at home and that would do nicely.

She rummaged around in her bag, pulling out her water bottle. It had barely an inch of water left in it, and that would be warm and horrible by now. She opened her purse, checking to see how much change she had. Mercifully it was just enough for a can of drink. She couldn't wait to get out of here and start earning some real money. When she was a rich and famous film star, money would never be a problem, and she would buy a big mansion a long way away from this place.

She waited for cars to pass on the High Street. Over at the police station, a man in blue overalls was replacing a window. Daisy crossed to the other side to the newsagent, whose window had also been smashed, a large piece of brown cardboard acting as temporary cover for the damage. She entered the newsagent, immediately grateful for the shop's air conditioning unit. She stood still a moment, basking in it. Mr Kareshi hastily emerged from the back room and took his place behind the counter.

'You seen this, huh? Have you bloody seen this?' The usually placid shopkeeper said, holding up a black and white image which, on closer inspection, Daisy could see was of a photocopied image of a bare backside.

'No, Mr Kareshi, I haven't,' Dasiy said, retrieving a can of ice-cold Sprite from the fridge and trying not to laugh, thinking that Mr Kareshi had no doubt shown this picture to every customer who had frequented his shop today.

'Sod smashed my bloody window,' Mr Kareshi said, jabbing a finger at the picture and then pointing at the damage behind him. A spider's web of cracks spread out from a cricketball-sized hole at the window's centre. 'Bloody bastard Douglas fling a bloody rock wrapped up in this filth. I chase him out of here last month. Sod bloody sitting with his bare backside on my new copier. Brand new piece of bloody equipment,' Mr Kareshi said, nodding over at his photocopier in the corner of the shop. 'Grabbed his filthy pictures and ran, laughing like a child. I chase him out with a bloody Broom, isn't it. You wait till I see Mrs Blouse. I tell her. I bloody tell her!' he said, waving an angry index finger. 'She comes in for magazines for bastard son today, I'll be sure to tell her!' he said, holding up a copy of Kerrang and WWF magazine respectively. 'Magazines come in this morning, but of her so far no bloody sign. Sergeant Alan said there's no sign of mother or bastard son at house or in the caravan. No doubt she is hanging her head in bloody shame,' he said, slapping the magazines down on the counter.

Daisy hadn't had a chance to get a word in amongst Mr Kareshi's relentless rapid-fire monologue. She stood before him holding her can of Sprite to her neck. 'I'm sorry to hear that, Mr Kareshi,' she said, feigning both interest and sympathy. 'He always was a bit of a wrong 'un, was young Douglas.'

'Ahh, young Douglas nothing. It was not just me he smashed in,' Kareshi continued. 'Police, fabric shop, signal box and church,' he said, counting them off on his hand. 'Bloody church! I see Reverend Hilda this morning when I deliver her paper. Smashed her stained glass bloody window of Christ himself right in the private parts!'

Mr Kareshi took a couple of deep breaths. 'You just want the drink?'

'Yes please,' Daisy said.

'55 pence please, love,' he said, holding his hand out. Daisy handed him a warm pound coin. 'You tell mum about bloody damage,' he said, scraping change out of the till. 'You tell mum and bloody council. I tell bloody police but police station window smashed as well. Sergeant Alan got big bloody problem, huh?'

'I guess so, Mr Kareshi. I'll let you know if I hear anything,' she said, heading for the door.

'Remember, you tell mum. Tell bloody council!'

'I will, Mr Kareshi,' she said, exiting the shop, grinning as she closed the door behind her. She opened her Sprite, taking two long swallows and only just dodging a brain freeze. She thought about Mr Kareshi's order. She wouldn't need to tell her mum, she would be well aware of the smashed windows by now. Her mum knew everything around here.

Daisy turned left towards the crossroads and the causeway, making for the ancient walkway's luscious canopy, taking in the familiar view of her village from beneath the shade of the tall trees: the old houses to her left, the allotments on her right; a view she had seen so many times, walking to and from the bus stop throughout her secondary school years. Now with those years almost behind her, she thought how she longed to be free from the place: the constraints of living at home with her parents in a small village where everyone knew everyone else's business. She didn't care what people round here got up to, she wasn't interested in them. Same old faces in the same old places. She had outgrown it all, and soon she would be far away from here. With her place at the Guildhall school of performing arts now assured, it was just a matter of time before she hit the big time. No more scrabbling about for a few quid an hour at 'Bean'eadz' coffee shop in town. In ten years' time that place would have a blue plaque on its wall telling everyone that 'Daisy Carr, world famous actress, worked here from 1991 to 1993.'

She emerged from the canopy of horse chestnuts where the causeway dipped down to be dissected by the road opposite The Crafty Digit pub. Her old primary school was on her right: the same school that both she and Douglas had once attended. She thought about Mr Kareshi angrily waving the photocopy. She'd seen Douglas's rear end before it had hair on it, and before it had the three little dots. Everyone at primary school had been subjected to an unwanted viewing of it at one time or another.

Though they were in different year groups, her being one year older than him, the school's small number of pupils meant that years 4, 5 and 6 would often have combined lessons or games. Douglas's favourite occasions to exhibit his backside was either on the home stretch during a game of rounders, trying not to trip as he came in to last base with his shorts at half-mast; or in the school's small outdoor pool, swimming with his polystyrene float held out in front of him, his bum cheeks just above the water line like a glistening pink jellyfish, always to the sound of either laughter or screaming. Either display would almost always end up with him being escorted away from the field or yanked out of the pool, giggling as he was led away to the changing rooms to dress on his own. Despite her own highly developed sense of sophistication and heightened maturity, Daisy couldn't help but smile at the crude memory of younger days.

She binned her empty can and turned left up Stocks Lane, heading for home and looking forward to the celebratory meal that had been promised to her by her parents tonight, and more importantly the drinks do afterwards – minus her parents – with some of her girlfriends at a bar in town.

As she approached the railway line, she could see that the barriers of the level crossing were upright and the lights were dull and inactive. Unlike the village's other crossing, this one did not have a signal box. She had thought about going the longer way home via the causeway level crossing, where the signal box was most probably being manned by Dan Fowler, current object of her desires. She would miss Dan when she left, and part of her wanted to go up and see if he was there, but she knew that her mum would want her home in good time today. She was getting a little old to be told what time to be home by, but in a way she didn't mind, it wouldn't be for much longer, and besides it would give her a chance to have a nice cool shower before trying on a few outfits for tonight with a cheeky glass of chilled sauvignon blanc.

She crossed the railway, descending the other side, giving a cursory glance over the brick wall into the adjacent allotments and doing an immediate double-take. She was stunned by what she saw. It looked like the place had been hit by a tornado: shed doors stood ripped open, hanging on their hinges; vegetables and plants had been ripped from their earthly wombs; and the entire area was littered with various gardening implements. She stood still, shaking her head in dismay and confusion. She turned to leave, thinking that she might phone her mum or dad and tell them about it when she got home. Then again, maybe she wouldn't. A bit of public concern might earn her a few extra brownie points, but on balance she didn't really care about the damage, and instead carried on. Then she heard him.

'OI, DAISY!'

The voice came from over the wall. She recognised it instantly.

Her suspicions were confirmed soon after as Douglas Blouse emerged from a ramshackle shed in the far corner of the allotment.

Daisy groaned inwardly. Of course, she should have known. Same old faces in the same old places. She wished now that she had gone the long way round.

*

Douglas came bounding over towards Daisy, appearing to be nursing a slight limp. It did not take her long to work out from his awkward stance and the slight bulge in his cut-off denim shorts that he was clearly nursing an erection. She did not wish to draw attention to it, however, nor to the fact that his shorts looked like they had been hacked at by Stevie Wonder, with one side of faded black denim clearly longer than the other. His Iron Maiden T-shirt looked as if it also had been subjected to a piece of DIY tailoring and was now without sleeves. She also noticed that – in stark contrast to his heavy metal T-shirt – he had on a pair of Mr Tickle socks, the elastic of which looked as limp and loose as the arms of the orange cartoon character himself. In one hand Douglas held a decapitated garden gnome, in the other a can of Stella Artois.

'All right, Daisy, how's it going then?' Douglas said, swigging from the can. 'Party time down here. Wanna come and hang out for a bit?' Blouse enquired before pushing his luck a little further. 'You're looking hot, Dais,' he said, using the abbreviated version of her name that she hated. 'Give us a kiss,' he said courageously.

Daisy threw her head back and laughed, immediately dampening the young Lothario's spirits and pouring cold water on whatever lustful thoughts Douglas might've had towards her. Her ponytail dangled behind her like a bell ringer's rope.

'Douglas, I am more likely to kiss the dog when I get home than I am to kiss you,' she said, smirking at him, a frown crinkling her sweaty brow. 'And anyway, I have got much better things to be doing than to stand around here talking to you. I might get arrested as an accomplice. Look at the state of this place. You know that everyone is after you for all those windows you smashed in, don't you? I just saw Mr Kareshi, he is not a happy bunny. What were you thinking? And now all this!' she said, sweeping her hand over the small walled area of destruction. 'Have you got a death wish or something?'

Douglas took another big swig from the can of Stella before smashing what was left of the garden gnome against the brick wall. 'Whoopsy Daisy!' he said, staring at her as pieces of the gnome's blue china overalls and brown wheelbarrow fell to the floor. Douglas smiled and swigged once more from the can before throwing it over his shoulder, the can circling end over end before landing in a small patch of radishes some distance away. Blouse burped loudly, staring at Daisy and smiling. 'Anyway, could've been anyone's arse, Daisy,' he said finally, with a poker face.

'Douglas, I'm serious. If I were you, I would just go home, go back to your little caravan, hide under the duvet and say that you've been there since the early '80s or something. The police are going to be looking for you;

they've already been round your house, Mr Kareshi said so. Good job your mum wasn't in. I hope she's got your excuses ready.'

Blouse looked down at the ground, wrinkling his brow, his mood taking on a brooding solemnity. 'Fuck the police,' he said. 'And anyway mum's gone away. Dunno where.' He paused, kicking at pieces of the broken gnome on the grass. 'I don't wanna talk about it.' He looked up, meeting her gaze once more. 'And you're not gonna say you've seen me, are you, Daisy? You're not gonna grass me up, are you?' he said, more as an order than a question.

'Tell people I've been with you?' Daisy said, eyebrows raised, chin tucked slightly into her chest. 'No Douglas, don't worry, I won't be doing that.'

'Cheers, Dais, I knew I could count on you,' Douglas said, perking up, pleased with her loyalty but oblivious to the mild insult marinating in the remark.

'Where you going anyway?' he asked.

'Douglas, I'm going home, I'm going out tonight with my parents for a meal, then I'm going out for drinks with my friends.'

Blouse lowered his head, frowning. He looked over towards the shed, and then to the railway. 'What you celebrating?' he asked suspiciously.

'Well,' Daisy said, drawing in breath, 'while you have been busy photocopying your spotty arse, smashing in windows, ripping up allotments and picking on defenceless garden gnomes, I have been at school making something of myself. Remember that place, school?' she said. 'That place you used to go. I passed all my A-levels, I just got my results back,' she said with a distinct air of smugness. 'Not all of us want to hang around here all our lives, you know. Just because you chose to drop out before you even made it to year 11,' she said. 'Mind you, the way you carried on, you probably would have been expelled long before you got anywhere near an exam desk. I can't imagine it must have been much fun for you being in the lower set for everything, surrounded by all the other special little boys,' she teased, reaching over the wall and pinching his cheek.

Blouse straightened up in defiance. 'Piss off, Daisy. And I ain't gonna live round here forever,' he said. 'And anyway, fuck school, it's a waste of time going through all that boring old bollocks. People bossing you about, putting you in detention. They act like they're your fucking mum and dad,' he said. 'As soon as I'm eighteen, I'll be coining it in on the dartboard down the pub. Either that or I'm gonna be a rock star, touring the world. Different girl in every town.'

'Anyway, bollocks to all that. You wanna celebrate, come have a drink with me, I got all sorts over in that one,' he said, pointing to a ramshackle shed in the far corner, its door hanging open precariously on its hinges. 'I need to get another one anyway,' he said. 'Come on, it's got a fridge in it and everything. Wine and all sorts there. Where do you think I got those beers? Think there's a bottle of champagne in there as well,' he said beaming, a mischievous glint in his eye. 'Wouldn't be a celebration without a bottle of bubbly, now would it, Dais?'

Daisy had known Douglas long enough to know that at least fifty percent of what he said was usually bullshit. But for the first time since her coming together with Steventon's most wanted, and emboldened mostly by the prospect of alcohol, she actually began to feel a little curious. In a strange way she kind of admired Douglas's rebellious spirit. She looked at her watch: she still had plenty of time before her parents were due home. Maybe she could have one here, as well as when she got home, who was to know? She sure as hell wasn't going to tell anyone she'd seen him, let alone *been* with him, and deep down she knew that he was pretty harmless, to her at least. She knew how to deal with him. Douglas had always had the hots for her. Ever since she gave him that one and only peck on the cheek during a game of kiss chase at primary school. Probably another reason why the bulge in his jeans had not decreased in size in all the time they had been talking.

She tilted her head, looking over Douglas's shoulder towards the beaten-up sheds and tatty vegetable patches. 'All right, so what's on offer at the Blouse bar today then? Is it happy hour yet?' she said, a little more enthusiastically than she might have liked. Her A-level results, the celebratory meal and drinks, and the fact that in a month's time she would be out of this place and away from all who dwelt here, filled her with a sense of reckless enthusiasm. It was more like a bizarre leaving do really, she thought. Why not?

Douglas's eyes lit up at Daisy's unexpected response. 'You better believe it's happy hour, Dais!' he said. 'Come on, I'll show you. It's over there.'

Douglas pointed towards a sad excuse of a shed, standing in front of a vegetable patch that was overgrown and suffering from serious neglect. Daisy's suspicions about the legitimacy of Blouse's claims resurfaced, but against her better judgement she went with him, walking along the side of the wall, crossing the brook that dissected the allotments and entering through a side gate.

Douglas led Daisy down the dusty narrow path, crossed back over the brook via a small wooden bridge and back in to the allotments. She could see the damage close up now. Adjacent to the ramshackle shed he was leading her to was a much nicer shed, one that had clearly benefited from more care and attention than its dilapidated neighbour. Unfortunately for whoever owned it, they would pretty much have to start again from scratch on it. The pristine white fencing that bordered a modest-size vegetable patch had been kicked in. Another member of the gnome family had done a kamikaze jump through the greenhouse, and pretty much all produce growing in the area had been ripped from the earth. Daisy saw the half head of another garden gnome looking up at her from the ground, a little brown pipe protruding from the smiling mouth of its smashed-in head.

'Douglas, you are going to be in so much shit for this,' she said. 'I would not want to be in your shoes when they find out about all this.'

If Douglas was at all bothered by Daisy's warnings, he didn't show it.

'Can't prove it was me. Same as the windows. Like I said, it could have been anyone's arse,' he said breezily.

From behind them the raucous warning sound of the level crossing broke the stillness of the afternoon. Douglas's head snapped round on his shoulders to face the direction the sound was coming from. The warning lights at the level crossing were flashing red. Moments later the metal barriers began their slow descent, rattling a metallic crescendo before settling on the hot concrete with a steely clank. Blouse turned away from Daisy, as if being drawn towards the sound by some unseen magnetic force.

'Douglas, if you're thinking of doing what I think you are, then I'm out of here right now,' she said. 'I did not come over here to watch you risk your life flashing your spotty little arse at a train,' she said sternly. 'Honestly, what is it with you? It's dangerous, it's illegal, and it's bloody well stupid!'

Blouse stood frozen on the spot, looking from Daisy to the railway and back again. He had the look of a desperate child at a funfair, unable to decide whether to go on the bumper cars or the fun house.

'I mean it,' she said, clarifying her threat. 'I've got better things to do. If this is more important, then you carry on, I'll be on my way. I shouldn't even be here after the way you've been carrying on,' Daisy said.

Blouse was breathing deeply, conflicted, nodding his head. The sound of the rails beginning to hiss became audible somewhere off to their right as the train approached from the direction of the bridge. Blouse's eyes began to dart back and forth from the barriers back to the noise of the train, before resting on Daisy. He let the train go.

The Intercity 125 hurtled past the allotments with a deafening roar as it clattered over the level crossing. Daisy winced at the sound, putting her hands to her ears. Douglas compulsively put his hands to his cut offs, gripping his waistband as if still determined to drop his shorts. He didn't. And the train disappeared from view as quickly as it came. Once again all was quiet in the allotment.

The barriers broke the silence as they clattered back to their vertical position. One car that had been waiting for the train to pass crossed the railway line. Thankfully for both Daisy and Douglas, the driver did not see either them or the damage.

Blouse broke from his trance, suddenly mooing like a cow in the direction the train had gone. 'Yeah, piss off back to Bridgend, you Welsh wankers!' he shouted, before adding, 'Love to dad and his fuckin' Welsh dragon!'

'SSSHHHHH, Shut the fuck up, Douglas!' Daisy whisper shouted, nervously looking around her.

'Welsh wankers,' he repeated, this time quieter, shaking his head with a contemptuous sneer.

'Come on then, Dais, let's have that drink', he said, taking her hand and leading her towards the shed.

Daisy withdrew her hand from his grip, but diverted Douglas's disappointment with a question. 'Do you see much of your dad these days then, Douglas?' she asked. 'You know, since he left.'

Blouse stopped on the dusty path, turned and looked at her. 'Who?' he said, appearing genuinely confused.

'Your dad. You mentioned him just then. Do you see him much? Have you heard from him at all?'

'Dunno who you mean, Dais,' he said. 'I ain't got a dad.'

Daisy shook her head, deciding not to pursue her line of enquiry.

As they approached the shed, Daisy could see that its attempted safety features were of little functional use, and that entry had been easily obtained. The rusted latch hung loosely against the wood. A small brass key with a plastic key ring name tag dangled from the padlock. The name BLUNSDEN was written on it in shaky faded blue biro.

'Key was already in it,' Douglas said.

'But you still broke it open, I suppose?' Daisy said.

'Yeah, didn't see the key at first. This one was easy, mouldy old piece of shit, really. And the padlock's all rusted, anyway. Wasn't even snapped shut. Asking for trouble, if you ask me,' he said in a safety-conscious tone, shaking his head. 'I mean, if it wasn't me, it would have been someone else,' he added, looking over his shoulder. 'It WAS someone else, OK, Daisy?'

Douglas opened the door. It creaked loudly on its aged, rusty hinges. Daisy peered in cautiously, her sense of adventure now being replaced by a disconcerting fear of being discovered. All remained quiet. Douglas held the door open. 'After you', he said chivalrously.

From where she stood in the dazzling afternoon sunlight, Daisy couldn't see much of the shed's darkened interior. She shielded her eyes and they slowly adjusted to the gloom.

Some hosepipe was coiled on the floor like a thin green dusty snake. Old gardening implements hung on the walls, as rusty as the nails they hung on. A small shabby armchair dominated one corner, and there was a bucket with a bunch of bamboo canes propped up in it. There were also what looked like pictures on the shed's left-hand wall, facing the armchair, though in the gloom she couldn't make out what they were exactly. She squinted. They were girls. Nude girls. But there was something odd about them. Their faces appeared to be covered over.

At the far end stood a small fridge that Daisy presumed was probably once white. Now it was a grubby grey. Some empty plastic plant pots sat on its dusty top. There were two cans of unopened Carlsberg on the shelf to her left. This must be the famous bar, she thought. Next to the cans were a large pair of gardening shears and two pieces of black cut-off denim of uneven size.

Makes sense, she thought.

Her eyes adjusted further to her darkened surroundings as she stepped into the warm quiet of the shed. The smell of dirt, dust and stale alcohol permeated the air. BLUNSDEN: she thought the name sounded familiar, but she couldn't place it. She thought she might have heard mum mention it before. There were more gnomes in the shed. Or at least there were bits of them. In their varying states of destruction, it was hard to tell how many there were or which was which. Daisy did not attempt an official body count.

She looked again at the images on the wall, the pictures now coming clear into focus. The bare-breasted pictures of naked ladies were plastered over almost one entire side of the shed. Some looked like page 3 girls from The Sun, others a little more hard core, revealing a lot more than just boobs. It reminded her of the car garages she had sometimes been to with her dad to collect the car. Pervy old men wallpapering their work places with pictures of unobtainable women. Sad old gits. It went some way to explaining Douglas's eternal trouser bulge though.

Daisy could see now what was covering some of the girls' heads. Pictures of tractors and other assorted farming machinery had been crudely cut out and stuck over the top of them. Half glamour model, half tractor. Like some kind of pornographic, agricultural hybrid. A perverted farming version of a mermaid. A dusty loo roll near to running out sat on the floor between the fridge and the armchair.

She began to feel deeply uncomfortable in the stuffy confines of the warped and seedy environment. She could feel her heart pounding in her chest. From behind her she heard the door creaking closed and the shed turned darker. The only light now being cast was the white beams of slanting sunshine that pierced the crooked slats of the building's tatty shell.

'Nice in here, isn't it,' Douglas said. Daisy couldn't tell if he was joking or genuinely trying to impress her.

'Douglas, this is fucking weird,' she said, trying to sound more assured than she felt. 'I'm out of here.'

'But you said you were gonna stay for a drink? You're not going back on your word, are you?' he said, pointing to the grubby fridge tucked away under some makeshift shelving. 'Open it, grab yourself a drink,' he implored.

Despite herself, Daisy clasped the plastic handle. It was warm and greasy. Her hand felt instantly filthy as she opened the door. Peering into the grubby interior, she saw that it contained nothing more than a piece of mouldy cheese, two more cans of Carlseberg, extremely warm by now no doubt, a sausage roll and two pieces of mouldy pizza.

'Not exactly the Ritz, is it, Douglas. I knew you were bullshitting!' she said, trying to maintain her composure, but feeling angry and a little anxious.

She slammed the door of the fridge, stood up and turned to face Douglas. 'Right, get out the fff...'

She was cut off mid-sentence by a warm spray of fizzing lager, shooting out of the can of Carlsberg that Douglas held. It soaked her face, her hair and the front of her top.

'Sorry, babe,' he said laughing, 'we've run out of wine.'

'You fucking idiot!' she shouted. 'Let me out of here now, you dick head! ... NOW!!'

Her heart pounded beneath her beer-sodden top. The warm lager dripped between her breasts. The look on Douglas's face did nothing to inspire confidence in her.

Outside, the warning sound of the level crossing, followed by the metallic rattle of the descending barriers, could once again be heard. Blouse again became distracted, and Daisy hoped that this time he would just run out the door; run onto the railway and get hit by the fucking thing, she didn't care. But he didn't. He seemed to be enjoying himself well enough, just where he was.

'Now now, Daisy,' he said, 'that's no way to talk to your host. I've gone to a lot of trouble here,' he said with a wry, sarcastic grin.

'Douglas, you are in a lot of trouble,' Daisy responded, making a mental inventory of the implements hanging on the wall. 'It's just a matter of time before they find you. Now let me out of here and I just might not say anything to anyone about this,' she said, her voice rising in defiance.

The ground began to shake as the train could be heard approaching. Nearing. Passing. The sound muted in the stuffy confines of the shed. The force of it could be felt as the ground rumbled beneath their feet, and gardening utensils hanging on their rusty nails rattled on the wall. Blouse's full attention, however, was on the beer-sodden girl standing in front of him.

Daisy Carr was pissed off, but Douglas stood in front of the door blocking her escape, and he was smiling. And he still had a bulge in his trousers.

'Blimey, Reverend, it's a bit warm for all that, isn't it?' Terence Russell called out over the dark green flat top of his perfectly manicured hedge.

Reverend Bowen, along with Moses her black and caramel King Charles spaniel, were passing the Morris man's bungalow on Castle Street en route to the butcher's. Bowen, deep in thought, was in no mood for conversation, but the jovial Morris man was not going to let her pas without a fight, it seemed.

'Good afternoon, Terence,' she said, a little startled to see that the Morris man was topless. She scanned his sizable, well-kept garden. 'Gentlemen,' she said with a crumpled brow, noting the assorted gaggle of fatigued dancers strewn around the garden like battle-weary soldiers, many of which were also topless.

Colin Blunsden was reclining on a deckchair, for once silent and inanimate. His shirt was fully unbuttoned, exposing his prodigious beer gut. A damp pink towel hung over his face and chest, making him look as if he was waiting to be worked on by a rather camp mortician. There was a crescent of empty beer cans scattered around his feet.

Bob Dobson leant forward on a white plastic chair, his straggly greying black hair wet with perspiration. He was holding a can of lager and wearing a blank expression. The other members of the group were stretched out on the lawn, most with cans in their hands. Among them an accordion lay discarded on the ground next to its case. A collection of white hankies, colourful ribbons and bells were strewn about the lawn, and florally decorated top hats sat on the lawn looking like stout black chimneys growing out of the flat green ground.

'Me and the boys are just taking a little breather, Hilda. Hard work in this heat, see. That's why I let's 'em take the old tops off. It's meant to be full dress rehearsal ready for Saturday, but I said, boys, you can take your shirts off but the Baldriks are staying on!' he said, with a smile and a dictatorial finger pointing skywards.

Terence Russell, although topless, indeed still wore the green and yellow Baldricks of his Morris man uniform, the colourful X criss-crossing his upper body like gaudy bondage gear. His impressive tan glowed beneath it and he held his top hat under his arm.

Reverend Bowen was a little taken back by it all, as if she had somehow stumbled upon some strange kind of rural S&M club, where leather, whips and chains were replaced by hankies, ribbons and bells. Terence, however, appeared completely at ease with how he looked.

'I can't believe you can walk around in all that black on a day like today, Reverend; you must be boiling. Especially with that waistcoat on n'all. You wanna get some of this gear on!', he said, proudly pointing at himself, before realising and changing the direction in which he pointed, 'well, some of that gear on,' he said, now cocking a thumb to the pile of white shirts on the lawn. 'Don't worry,' he said, 'that'll all be in the wash tonight ready for the weekend,' before adding, 'won't it, boys?' Russell received a round of non-committal groans from his weary troops. 'I always washes the kit before the big shows,' Terence said proudly. 'Too good to you, en I, boys?' More mumbling sounds came from his men.

'Yes, well, very nice, Terence,' Bowen said, still a little bemused by it all. 'But as a matter of fact I rather like black,' she said. 'Although I must say I am beginning to regret coming out in the waistcoat as well,' she said, rolling her shoulders under the black leather waistcoat of her 'CROSSROADS' Christian motorcycle club uniform, hanging heavily on her shoulders, a bit like all her other concerns at the moment. Her imminent eviction from the vicarage was second only to the wanton act of vandalism committed against her stained glass window. She wore the waistcoat because to her it represented freedom, freedom from her worldly cares. When she was out on her trike, she felt like she could out-run anything. And after her supper with the bishop later, that is exactly what she intended to do.

‘Hey, give us a look at that a minute, Reverend,’ Terence Russell said, noticing the embroidery on the reverse of Bowen’s waistcoat. ‘Come on, Reverend,’ he said, ‘don’t be shy, give us a twirl!’

Bowen wearily did as she was asked, showing the Morris man the crucifix design that was the club’s logo on the rear of the waistcoat.

‘Hey, now that’s clever,’ he said. ‘Well, look at that, CROSS – ROADS,’ he said. ‘Hey, Gerry, come over here and look at this,’ Russell said.

Another topless middle-aged man walked over to join them.

‘What’s that then, chief?’ he said enthusiastically.

‘What’s that then, chief?’ came the muffled, mocking voice of Colin Blunsden from under the pink towel.

Hayman, topless but still wearing his baldricks, and also his top hat, rested an elbow on his lead dancer’s shoulder.

‘Look at that,’ Terence continued, marvelling at the emblem’s design. ‘A crucifix, look, Gerry. You got C-R-O-S-S going along there,’ Russell said, tracing his finger across the horizontal, ‘and then R-O-A-D-S coming down there,’ now tracing the vertical word, ‘and the O in the middle works for both of ’em. Well I never, now that is clever,’ he said, smiling and wiping his brow.

‘That is clever, chief,’ Hayman agreed, ‘very clever.’

‘And what does that say across the bottom there, Hilda? “Thy Wheel Be Done.” Hey, now how about that?’ he said. ‘You see it, Gerry? Wheel,’ he said, looking amazed at his friend, ‘like Thy Will Be Done, from the Lord’s Prayer, but it says Wheel instead, coz they’re into their motorbikes.’

‘Very clever, chief, very clever indeed.’

‘Oh, stop calling him chief, ya twat,’ came the voice from beneath the towel again.

Moses, at Bowen’s feet, began to whimper. Terence looked down sympathetically at the King Charles spaniel.

‘And look at little Moses’ collar there,’ he said, ‘look, it’s just like yours, Reverend, got the little white bit on the front and everything, ent that neat, Gerry?’

‘Very neat that, chief,’ Hayman agreed.

Reverend Bowen was beginning to feel like an unwitting fashion model, and was becoming increasingly bored with the scrutiny afforded to her and now to her dog also, by the topless Morris dancers. And the heat wasn't helping. She attempted to extricate herself from proceedings. 'Yes, all very good indeed,' she said, as patiently as she could muster. 'Now if you gentlemen will excuse me, I must get to the butcher's before they close. I've got the bishop round for supper tonight and I'm sure you gents will want to continue with your preparations for the big day.'

'Ohh, absolutely, Reverend,' Terence said. 'My boys are raring to go, aren't you, boys?'

A faint murmur of half-hearted affirmation came from over Terence's shoulder, and his smile dropped slightly. He lowered his voice, leaning in towards Reverend Bowen. 'Bad business about your window, Reverend,' Terence said gloomily. 'They got who done it yet? Put a few through, so I hear.'

'The police are looking into it,' she said.

'What, the hole?' came the muffled voice again, as Colin Blunsden began to crow with laughter under the towel at his own joke.

'Shuddup, you,' Terence said over his shoulder. 'Well, you go and get on your way, Reverend, don't let us stop you. You go and have a nice evening with that bishop of yours.'

'Indeed,' she said, 'and good luck with your preparations. I look forward to seeing it all come together on Saturday,' she lied.

She turned and continued on her way, Moses by her side panting in the heat. Stroking the dog's small head and soft floppy ears, she said, 'Shall we go and see Eric then?' The dog immediately perked up, seemingly aware of the destination and the potential rewards of such a journey.

'Right, come on you lazy bunch of sods, on your feet,' she heard Terence say to his gang of not so merry men as she put distance between herself and the dancers. She continued on down Castle Street, rounding the corner onto Stocks Lane and towards the railway. She was just about to thank the Lord for the level crossing's barriers being up, when the shrill sound of the warning alarm sounded, and so instead she quietly cursed Him.

She contemplated turning round and making for the farm track that led up to the top end of the High Street, but weariness overpowered her, and so she waited at the barriers. She turned to Moses, who was beginning to appear somewhat distracted and emitted an audible whine. 'Patience is a virtue ... apparently, isn't it, boy', she said, but the dog was not looking at her; instead, Moses' attention was focused towards the wall on the other side of the road. The dog began pulling at the lead, whining further. Reverend Bowen compliantly walked with the dog towards the wall that bordered the allotment, and was aghast at the sight of destruction as she looked over it.

She gasped, held her breath and expelled. 'What the hell is going on around here?' she said. The image of the smashed stained glass window and the photocopied backside came to mind. Her blood began to boil as the image of Douglas Blouse's smirking face formed in her mind, grinning with pleasure at his loathsome achievements. And he had done this to the allotments also, she was almost certain of it.

Moses, still whining, began scratching against the wall, as if in a futile attempt to climb it. Reverend Bowen could sense that something had spooked him. She heard what sounded like voices emanating from one of the sheds at the far end, and immediately knew that her instincts were correct. He was here.

The hiss of the rails, signalling the arrival of the train, discordantly harmonised with Moses' whinings. The train came into view, thundering past the vicar, who continued to look distractedly over the wall at the damage.

The train passed and the barriers lifted, but Reverend Bowen did not cross. Instead she turned and made her way back towards the small gate that led into the allotments, spurred on by the sound of the voices coming from the ramshackle shed that were becoming louder and louder the closer she got.

Bowen could see a key jammed into a discarded padlock a couple of feet from the shed. She picked it up. On it was the name BLUNSDEN. For a brief moment she actually felt mild amusement: the old drunkard lying under the pink towel laughing at her window. Just one of many villagers who had strayed from her congregation. In Blunsden's case, choosing to worship at the alcoholic altar of the Crafty Digit public house.

She heard banging and muffled voices. Reverend Bowen knew HE was in there. Her pulse quickened with the sudden rush of adrenalin that coursed through her. The sound of something thumping against the flimsy shed wall startled Moses, who began scratching against its closed door, barking incessantly.

Bowen harnessed her adrenalin. 'All right, come out of there!' she called to the shed's unseen occupants, her heart beating loudly in her chest. Moses was still scratching wildly at the door.

She banged on the door, unsure whether to open it, worried about what she might find.

'I said come ou ....'

Before she could finish the sentence, the shed door flew open, hitting the dog full in the face.

'Moses!' she cried.

Douglas emerged from the shed, squinting, staggering into the daylight, dazed and uttering a strange, nervous laugh. He stumbled, taking in his surroundings, and the new company. His head recoiled slightly at the sight of Bowen, and his strange, panting laugh dissipated, morphing into a low growl. A crumpled sneer formed on his lips as he backed away from the startled vicar. He looked down at the whimpering dog laying dazed amongst the broken remains of a smiling garden gnome, looking contemptuously at the stunned animal, and uttering a childish titter of laughter. Reverend Bowen stood looking on, shocked.

He barged past the vicar, making a run towards the farm track and away from the allotment. The shove that nearly knocked her to the ground startled Bowen from her momentary immobility, and she finally regained her senses. As the shock alleviated and reality crept back in, she called after him. 'You smashed my window, didn't you, you little sod! And you're going to pay! As God is my witness, you're going to bloody well pay!'

She watched Douglas make his escape. The sound of his manic, tittering laughter faded as he ran. Rage consumed her.

She turned her attention to Moses, who was unsteadily getting back to his feet, sidling up needfully to the vicar. She stroked the dog, soothing him, noticing the trickle of blood coming from his little black nose.

'Bastard', she said, watching Douglas flee.

The shed door creaked open on its rusty hinges, and Reverend Bowen's nose wrinkled as the smell of stale alcohol and mouldy food wafted up her nostrils. She heard a shuffling sound coming from inside the shed, whose interior was now partially lit by the sagging open door. Daisy Carr emerged, an open pair of garden shears dangling from one hand. She didn't appear to be hurt, but she was breathing heavily. She dropped the shears onto the shed's rotten wood floor. They landed with a dull thud.

Reverend Bowen looked Daisy Carr up and down. The front of her white top was a dull yellowy brown, her long blond hair was streaked with sweat and cobwebs. Her chest was pitching up and down, but decreasing as her breathing slowed to a more regular pace. Out of the corner of her mouth, she blew a straggly lock of hair from off her face.

'Good Lord,' Reverend Bowen said.

Douglas made his escape up the farm track, heading towards the main road, stopping halfway up its moderate incline as tiredness overwhelmed him. Panting, he bent over, putting his hands on his knees, nearly throwing up, as sour, lager-tasting bile rose in his throat. He spat a ball of light brown saliva at the dusty track. Mercifully the booze stayed down.

'Fucking nosy cow,' he swore breathlessly, cursing the vicar for blowing his chances. God, Daisy was sexy when she was angry, he thought, certain within his own deluded mind that had they not been so rudely interrupted by the snooping vicar, his attempts at a sexual conquest would have eventually led to success.

He felt a confusing mixture of sexual arousal – still thinking about Daisy – and bitter resentment towards the vicar for ruining his chances, and he cursed both Bowen and her yappy dog. She was bound to grass on him. Daisy wouldn't, but that meddling God-botherer would be straight down to tell the old bill. Well, bollocks to her and the old bill. He didn't care.

He was sweating profusely, glad that he had made the alterations to his jeans. Christ, that shed was hot, he thought. But how sexy did Daisy look in that wet, white top of hers after he'd opened that can of lager on her, like a victorious Formula 1 champion. He'd glimpsed the proud protrusion of her nipples beneath the damp white cotton of her top. Five more minutes and he would have been in there for sure.

Nosy God-bothering cow, he thought, thinking he might have to pay her precious little church another visit. All he needed was more ammo, and there was plenty of that on offer, he thought, looking at all the ballast on the railway line.

He stood up straight, feeling a little better at the prospect of revenge, and made his way over to a nearby blackberry bush, selecting four decent-looking candidates. He put them all in his mouth at the same time, and winced as he realised that at least one, maybe two, were still well under-ripe. Nevertheless he swilled the berries into a liquid before punching himself in the face, swishing his head dramatically to one side as if he had just been landed a good one by Rocky Balboa, and spitting out the liquidised blackberries in a dark jet of fake gore.

He heard a hiss. After so many years of living near the railway, his ears had become sensitive to its sounds, and he could detect that old familiar sound a mile away. He wasn't sure if he could make it down onto the line in time from where he was, but undeterred he wiped the residual dripping blackberry mess from his mouth with the back of his hand and darted towards the railway, easily bypassing the ineffective wire fence. He popped the button on his shorts as he ran.

He'd scurried halfway down the railway embankment as the thunderous sound approached and the train came into view from the west. Knowing he would not make it to the track in time, he dropped his shorts on the embankment and lowered his boxers, turning his backside towards the railway line just as the Intercity train hurtled past. He slapped his bare bum cheeks with both hands, reeling off a string of profanities as he did so, his words drowned out by the noise of the train. He hoped that whoever was on it got a good look. He nearly lost his footing, coming close to over-balancing. Alarmed, he leant forward, steadying himself as the train disappeared towards London and out of sight. He slumped down on the embankment, a feeling of partial release flowing over him. It wasn't quite the rush you felt when you had both feet firmly planted on the sleeper, but it was OK. It was better than nothing, and he felt the anger in him begin to subside. He rolled over, attempting to fasten his shorts, and was stung by a nettle. It was not entirely unpleasant. He masochistically rolled again, and was stung many times on his exposed rear end, the pain providing a perverse kind of physical outlet for his frustrated mind. It felt good. Sometimes, even though it hurt, pain felt good. But not as good as getting even with that nosy God-botherer was going to feel.

He lay on the railway bank a while, his mind slowly beginning to calm. The pain of the stinging nettles subsided to a soft buzz. He felt safe. He could not be seen from here, even if someone were to walk down the farm track. He dozed a while, ignoring the passing trains that hurtled by at staggered intervals, his compulsions temporarily dowsed by brooding thoughts of resentment and revenge.

He nodded off, for how long he wasn't quite sure. When he woke a little while later, he got up, brushed himself down, ducked back through the fence and walked up the farm track's short incline towards the main road. Upon reaching it, he turned left and headed back into the village.

In the eighteen years that Daisy had lived in Steventon, she'd never once stepped foot inside the police station; and were it not for Reverend Bowen, now seated beside her insisting she did so, Daisy would have preferred to have kept it that way. She sat at the desk facing Sergeant Frisk, who was currently trying to prevent a mini-mound of paperwork from being blown away by the oscillating tower fan beside his desk. Pieces of railway ballast sat atop them, acting as improvised paperweights.

'OK, Daisy,' Sergeant Frisk said, 'just try and relax and tell me from the start exactly what happened. I think you probably know by now that Douglas is someone we are extremely keen to speak to in connection with the recent incidents reported around the village. If you can help us with that in any way, help us find him, I think that would be of great benefit to us all right now. I've got statements here from all the people we think have so far been the victim of his little crime spree. With yours and the Reverend's testimony, that will lend a lot of weight to our cause.'

Frisk's smooth reassurance made Daisy feel at ease in his presence. The fan beside his paperwork-strewn desk brought a most welcome breeze to her face, which she had just splashed with cold water in the police station's small toilet, trying to regain a little composure in preparation for the imminent inquisition. She took deep breaths, in and out, aware that the need to think clearly was now of critical importance. She fidgeted in her seat, readying herself for the performance. She was going to need all her acting skills if she was to get out of this looking like the innocent damsel in distress, whose only crime was finding herself in the wrong place at the wrong time. And she was probably going to need her secret weapon too. Composing herself, Daisy sipped the glass of water in front of her and began to relay her story, taking Sergeant Frisk up to the point where she crossed the railway line, going on to describe the scene of carnage she had been confronted with at the allotment.

'So I went into the allotments to have a closer look,' she said. 'There didn't appear to be anyone around, or at least not that I could see. Just stuff everywhere and all that damage. Doors ripped off their hinges, plants and vegetables uprooted.' She paused, taking a hitching inward breath. 'I saw a smashed garden gnome, and ...' she faltered, 'I don't know why, it sounds silly, but it was holding a little sign that said 'Gnome, Sweet Gnome' on it. Only its head had been cracked open and I, I felt so sad. I know it's stupid, I know it was just a silly gnome, but…', the tears began to come, 'it just got to me.' Daisy sobbed. Her ability to cry on command had not eluded her, even under pressure. Reverend Bowen stroked her back, soothing her, staring at Sergeant Frisk who listened intently.

'I wish I'd never set foot in that place now,' she said, a touch more defiantly. 'I should have just gone home and phoned the police, I know that now, but I thought that whoever had done it might still be around, and that maybe I could, you know, make a ... what do you call it?'

'A citizen's arrest?' Sergeant Frisk said, raising his eyebrows.

'Yeah, exactly, you know, do the right thing. Be a bit of a hero, I suppose. Stupid, huh?'

'An admirable attitude, Daisy,' Frisk said, smiling.

'So I went into the allotment, and there was this one shed at the far end. You know, the allotments by the railway aren't as big as the ones by the causeway, but it was about thirty feet, I guess, from the gate. Anyway, I thought I could hear noises coming from it, so I went up to it. The door was hanging open on one hinge. I thought it was going to fall off. It looked like a big mouth, yawning open, like the entrance to a haunted house or something, I was pretty scared, to be honest,' she said, rather pleased with her spooky piece of improvised dialogue. 'As I got right up to it, the noises, it sounded like low murmuring and faint banging, well they stopped, I didn't know what it was. Now I wish I'd never found out,' she said, rubbing her eyes. 'I went inside to see if I could find out what was making the noise, but it was dark in there and I couldn't really see anything, only those weird pictures on the wall.'

'Weird pictures?' Frisk asked.

'Yeah, like, nude women. Like you see on the walls in garages, only some of them had, like, pictures of tractors and stuff taped over their faces. It was really odd.'

'It certainly sounds it,' Frisk said. 'Go on, Daisy, you're doing fine,' he said encouragingly.

'So I stood there, kind of mesmerised, and a little appalled, to be honest. I'd never seen such strange pictures. I was already feeling uneasy by that point, and that's when I, I heard the door creaking on its hinges.' The tears began to come again. 'It was being pulled shut. By someone in the shed!' She said, veering into mild hysterics. 'It slammed shut, and that's when I knew I wasn't alone. I don't know whether he was already in there with me and had been hiding, or whether he'd been outside and come in, I just, I just don't know. Then he spoke.'

'What did he say, Daisy?' Frisk asked calmly.

'He just said "Hello ... Hello, Dais." That's what he calls me even though I don't like it. Only the way he said it was really creepy, like something out of a horror film. That's when he moved into a slit of light and I saw for the first time who it was. I saw who it was, and it was Douglas.'

'Douglas Blouse?' Frisk asked for confirmation.

'Yes, of course, Douglas Blouse!' she said in a rising, angered voice. She put her face in the flat of her palm as the tears rolled down her cheeks, Reverend Bowen once again soothing her.

'Daisy,' Frisk said softly, 'I know it's hard for you, but it really is best to talk about it while it's still fresh in your mind.'

'I'm OK,' she said, wiping her eyes and straightening up in her chair. 'So he opened this can of beer. I think he'd already been drinking, it stank of booze in there. He started telling me how pretty I was, how he fancies me, how he's always fancied me. He offered me the can, which I refused. That seemed to annoy him. He came over, telling me to have a drink with him, getting angry. I refused again, but he wouldn't take no for an answer.' The tears welled in her eyes and rolled down her cheeks. 'He put the can up to my mouth and started to pour it down my throat. Getting me in a kind of headlock. I choked and I spluttered on it, it was horrible, warm and sickly, it went all down my top. The beer was coming out of my nose, and then the next thing is he comes right up close to me and,' ... she faltered ... 'he let go of the headlock. I was scared rigid. Frozen on the spot. He put his arm round my shoulder.' Tears. 'He moved his hand down my back.' More tears. 'And then he ... he ... he touched my bottom!' (I'd like to thank the academy.)

Daisy Carr buried her head in her arms, weeping on the desk like a pupil who had just finished an exam they knew they'd already failed. Only now they were tears of laughter. She'd tried her best to keep herself together throughout the whole absurd performance. But that one little B word had set her off, and if she gave herself away now it would be curtains for sure. The air came rapidly in and out of her nose, her breathing muffled by the arms that hid her grinning face. Her shoulders rising and falling with every insincere sob.

Reverend Bowen tutted loudly, appalled at what Daisy was describing, completely oblivious to its deceit. 'Ohh, sergeant, really, that's enough now, can't you see she's upset?' Bowen said, rubbing Daisy's shuddering back.

Daisy stayed down, valiantly trying to overcome her giggling fit. Eventually she came up for air. 'I'm OK, I'm OK,' she said, trying to reassure herself as much as anyone else.

'Then what happened?' Frisk asked.

'Well, that's when I heard the barking outside,' she said, looking at Moses contentedly sat in Bowen's lap, 'and the scratching at the door. I knew that someone must have been outside, and so did Douglas. I think that's what must have scared him, because that's when he bolted for the door. I guess he thought he was in enough trouble as it was, without hanging around for more. I picked up a pair of gardening shears off the table in the shed, I don't know why, some kind of last-ditch, feeble attempt at self-defence, I suppose. It was a bit late for that, though. That's when he ran off across the allotments and up the track.'

Frisk turned to Bowen. 'And that's what you saw, Reverend?'

'Yes, Sergeant', she clarified. 'Like Daisy said, he came bursting out the door like a man possessed, and for what it's worth, I believe that's exactly what he is. He bashed poor Moses here right on the nose,' she said, stroking the dog. 'He gave me the filthiest look and was giggling like a little child. God knows what was going on in that deranged mind of his, or where he is now for that matter.'

'That's for us to deal with, Reverend,' Frisk said, before taking a long deep breath. He looked at Reverend Bowen. 'So you didn't actually see Douglas engaging in any type of inappropriate behaviour with Daisy, Reverend?'

Daisy looked pleadingly at the policeman. 'What are you saying? That I'm making all this up!?'

She nearly started again at that one, and had to hold a hand to her mouth to shield a grin.

'No, Daisy, I'm not saying that for one moment. You have clearly been through a very traumatic experience, and I for one am grateful to you for having the courage to relive it so soon after it happened. It's just that without any witnesses to an actual crime having taken place, it is going to be hard to prove any wrongdoing. It's your word against his at the moment, I'm afraid. I know that's not what you want to hear, but until we can get our hands on him, that's just how it is,' Frisk said, looking down at the papers on his desk. 'Which we will,' he said, looking back up at her.

Daisy slumped back in her chair, wearing a look of mild exasperation on her face, glad that for now at least, the show was over. She just wanted to get out of here and forget that all this had ever happened.

'How is your window, Reverend?' Frisk asked. 'Any news on getting it fixed?'

'It's a specialist piece of 18th century stained glass, Sergeant, I can't just pop down to B&Q for a new one, now can I?' she snapped, shaking her head. 'I think that whatever we raise at the fete on Saturday is going to have to go towards replacing it, and I doubt very much that even that will be enough. We'll just have to wait and see, won't we,' she said, crossing her arms and looking disdainfully at Sergeant Frisk, as quiet descended in the office.

The quiet was short-lived, as seconds later, the flapping, walking maelstrom that was Petra Carr burst into the office. Daisy wilted in her seat and shut her eyes.

'Where is she? Where's my daughter?' Petra said in clipped, panicky tones.

Daisy sat back, waiting for the inevitable interrogation that was sure to follow.

Sergeant Frisk pinched the bridge of his nose, rubbing it gently.

He looked about as pleased to see her as she was.

Butch Ransom had wood. Quite literally.

While Daisy was giving her one-woman performance down at the police station, Butch was a little further up the High Street, helping his old friend Barbara Rix board up the broken window of her fabric shop.

Fabsolutely Babulous was not big, from the outside at least, but inside it was like a Tardis. Balls of wool and rolls of fabric were stacked high and deep, belying the building's petite-looking structure. The window had been smashed dead centre. A hole of roughly two inches pierced its glinting surface, and cracks spread out like a spider's web for a couple of feet from its central point. Butch held up a thin piece of chipboard, placing it portrait ways over the middle of the window, covering the full extent of the damage.

Butch stood on a small stepladder in the boiling afternoon sun holding the chipboard. Finn dozed idly by in the shop's doorway, looking decidedly uninterested. They were both startled by the sound of a Volkswagen Polo blaring its horn as it passed the shop. Startled by the noise, Butch nearly hit his thumb with the hammer.

Wearing his khaki shorts and white vest, Butch turned in the direction of the car now disappearing up the High Street. His eyes squinted behind his wire-rimmed spectacles that were being held in place by a geeky-looking beige strap that ran round the back of his sweaty short-haired head.

'Friend of yours?' Barbara asked, sticking her head out the door.

Butch smiled, imagining the seductive gaze of those beautiful hazelnut eyes undressing him in the Polo's rearview mirror. 'I've never seen that car, or the pretty brunette behind the wheel of it before in my life, Barb,' he said.

'Yeah, right,' she said, smiling suspiciously.

The car in question belonged to a local lady called Lisa, whom Butch had met at a pub quiz one night up at The Crafty Digit during lambing season.

Butch had worked his magic on her, eventually enticing her back to Ransom farm for what turned out to be a marathon six-hour sex session, punctuated at 2 a.m. by a trip to the sheds, where Butch brought another two lambs into the world before continuing their love-making in the soft straw of an adjacent pen.

Barbara came out of the shop holding a small tray, bearing two glasses of ice cold lemonade. The costume jewellery that adorned Barbara's wrists and nearly all of her fingers gleamed in the sunshine as she stepped over Finn with an agility that belied her progressing senior years.

'I'm so grateful to you for doing this, Butch,' she said.

'No worries, Barb,' Butch responded, smiling down at the lady who had become like a mother to him. 'Happy to do it, you know that,' he said, banging the last tack into the board, temporarily concealing the damage.

It was true, Butch was more than happy to do it. And he was always happy to put himself in the shop window, literally in this case, to members of the opposite sex such as the beautiful Lisa. Plus a good public display of human decency did his credibility around the village no harm whatsoever.

'It was such a shock this morning when I saw it,' she said. 'I couldn't believe it when I walked up and down the High Street. If it's Douglas who's done this, well, I hope ....' she trailed off. 'Well, I don't know what I hope, Butch, to be honest,' she said, shaking her head. 'But I think the boy needs help, let me put it that way.'

'What he needs, Barb,' Butch said, descending the small ladder and gratefully accepting the glass of lemonade, 'is a good kick up the arse.' Butch wiped the sweat from his brow with the hem of his vest, revealing a chiselled set of abs.

'Oh come on now, Butch, I don't think that's the answer. Violence won't solve anything. No, what I think he needs, and it's obviously something that's been lacking in his life, is a positive male role model – someone like you.'

Butch nearly spat the last of his lemonade out. The thought of being a mentor to someone like Douglas Blouse did not appeal in the slightest to Butch, who was more than happy in his childless, bachelor lifestyle.

'You gotta be joking, Barb! He comes anywhere near my farm and I'm gonna be reaching for my gun. Fill that famous little arse of his with two cartridges of buck shot. Then the bloody thing really would look like the moon!'

Butch held the empty glass of lemonade up to the sun, the ice cubes in the bottom visibly melting in the heat. He tipped the cold transparent cubes into his hand, throwing them to Finn in the doorway. Waking from his doze at the sound of the cubes hitting the pavement, Finn gratefully crunched on the ice before resting his head back on the pavement.

'Don't suppose you've got anything stronger, have you, Barb?' Butch enquired, holding up his empty glass and giving it a little shake.

Barbara frowned suspiciously at Butch, then smiled. 'I might have something out the back, I suppose,' she sang back. 'Seeing as you've done such a good job. Truth be told, Butch, I had one earlier myself to steady my nerves. I know it was a bit early but, well, like I said, I was in shock.'

'At a girl,' Butch said, folding the ladder and leaning it against the shop before retreating back into the shop with Barbara. Finn rose and followed on behind them.

Butch leant up against the shop counter, looking at the broken window from inside. It was so much gloomier in here with the board now covering over two-thirds of the window. The vibrantly coloured rolls of fabric, balls of wool and other sparkly accessories housed within Barbara's Aladdin's cave of colourful creation were now decidedly subdued in the half light afforded by what glass remained uncovered.

A woman walking past caught his attention, disappeared out of sight, momentarily obscured by the chipboard, before popping out the other side. She stopped outside the shop, hesitantly, before giving the door a gentle push.

'Hellooo', she said, poking her head into the darkened shop.

'Good afternoon, madam. And how may I help you on this beautiful afternoon?' Butch said in his best salesman's voice, beaming a broad grin at the woman's long, sandy hair, violet tie-dye vest top and flowing white skirt.

'Oh, I'm sorry,' she said, frowning, 'do you work here?'

'More of a supplier, if truth be told. That's some of my produce over there,' Butch said, pointing to the balls of wool stacked high on the wall next to the counter. 'Butch Ransom, owner of Ransom farm,' he said, offering his hand to the female stranger.

'Oh, nice to meet you, Butch,' she said. 'I'm Trudy, Trudy Ryan, I live on the causeway, just over the railway. I'm actually still quite new to the village.'

'Ahh, weren't we all once, Trudy, weren't we all,' Butch said with a smile. 'But once you're in, you're in,' he said, trying to put Trudy at ease.

'Oh hello, Trudy dear, I didn't hear you come in,' Barbara said re-appearing, holding another tray of drinks.

'Barbara, are you OK? I wasn't sure if you were going to be open,' she said. 'I've seen the damage to the signal box across from the house and the other places on the High Street on my way up. Isn't it awful?' Trudy said with concern. 'Have they found out who did it? Do you think they might be connected?'

'Local arse hole did it, Trudy', Butch said, very matter of factly. 'And yeah, they're as connected as my foot and Douglas Blouse's arse are gonna be if I get to 'im before the bloody police do,' Butch said.

'Ohh Butch, sshhh, that kind of talk's not going to help, is it?' Barbara said. 'I'm fine, Trudy dear, thank you for asking. It's just a window that's broken and it is insured. I'll hope to have it replaced by tomorrow, morning time they said. Meanwhile I've got my Kiwi superhero to help me, eh, handsome Ransom?' Barbara said flirtatiously to Butch.

'At your service, m'aam,' Butch replied, curtseying dramatically, sounding like one of his sheep. 'So you're new to these parts, eh, Trudy?'

'Yes, we moved into a place on the causeway next to the railway a couple of months ago. We're still finding our feet a little. It's taking a bit of time to adjust to the noise of the railway, but I think we'll get used to it eventually, and the house more than makes up for it. It really is lovely.'

'Well, you're most welcome,' Butch said. 'We were just toasting Barbara's misfortune, Trudy, if you'd care to join us for a G&T?' he said, smiling. 'Plus, don't forget Barb,' Butch said, 'we're also celebrating the successful completion of my lovely little surprise for the fete on Saturday, aren't we?' he said beaming. 'Or at least we will be when I finish the bugger!'

'Oh yes, I'd almost forgotten,' Barbara said, 'I can't wait to see how you've got on. My little student. You'll be working for me soon. Mum's the word until Saturday though, eh, my darling?' Barbara said, tapping her nose. 'Wouldn't want to spoil the surprise now, would we?'

'Better bloody believe it,' Butch said, grinning from ear to ear. 'So how about it, Trudy?' Butch asked. 'Drink?'

Looking a little taken aback, Trudy pondered, before happily accepting the offer. 'Yes, OK. Love one, thanks,' she said gratefully.

Barbara disappeared out back once again, leaving Trudy and Butch alone in the dim light of the shop.

'So you live on the causeway then, Trudy?' Butch enquired.

'That's right, Rose Cottage,' she replied.

'Ahh, yeah, nice place. By young Dan there in the signal box. I go past there all the time. My farm's up past the church. Got a hundred or so sheep up there. At least I did last time I counted. Mind you, I did fall asleep halfway through, so there could be a few more,' he said, laughing at his joke. 'Young Barbara there gets most of her wool from me, y'know. Very talented spinner is our Barbara,' Butch said. 'So what do you do, Trudy?'

'I'm actually just starting up my own Aroma Therapy and Holistics treatment studio in one of the spare rooms at home. It's why I've been plundering this place so much, putting all the finishing touches on the cushions and decor. You drive a red Toyota pick-up, right?' Trudy enquired, scrutinising Butch's face.

'Correct,' he replied, 'although Finn there sometimes drives it home when I'm too pissed' he said, with a straight face.

For a moment it looked as if Trudy almost believed him, until Butch gave himself away with a smile that made both of them laugh.

'I think I've seen you waiting at the level crossing. I recognise your dog as well.'

'Yeah, Finn here's a local legend, aren't you, boy?' Butch said, stroking his loyal sheepdog.

'Here we are then, dear,' Barbara said, re-appearing for the second time, gin and tonic in hand for the group's newest member.

'Thank you very much, Barbara,' Trudy said, gratefully accepting the ice cold drink and taking a sip.

'So who did break all the windows?' Trudy asked.

'Local fruit loop by the name of Douglas Blouse,' Butch answered with an air of exasperation. 'Always was a bit of a loony tune around here, but he seems to have stepped it up a gear recently.'

'Allegedly, Butch,' Barbara said. 'Allegedly. We still don't know for sure it was him.'

'Oh come on, Barb,' Butch said. 'You saw what was wrapped around that bloody missile. Kareshi said he chased him out of the shop for photocopying his arse there last month. Then it comes smashing in through your window! Now I'm not exactly Sherlock Holmes,' Butch said, stroking his chin, 'but I'd hazard a guess that it might be him.'

'It's his poor mother that I've always felt sorry for,' Barbara said. 'Especially after dad left. Before that they seemed fine. She used to come in every couple of weeks for wool when Douglas was a young boy, knitting him all those Mr Men jumpers. They were his favourite. Had a lovely little collection of them, he did. Used to pass the shop holding mum's hand on the way to school. Always in one of her jumpers, he was,' she said with a smile. 'Mr Bump, I remember she used to call him, on account of all the trouble he'd get into. Knee scrapes and bangs on the head. She'd always stay and talk a while in here when she bought things. But after dad ran off to Wales with that woman off that TV programme, she pretty much stopped coming in here. And Douglas was getting a bit old for Mr Men jumpers by then as well, but that's definitely when I'd say he started to go downhill. That was when he started secondary school as well. All the trouble he got himself into. I used to hear a bit of gossip from the customers about him, and then of course when poor Peter Glass died in that car crash with the police...' She paused, sighing. 'Closest friend Douglas ever had around here was Peter,' she said. 'Edna will tell you that.'

A long pregnant pause filled the shop.

'And the rest is history, I suppose,' Barbara said philosophically. 'Sergeant Frisk said he's been down their house twice already today. There's no sign of them. Doors are all locked, curtains closed. The caravan was open, but there was no sign of Douglas. Although it was a total mess by all accounts.'

Trudy nodded along. 'It sounds like he's had quite a lot to deal with,' she said. 'Trauma at an early age can be very damaging, particularly when a parent leaves. It can leave the child feeling abandoned, and worse still, like they're somehow to blame. Does he have any brothers or sisters?' she asked.

'No, Trudy love,' Barbara said, 'he's an only child.'

Butch finished his drink and placed the empty glass on the counter, turning to Trudy.

'So what are you saying there, Trudy Freudy?' he asked, cynically mocking her pseudo psychoanalysis. 'We should all pop round his place and give him a nice little hug? Little sing song maybe, eh? "Hey, Douglas, I know you caused thousands of pounds' worth of damage around here this past couple of days, and pissed loads of people off, but maybe we can use this opportunity to fix them together?"' he said, sarcastically. 'In fact, I've got it, I know how this all works,' Butch said, clicking his fingers. 'Douglas IS the window, right!? … I mean, figuratively speaking. Broken? That's how this sort of thing goes, isn't it?'

'Butch, calm yourself down,' Barbara said.

'I'm not saying that at all,' Trudy countered. 'I'm just saying that sometimes it's better to try to understand the individual and treat the cause, rather than having to endure the effects. I did a bit of counselling at my local youth centre in my twenties and I had to deal with a lot of young kids and adolescents from similar-sounding backgrounds. It's not uncommon behaviour.'

Butch laughed. 'Put him on the couch and see what you get out of him then, Trudy,' he said, 'coz I'll tell ya, he's more likely to get a stiffy listening to the trains go by than he is talking about his bloody feelings.'

'All right, Butch, that's enough now,' Barbara said, intervening. 'It's not poor Trudy's fault. Now come on, we're all friends here. I'm just grateful that

I've got good friends around me at a time like this. That's more than can be said for Douglas.'

Butch ran his hand over his sweaty head, feeling a little ashamed of his outburst. 'Yeah, listen, I'm sorry, Trudy, didn't mean to get at you there, it's just, well, Barbs has been like a mum to me since I came here, and it breaks my heart to see her treated like this.'

Trudy smiled. 'It's fine, Butch, honestly. Don't worry.'

He turned back to Barbara. 'Gonna be a bloody hot one for the fete on Saturday, eh, Barb?' he said, turning to cheerier subject matter. 'Gonna be a sweaty one, shearing all those woolly buggers of mine, that's for sure. Still, it'll give you some good stuff for your spinning, won't it?'

'Absolutely, my love,' she replied. 'Always love doing the fete, don't we, doing the little displays for the kids. I'm hoping I might do some in the back room here before the summer holidays finish as well,' she said, 'although I might need a new air conditioner if this bloody weather carries on,' she said, putting a hand to her mouth.

'Language, Barb, ladies present,' Butch said.

They all smiled.

'I'd love to bring my two up here some time, Barbara,' Trudy said. 'Anything to keep them occupied over the holidays is an absolute God send. And as for Saturday, you can be sure 'wool' be there to see 'ewe' both in action.'

'Good one, Trudy Freudy,' Butch said, nodding appeciatively.

'Tell you what, ladies,' Butch said, clapping his hands together, 'what say we finish up here then sneak off for another little drink down the Digit, eh? Little afternoon refreshment in the sunshine. Bit of team building, eh? It's good for morale,' he said smiling, eyebrows raised, looking at both ladies.

'That sounds very nice, Butch,' Barbara said, 'but I've got to stay here and do some admin while i wait for the glaziers to call to confirm when they're coming. And I must phone the insurance company again with some more information, you know what they're like. Blood from a stone sometimes, they are. No, you two go, enjoy the weather,' she said, smiling at them both.

Butch turned to Trudy, hands on hips, breathing in deeply, exhaling, he asked, 'So whadda ya reckon then, Trudy Freudy? Thirsty? Or have you got plans?'

She stared for a moment. Butch felt her quietly appraising him. 'Actually, no, I've got no plans,' she said finally. 'The girls are having an early tea round at a friend of theirs, and Jeremy won't be back till about seven, so yes, I think I could be persuaded.'

Butch felt an internal thud. Jeremy. He should have seen that one coming. Still, married women did not necessarily mean off limits. Not that he thought Trudy would be a push-over. She obviously knew her own mind, and Butch liked that about her.

'At a girl!' Butch said, not drawing attention to the issue. 'After you,' he said, leading her out of the shop, Finn following on behind them. 'And hey, Barb!' he called, poking his head back round the door. 'Anyone messes around with that window who isn't a double glazing salesman and they'll have me to bloody well answer to, right?'

'Butch, language,' she said. 'But thank you,' she added with a maternal smile. 'You two go and enjoy the weather. Have a lovely afternoon.'

'Cheers, Barb!' Butch said, giving her a cheeky little wink as they left. 'We will!'

'Where are you, you little sod?' Reverend Bowen said to herself, leaving the police station, crossing the High Street to the butcher's opposite. Moses as always was by her side.

Bowen was trying her best to hold herself together, but the heat was not helping. She slung her leather waistcoat over her shoulder and loosened her chafing dog collar round her neck, its constriction an appropriate metaphor for her current state of mind; really starting to irritate her. She longed to get out on her trike later, but her meeting with the bishop had to be dealt with first, and it was really beginning to play on her mind. The thought that she might soon find herself ousted from her beloved vicarage – her home for almost twenty years – and be forced into a smaller new-build on the new housing development at the edge of the village troubled her deeply. In fact it did more than that. It disgusted her. She could try and butter the bishop up with as much steak and red wine as she liked, but she felt in her heart that the outcome would be the same. They would sell the vicarage off to the highest bidder in order to swell the church coffers, and she would be forced into the smaller, soulless new build. She was fast losing grip on what little faith remained. And that wild-eyed smirk of Douglas Blouse emerging from the shed was still burning at the forefront of her mind.

She saw Butch Ransom turning left off the High Street onto the causeway. Unsurprisingly he was with a female companion. A ripple of resentment ran through her as she thought of another thing she had sacrificed in the name of her religion.

The sign in the door of E Bumsteads family butchers, hanging slightly to one side, said open, much to Reverend Bowen's relief. Unfortunately next to it was a hastily scribbled note written in pencil that read, 'Back in five minut', the tail of the T trailing off leaving the word unfinished. It seems that whatever had temporarily called the butcher away must have clearly been a matter of some urgency.

She tapped her foot with impatience, wondering how much of the 'five minut' had already elapsed. Moses looked up expectantly at her and began to whimper.

'Don't blame me,' she said, tying him loosely to the newsagent's swing sign next door. She went for another look in the window, cupping her hands around her face to restrict the glare of the sun, trying to see if there were signs of life inside. Nothing. In fact quite the opposite, she thought, looking at the rows of dismembered animals on display. She leant against the door, immediately startled to feel it give way under her weight. She stumbled into the butcher's, nearly falling flat on her face in the process.

'Knock, and the door shall be opened, eh, reverend?' Eric Bumstead said smiling, wiping his hands with a blue paper towel as he emerged through the silver and green chain link partition from the rear of the shop.

Bowen composed herself, regaining her balance. 'Eric, you left your door unlocked. I could have been anyone. You're not very safety-conscious, are you,' she said, wrinkling her brow. 'You should think about that, considering all the trouble we've been having. Count yourself lucky that little sod didn't put your window through.'

'I know, Reverend, I heard about all that. Perhaps young Douglas thought he'd spare his old boss the trouble. I see old Mr Kareshi this morning. Not a happy camper,' he said, exhaling and shaking his head. 'I know I shoulda locked the door n' all, but it was a bit of a do or die situation, if you know what I mean. Got a bit of irritable bowel syndrome, think it might've been some out of date pate I had for my tea last night. I won't go into details, Reverend, wouldn't want to put you off your dinner,' he said, with a wry grin.

'Very considerate of you, Eric,' she said. 'Well, I'm glad I caught you anyway. Time is getting on. I thought I was going to be forever at that police station.'

'Police station?' Bumstead enquired. 'You not given a statement already about your window? Everyone else has,' he said, 'Sorry to hear about that, by the way, reverend,' he added as a sympathetic afterthought.

'I gave my statement about the window to Sergeant Frisk this morning, Eric, yes, foolishly thinking that that would be the end of it, but how wrong I was!'

Bowen went on to fill Bumstead in on the more recent events concerning herself, Daisy and Douglas.

Eric Bumstead grinned, stroking the ginger stubble on his chin as he listened to Bowen's story.

'Yeah, he always was a bit of a strange one, was our Douglas,' Bumstead said, pushing up the thick rimmed glasses on his big flat nose. 'Decent worker when he wanted to be, though, and my girls seemed to like him when he worked here with them on Saturdays. Course he worked the odd weekday as well after he packed school in. Think they had a bit of a thing for him, if truth be told. Couldn't tell you why, mind,' he said, scratching his bristly chin again in absent- minded contemplation. 'But they do say that girls like a bad boy, don't they, Reverend?'

Reverend Bowen knew the Bumstead twins, as she did nearly everyone in the village in her role as parishioner. She had the pleasure of baptising the twins when they were still babies, remembering how they felt like a pair of cross-eyed bowling balls in her arms as she struggled with them at the font. Both girls had been born slightly cross-eyed, Mandy's right eye looking towards her rounded nose, Donna's, her left. This was the only distinguishing feature that set them apart as identical twins.

'I wouldn't say I approved of them going down to that caravan of his,' Eric said a little warily, reaching into the meat counter to retrieve two fillet steaks. 'He always used to boast to them about having his own place. Never mind the fact that it was that tatty old thing. They'd work together some Saturdays when it was busy,' he said, weighing the vicar's meat. 'I'd send him out on the bike to make deliveries round the village, and the girls would help me in here. Took his time some days, mind, pushed his luck a bit, did our Douglas. That bloody railway, wasn't it?' he said, shaking his head with a wry grin. 'Easily distracted, shall we say. Well, in the end he just stopped turning up, and I had the girls to lend a hand if we were busy. I still sorted his mum out with a few sausages from time to time, when they was a bit short of cash, which of course they mostly were after Bertie buggered off,' Bumstead said. He apologised, realising his bad language. 'Nice lady though, Alice. She's had a lot to put up with.'

Poor her, Reverend Bowen thought unsympathetically, digging into her purse for a ten pound note. Most people had problems in their lives. She was currently facing the biggest spiritual and domestic crisis of her life, but that didn't mean that it gave her licence to put people's windows through with rocks wrapped in dirty pictures of their backsides and holding young girls hostage in garden sheds.

As if reading her thoughts, Bumstead said, 'You seen them pictures, I suppose, Reverend? Of his arr…' he paused, 'of his backside? Done the old dot to dot on it yet?'

Bowen frowned. 'I'm sorry, Eric, I don't quite follow you,' she said.

'Girls told me about it. Few years ago now, I suppose it would have been. When Douglas was still going to school,' Bumstead said. 'On the bus. My girls got on the same one. Young Douglas thought he was a bit of a lad, didn't he. Well, a big fish in a small pond round here he might well be, but there was bigger fish elsewhere, especially on the bus with all them lads from the other schools. They used to tease him something rotten by all accounts,' he said, wrapping the steaks in paper. 'They went to different schools but they all still got on the same bus, didn't they. Recipe for disaster, if you ask me. Calling him Douglas the big girl's Blouse. Easy target really, with a name like that. My girls got it n' all. On the bus and at school. The Bumstench twins, they used to call 'em. Kids can be right bastards sometimes, Reverend, pardon my Dutch.'

Bowen nodded, the image of Douglas grinning as he emerged from the shed coming to mind. 'Indeed they can be, Eric,' she said.

'They used to tease my girls because of their cross-eyes as well, or their asthma. Nicking their inhalers and lobbing them about the place. Sometimes it was cuz of their size. You know my girls are a bit on the large side, shall we say, Reverend. Not their fault they eat well, is it? If it weren't that, then they'd have a go about me and their mum just because we had 'em a bit later on in life. "How's your Nan and Grandad?" they'd ask 'em. The girls were worse than the boys for the teasing. Little cows,' he said. 'My girls might not have been blessed in them departments, Reverend, but they're more loved than any of them little trollops on that bus or in that school, I can tell you that,' Bumstead said proudly.

Bowen gave him a wan smile, wary of the time but strangely fixated by the butcher's story. 'And what's all this got to do with Douglas, Eric?'

'Well, one day a bunch of lads all got Douglas on the back of the bus. Laid him face down across their laps on the back seat, that's where all the so-called bad boys likes to sit, isn't it?' he said.

Bowen didn't, but took his word for it.

'Anyway, he had his darts on him, didn't he, silly sod. You know he used to call me Mr Bristow, on account of my first name, see. Hero to our Douglas, was Brizzy. The Guv'nor. Anyway they got him across the back seat, held him face down, arms and legs stretched out like bloody superman. Then they pulled down his trousers and pants and stuck them darts right in his arse cheek, didn't they, the savage little bastards. Shouted the whole bus down, Douglas did by all accounts. My girls were sat near the front, less trouble there, away from all that kind of thing, you know, but they sees what them lads are doing to him. Left him with the scars to prove it n' all, well, three little dots. I noticed them when old Mr Kareshi showed me that photocopy this morning. Bit hard to spot amongst all the, well, the spots,' he said, 'but you can still make 'em out.'

Reverend Bowen found herself completely absorbed by Bumstead's story, and now, knowing all that, she finally had evidence to link Blouse to the windows. She quickly paid the butcher, thanking him before dashing towards the door.

'Hey, Reverend,' Bumstead called out as she pulled the door, 'perhaps that's why Douglas's got a bit of an axe to grind with you.'

'I don't quite follow, Eric,' she said.

'Well, your surname. Bowen. Like Jim Bowen off *Bullseye.* If it hadn't been for old Bertie going on there, he wouldn't have met that Welsh tart and fuh..., err, left the way he did, if you get my meaning, Reverend.'

'A distinct possibility, I suppose, Eric,' Bowen said, her hand on the door handle. 'Now if you'll excuse me, I really must be going.'

'Good luck, Reverend! Hope you enjoy them steaks. See you Saturday at the fete... God bless!'

The fete. Indeed. She couldn't risk having that lunatic boy running around unhinged with the fete only two days away. At least now, after Eric's potted biography of Douglas, she finally had some real evidence. All they needed to do now was find him and prove it.

Reverend Bowen dashed out the door, steaks dangling beside her in the blue and white striped carrier bag. She looked both ways at the High Street before crossing.

Then she remembered: Moses!

She'd left him tied up to the swing sign outside the newsagent. Hastily, she turned around, cursing herself for being so forgetful.

And then her heart sank. Because Moses was no longer there.

10

Butch, Trudy and Finn walked the cobbled causeway beneath the shade of the horse chestnuts towards The Crafty Digit. Something in Butch told him they should be holding hands. Something else told Butch that if he tried, she would not resist. In the short time he had known her, he had become quite smitten with Steventon's newest resident. Although he was moderately disappointed to find out her marital status, he didn't let it dampen his spirits, or let it spoil the enjoyment he felt in her company. He thought once more about reaching out to hold her hand. But to be on the safe side he kept it in his pocket. Butch liked what Trudy had to say. He admired the fact that she was clearly a strong-minded, independent woman with her own ambitions. He also liked the Aroma Therapy part, thinking he might get himself booked in for a massage some time. Although unfortunately he doubted it would include the happy ending he hoped for.

Halfway down the causeway was the small village shop that, along with Mr Kareshi's newsagent, served as the general store to Steventon's residents. Like Fabsolutely Babulous, it was bigger than it looked from the outside, and you rarely left without whatever you had come in for.

Butch told Trudy to wait outside, before skipping up to the shop like an exited child. Two minutes later he re-appeared, holding his hands behind his back and grinning a broad, dopey grin.

'Left or right?' he said, standing in front of her.

'I'm sorry?' she replied, a little confused.

'Don't be. Come on, time is somewhat of the essence here, Trudy Freudy. This could be the most important decision you make all day. Now, left or right?'

Trudy wore a quizzical grin, her eyes glinting in the sun. 'Lift!' she said, mimicking Butch's accent.

‘Ooooohh, Trudy,’ Butch said, amused at her bravado, ‘Taking the piss, are we?’ he said in good humour, before drawing his arm round from behind his back. ‘Good choice that, lady!’ Butch said, holding out an orange Callipo. Trudy let out a surprised laugh.

‘Welcome to Stivvy!’ he said, grinning. ‘But don’t look too happy just yet, Trudy,’ he said. ‘Look at what you could’ve won, as Douglas’s favourite gameshow host would say.’

From behind his back he revealed an identical Callipo. Trudy laughed as Butch ripped the foil from it, proudly holding it aloft. ‘Cheers!’ he said to Trudy, smiling.

In tender cooperation, Trudy held her own Callipo aloft, tapping it against Butch’s before walking the last hundred or so yards to the pub.

11

On the High Street Douglas could not believe his eyes. He cautiously slowed his pace as he approached the row of shops, not because he was now opposite the police station, where unbeknown to him he was being lauded as Steventon's most wanted. Not that he would've cared about that. He was walking cautiously because he didn't want to spook the dog: the nosey little shit that had given him away earlier, when he was moments away from getting it on with Daisy.

The dog had taken a hit to the nose earlier from the shed door, and Douglas hoped it didn't recognise him and start barking. Then he remembered, feeling the lump in his back pocket and smiling. Dogs were basically stupid, Douglas believed. Although they acted like they loved you or showed some genuine affection, all they were usually after was food. 'I hope you like sausage rolls,' he said in a low voice, eyeing up the tethered dog lying sedately in the shade of the newsagent's. He had to be careful. Douglas was reckless, but he wasn't stupid, and were he to be given away now with the police station directly opposite, it would be curtains for sure. They'd be on him like a King Charles spaniel on a sausage roll, he thought, looking at the dog and smirking.

Douglas walked slowly, passing the garage where he occasionally got petrol for his generator. A man he didn't recognise was filling up a beige Skoda, but apart from that all was quiet. He looked in the window, seeing the solitary, lazy figure of the garage's owner, Gary. He was slumped behind the counter reading a newspaper. No customers were present among the videos, pick and mix and car accessories. Perfect, Blouse thought, gliding stealthily past, reaching into his pocket for the warm crumbling pastry of the sausage roll.

The dog, thankfully, was still oblivious to Douglas's presence. He peered in through the bottom corner of the butcher's window, his already pounding heart rate increasing as he saw the black shape of Reverend Bowen. The nosy cow had her back to the window and was deep in conversation with his former employer. Eric Bumstead's eyesight was poor, as the thick-rimmed glasses and scarred index finger on his left hand would attest to, and he did not see Douglas lurking by the window. Given his poor eyesight, combined with the array of lethal implements he wielded daily in the shop, it was a surprise that the butcher had not lost more of his anatomy. Blouse recalled the day Eric had chopped the top of his finger off. Bumstead had hacked it off with a cleaver whilst butchering a beef carcass out the back. He remembered being fascinated by all the blood and panic, and the manic efforts made to preserve the detached finger. Lucky they had so much ice to freeze the finger immediately, making re-attachment an uncomplicated procedure later on. Bumstead would be forever ribbed by the patrons up at The Crafty Digit for his injury, with threats to change the picture on the pub sign frequently voiced.

Mandy and Donna had been drafted in to mind the shop, while their father was up at the hospital having his finger sewn back on. Douglas had used the opportunity to slope off, leaving his not so secret admirers to run the show. He left that afternoon with two packs of sausages, three sirloin steaks and the blood-stained meat cleaver responsible for separating hand and finger.

Thankfully for Douglas, Reverend Bowen's conversation continued. He felt that as long as she stayed with her back to him, he could remain undetected. He glanced over the road a little nervously at the police station. All quiet there, it seemed. He had to walk past the butcher's window to get to the dog tied up outside the newsagent, with the no doubt still irate Mr Kareshi lurking within. He backed away, standing with his back to the wall, pulling the sausage roll from his pocket. The dog raised its head from its lazy doze, appearing to detect the scent of the stale snack almost immediately.

Fuck it. Now or never, he thought, as he walked past the window. In one smooth motion he stooped down to the dog, holding the sausage roll out.

Moses greedily began nibbling on it as Douglas fumbled at the lead, trying to undo it from the swing sign. He untangled it easily enough. Mercifully Moses did not seem too perturbed by his sudden appearance, nor did there seem to be any trace of recognition. The greedy dog was only interested in his sausage roll. Proving Douglas's earlier theory correct.

'Good boy,' Blouse said as the dog began tucking into the sausage roll. 'Good nosy, snooping yappy boy,' he continued, stroking the animal's chin and noticing the collar Moses wore, identical in design to that of his soon to be former owners. Thankfully, the dog made no sound, and the small metal name tag that dangled from it did not jangle too much. Not enough to be detected anyway. He thought it best to get away as quickly as possible.

The dog had already devoured half of the sausage roll. Douglas knew that if he wanted to keep it quiet he was going to need more food. He stood up, being sure to keep clear of the butcher's window, and assessed his options. He pocketed what was left of the sausage roll, keeping it as incentive for the dog. It whined quietly as they began to walk away from the butcher's. There was more food back at the shed, he thought. And more booze. But was it stupid to go back there so soon? ...Who cares, he thought, licking his lips, suddenly very thirsty. He looked down at the dog and smiled, 'So ... you wanna come get slaughtered with me then, shit bag?'

12

Entering the beer garden, Trudy Ryan began to upend the cardboard carton of her orange Callipo.

'Ah, bab, bab!' Butch cried, holding his hand to the slowly rising packaging, lowering it down and safely away from her mouth. 'Don't drink all the good shit at the bottom, Trudy, I've got plans for that,' he said, holding onto his own carton. 'Go grab a bench,' he said, relieving her of the cardboard packaging and waving her away.

Butch walked towards the hatch that served the patrons in the beer garden. Finn followed on faithfully behind. 'Stick a couple of voddys in there, would you please, Pat, my love?' Butch asked, holding out the two orange cartons.

Patricia Wilkes, co-owner of The Crafty Digit, duly obliged, taking the tapered cartons from Butch, grinning at the Kiwi's odd request, adding the shot of vodka to the melted orange liquid pooled at the bottom. He took them from her smiling.

'Cheers, Pat', he said, holding both cartons in one hand and fishing a ten pound note out of his pocket with his free hand and placing it on the counter. 'The old man working today?' he asked.

'Yep,' Pat said.

'Get the old boy to knock us up a pizza, would you?' he said.

'Bernard!' she shouted over her shoulder. 'What one do you want, Butch?' she asked in quieter tones.

'Twelve-inch Hawaiian,' he said smiling.

'Wouldn't we all, sweetheart,' Pat said, returning his smile.

'Bernard! Twelve-inch Hawaiian for Butch.'

'Pervert,' came a soft muffled voice from the pub's small kitchen.

Butch took his change and walked back over to the bench where Trudy sat, shaded under a large Stella Artois umbrella. Taking his seat, he handed the ice lolly carton back to Trudy, raising it in the air a second time. 'Here's to Stivvy part two,' he said, smiling. 'And to new friends,' he added.

'To Stivvy, and to new friends,' Trudy said in agreement, before up-ending the carton and giving a little shudder. 'Mmm, interesting,' Trudy said. 'Vodka and callipo, that's a new one on me.'

'God, that's good,' Butch said, wiping away the orange crescent of syrup from around his top lip. 'Shit, should've got a couple of pints in while I was up. What'll it be, Trudy?' Butch asked, rising from the bench.

'No no, Butch, sit down, my round, I know protocol. What would you like?' she asked.

'At a girl!' he replied. 'Lager, cheers, Trudy.'

'Coming up,' she said, rising from the bench and taking the empty Callipo cartons to the serving hatch. She soon returned, placing one and a half pints of amber nectar on the bench. Butch looked at his pint admiringly.

'Cheers,' he said, raising his glass.

'Cheers,' she said, clinking glasses with him.

'So, Trudy Freudy, how are you settling into our little community?'

'Pretty good, actually,' she said, sipping her half. 'It's such a lovely place, and everyone seems so friendly. It's not like London, everyone running around all stern and anonymous.'

'Posers,' Butch said, taking a mouthful of lager.

'I just can't wait to get started with the Aroma Therapy and the Holistic practice now i'm qualified. It's something I've wanted to do for so long. I just never felt that London was the right place to do it. Here feels so much more conducive to that sort of thing. Much more peaceful,' she said. 'Jeremy isn't exactly overjoyed with the added time to his commute from moving here, but we both agreed that we didn't want the girls growing up in London. I always imagined a place just like this for them when they were young. Idyllic, peaceful,' she said as a frown creased her forehead, 'well, apart from the railway perhaps,' Trudy said, sipping her drink. 'Tell me, Butch, this

Douglas, he isn't, well, dangerous is he? You know, I worry about the girls, that's all.'

Butch took a big swig of his pint. 'No, Trudy, you don't have to worry about that. Douglas may be a lot of things, but he's not a nonce. Arse flashing, railway trespassing, window smashing, caravan dwelling little bastard he may be. But dangerous, no, I don't think so.'

'Not quite what I meant, but reassuring all the same, I suppose,' she said with a little smile. 'No, I just love it here. I can't wait to start walking the kids to school in September,' she said, nodding to the charming 19th century red brick primary school opposite the pub, resplendent with its quintessential bell tower. 'And going for walks, getting the business up and running, all of it. I think we're going to be very happy here,' she said with a smile. 'So anyway, that's enough about me, tell me about you. What brought you to these shores, Mr Kiwi sheep farmer extraordinaire?'

Butch contemplated the question for a moment. 'You promise to buy me another beer after?'

'Mmm, OK. Deal.'

Butch took a deep intake of breath and another large gulp of lager. 'I came here after my wife died of cancer back in '84,' Butch said, getting straight to the point. 'Couldn't hack it back in New Zealand without her, everything just reminded me of her. So, I did the only sensible thing I thought I could do. I sold the farm back home and I ran halfway around the world. After freelancing for a while down along the south coast area, I came inland a bit and found myself here. Bought the farm in '86 and never looked back. Got Finn here thrown in with an old motor home I bought off a guy down in Kent. His dog had just had a litter. Best freebie I ever had, isn't that right, boy?' Butch said, rubbing Finn's belly, the dog rolling over under the bench to receive the adoration.

'And you didn't remarry? If you don't mind me asking.'

'No, I didn't remarry. Kinda got used to the bachelor lifestyle again, if you know what I mean,' Butch said with a little cough. 'And no one'll measure up to Trish,' he said, raising his glass to the sky. 'Love you, girl.'

A gentle but comfortable silence settled between the two before Trudy asked, 'Apparently this place used to have its own railway station?'

'Yep. Up until the sixties, I think, then they got rid of it. No call for it any more.'

'That's not what Jeremy would say. He'd love to be able to get on the train two minutes from the house. I think he's a bit resentful, you know. He's the big city breadwinner, you see, and I'm the stay at home housewife trying to make a go of her "Woo woo hippy stuff", as he likes to call it. I think he'd prefer it if I was just a full-time mum; after all, as he's so fond of telling me, on the money he earns, we could afford it. But that's not me, you know. I've always had my own hopes and aspirations and I'm gonna show him that I can make a go of things.'

'Here, bloody here!' Butch said.

'Blimey, listen to me getting all squiffy and brave,' Trudy said checking her watch. 'Better rein it in, I've got to go and get the girls in an hour. They've already made friends in the village too, and I don't want to get a reputation as an alkie with the other parents this early on.'

Butch drained his pint. 'You might not, but my reputation around here is already firmly established,' he said jovially. 'Now go and get me that bloody beer!'

13

Sergeant Frisk was close to tears. If Petra carried on, he would surely end up displaying the same kind of emotions her daughter had earlier on.

Seated in the chair previously occupied by Reverend Bowen, Petra was now bombarding him with a series of questions relating to the recent decline in law and order, and the subsequent whereabouts of the individual suspected as being responsible for it. She also demanded to know what, as a Sergeant, he intended to do about addressing the delicate matter of public safety, should Douglas Blouse continue to evade capture; particularly with the village fete a mere two days away.

'With a maniac like Douglas Blouse on the loose, Sergeant, I am seriously considering postponing the entire thing!' she said dramatically. 'I mean, what more is he capable of? He needs to be found. He's out there somewhere, getting up to God knows what. Who is he going to target next? It's down to you to find him, Alan!' she said, pointing her skinny finger at him, wild and judgemental.

Daisy squirmed, clearly embarrassed by her mother's behaviour.

The unfortunate truth, Frisk knew, was that Petra was right. Douglas did need finding, and the sooner the better. Perhaps if Petra realised that she was actually hindering rather than helping him, then he might be able to get out there and find him. It was just a shame that it had to have been Daisy that had been on the receiving end of Douglas's charms. If it had been anyone else in the village, you could guarantee that the likes of Petra Carr wouldn't give it so much as a second glance. Losing his patience, he was on the verge of telling Petra Carr to button it, but as he opened his mouth to do so, the doors of the office burst open and a visibly distressed Reverend Bowen rejoined the proceedings.

My God, what now? Frisk thought, wilting a little more inside.

'He's taken him, Alan. He's taken him, I just know he has ... Jesus Christ, what next!?' Bowen shouted blasphemously as she entered, swinging a blue and white plastic bag. 'We've got to find him, Alan. We've got to find him, and quick!'

'OK, OK, Reverend, slow down, what's happened?' Frisk asked, raising his palms to the panicking vicar in an attempt to placate her.

'Moses, my poor Moses!' she shouted, before giving a distressed account of what had just taken place. 'I've been up and down the High Street. I've been in the shop, the garage. No one's seen him. My God, what's he going to do!? He's got it in for me, and now he's going to take it out on my poor dog. I just know he's going to do something stupid, Alan.'

Petra Carr gave Sergeant Frisk her most potent, withering look, shaking her head. Choosing to ignore it, he continued addressing the vicar.

'Well, Reverend, like I said, we still can't be sure it was Douglas who smashed the windows.'

'Oh bollocks, Alan!' Bowen shouted, startling them all with her colourful outburst. 'Don't give me that. What kind of idiot do you think I am? Of course it was him. And I'll prove it.'

Reverend Bowen reached between Daisy and Petra and on to Frisk's paper-strewn desk, grabbing at a small pile of crumpled A4 pages being held down by a piece of railway ballast and selecting the top piece of paper. The remaining paperwork on Frisk's desk was blown to the floor by the fan.

'Oh thanks, Hilda,' he said, scrabbling to pick them up.

Ignoring him, Reverend Bowen placed the crumpled piece of paper on the desk, flattening it out as much as possible, attempting to iron out the creases and crinkles to make identification an easier task. She pointed to a faint row of dots on the right-hand cheek.

'There! There is your proof, Sergeant,' she said, relaying Bumstead's story to the increasingly bewildered Frisk. 'Puncture wounds. Scars. Just like Eric said! That is Douglas Blouse's bottom!'

Squinting at the image, Frisk was initially confused, wondering how many more times he would have to scrutinise this bizarre image. At first the pattern seemed a little indistinct amongst the creases and blemishes, but eventually he could see something there.

'Where is your car, Sergeant?' Bowen said, her eyes wild in their sockets.

Petra Carr, still seated, had gone noticeably quieter in the presence of the maniacal holy woman, presumably enjoying watching the Sergeant squirm as more trouble was heaped on him.

'We need to find them, Alan.' Bowen said.

Frisk agreed, but they all needed to calm down. He had taken quite enough from these hysterical women. He needed to regain control. 'OK, Reverend, OK, we'll go and look for him,' he said, trying to reassure her, thinking of a plan that might be good for all of them. 'What I suggest is,' he said, looking at the livid grimace on Hilda Bowen's face, 'you come with me in the car and we go for a drive round the village and try to find him. Petra, Daisy, you come as well, I can drop you home on the way round. I have enough information from you both for the time being,' he said. What he really wanted to say was, I've taken quite enough crap from all of you for the time being, but he held his tongue.

'Fine,' Petra said rather petulantly, crossing her arms. Daisy next to her looked relieved at the prospect of going home.

'Yes, right ... OK,' Reverend Bowen said, appearing to calm a little.

'Dennis, can you stay here?' Frisk said to his young Police Constable seated at the desk in the corner of the office. 'I'll check out the damage to the allotment after I've done a circuit of the village,' he said. 'That is, if we don't see anything of Douglas or Moses in the meantime.'

'Yes, Sarge,' Binsley said.

Reverend Bowen became increasingly distressed at the mention of her dog's name. 'Sergeant, please,' she said to Frisk, who was retrieving the van keys from a small glass-fronted cupboard on the office wall. 'Sergeant please, for God's sake hurry,' Bowen demanded. 'My dog's life is on the line here!'

She didn't know just how right she was.

14

Butch Ransom demolished the twelve-inch Hawaiian pizza almost single-handedly, Trudy only lending marginal support by eating two slices. He drained his second pint of the afternoon before belching rather unceremoniously, apologising to Trudy, who was now on water, for his uncouth behaviour.

Like most dogs when food is around, Finn had been sat upright beside his master the whole time Butch ate, venturing out from the shade of the bench to brave the heat of the garden, and receiving the odd tidbit of pizza for his troubles. The dog hungrily devoured it before lapping up water from the bowl that Butch had put under the bench for the panting dog, the ice cubes he'd requested in it long since melted.

'So why did you call him Finn?' Trudy asked. Butch gave her a rather confused look for her troubles.

'I'll tell you a little story in answer to that question, Trudy,' he said, smiling and gently wagging his finger. 'Not so long ago a music journalist asked Paul McCartney, "So, Paul, what's it like being the greatest living song writer?"' Butch said, holding an imaginary microphone to the invisible mega star seated next to him. 'And you wanna know what he said to that? What Paul McCartney said to that question?' Butch said, ramping up the drama. 'He said,' effecting his best McCartney accent, '"I dunno, you'd better go and ask Neil Finn."'

Trudy stared blankly back at him and said nothing, only shaking her head a little.

'You're joking me,' he said. 'Neil Finn, Trudy ... of Crowded House? Crowded House! New Zealand's greatest band? Ring any bells?' he said, failing to comprehend Trudy's ignorance.

She shook her head and stuck out her bottom lip. 'I'm sorry, Butch, the name doesn't mean anything to me,' she said, almost in apology.

'The name doesn't ...?' Butch trailed off in incomprehension, looking around the garden.

Trudy gingerly sipped her water. 'Sorry,' she said, smiling as if she had been told off by her parents but couldn't help laughing.

'You've got a lot to learn about music, young lady,' Butch said, just about managing a smile himself. 'You do know who Paul McCartney is, don't you?' he said, now sounding genuinely concerned.

She again looked blank. Butch looked like his eyes were about to pop out of his head.

She burst out laughing. 'Yes of course I know who Paul McCartney is, you wally. I guess it's just New Zealand bands I struggle with,' she said, grinning. Ransom smiled back.

Over Trudy's shoulder Butch saw a small white Fiat Panda coming down Stocks Lane before turning left into the pub car park. The car looked crammed full. From the back seat an elderly gentleman who looked a little worse for wear leaned forward over the front passenger's left shoulder, trying to gulp down air from the open window.

'Oh here they are!' Butch said, grinning as the doors of the Fiat opened and Terence Russell and Gerry Hayman got out, before pushing the two front seats forward to release the men trapped in the back, struggling to breathe.

'JesusChristlemmeout ... lemme out ...' Colin Blunsden uttered frantically, panting like a dog, almost crawling to the serving hatch. 'What you 'avin, Bob?' he asked, gulping in air, 'whatchoo'avin?'

'Pint,' came the one-word reply from the man clambering out from behind the driver's seat. Both of them wore vests, shorts and sandals. Blunsden's was a white string vest, and he had a wet tea towel on his head.

'Been working them hard today, have we, Terence?' Butch asked, as the lead Morris dancer made his way over to the Kiwi's table with Gerry.

Both men wore short sleeved shirts, unbuttoned to the navel, their grey hairy chests on display. The shorts they both wore just about maintained their modesty. Hayman wore a faded blue cap with an embroidered Esso logo on the front.

Terence beamed, before winking at the Kiwi. 'Big day on Saturday, Butch, you know that,' he said, placing one foot up on the bench, and putting Trudy Ryan in serious danger of eyeing up the antiquated contents of his shorts. 'Last practice before the big day, no room for error,' he continued. 'Got to have them well drilled. People round here expect a certain standard from the headline act, don't they?' he said, smiling proudly. 'The gear's all in the wash. I'll be back to hang it out once me and the boys have had our refreshments. God knows we've earned it,' he said, licking his lips. 'I'll run the iron over 'em a couple of times tomorrow and dish it back out to the boys at the meeting,' he said. 'I want them all looking their absolute best for Saturday. I want us all to be at our very best,' he said. 'It's a big ...' Terence faltered a little, 'it's the first...' He paused, composing himself before continuing. 'It's the first since Iris ... last year, you know, since she went. I've had to get used to taking care of myself this past year, Butch,' he said. 'Wel, you know what that's like,' he said, nodding at Butch who smiled, nodding back. Terence faltered, the words sounding strangled in his throat. 'And I ... I just want to look my best for her,' he said. 'I wanna look my best.'

'You will, chief, you will,' Gerry said, putting an arm around his lead dancer.

'Poof.'

They all ignored Colin's comment from over at the hatch.

'Iris,' Butch said, holding up his glass as they collectively toasted her memory.

Butch looked over at the shambolic figure of Colin Blunsden over at the serving hatch, looking far from his best. 'Old Colin there gonna be OK, Terence? Looks like he can barely stand up,' he said. 'Mind you, not much change there.'

'He's all right, Butch. Be right as rain after a little rehydration. Him and Bob both.'

'Better keep an eye on 'em, Terence. You know what those two are like,' Butch said cautiously.

'Professionals, Butch,' Terence said, in more spirited tones. 'They won't let me down,' he said. Although Butch didn't think Terence sounded quite as confident as he'd perhaps hoped.

'That's why I drove down here, see,' Terence continued. 'Saving up their strength. The boys deserve a drink for all the effort they put in today. Should be a good one, Saturday,' he said. 'It will be a good one, Saturday.'

Trudy Ryan, looking a little out of the loop, leaned into the conversation. 'Pardon me, Mr uhh ...?

'Russell, miss, Terence Russell,' he said smiling, turning to face her properly for the first time.

Butch interjected. 'Yeah, sorry, Trudy, should have introduced the pair of you. Trudy here's new to the area,' he said. 'Terence is in charge of these reprobates,' he said, pointing at the Morris men now dispersed around the garden. 'Lead dancer of the Morris men. Going to be performing on Saturday at the fete, eh, Terenece?' Butch said, gently slapping Russell on the hip.

'Abosolutely,' Terence said, grinning from ear to ear.

'How wonderful,' Trudy said. 'I very much look forward to my first fete here as an official Stivvy local,' she said, before adding, 'My first of many, I hope.'

'And we'll be happy to have you there, my dear,' Terence said warmly.

'No, what I was wondering was,' Trudy said, 'it's just, is that man all right?' she asked, gesturing towards the figure of Bob Dobson, seated on a bench a short distance away from them, wearing his usual dumb-founded expression.

'Bob?' Terence said breezily. 'Ohh, he's fine. Just he's had a bit of a bad time recently. Got made redundant, poor bloke. He's still struggling to adjust.'

'Oh, I see,' Trudy responded, sipping her drink. 'When did this happen?'

'Last year,' Terence said.

Trudy nearly spat out her mouthful of water. 'Last year?' she asked in disbelief.

'Bob sure loved that brewery,' Butch said, laughing and looking over at the redundant figure.

'He only properly stopped talking a couple of months ago. Still a great dancer, mind,' Terence said confidently. 'Just as capable as any of my boys,' he said, looking over at the hatch where Colin Blunsden was up-ending a glass of water over his tea toweled head as two full pints were placed in front of him.

'I got four more lads for Saturday,' Terence said, 'taking us up to eight. Another two dancers and two musicians, accordion and violin. They shot off back home. I'll be playing the old squeeze box myself for the young 'uns from the school,' he said, nodding across to the primary school opposite. 'Gonna be doing some traditional stick dancing. Basic stuff, really, but it's nice for them to get involved and for the mums and dads to watch 'em. Always good to start recruiting the next generation as well.'

'Gotta keep an eye on them two, mind, eh, Terence?' Butch said.

'Just a couple of shandies down here beforehand to settle the nerves, Butch. That's the tradition and that's all they'll need,' he said. 'It's going to be a proud day for us all.'

'Too bloody right, Terence,' Butch said. 'I'll be down here. Might even have a little surprise for you all as well,' he said, smiling at Terence and winking at Trudy.

Colin Blunsden took a tray of drinks from the hatch and ambled shakily back over to his mute dancing companion. Butch counted four pints that miraculously remained unspilled on the tray, plus two chasers of clear liquid. He looked back at Terence with a raised eyebrow.

'It's been a long day for them,' he said, laughing a touch nervously. 'Besides, they've got tomorrow off to recover. Only the meeting in the evening,' Terence said. 'You coming?' he asked.

'Absolutely, Terence,' Butch said. 'The traditional pre fete AGM. With such interesting subjects as, How much air is going to be in the bouncy castle? What constitutes a true garden on a plate? Is the lucky dip really lucky? I wouldn't miss it for the world,' Butch said. 'You should come, Trudy Freudy.'

'Maybe I'll try,' she said. 'Depends on Jeremy really.'

'Ello ello ello, wossallllisssen?' Colin Blunsden said, looking down the causeway, belching a full stop at the end of the sentence.

They all turned to look towards the police car that was slowly driving up from the direction of the High Street.

Like Terence Russell's Fiat Panda earlier, the police car had the same number of occupants, only this one had four doors, and so, unlike the suffocating Blunsden earlier, those seated in the back had access to their own windows... And in this instance, were not elderly degenerate alcoholics.

Sergeant Frisk drew up to the pub, stopping outside but not getting out. He leaned out of his wound-down window.

'Bugger me, Alan!' Butch quickly piped up, clocking the car's all female occupants. 'You're a married man,' he said. 'Does your missus know you're driving around with three other women?'

Before he could respond, the back window jerkily began to wind down further. Petra Carr stuck her head out, pointy nose first. 'That's right,' she said accusingly, wasting no time, 'you lot just drink away your cares. Never mind the fact that there is a mad man on the loose in our village,' she said. 'Vandalism, sexual assault, and now kidnap ... well, dog nap,' she said, correcting herself. 'Anyway, whatever. This village is in the midst of a crime epidemic and all you can do is drink,' she said, adding with a final judgemental flourish. 'Disgusting!'

'Hello, Reverend!' Terence called out, waving to the vicar in the passenger seat. 'Still got that waistcoat on, I see.'

Bowen ignored him. Daisy Carr was slumped in the back seat beside her mum.

Frisk finally managed to get a word in. 'Oh, didn't you know, Butch? Thames Valley taxi service now,' he said. 'We've diversified in order to generate extra funds. Just doing the rounds,' he said, cocking a thumb at his passengers. 'Have any of you seen a certain Mr Blouse on your travels?' he asked with an air of exasperation. 'Possibly with a dog,' he added.

'You mean one uvver'en them ones you got in there?' Colin said, pointing at the police car and laughing.

Petra leaned further out of her window. 'You dirty drunken old man,' she spat. 'You won't be laughing when you see what state your allotment's in. Don't think we don't know all about you and your foul perversions,' she said. 'Naked ladies and tractors indeed,' she said, shaking her head. 'You should be arresting that man for public indecency, Sergeant,' she said, tapping Frisk on the shoulder. Frisk ignored her.

'Not seen a thing, Sarge,' Butch said. 'Been very quiet round here,' he added. Everyone else nodded in agreement.

'Well, if any of you do see him, you let me or someone back at the station know as soon as possible, please. We've had a bit of trouble with him today,' he said, 'and not just the windows either.'

'So what's new?' Butch said.

'Sergeant, we must go!' Reverend Bowen yelled from the passenger seat.

Frisk exhaled. 'Enjoy the rest of your day,' he said, pulling away from the pub.

'Naked ladies and tractors? What's all that about then, Colin?' Gerry Hayman asked, smiling suspiciously at the now extremely sheepish looking Colin Blunsden.

'Piss it off, you', came the curt response.

15

From a small gap in the shed door, Douglas watched with amusement as the police car drove slowly past the allotments. The blue lights on the car's roof protruded just above the allotment wall, but were inactive. It continued down Stocks Lane, coming into view where the wall became metal railings. He could see Reverend Bowen sticking her head out the passenger side window, moving it frantically from side to side. She did not look happy, Douglas thought to himself.

'I wonder what her problem is?' he said, smiling down at Moses.

He could just make out the long blonde ponytail of Daisy Carr in the back seat, and prickled with lust and frustration at the teasing glimpse of his would-be lover. She was sat next to what he supposed was probably her mum. He couldn't quite make her out. She was another busybody. Never happy unless she was sticking her pointy nose into other people's business. She would try and come between him and Daisy, no doubt about it. Perhaps it was for the best they stayed apart. She would be a crap mother-in-law anyway.

Douglas watched as the police car veered round the corner on to Castle Street and out of sight. He opened the door and stuck his head out, confident now that they were out of sight. He yanked Moses' lead, causing the dog to emit a soft yelp. 'Looking for something?' he said to the now empty road.

Moses had finished the sausage roll that Douglas had used to lure him away from the butcher's. Luckily for him, within the musty confines of Colin Blunsden's broken mini fridge there lurked a couple of slices of pizza and another sausage roll. Only a small amount of mould had begun to form on the crust of the pizza. Moses didn't mind, exhibiting the same enthusiasm for it that he did towards the sausage roll. Only this time the dog had something to wash it down with. As well as mouldy pizza and sausage rolls, it turns out that dogs are also quite fond of warm lager on a hot summer's day. Moses had lapped up a fair amount of Carlsberg export from the empty ice cream tub Douglas had found, blowing the dust and cobwebs from it before pouring in nearly half a can.

'We could have been good friends, you and me,' he said, looking at the now slightly wobbly spaniel, who continued to look up expectantly at the pizza Douglas was waving. 'If only you and your holy roller mummy weren't such a pair of nosy little sods, eh?' The dog yelped again. 'Just like every other piss 'ead around here, aren't you?' he said.

With comic timing, Moses began to urinate on the rotting wooden floor. The smell immediately filling the hot shed with a cloying sour reek.

'Oh, you dirty bastard!' Douglas said, pulling the neck line of his T-shirt up over his nose. 'Right, that's it, we're out of here,' he said, kicking the creaky door open and finally off its last remaining hinge. He walked over the door, like a drawbridge, pulling the dog along with him. The dog resisted.

'What?' he asked, then he remembered.

He went back into the shed and picked up the piece of stiff, stale pizza, Moses immediately standing to attention. Blouse pulled a bamboo cane from the bucket in the corner and skewered the pizza, holding it out in front of the dog. Moses tried in vain to get at it, Douglas holding it tantalisingly close, just out of the dog's reach. He grabbed another sausage roll for insurance. 'Perfect,' he said as he led the hungry dog out of the allotment and up towards the level crossing.

He crested the incline onto the railway, ignoring for the thousandth time the NO TRESSPASSING sign and the threat of the £200 fine that went with it.

'Forgive us our trespassers, eh, shit bag?' Douglas said, looking down at Moses. 'That's what mummy would say, wouldn't she.'

He stepped off the crossing and onto the railway line, stepping one-footed from sleeper to sleeper, Moses by his side myopically followed the dangling slice of pizza.

He had barely walked ten yards when the warning signal sounded and the barriers clattered down. He looked up to the heavens, smiling. 'Thank you,' he said. Mooning the train from the bank earlier had been OK, but it wasn't the same feeling as doing it standing on the tracks. Peter had told him once that was why old men flashed women in the park. For the buzz of excitement it gave them. Douglas had been quick to defend himself, telling Peter he wasn't a dirty old man, and that mooning trains was completely different. Douglas missed Peter. He thought about Sergeant Frisk driving the police car past the allotment with the vicar and the others and wondered whether that was the same car that was involved in the chase on the night Peter was killed.

Fucking old bill, he thought.

Douglas was snapped out of his thoughts by the HST he saw in the distance, coming from the east heading towards the railway bridge.

Moses. Shit. Best keep him out the way, for this one at least, he thought, quickly assessing his options. He quickly staked the bamboo cane in the railway's soft verge beyond the edge of the ballast. Standing erect, the cane looked like a lop-sided corner flag on a football pitch. Moses looked up at it with the same hungry eyes that most drunks have when food is on offer after a long day on the piss. The dog's energy levels did not match its appetite, however. Douglas reached into the pocket of his shorts and pulled out the flaky sausage roll. 'Here, get on that, you greedy little bastard,' he said. 'Stay out the way, I'm a bit busy here,' he said, tossing the pastry to Moses, who lazily began to munch on it.

The train was now passing under the railway bridge. He unbuttoned his cut-off shorts, feeling the first soft rumble beneath his feet. The driver had spotted him. The horn of the train blared deafeningly as it headed towards him. In between the blasts of the horn, Douglas could hear the soft seductive hiss of the rails getting louder. Like the snake working its manipulative magic in the Garden of Eden. *Moon it Douglas ... moon it,* those long steel snakes seemed to whisper to him. Giving into temptation with zero hesitation he did exactly that. His thumbs were tucked into the waistband of his cut-offs and his boxer shorts, and he pulled them both down, revealing the backside that had become so familiar to drivers who worked this stretch of line. Looking through his legs, Douglas viewed the train from upside down. He smacked his bare bum cheeks, the white spotty flesh reddening with every impact, the three faint dotted scars softening into obscurity as the moon's white surface turned a Mars-like red. The sound of the horn was deafening now, and the ground thundered beneath his feet. He could almost make out the upside-down face of the driver, see the panic in his eyes and the terror on his face.

Now! he thought, just as the front of the train consumed his field of vision.

With only split seconds to spare, Douglas shifted his weight to one side, falling over and out of the train's way on to the hard, knobbly ballast. He just missed landing on Moses, who was nibbling on the last crumbs of the sausage roll, totally uninterested by all the noise happening right next to him. Douglas's heart thumped in his chest and the adrenalin surged through his body. He lay beside the railway on the warm ballast, tilting his head to watch the train continue on its way, diminishing in size until it was just a dot on the western horizon. Then it was gone.

'Textbook,' he said, laying on his front and panting from the rush, his backside still exposed and pointing to the sky. 'That's the way to do it!' he said to Moses in his best Mr Punch voice. He heard the sound of the barriers rattling back up. A couple of cars went over at each crossing, but no one saw him in his reclined position between the crossings. He looked at Moses, lying on the verge in the sunshine, full from the sausage roll and sleepy from the drink. The bamboo cane staked in the ground had tilted over slightly from the rush of air from the train, but it had not gone over completely. The pizza skewered near the top held firm, baking in the sun. Still lying on the ballast, Douglas pulled his shorts up, zipped his fly and fastened the button. The world started to return to him as the rush began to dissipate.

He looked at Moses again. 'Oi, wake up!' he said. 'It's your go next.'

16

After dropping the mother–daughter duo of Petra and Daisy back home, seeing them to their front door and gladly discharging them from his care, Sergeant Frisk now made his way back towards the police car and to the increasingly anxious Reverend Bowen, who was more than a little distressed by the sound of the blaring horn heard coming from the railway moments ago.

'If that little sod has hurt a single hair on that dog's head, Alan, I will personally crucify him,' Bowen said as Frisk climbed back into the police car and buckled his seatbelt. He looked over, aghast to see what Bowen was doing to the carrier bag containing her steaks. With robotic repetition and growing fury, her fist had pounded through the thin plastic carrier bag, and through the paper the steaks were wrapped in, her bloody knuckles making a cold dead slap against the flattened meat in her lap.

'That horn, Alan. You heard it. I know it's him,' she said. 'I know it's him.'

'We'll find him, Hilda,' he said. 'And when we do, Douglas bloody Blouse is going to be in a lot of trouble, let me tell you. But in the meantime, let's just try and stay calm. Besides,' he said, trying to introduce a bit of levity, 'did Jesus not teach us to forgive our enemies?'

*

The church came into view a hundred or so yards away on their left. Even from this distance, Reverend Bowen could make out the hole in her stained glass window. She bristled, as her collective woes fizzed through her like electric current. She looked at her vicarage opposite the church, knowing it would not be her home for very much longer. She thought about Moses, lying in his bed in the kitchen: her beautiful dog that had never hurt anyone in its life, now being held captive by a feral lunatic; by a boy whose behaviour was symptomatic of a wider decline in public morality. She had watched from her pulpit week in week out as her congregation steadily dwindled, all of them slowly succumbing to the pleasures of the material world: mesmerised by cheap thrills and empty promises; straying from the word of God at the expense of their spiritual evolution; drinking; cavorting; indulging in all kinds of carnal behaviour. Amongst it all, she was left alone trying to hold onto her faith like a slippery rope in a turbulent sea, and the worst thing was that she was beginning to think they might be right. The hole in the window that punctured the groin of the crucified Christ was like the hole in her soul; the image a perfect representation of her inner spiritual conflict.

She longed to get out on the trike; to distance herself from the feelings that seemed to stalk her at every turn; to be with the ones who would understand her despair and disillusionment towards her sinful, dwindling congregation; where a swift consensus could easily be reached as to where all those lost souls were heading, were they not to change their sinful ways. She longed for the company of the Crossroads Motorcycle Group. Thy wheel be done.

Bowen heard a distant voice. Snapping out of her vengeful daydream, she realised it was the voice of Sergeant Frisk beside her.

'Reverend? ... Reverend, are you OK?'

She turned to him slowly, remembering the pitiful question of forgiveness he had asked her a moment ago. She raised her hand and pointed a finger. Her knuckles were a light red from pummelling the steak in her lap. She fixed her gaze on him.

'Sergeant,' she said, 'forgiveness is for idiots.'

17

The urgency with which the train had sounded its horn caught the attention of everyone in The Crafty Digit's beer garden, but most soon returned to the more important business of steady intoxication once it had stopped. Everyone except Trudy Ryan.

'Butch?' she called from the bench.

Butch was currently being hemmed in by Terence and Gerry. He only went over to say goodbye to them. That had been ten minutes ago. Butch looked over at her, smiled and nodded before doing the same to the two chatty Morris men, politely extricating himself, thankful for Trudy's intervention. He walked back over to where they had all been sitting. Finn following on behind.

'You did me a bloody favour there,' he said. 'I thought those boys would never stop. Don't think I even need to see the bloody dance on Saturday after that blow by blow account,' he said, turning his attention back to Trudy. 'What is it, Trude?' he asked.

'Butch, did you hear that horn? That's not normal, is it?'

Butch, remaining characteristically upbeat, replied. 'You get used to that kind of noise around here, Trudy,' he said. 'You'll find that out the longer you live here.'

'How do you mean?' she asked, wearing a frown of worry.

'You asked me earlier if Douglas was dangerous, and I said no. Well, that was sort of a lie, he is a danger. A danger to his bloody self, pissing about on that railway line. The kid's got a bloody screw loose,' he said, twirling a finger at the side of his head. 'One day his luck is going to run out,' Butch said. 'It's been fairly quiet around here for a while as well. That all seems to have gone out the window these past few days,' he said, grinning. 'Or should that be through the window.'

Trudy did not share in his amusement. 'You don't think it's got anything to do with what the police officer was saying earlier, do you? You know, about the vicar's dog and what that other lady in the police car was saying, about the vandalism at the allotment? And the windows?'

'Very possibly, Trudy', Butch said, matter of factly. 'But Alan'll catch up to him soon enough.'

Trudy's insides constricted, and she thought of her new home slap bang next to the railway. Was he there now? She hadn't heard the smashing of the signal box window last night, probably due to the fact that she had taken to wearing earplugs at night to combat her husband's incessant snoring and also the railway, which was now by comparison the quieter of the two.

'I think I'm going to make a move, Butch,' Trudy said, rising from her seat. 'I want to go and make sure everything is OK at home. Plus I'll need to go and get the girls soon,' she added.

'If there's anything wrong, Trudy, Alan'll sort it out,' Butch said. 'Especially seeing as he's got the combined powers of the parish council and the Church of England on his side,' he said, laughing. 'God help Douglas Blouse, that's all I can say. And hey, let's face it, it could be nothing. Those drivers blare their horns coming through here all the time. But I tell you what, if you are worried, I'll come up with you. I gotta go past your place to get back up the farm anyhow. Got some stuff I need to be getting on with myself. Got a date with a sewing machine,' he said, winking.

Trudy looked quizzically at Ransom. 'A sewing machine? This wouldn't have anything to do with the surprise you mentioned up at Barbara's earlier, would it?'

'It might have,' Butch said with a poker face. 'But don't try getting anything out of me, because it's top bloody secret. You try it,' he said, motioning towards the bar. 'Buy me another beer, I'm telling you, it won't work.'

Trudy smiled, seeing through Butch's plan.

'No, I believe you,' she said. 'I can wait.'

'Then let's get out of here,' Butch said. 'With a little luck, if there is any action going down, we can go and get a good view, what d'ya say?'

Trudy sincerely hoped it was nothing; her intuition, however, told her it wasn't.

Butch drained his pint. 'Come on then, young lady,' he said. 'Let's go and see what all the fuss is about.'

18

Having pulled his shorts up, Douglas Blouse was back on his feet, still equidistant between the two level crossings. Moses moved sluggishly by his side, still motivated by the skewered pizza that Douglas continued to tease in front of the dog's nose. Ahead he could see the signal box, and the brown rectangle that had been placed over the window he had smashed earlier this morning. He thought about Dan Fowler up in the signal box. Mr Big Shot, thinking he was so cool. Muscling in on Daisy. He'd seen Dan standing on the steps of the signal box wearing his silly sunglasses, smoking and trying to chat her up.

'Don't worry, Dan,' he said, looking at the endless miles of ballast ahead of him. 'I've got more stones than you've got windows, you prat.'

Moses moaned by his side, evidently tiring of chasing the elusive slice of pizza, perhaps finally figuring out how the futile charade was rigged against him. Douglas threw him a small piece to keep him interested, but he was becoming increasingly bored of the dog. He was walking on the railway line like a tight-rope walker, balancing on the narrow steel, skewered pizza cane in one hand, dog lead in the other. He could walk all the way to Wales if he wanted to. Go and visit his dad, shacked up with that tart in Bridgend. Moses twice barked loudly, distracting him from his looming misanthropy.

'Right, I've had just about enough out of you,' he said, looking down at the dog. 'Get a drink down you and you turn in to a chopsy little nob 'ead, just like everyone else around here, don't you,' he said, looking at the groggy, panting dog.

Blouse again staked the bamboo cane in the ground, far away from Moses, and knelt down beside the railway line. He looped the plastic handle of the dog lead underneath the rail, digging out some ballast to allow the chunky black handle enough room to pass through.

'And tell me, Douglas, what is it that you're doing with your dog these days?' he said, remembering an episode of *The Young Ones*. He began to sing: 'I'm tying my dog to the railroad track, uh huh, choo choo train's gonna break his back, we used to call him Spot, yeah, but now he's called Splat, that's the kind of person we are ... Ohh, Daisy, won't you come home with me,' he sang, looping the lead over and under the rail, making sure it was secure. The dog still had some slack from the lead that fed out from the handle, but if Douglas's plan was to work the way he hoped, the dog would not intend to move far. He stood up a bit too quick, feeling light-headed. He remained motionless on his feet as the dizziness passed. In stereo, between the two crossings, the warning alarms sounded and the barriers once again rattled down. Moments later, he heard the clacking splutter of a diesel engine coming from beyond the railway bridge. Good timing, he thought, looking at Moses with a broad grin.

He unstaked the bamboo cane from the ground and squatted beside the railway, the sun beating down on his back. He held it out to Moses, seated on the sleeper, slap bang in the middle of the railway line. Douglas finally allowed him to nibble on the pointy end of the pizza triangle.

His luck was in. The train was on his line. Only this time it wasn't going quite so fast. Far from it, in fact. Douglas could see it was a big class 37 diesel engine, probably pulling a load of petrol tankers, or a car transporter. Car transporters were always fun. Especially if you had a catapult.

He couldn't gauge the engine's speed exactly, but it was going pretty slow. An educated guess suggested that it was probably just pulling out of the sidings on the other side of the bridge, where the two lines that ran through the village split off into four, allowing goods trains like this to pull in and wait for the more important passenger services to pass. It had probably just been given the green light to continue its journey after the HST he had mooned previously had got safely out of sight.

'Oh well, never mind', he said philosophically to Moses as he watched it approach. 'It'll be good practice for a beginner like you, I suppose.'

He continued to dangle the pizza, Moses still drunkenly devouring the stale slice of pepperoni, happily sitting on the warm sleeper, blissfully unaware of the imminent danger it was now in as the train came slowly but steadily towards them.

'I said it was your turn next, didn't I, boy,' he said, looking down at the drunken dog. 'So now it's time for you to show me what you're made of,' he said, 'literally.'

19

Sergeant Frisk was contemplating Reverend Bowen's cold, unsympathetic words as they approached the causeway crossing. Reverend Bowen, motionless next to him, looked straight ahead. She was silent, and making Frisk feel distinctly uneasy. The pounded meat in the crumpled carrier bag sat in her lap, warming in the hot police car. The coppery smell of bloody meat wafted up in to Frisk's nostrils. His window was all the way down, as were all other windows in the car, but the smell of the raw meat persisted.

As they crested the incline onto the railway, Bowen and Frisk both turned their heads to look out of their respective windows. Bowen to her left looked west, seeing nothing but endless empty railway, gleaming in the afternoon sunshine. Frisk looked out of his towards the east, towards the other level crossing and the bridge. Something caught his eye, or more accurately someone, positioned between the crossings. He didn't need to look twice to know who it was.

'There he is,' Frisk said, keeping his tone as neutral as possible in order not to alarm the vicar. He continued over the railway, descending the other side of the level crossing.

'What? Where? Where is he, the little sod? Has he got Moses? Alan, why aren't you stopping?' Bowen asked in rapid bursts.

'It'd be rather stupid of me to stop on the railway line, now wouldn't it, Hilda?' he said as he pulled the car over to the side of the road a short distance from the railway. Down the causeway, he could see Butch Ransom heading in their direction. He was with a female. Typical Butch, Frisk thought, before his mind snapped back into sharp focus at the sound of the level crossing's warning alarm.

Reverend Bowen looked over her shoulder, towards the railway. Her slippery, blood-stained fingers grappled madly at her seatbelt.

In the police car's rearview mirror, Frisk saw the flashing lights of the level crossing, and watched grimly as the barriers descended. Ohh perfect, he thought, switching off the engine and unfastening his seatbelt.

*

Douglas shouted profane words of encouragement at the heavy goods train as it rumbled towards them. Moses still sat contentedly on the sleeper, nibbling the pizza. Douglas was lying flat on his belly, hoping the driver would not see him. Though the engine was still going too fast to stop entirely, it was better to remain hidden and let him pick up pace. Moses was unlikely to be spotted. Not before it was too late, anyway.

Blouse looked at the docile dog between the rails, and a thought suddenly occurred to him. If Moses stayed where he was, then the train would surely just pass over him. In his current state he didn't look like he was in the mood for much excursion. The dozy thing probably wouldn't even notice as the hundred-ton engine and twenty odd petrol tankers rumbled over his little drunken head. No, he needed a change of plan.

The ground began to rumble as the trundling goods train made steady progress towards the Stocks Lane crossing, and the rails began to hiss. Douglas lifted the pizza slice away from the dog. The animal's drunken, droopy eyes looked up in bleary confusion, lazily following it as Douglas drew it away. Moses rose sluggishly to his feet, a little unsteadily, moving towards the outer rail that separated him from Douglas.

The engine driver detected the movement on the tracks and at last began to sound his horn. The noise did not appear to bother Moses though, who began munching away at the outstretched pizza once again. He settled down to continue his feast. Only now his neck was resting on the hissing rail.

*

Sergeant Frisk jogged towards the barriers. He was not quite as fit as he might have liked these days, and was carrying a little extra weight as he approached forty, but he could still move when he wanted to. Or in this case, had to.

Frisk ran up the incline towards the level crossing, hoping to jump the barrier in one smooth, graceful motion, like the professionals might have done back in the day. Problem was he was neither Bodie nor Doyle and this wasn't London. It was Steventon. He swung his right leg at the barrier, hearing a tear as his trousers ripped open at the crotch. He slammed his palm against the barrier in frustration, fingering at the hole in the torn trousers. Oh great, he thought. And clean on today as well. His other pair were sitting in the linen basket at home. 'Bollocks,' he said to himself before attempting to clear the barrier once more, clambering over it successfully, if a tad ungracefully on the second attempt.

Frisk saw Dan Fowler standing on the signal box's top step, Fowler no doubt panicking at the sight of the police. Sergeant Frisk had already cautioned him for possession of marijuana, and had warned him that any further use of illegal substances consumed on the job would be dealt with swiftly, and his employers would have to be informed.

'Keep them bloody barriers down, Dan!' he said. The signal man's brow crumpled in confusion.

'What's the problem, Sarge?' Fowler asked, poking his head out the signal box door, looking perplexed as Frisk made his way onto the crossing.

'That's the frigging problem!' Frisk said, pointing towards Douglas and Moses and the diesel engine coming towards them.

'Oooofff!' Fowler said with mild alarm, looking east.

A figure in black lithely leapt the barriers, making Frisk's attempts look decidedly pathetic. It was Reverend Bowen, making her own dash onto the railway line.

'You don't see this shit every day,' Fowler said to himself as Bowen began to make up ground on the policeman.

'Go on, Reverend!' Fowler shouted from the top of the steps.

*

Jesus, this was going to be close, Frisk thought as he stepped from the level crossing onto the crunching ballast of the railway embankment, his heart pounding hard in his chest. The ballast was banked up alongside the railway line, making for cumbersome running. He nearly fell as the ballast gave way on him, and he slipped down on one knee. He decided that if he was going to make it to Douglas and Moses in time, he would have to run on the level ground of the railway line itself. Frisk switched over onto the line, carefully hitting every other sleeper as he closed the gap between himself, Douglas and the dog, running head on towards the diesel engine that was growing in size ahead of him, fully concentrating on his footing. He didn't dare think what a slip could mean for him at this stage.

He could hear the loud clacking flap of the engine, and smell the fumes that spluttered from the diesel's roof. The ground was rumbling beneath his feet and the driver once again sounded the horn in futile alarm. Frisk could see that Douglas was waving at the engine. Crouching down, waving with one hand and holding something out for the dog with the other. Frisk now saw with horror how Moses was positioned. His head was on the railway line, and he was eating whatever it was that Douglas was holding out for him.

Among the sensory maelstrom, Frisk detected movement: footsteps other than his own gaining on him from behind. He looked over his shoulder, startled to see Reverend Bowen running at full speed, her wild eyes fixed on Douglas. She was almost neck and neck with him. The look on her face sent a shiver down his spine. You are in deep trouble, Douglas, my friend, he thought, looking from the vicar to Douglas, who was still waving at the engine.

'I'll get the dog!' he shouted over the sound of the blaring horn, the clacking diesel, and the hissing rails. He didn't know if Bowen had heard him, though he needn't have worried, there was little doubt who the vicar had her sights set on.

Douglas looked round, noticing at last that he had company. He did not run, however; merely started nodding his head, as if mentally trying to spur the engine on, his head looking rapidly between the dog and the engine.

The diesel engine was ginormous as it came upon him, but the adrenalin coarsing through Frisk's body overcame his terror. In one final surge of momentum, he scooped Moses up off the railway line, seizing the dog like a scrum half would pick up a rugby ball at the back of a scrum, kicking through the bamboo cane Douglas was holding and diving out of the engine's path with barely a second to spare. The engine's horn was ear-splittingly loud as the oily buffers flashed past his head only inches away.

The dog lead screamed out from the plastic handle's housing as he tumbled down the verge and away from the railway line with Moses in his arms, like a fish taking a giant baited hook. The lead snagged, and Frisk was jolted as the plastic handle pulled against the inside of the rail, only to tumble further a split second later as the lead was severed by the numerous steel wheels running over it.

Frisk and Moses landed in a crumpled heap in a patch of stinging nettles at the bottom of the verge. Through the hole in his trousers, a nettle stung his inner thigh, and his forearms buzzed from the numerous other stings already inflicted on his exposed flesh.

He hadn't seen what became of Douglas or Reverend Bowen after he'd grabbed Moses; hadn't seen how Bowen had speared the squatting Blouse in a crunching tackle, splaying him out beside the railway line as the tankers clattered past dangerously close to them. Hadn't seen how she had tried to hold out Blouse's arm towards the clattering wheels in an attempt to dismember the limb of her dog's tormentor, Blouse only just strong enough to resist the deranged vicar's maniacal advances and regain possession of the bamboo cane that Frisk had kicked out of his hand. He saw them now, though. They were both on their feet as the last of the tankers disappeared from view, and all he could hear now was the crunching of ballast under their feet, the furious panting of both combatants, and the swishing, thwacking sound of the bamboo cane.

Bowen had one hand around Blouse's throat, her other hand attempting to bat away the rapier-like blows of the cane that now peppered her arms, neck and face. Blouse's face was a mixture of terror and hysteria as he tried to beat his way free from the vicar's grip.

The cane thwacked mercilessly one last time across the right hand side of the vicar's face and Douglas was free, Bowen releasing her grip and raising her hand to her cheek. Douglas tripped her, causing her to tumble backwards onto the ballast, not hesitating in seizing his opportunity to escape, running like hell from the vicar but still having the presence of mind to flick the Vs at Sergeant Frisk who was stumbling out of the nettles and back up the verge with Moses, wincing from the pain of the stings and struggling to keep his balance.

Reverend Bowen was sat up on her elbows beside the track, watching Douglas run off into the distance. She was breathing hard and Frisk could already see the red welts from the cane beginning to form on her face. Panting heavily and in considerable discomfort himself, he made it back up trackside with Moses. If he had handed the dog over five seconds earlier, it would have been Reverend Bowen that Moses would have vomited on; as it was, it was the buzzing right forearm of Sergeant Frisk that suffered the further indignity at the hands of the drunken spaniel. He sighed, holding out the dog to the battle-weary Bowen.

'I believe this belongs to you,' he said.

Sergeant Frisk and Reverend Bowen walked in silence back towards the level crossing. Relieved that Moses was safe and back in the arms of his rightful owner, but dejected as the dog's tormentor had once again evaded capture. Dan Fowler, still at the top of steps of the signal box, clapped the weary duo home. 'Bloody hell, that was close, Sarge!' he shouted. 'Don't worry, I've radio'd control and told them to halt all services in the area until further notice.'

Frisk raised his hand in recognition. 'Thanks, Dan, good work,' he said, wiping his brow. 'Let 'em up.'

Fowler did as he was instructed, ducking back in and raising the barriers, allowing the waiting traffic that had built up to cross at last. There were half a dozen cars, the drivers of which had all exited their vehicles, straining a look over the barriers to see what was going on further down the line. They now returned to their vehicles and continued on their way.

Frisk detected a cheeky smile and a little nod from Fowler to someone, before the signal man had gone back in to raise the barriers. He and Bowen stepped from the ballast of the railway track back onto the concrete of the level crossing, walking wearily back towards the police car. The sight that greeted them took them both entirely by surprise. Squirming in Butch Ransom's arms was a distinctly worried-looking Douglas Blouse.

'Would you believe it, Sarge,' Butch called out with his usual jovial enthusiasm, 'he just jumped into my arms.'

Frisk, tired from his excursions, sighed with relief, even managing a little smile as he bent over, placing his hands on his knees. But underneath his relief, there was also anger.

Reverend Bowen, holding Moses, did not laugh. Only stared. Stared into the eyes of the squirming boy who had brought so much havoc into her life. She softly stroked Moses, her hands covered in the dry blood of the pummelled steak that the dog now began to lick clean.

'So,' Frisk said, still a little breathless, 'it's not just the women that throw themselves at you then, Butch?'

PART 2

21 *Friday, August 13*

After throwing Douglas in the police cell, following their collective near-death experience on the railway, Sergeant Frisk had taken another brisk walk down to the Blouse family bungalow, determined to let rip at Alice about her son's demented actions, only to be greeted by the same situation as his two previous visits. All was quiet. Douglas, who had offered little resistance to his arrest and subsequent incarceration, had been very reticent on the subject of his mother's whereabouts.

'She's tired, and she's gone. I don't know where,' was all he had to say on the matter.

After locking him up, Frisk had decided he wanted nothing more to do with Douglas, only for the time being though, unfortunately, and had told the two incoming officers handling the night shift exactly that. Thanks to Douglas's day of destruction, he'd been unable to go back home as he'd planned, to try and catch Jenny and Sophie before they went off for the weekend. By the time he did get home, just after 6 p.m., the place was as quiet and deserted as the Blouse bungalow from which he'd just come.

After trudging lethargically into the kitchen to get a beer, he had been greeted by a single yellow post-it note stuck on the fridge door:

Gone a cpl days.
Lasagne X 2 in fridge.
Will b in touch.

Will be in touch? he thought, popping the top off a blessedly cold bottle of Becks and taking a long swallow. Well that's OK, he thought, I'll just sit here and twiddle my thumbs until you're ready to call. He had more than enough on his plate right now, more than two poxy lasagnes, that was for sure.

After retrieving his other pair of work trousers from the linen basket and setting the ripped pair aside for eventual repair, Frisk had endured a lonely evening and a restless night's sleep, as the thundering diesel engine blared its horn as it bore down on him in his dreams, only with Douglas driving it, a mad grin on his face. When he went back into the station, he wanted to make it perfectly clear that he was in no mood to pussyfoot about.

*

'All right, Douglas,' Frisk said, striding into the police station's small interview room holding a crumpled piece of paper in one hand and a piece of railway ballast in the other. 'Let's see that famous backside of yours.'

In the claustrophobic confines of the interview room, an alarmed look of confusion flashed across Douglas's face, his blinking eyes darting back and forth between Sergeant Frisk and PC Dennis Binsley, who was leaning against the wall in the corner of the room grinning. In the heat of the small windowless room, Frisk could detect the funky smell emanating from his crumpled trousers.

'Well,' Binsley said, 'do as the Sergeant says, Douglas, there's a good boy.'

Douglas, wearing the same clothes he was captured in, remained motionless in his seat, his chin resting in the palm of his hand, appearing not to comprehend the instruction. He gave a little smirk. Frisk slammed his fists down on the desk, staring daggers at Douglas, who jumped at his sudden flash of anger.

'I am in no mood for any more of your fun and games,' he said. 'Now get on your feet, come round here and drop your shorts. I will not tell you again!'

'Why do you wanna see my arse, you gaylord?' he said, brow crumpled.

Calming a little, Frisk smiled at Blouse's cocky question. 'No, Douglas, sorry, you misunderstand me. Believe it or not, this is actually official police business,' he said. 'You see, in the light of new evidence, we're going to have ourselves a little identity parade. Frisk began to pace in the small room. 'I've got you for trespassing, so that's £200 you owe me straight away. And as for what you did to Reverend Bowen with that cane, and trying to kill her dog,' he said, 'well, take your pick. But for now, for the sake of chronology, let's just stick with the windows, shall we? You see, I think I can now confidently pin that one on you as well, despite your continued repeated denials to the contrary.'

Frisk flattened the piece of crumpled paper out on the table in front of Douglas. 'You see, I've had some very distressed people coming to me over the past couple of days, Douglas: all of them with the same complaint, the same story, and all with the same little souvenirs,' he said, placing the piece of ballast down on top of the photocopy. 'And it's my job to get to the bottom of it,' he said with a little laugh. 'Which brings us nicely back to you and that troublesome backside of yours. Now get round here,' he said, pointing to the spot on the floor directly in front of him

Douglas looked first at the two items on the table, then back at Frisk, giving little away. Frisk was sure he detected another smirk, just dying to emerge.

PC Binsley grabbed Blouse under the armpits, pulling him to his feet and dragging him round the desk.

'Turn around and bend over the desk please, Douglas,' Frisk asked, pleasantly.

'Piss off, you big gay boy,' Blouse said indignantly. 'What is this, Deliverance? Pair of homos.'

PC Binsley swung a fist into Douglas's stomach, drilling him hard and knocking the wind out of him. He manhandled Blouse round to in front of Frisk, who gave his wily PC a look of disapproval for his heavy-handed display. Binsley bent Douglas over the desk.

'Hold him down please, would you, Dennis?' Frisk said.

Douglas was coughing and spluttering over the desk, trying to get his wind back, his face pressed hard against the desk under Binsley's rigid forearm. Douglas's jagged exhalations fluttered the edges of the weighted piece of paper beside his head.

'Now, Douglas, this won't take a moment,' Frisk said, 'we just need to check something out, OK?'

'Piss off, you rapist!' Blouse coughed in muffled response from under Binsley's forearm. 'Let me up!'

Sergeant Frisk ignored his request and pulled down Douglas's denim shorts.

Douglas began to kick out violently, so Frisk decided it would be safer to cuff Blouse's ankles. He then lowered the young man's boxer shorts, revealing the infamous pasty backside. PC Binsley continued to apply his weight to Blouse's head, pushing him down hard on the table, grinning as he did so.

Frisk picked up the crumpled piece of paper from off the desk, holding up the black and white image of the photocopied bum cheeks just beneath the real thing. He had no problem identifying the trio of scars. The line of three dots that Reverend Bowen had told him about yesterday were clearly visible on Douglas's right cheek.

'You see, Douglas, I heard a little story about you yesterday,' Frisk said as he scrutinised the picture. 'It seems those darts of yours landed you in a bit of trouble a while back, didn't they? Your girlfriends, the Bumstead twins, said some lads tried a bit of amateur acupuncture on you on the school bus one day. Or at least Eric said that's what they told him. Is that true?'

'They ain't my fucking girlfriends,' Douglas said defiantly, getting his wind back. 'Pair of frigging heffers. Wouldn't be seen dead with 'em.'

'No?' Frisk said, eyebrows raised. 'Eric said you had them down the caravan a couple of times. He said they had a bit of a thing for you. In fact the way he was talking, it sounded like you enjoyed nothing more than to play a bit of hide the sausage with the Bumstead twins after a tough day at the butcher's?'

'You're full of shit, and so is he. Everyone round here is,' Douglas said, trying to straighten up, Binsley ensuring he was unable to do so.

'I think he's right, you know, Sarge,' Binsley said. 'After all, he's gonna marry Daisy. Isn't that right, Douglas?' Binsley said, pinching Blouse's cheek. 'That's why he smashed in Dan's window up at the signal box, isn't it,

Douglas?' he said, sounding like he was talking to a two-year-old. 'Because Dan's been fingering your girlfriend,' he sang.

'Ahh, is that right?' Frisk cooed. 'Well, don't give up on her, Douglas. I think she really likes you. And I know that Petra would love to welcome you into the family.'

'Yeah, maybe you could go and live with them, seeing as how you're officially a bastard now,' Binsley said. 'Why won't you tell us where mum's gone, eh, Douglas?' he said. 'Maybe he killed her guv?' he said. Binsley put his face close up to Douglas's. 'Where did you bury her, Douglas?' Binsley asked. 'Where did you bury mum, eh? Shall we go and get a couple of spades and do a bit of digging in your back garden?'

'Prick!' Blouse said, trying to kick out, jerking wildly like a cuffed bucking bronco. Binsley continued to push Douglas's face into the table, his superior strength ensuring Douglas stayed exactly where he was.

Sergeant Frisk scrutinised the picture. 'Those dots look like Orion's belt, don't they? Frisk said, holding up the picture. 'Anyway, Douglas, at least they didn't stick them up your bum,' he said. 'You could've had a one-fifty checkout up your brown bullseye!' Both policemen laughed.

'How can you laugh, Binsley, you murdering bastard?' Douglas said from the desk. 'You allowed to drive that car yet, murderer?' He looked to Frisk. 'Is he allowed to drive yet, Sarge? After he killed my fucking mate?'

'Shut up,' Binsley said. His smile had disappeared.

'Sarge! Sarge! There's been an accident, but it wasn't my fault, honest! I just killed an innocent lad, but it wasn't my fault. Please tell them it wasn't my fault,' he said, before adding, 'My mum and Edna told me all about you.'

The smile on Binsley's face had been replaced by a grimace of disdain. He released his weight from on top of Blouse, who immediately stood up straight, his shorts around his cuffed ankles and his bum cheeks peering out from his lowered boxer shorts.

Binsley reached down to his own trousers. 'I'll show you Orion's belt, you little shit,' he said, unbuckling the heavy leather belt from around his waist, removing it from the loops of his trousers in one smooth swishing flick. He wielded it above his head like a whip, bringing the belt down straight across

Blouse's exposed rear end. Douglas screamed, but then began to laugh, his hands instinctively moving to his stinging cheeks.

Binsley swung again, this time catching Blouse on the arm. 'Not nice, is it, you little bastard?' Binsley bellowed.

Frisk had to duck to escape the wild antics of his enraged constable, whose sudden actions had taken him completely by surprise. 'Dennis, get a hold of yourself!' Frisk said.

'Yeah, Dennis, get a grip, you're all over the place.' Douglas was now laughing madly and holding an invisible steering wheel.

Binsley continued to chase Douglas, who hopped around the small desk, ankles cuffed like he was in some kind of lewd sack race, minus the sack.

Frisk caught hold of Binsley's arm. 'Dennis, stop it!' he shouted. 'That's an order.'

Binsley, breathing hard reluctantly did as he was told. 'By the time I've finished with you, boy,' Binsley said, holding up his belt, 'you'll make Hilda Bowen look like Cindy fucking Crawford!'

At that moment the door to the interview room opened, and a black shape appeared.

'Did someone say my name?'

'Speak of the devil,' Blouse said, smirking and looking up at Reverend Bowen standing in the doorway.

22

'Put it away, Douglas, for heaven's sake,' Reverend Bowen said. 'Honestly, we've had quite enough of that hideous thing to last us a lifetime.'

Sergeant Frisk, looking a little startled by the vicar's unscheduled appearance, quickly unlocked the handcuffs from around Douglas's ankles and instructed the young man to pull his shorts back up. Douglas did as he was told, sneering at the vicar through the wincing pain of his stinging rear end.

In the doorway, Bowen smiled back at Douglas. 'I'm glad to see my information was useful to you, Alan,' she said, nodding at the photocopy on the table.

'A little unconventional, Reverend, but yes, helpful nonetheless,' Frisk said.

'I'm glad to hear that,' she said. 'Sergeant, I wonder if I might have a word with you in private?'

'Of course,' Frisk said. 'Put him back in his cell please, Dennis,' Frisk said over his shoulder as he led Bowen down the short hall way and through to the office. 'And no nonsense.'

Reverend Bowen was trying to maintain an appearance of external calm, serenity even. She was still seething at Douglas's actions from the previous day, and seeing him again had re-ignited that anger. But if she was to achieve her primary objective, a level head was what was required, and that was a hell of a lot easier said than done considering what she was up against.

Her meal with the bishop had been a disaster. Bishop Howard Trimble, though sensitive and sympathetic to her ordeal, and clearly aghast at her injuries, did not shy away from spelling it out to her in no uncertain terms that the vicarage would be going up for sale – and soon – just as she knew it would be. She had been mentally absent for most of the evening, her mind still overwrought by the events replaying over and over again in her mind. The bishop was complimentary, however, on the tenderness of his steak, even if he did pause on more than one occasion to prise pieces of melted plastic from the pummelled meat.

As planned after dinner, Reverend Bowen had fired up her trike to attend the weekly meeting of the Crossroads motorcycle club, arriving at the bike meet just after half eight. It had taken her ten minutes or so to relay the details of her horrific day to the other members of her exclusive club, though plenty more unaffiliated bike enthusiasts leant in to eavesdrop.

Her Crossroads brothers and sisters were as unanimously sympathetic towards her as they were disgusted by the actions of Douglas Blouse, and were all in agreement that something must be done. But no one, especially Reverend Bowen, was exactly sure at that point what that something should or could be. Until later that night, when a man wearing red and white leathers asked her if he could have a moment of her time. The man had told her a bit about himself; also about how sorry he was to hear her story, and how he might be able to help her. It turned out he was also a policeman, and when he flipped open a black leather wallet with a Thames Valley police badge on its front, Reverend Bowen saw two things: a police warrant card was one, and the other was a picture of a sleek-looking German Shepherd. The name on the warrant card was Sergeant Laurie Knox.

23

Reverend Bowen settled herself opposite Sergeant Frisk in the same seat she had occupied yesterday afternoon while offering moral support to Daisy Carr. The small office was just as stiflingly hot and the rotating fan next to Frisk's desk did little else than cause the edges of the statements and other assorted bits of paper being held down by Douglas's ballast to flutter in its breeze.

'Sergeant, I happened to bump into a colleague of yours last night whilst up at my meeting,' Bowen said, composing herself. 'A Sergeant Knox, police dog handler. I seem to remember him from last year, although I don't believe I actually had the pleasure of meeting him personally on that occasion,' she said. 'I understand that he is going to be involved in the police dog display tomorrow?' she said, eyebrows raised.

'He will be, Reverend, yes,' Frisk said. 'The dog display's always a big favourite with the locals, and this year will be no exception.'

Bowen smiled. 'Well, quite. And it is my understanding that Sergeant Knox will also be attending tonight's meeting at the village hall?'

'As far as I know he will be, yes. Got a few things I need to discuss with him about the display, and one or two personal issues I need to have a chat to him about. I don't know how much he told you,' Frisk said, lowering his voice, 'but he's had a bit of a bumpy year. He lost a dog in the line of duty last year and I also believe he's had a relationship break-up on him.'

'Over Christmas, no less,' Bowen said. 'Threw her out into the street. I can't say it was a particularly Christian thing to do, given the season and him being a practising Christian, but one cannot argue with the commandments, I suppose.'

'So you do know,' Frisk said.

Bowen smiled.

'Anyway,' Frisk said, 'by all accounts he's been throwing himself into his work, training this new dog of his.'

'Gooch, I believe his name is,' Bowen said.

'Yeah, that makes sense, his last one was called Beefy. Obviously keeping the cricket theme going. But yes, Hilda, he'll be down the hall tonight, and I know Petra is going to want to know the ins and outs of our every last detail, you know what she's like.'

'Indeed I do, Sergeant,' Bowen said, with a trace of a smile. 'In fact I have spoken to her already this morning,' she said. 'Just a preliminary call to discuss a few things concerning the fete.'

Frisk frowned. 'You're sure you're still up to it, Reverend?'

'Don't worry about me, Sergeant, I'll be fine. Tough as old biker boots,' she said with a thin smile.

A tuneless whistle began emanating from the direction of Douglas's cell. He was whistling 'How Much Is That Doggy in the Window', badly. Bowen could pick out the tune, despite Douglas's poor rendition.

'As for him,' Frisk said, cocking a thumb towards the cell, 'have you thought any more about pressing charges?'

Bowen shuffled in her seat, settled again and looked Frisk in the eye. 'Sergeant, I've had an idea about that; about how we might perhaps be able to deal with the wayward actions of that lost soul in there ourselves,' she said. 'Outside the boundaries of conventional justice. Let's call it ...' Bowen's eyes circled the room, searching for the right expression, 'community service.'

'I don't quite follow, Reverend,' Frisk said.

'Our young friend down there has his whole life in front of him, wouldn't you agree, Sergeant?' Bowen said, not pausing to allow Frisk to answer. 'I think it would be a shame for him to begin his adult life behind bars, or in some young offenders' institute. Perhaps what would be best for all of us, to help us move on from all this recent unpleasantness, would be for Douglas to undergo what we in the church call "atonement".'

Frisk sat up straight in his chair. 'Go on,' he said.

'I believe that Douglas should be given the opportunity for public atonement for his behaviour. I think it would be good for the village as a whole, and I also think it would be good for him: to understand that his actions have consequences; that, as our Heavenly Father so rightly taught us, you do indeed reap what you sow. I think that between us we can do that, Sergeant. And what better timing?' She continued breezily, 'Given the fete is tomorrow and everything is already in place, a simple switch of personnel is all that's required. After all,' she said with a hint of menace, 'every good police dog needs a criminal to chase.'

24

'So we're gonna lose our spot!?' Terence Russell said to Sergeant Frisk, descending the small set of steps at the side of the village hall's stage. Petra had barely brought her limp-wristed gavel down on proceedings, officially brining the meeting to a close, when Sergeant Frisk was confronted by the aggrieved lead Morris man.

'We're gonna lose our spot? Is that how it is now, Alan? Bloody home town show and we get bumped down the bill because of some juvenile bloody delinquent!? Rewarding bad behaviour, that is. Rewarding-bad-behaviour,' he said, jabbing his index finger into Frisk's chest with every enunciated word. He turned his head to Gerry Hayman behind him. 'Bloody rewarding bad behaviour, isn't it, Gerry,' Terence said over his shoulder, shaking his head disconsolately.

'Be sending him to Butlin's next thing you know, chief,' Hayman said.

I hardly think being forced to take part in a police dog display is exactly rewarding bad behaviour, Frisk thought. Padding or no padding.

'You know how hard we've been practising for this one, Alan,' Terence said, looking like he was about to cry. 'You know what it means to us, the big home town show. What it means to me. What it would have meant to my Iris!'

Frisk was getting a little tired of Terence's stroppy diva antics, and now he was trying to blackmail him emotionally by bringing his dead wife into it.

'Terence, come on,' he said, irritated at the old boy's exaggerations. 'It's just half an hour or so earlier, that's all. You still get to perform. It's gonna be the same as it is every year. It's just that we're gonna do our display last this year. Not too much to ask, is it?' Frisk said, exasperated at having to explain himself at all. 'After everything that's happened, myself, Hilda and Petra think it would be appropriate,' he said, pointing towards the stage.

Reverend Bowen, still seated at the long green table, was speaking to Sergeant Knox. Petra was standing in front of the stage holding court to a small group of women who surrounded her in a small semi-circle. Probably talking about jam, Frisk thought.

He continued, 'That boy that I've got locked up down the road put them through hell yesterday, Terence. Not to mention all his other misdemeanours. Douglas is going to take part in our display by way of a public apology,' he said. 'And Reverend Bowen is going to drop all charges against him if he cooperates, which he's already assured me he will,' Frisk said. 'Do you want to go and tell Petra over there that you think you and your lot are more important than what Douglas did to her daughter?' Frisk asked. 'She's as enthusiastic about it as Bowen is. Thinks it's a great idea. Maybe you want to tell Hilda that her dog's near decapitation doesn't justify changing the running order? Not to mention me putting my own life literally on the line to save it.'

Frisk felt anger rising in him. 'Maybe you'd like to go and tell her your little dance is more important, Terence. Because I sincerely doubt that those two will see it quite the same way,' Frisk said, now poking his finger into Terence's chest.

Terence winced, shrinking back from Frisk's outburst. Gerry by his side remained silent and pensive.

'I suppose they have been through a lot,' Terence said, looking up at the stage, beginning to mellow. 'And don't forget what that little sod done to old Colin's allotment. That's why he's taken so much of the drink yesterday and today, after the shock of what Douglas done up there.'

Frisk sincerely doubted that Terence's claims were the reason for Blunsden's heavy drinking. Colin didn't need a reason to drink: a Y in the day of the week was enough for him, though the vandalism was probably helpful as a convenient excuse.

'Well, I must say that despite the uhh…' Terence searched for the right word, ' disruption ... shall we say, to the line-up, I suppose I'll be happy to see that little sod get what's coming to him.'

Frisk exhaled. 'Well that's it, Terence,' Frisk said, pleased at last that the lead dancer was coming round. 'The boy needs to learn that he can't go on behaving the way he does. Not any more. He's a loose cannon, and I for one am tired of it. I hope that this experience might just shock him into changing his ways. God know's he bloody well needs it.'

25

Tony Gables bounced into the village hall with an energy that belied his sixty-two years. He was wearing a crushed velvet scarlet jacket, black corduroy trousers and a white shirt, the neckline of which was damp with perspiration. He looked taller in his cuban heels and younger thanks to the botox. His pearly white teeth were proudly all his own, and they gleamed as he made his way into the crowded hall.

'Well, well, if it isn't Bruno Brooks's tea boy,' Butch said. 'You're a bit late, Tony, you've missed all the fun.'

'Oh no, really? Bar's still open though, isn't it?' Tony said, looking at his watch, making his way towards Butch and his little crowd. 'Is Edna not working tonight?'

He looked over at the bar where Edna Glass was biting the tip off a triangle of Toblerone. Tony raised an invisible pint glass to his mouth and tapped his watch. Edna gave him a flinty look in return. She swallowed her chocolate. 'If you're quick,' she said, sounding none too pleased.

The meeting had been officially brought to a close fifteen minutes ago. Now the villagers who had chosen to stay on for a quick drink were discussing tomorrow's big day over refreshments.

'Ready and raring for tomorrow then, Tony?' Butch asked.

'Oh, you bet, Butch. Just been getting some last-minute practice in at a private do at the rugby club in town,' he said with a wry smile. 'Spinning some tunes as a favour to an old friend from the 'Sounds Good' radio days. Just did an hour guest slot for him. It was a bit of fun actually, joint mother, daughter, granddaughter party. Her sixtieth, her daughter's fortieth and her granddaughter's twenty-first,' he said, concentrating, counting off the numerical sequence on his right hand. 'Talk about the generation game.

Some hot stuff about down there, mind, Butch, you'd've loved it,' he said, snatching Butch's half-full pint glass from the table and taking a swig.

'Get out, you cheeky bastard! Go get your own, you tight arse,' Butch said, reclaiming his pint from the grinning Gables. 'Must have been one hell of a party if it finished at ten o'clock, mate,' Butch said sarcastically. 'Then again, I suppose they've all got to get back to the nursing home, eh.'

'Very funny, Butch. Actually I think some of them were breaking off to go into town to carry on for a bit. I left them in the not so capable hands of some tradesman DJ they probably got out of the Yellow Pages. Terrible equipment. I was tempted to go off with them, and they did ask, but I thought it best to get an early night so I'm fresh for tomorrow.'

'Gone to that new OAP strip joint in town that I've heard so much about, have they? The one with the world's longest striptease, coz the old fogies have got about fifteen layers to take off first!' Butch said, bringing ripples of laughter from the assembled crowd. Barbara Rix sipped her drink and slapped Butch on the arm.

'So it was nice to have some women your own age flocking round the DJ booth tonight then, Tone?' Butch said. 'Lots of requests for Dame Vera Lynn and Bing Crosby, I bet,' he continued. 'Get a couple of 'em behind the booth, did ya?' Butch said, leaning in. 'I hear it's really good when they take their teeth out,' he said with a wink.

'Butch!' Barbara said, hitting him harder.

'Hey, I can still work a bit of the old magic with the younger crowd, don't you worry about that. I'm not over the hill just yet. In fact I got a couple of numbers tonight, I'll have you know,' Gables said smugly.

'Oh yeah?' Butch said. 'What were they, Tone? Numbers for the next of kin, for when the old codgers pop their clogs on ya?'

'What's your favourite position, Tony?' Colin Blunsden asked drunkenly from out of nowhere, over by the bar.

Butch beat him to the punch before Tony could fire off a response. 'The recovery position, I imagine,' he said to a roar of laughter.

'Yeah, ha ha, Butch, very good,' Tony said sarcastically as the laughter died down. 'It's true. In fact this separation from Karen is probably the best thing that could have happened to me right now. There's plenty more fish in the sea, Butch, you know that better than anyone round here, you old slapper.'

Butch leaned over and grabbed Tony's arm. He held up Tony's fingers to his nose, breathing in deeply. 'Blimey, Tony! You're not wrong there!' he said, looking round. 'Where have these fishy fingers been tonight, eh, Captain Birdseye?!'

Tony snatched his hand back from the wise-cracking Ransom as laughter erupted once more. Almost blushing the colour of his jacket, he swept Butch's pint off the table, away from the jovial Kiwi, who was looking round soaking up the adulation, and drained what was left of the lager in two gulps.

'You cheeky little shit!' Butch shouted at the grinning Gables, who smugly placed the empty glass back in front of Ransom before burping.

'Ooh, excuse me,' he said, grinning, as a hand clamped him firmly on the shoulder. He turned to see the smiling face of Sergeant Frisk.

'Ello ello ello, what's all this then, Mr Gables?' Frisk said. 'I hope you're not doing what I think you're doing,' he said. 'Wouldn't want to have to take your driving licence away again now, would I? You've only had it back six months. Can't be easy being a DJ and having to carry all those records on the bus, can it?'

'I should sue you lot for loss of income,' he said. 'And actually I haven't touched a drop tonight, if you must know, Sergeant,' Tony beamed smugly, and for once truthfully.

Frisk gave a suspicious look at the empty pint glass in front of him.

'Other than that little quaff, of course, but that was only to get back at that smug little sheep molester,' he said, pointing at the still smiling Ransom.

'I'm glad to hear it, Tony, glad to hear it,' Frisk said.

'So, Sarge,' Butch said, 'sounds like young Mr Blouse is going to find out that your bite is worse than your bark tomorow, eh?' Ransom said. 'Gonna be interesting.'

'In a manner of speaking, I suppose, Butch,' Frisk said. 'A little bit of community service, as Hilda and Petra are so fond of putting it. Hilda said she's not going to press charges, Petra likewise, which saves me a lot of hassle on the paperwork. Not that Petra actually had any charges to press in the first place, but you know her. Doesn't like to be outdone, does she?'

'What's all this?' Tony asked.

'Feeding Douglas to the lions tomorrow,' Butch said. 'Well, police dog. Sounds a bit like ancient Rome to me.'

'It's not quite that extreme, Butch,' Frisk said. 'We're not sadists. He's going to have all the proper protective clothing. Dennis did it last year, and the year before that come to think of it. Laurie over there is gonna be doing it as usual, and he's as experienced as they come,' Frisk said, pointing towards the police dog handler seated beside Reverend Bowen. 'Gonna give this new dog of his its first proper run out. I think the elders just want to put the frighteners on Douglas a bit,' Frisk said, nodding towards Carr and Bowen respectively. 'He went too far yesterday, I can vouch for that just as well as anyone,' he said. 'I think Hilda's been at her Bible again, you know, "Do unto others" and all that. I think she sees Douglas being in our display as an appropriate form of punishment after what he did to Moses. We'll get through it and hopefully they'll all be appeased,' he said. 'If his mum hasn't shown up by Monday, I might have to start making a few phone calls though. He's costing us a fortune to feed. I need to see if there're any other relatives around who might take him. Might even have to give social services a ring, if all else fails. Mind you, he's old enough to look after himself, if only he bloody acted like it.'

*

From the bar, Edna Glass stared at Sergeant Frisk, grateful only for the fact it was him here tonight and not that reckless coward Dennis Binsley as well. Frisk looked over, meeting her gaze. As if sensing the frosty chill in her stare, he quickly turned away.

The bastards, she thought. So quick to forget.

She looked over at Petra Carr, the snobby cow. She thought about what it would have been like if it had been Daisy who had died that night. Whether Petra would be able to swallow an accidental death verdict like she'd had to. I don't think so, she thought. Somehow I seriously don't think so. An afternoon in a shed with Douglas was nothing compared to what happened to her Peter. And here they all were now, cozying up to each other. Throwing their weight around. Making the rules up as they went along. Douglas might have been a bit of a strange boy, but this was all getting to be a bit sick, she thought, as she looked around the gloating throng of villagers who had offered nothing in the way of opposition to the sadistic freak show that was now officially scheduled to take place tomorrow afternoon, and she didn't have a clue where Alice was in all this. She'd not seen her in over a week. They didn't tend to see so much of each other outside the steamy confines of the primary school kitchen where they both worked. And as it was summer holidays, she hadn't thought much of it. But now with everything that was happening with Douglas, she was really starting to worry. She knew Alice had a sister somewhere. She'd apparently offered on more than one occasion to put her and Douglas up after Bertie left, but Alice had turned her down, determined to raise him on her own, with Douglas becoming increasingly isolated as he progressed through his teens. Nothing like the hyperactive trouble-maker that she had babysat for when he was still in single digits. But even through those difficult teenage years, he'd still had Peter's friendship to fall back on, and his mum's enduring love and support was without question. So where the hell was she? If she had gone to stay with her sister, she hoped she would at least be back before term began again in a few weeks. The last thing she needed was trying to run that kitchen single-handedly with all those hungry mouths to feed.

She and Alice had never had much. They'd both had to scrimp and save to feed and clothe their children. But one thing they did have, and it was something that the sickos in the hall here tonight clearly underestimated, was an unconditional love for their sons.

26

'Wakey wakey!'

'What the fff...', Edna said, startled out of her thoughts by the sound of banging on the bar.

'Hey, Edna!' Tony said, now clicking his fingers in Edna's face. 'Hey, come on, wakey wakey, Edna, are you with us?'

'What? Yes, all right, piss off will you, Tony,' she said, waving Gables' hand away like she would a tedious fly. 'What do you want? The bar's closed, I told you to be quick.'

'No no, that's all right, Edna, I'd better not,' he said. 'Not with the long arm of the law in attendance.'

She would have taken a six-month driving ban over a dead son any day, she thought morosely.

Gables took a step back from the bar, eyeing Edna up in her black low-cut dress, his eyes resting on the swell of her formidable breasts. 'And may I say you're looking as lovely as ever tonight, Edna.'

Glass shook her greying snowball of frizzy hair, frowning. 'Oh bollocks, Tony,' she said, tired and irritable. 'What do you want?'

'I wondered, will you be opening up the football club tomorrow? It's just I have to bring my stuff down for the show and I'm going to need to get it all up and running to make sure it's all F.A.B before things get underway,' he said, giving her a double thumbs up. 'I'll have my decks and my music with me obviously,' he said. 'By the way, are you any good at putting up gazebos?'

Edna gave him an icy stare.

'Never mind,' he said.

Edna took out a cigarette from her gold packet of Benson and Hedges on the bar and lit it. She took a long drag and exhaled deeply. 'Yes, Tony, to answer your question, I will be opening up the football club tomorrow,' she said out of the corner of her mouth not holding the cigarette. She puffed away no-handed, removed it and held it between her chubby fingers. 'After opening it up once already today so the bloody Fuzz over there could put their little Crufts display apparatus in there while I restocked the bar and cleaned the place top to bottom. I've also got to clear up here after this lot eventually sod off. Then I get to come back down here in the morning and do it all again. Aren't I just the lucky one?' she said irritably, pulling deeply on her cigarette. 'So yes, Tony, does that answer your question? I will be opening up the football club tomorrow, and I simply cannot wait to see you there in all your finery with all your lovely records, some snazzy bloody shirt and your magical pissing gazebo,' she said, crushing the cigarette out in the ashtray and blowing the last of the smoke in Tony's face.

Gables smiled and leant on the bar. 'Edna,' he said, winking.

'What?' she said frostily.

'Give us a gobble.'

Glass tutted, shook her head and raised both meaty arms in the air, grabbing hold of the metal shutters and slamming them down in the disc jockey's hopeful face, narrowly missing his fingers. The bar was now officially closed.

*

The village hall was now steadily emptying. The moulded plastic chairs that Edna would have to stack and put away littered the floor at odd angles.

Butch Ransom went out the same way he came in, arm in arm with Barbara Rix to return to the farm to check on Finn and gaze admiringly at his outfit. He would be back at the hall earliest of all tomorrow with all his equipment.

Reverend Bowen, Petra Carr and Sergeants Frisk and Knox were all now making their way to the village hall's double-doored exit. The Morris men passed them as they made their own way out into the warm darkness of the summer's night. The butterflies were starting to flutter in Terence Russell's stomach, particularly after the last-minute change to the line-up. He tried to put it from his mind as he chattered excitedly with Gerry Hayman, who peered into the carrier bag just given to him by his lead dancer, smiling appreciatively at its contents. Colin Blunsden and Bob Dobson ambled behind them, holding their carrier bags containing the freshly washed, dried and ironed Morris outfits they would all be wearing tomorrow for the big show. Colin and Bob left the hall looking like two drunk children who had just been given an oversized party bag each to take home.

'Well, ladies, I will bid you good night,' Sergeant Frisk said to Petra and Reverend Bowen. 'Better go and drop the van off up at the nick. The night shift will be keeping an eye on our little volunteer until Dennis and myself go back in in the morning. Laurie, I'll see you at the station with Gooch at about eleven tomorrow, OK?'

'Sounds good, Alan,' Knox replied, now half zipped up in his red and white bike leathers. 'I know Gooch is really looking forward to it,' he said with a smile.

After returning the police van, Frisk made his way on foot back to the deserted house that – without his wife and daughter – did not feel at all like home.

Petra got on her push bike, switched her lights on and cycled back up the causeway to Castle Street and her own family.

Reverend Bowen and Laurie Knox's keys jangled as they inserted them into the ignitions of their respective vehicles. From astride her trike, Bowen looked over at Knox, the red criss-crossed facial abrasions barely visible in the gloomy orange light cast by the village hall's meagre exterior illumination.

'Douglas likes to mess about with dogs, does he?' she said grimly, looking at the smirking Knox, seated on his own motorcycle... 'Well, we'll just see how much he likes messing with dogs after tomorrow, won't we.'

*

The night descended into still, tranquil black, and the majority of the villagers slept peacefully that night. In homes all over the village, duvets and sheets were kicked to the floor, and bedroom windows were open to their fullest, their occupants welcoming any breeze that might pass through on this muggy summer evening. Every blade of grass on the village green breathed a collective sigh as night cloaked its scorched surface in its vast black pall.

There was no sound of windows being smashed; nor from the railway could you hear startled train drivers sounding their horns in alarm; nor broken garden gnomes and creaking shed doors; nor swishing bamboo canes and crunching ballast.

The barriers at both level crossings would remain erect and motionless until the first service passed through in the early hours of tomorrow morning. The endless miles of steel rails were once again cool to the touch.

The generator next to Douglas Blouse's caravan was silent. The shabby caravan as dark and abandoned as the bungalow on whose driveway it stood.

The Crafty Digit pub was silent, standing like a dark, disused film set, devoid of life until money once again changed hands tomorrow, bringing the old place back to life.

Some villagers slept with their wives or their girlfriends, as they had done for months, years or even decades previously. Some slept alone. Some tossed and turned while others sank easily into the black void of sleep. Some had dreams, some had nightmares. But all would be quickly forgotten, as dawn consumed the images of their fleeting subconscious. All who slept and dreamed that night, however, would have a much harder time forgetting the waking nightmare that the new day would bring.

27 *Saturday, August 14*

Sunrise came at 05.38 a.m. on the morning of Saturday 14 August, and Butch Ransom was up bright and early to meet it. Early mornings didn't bother him, as the black night sky slowly began to turn a silvery blue at its furthest easterly horizon. He'd already been up for nearly an hour, attending to the usual list of seemingly endless jobs that were part and parcel of the farming life.

His flock were in good shape and appeared well rested. Later he would select the nine lucky volunteers that would accompany him down to the fete. In the meantime he loaded up the disassembled steel sheep pen and other pieces of apparatus into the animal trailer he would be needing to bring the sheep back in later, coupled to his battered Toyota pick-up truck.

He was excited. The village fete was always great fun, and he loved giving his sheep shearing demonstrations to groups of enthralled youngsters, and letting those who were keen enough have a go at shearing one of the sheep themselves, while he held the animal steady. It was always a great way to show off to the yummy mummies as well, giving him the perfect platform to get hot and sweaty in front of a swooning crowd of females as the shears buzzed and the sweat dripped. Having listened to the early morning forecast, the outlook was good again, though there had been warnings in the south of sporadic pockets of heavy rain and possibly thunder by late afternoon. None the less, Butch hoped to be topless by midday.

Now at 6.30 a.m. and with the sun rising steadily into a clear blue sky, he and Finn began their journey from Ransom farm, trundling down the farm track to the village, the trailer rattling as they bounced up and over the speed bumps. He passed the church, noticing that the door was slightly ajar. His progress was impeded at the railway line. The barriers were lowering just as he approached. He was the only vehicle waiting. He switched off his rumbling engine, as was the habit of most locals when waiting at the level crossing. Butch looked up at the signal box, picking out the shape of Dan Fowler stirring a cup of something inside. Dan waved, noticing Butch, who stepped out of his vehicle. He rested his arms on the roof, looking up at the signal box, and with scant regard for the early hour gave a short, sharp wolf whistle. Finn, seated in the vehicle's passenger seat, automatically looked over at his master, expecting a command.

'Not you,' he said through the open driver's side window. 'Oi, Dan! … Get these bloody barriers up, mate!' he shouted. 'My adoring public awaits me!'

Dan opened the door of the signal box smiling, holding his steaming mug in one hand and a roll-up cigarette in the other. He walked out onto the small platform at the top of the building's set of steps, taking a slurp from his mug before placing it on the newel post at the top of the steps.

'Your adoring public are all still tucked up in bed with their hands wrapped round their little willies,' he said. 'Somewhere I wish I was as well,' he added, 'rather than on earlies for four days,' Fowler said, rubbing his bleary eyes.

'Unlucky,' Butch said. 'And hey, it's not my fault if the blokes find me attractive too, Dan. After all, I can always pass their numbers on to you, mate,' he said, grinning.

'Puss off, you cheeky luttle shut,' Dan said, mocking Butch's accent and dragging a pink-headed Swan Vesta across the dry wood of the signal box and holding the flame up to his cigarette.

Butch looked up suspiciously at him. 'I hope that's not what I think it is, Danny boy?' he said.

'Nah, sod that, Butch,' he said, waving the match out and dropping it over the edge of the stairs. 'Bit early for all that anyway, plus you know I've had a warning,' he said, like a naughty schoolboy. 'Anyway, back to the subject, I'll have you know it might be my lucky day if things go to plan a little later on,' Dan said, tapping his nose with his index finger and wearing a cheeky grin.

'Oh yeah?' Butch said inquisitively. 'Well, whoever he is, he's a very lucky boy. I shall ask Hilda to prepare the altar when I see her.'

'Yeah yeah, whatever,' Dan said.

'Where the hell's this bloody choo choo anyway? Got shit to do, eh.'

'Shouldn't be much longer. Slow one. Tankers. Like the other day, minus the drama. That was bloody funny,' he said. 'You off to set up then?'

'Yeah, just going down to drop off some of the hardware before I come back to get changed and get the kids,' Butch said.

'Ohh yeah, I heard you were up to something, you pervy little weirdo.'

'Hey', Butch said, 'all the girls love a bloke who's in touch with his feminine side.' They both laughed.

To Butch's right, a window creaked open. He turned and realised for the first time that he was standing outside his new friend Trudy Ryan's house.

'Oi!' the stranger's voice called out, in a shout poorly attempting to be a whisper. 'Joe fucking Mangel! Keep the noise down, will you?' he said. 'I've got kids in here, some of us are still trying to sleep. Bloody wolf whistling and mouthing off at this time in the morning,' he said, stifling a yawn.

'So this must be the famous Jeremy,eh,' Butch said quietly to himself. 'Yeah, looks like a dick head.'

'And oi, fat controller, can't you turn the bloody sirens down or off on them things?'

'Sorry, sir,' Fowler replied in a professional tone from the top of the steps. 'But public safety isn't something you can just turn on and off,' he said deadpan, winking down at Butch.

The familiar sound of hissing tracks could now be heard from the railway line, and the flapping sound of the diesel engine drew nearer.

Before Jeremy could react to Fowler's thinly veiled sarcasm, Butch interjected, 'Yeah, sorry about that, handsome, no harm meant, eh.' Butch leant against the side of his truck, facing the man at the window. 'Didn't mean to disturb your beauty sleep there,' he said as the train came loudly upon them. 'Speaking of beauty sleep,' Butch continued as the train clattered past, his words deliberately drowned out by the rumbling thunder of the passing tankers, 'what I'd really like to do is get your missus in the sack. I like to make love to women in their own beds given the choice, see, where more often than not their sexually inadequate husbands fail to give them even the minutest bit of erotic gratification, with their equally miniscule genitalia,' Butch said, grinning as the tankers continued past, 'and I'm sure in your case both strongly apply.'

Jeremy Ryan leant out of his window, attempting to decipher what Ransom was saying over the noise of the train. It was useless, but Ransom continued regardless. 'Let's hope she'll then leave you and take the kids, and you'll spend the rest of your life draining your little balls and crying yourself to sleep every night, all on your lonesome.'

The last tanker passed from view. Jeremy Ryan was only able to catch the last sentence: 'In what I must say is a very very lovely house, sir!' Butch finished off.

Jeremy Ryan squinted, shaking his head. 'Yeah well ...' he said, a little confused and none the wiser. 'Just keep it down in future, yeah.'

'You got it, mate,' Butch said, giving him the thumbs up and trying not to laugh. 'Maybe see you and the missus down the road later on, eh?' At which Butch returned to his truck and started the engine.

'Come on, young Dan,' he called out. 'Get these bloody barriers up, I've got a sheep pen to assemble!'

Dan raised the barriers, smiling down at Butch and waving as he crossed.

Jeremy Ryan closed the window and went back to bed.

Reverend Bowen sat up against the front wooden panel of her church's right-hand pews. Bride or groom? she thought. Her legs were splayed out in front of her, forming a flat V. A tatty Bible sat between them with a crumpled piece of paper wedged in its pages serving as a bookmark. Her back felt good against the cool hard wood; the smell of her leather waistcoat draped over it next to her mingled with the smell of old wood and the musty paper of hymn books and Bibles. The church's interior was as quiet as the dead who slept beneath its churchyard's dewy green surface. The morning sun cast light on the stained glass of the east window, bringing the first rays of technicolour illumination to the church's gloomy confines. Moses was scampering up and down the central aisle, his little claws scratching on the cold black and terracotta tiles, ducking into pews to sniff at the embroidered prayer cushions that hung on small hooks in front of the hard bench seating.

Bowen had not slept well. Her mind was still a maelstrom of emotion following the events of the past couple of days. Thank God for Laurie Knox, though, she thought: one thing she could at least be thankful for. Her chance conversation with him at the bike meet on Thursday night had seemed almost pre-ordained, even if her belief in that sort of thing was becoming more and more strained with every passing day. Laurie was a kindred spirit; someone who, much like herself, had been through hell, and was still going through it. She'd spoken with him a great deal since meeting him on Thursday night. He was, again much like herself, unanchored and adrift in a shifting world devoid of any fixed reference points. A lost soul.

She thought about those words. Rolled them around in her head. Kindred spirit. Lost soul. Could lost souls be kindred spirits? Was there redemption to be found in the reconciliation of two lost souls? Did the combination of two lost souls make you by default kindred spirits? Did she even believe in such things as spirits and souls any more? One thing that she was sure of was that Laurie had been sent to her as an angel; not of mercy, but of retribution.

A distant rumble disturbed the silence of the church, as the sound of a train rumbling through the village came from down the causeway, and up through the hole in Jesus Christ's groin. Her heart raced at the noise as her mind returned to the events of Thursday afternoon. She shuddered, instinctively raising her hand to her face, touching the thick red marks that still stood out there nearly two days later. Silence returned as the train continued on its journey.

Moses came and sat next to her as she looked up at the elegant altar in front of them, with its ornate gold candlesticks and plush red carpeting. To the left of it, in the corner of the church, stood, quite literally, an old rugged cross. At nearly ten feet tall, it was an imposing piece of interior decoration that she thought would look a lot better with Douglas Blouse nailed to it. Still, she would have the next best thing waiting for him down at the fete later on.

Directly above the altar was the vandalised image of Christ hanging from a similar piece of wood in the stained glass window. He looked downcast, sad. The hole where Blouse's rock had struck let in a shaft of weak early morning sunlight.

'That was always your problem, wasn't it,' she said, looking up at the desecrated image, her voice reverberating off the church's cold stone walls. 'No balls!' she said, emitting a pitiful laugh. 'Love each other,' she said, 'love thy neighbour, show mercy... be nice?!' she said, raising her voice. 'And where does it get you?' she asked, looking into the downcast eyes of Jesus Christ, an empty silence filling the church ... 'Nowhere, that's where,' she said flatly. 'They walk all over you. They take advantage, and they run amok. A few might come crawling back to you on their deathbeds, but only if the pubs are shut or there's nothing good on telly,' she said with disdain. 'You might as well have just kept quiet.'

She looked across to the pulpit where she delivered her sermons, wondering what the faces of her parishioners would look like if she gave this kind of sermon tomorrow. That's if she could even be bothered to come in. Maybe she would have a day off like all the other lazy sods in the world. Have a nice long lie in. Her first Sunday off for God knows how long. A day of rest at last.

'It was better before you came along,' she continued. 'Old Testament. They were all for it then,' she said. 'I preferred your old man back then. Wrath of God, that was much more like it. A vengeful God. A GOD WITH BALLS!' she shouted. The smile disappeared from her face, her raised voice echoing all around her. Moses looked up briefly before resting his head back on the floor.

She smiled again, beginning to feel the first flickers of anticipation stirring as her thoughts turned to the fete. And revenge. Oh yes, the old ways were the best ways, and today there would be a little trip down memory lane for those who might have forgotten their lesson. A fire, long since doused by doubt and confusion, began to flicker back into life. Today it would ignite, and the flames would consume the soul of Douglas Blouse. And all those who looked upon it would fear; fear the coming of the Lord.

Bowen opened her Bible and took out the photocopied image of Douglas Blouse's backside. She crumpled the piece of paper into a ball and threw it over her shoulder.

'Vengeance is mine,' she said. 'And I will repay, saith the Lord.'

29

Trudy Ryan had removed her earplugs, catching the last verbal exchanges between her husband and the man she knew to be Butch Ransom outside. It was still early, but she didn't mind. With two young daughters, she was used to early mornings. And Jeremy deserved it after he'd come home drunk and late again from another Friday night's boozing with the city boys; no doubt continuing the party in the glamorous surroundings of the Intercity 125 buffet car on the commute back to Didcot. By the time he'd staggered into bed, struggling to undress himself and chauvinistically complaining about the lack of food in the house, it was approaching eleven o'clock, by which time Trudy and the girls had all long since gone to bed. They had exchanged words, but nothing that her husband would remember this morning. She had put her earplugs in within thirty seconds of Jeremy collapsing into bed in an attempt to block out his snoring, which always got worse if he'd been drinking. She'd breathed in deeply, in and out, in and out, a simple exercise she had found helped her get off to sleep. Miraculously, despite the window-rattling noise being made next to her, she had managed to drift off again, being woken again in the early morning daylight by the conversation between her husband and Butch.

Jeremy closed the creaky window and crossed gingerly back to the bed, holding his hand to his head. 'Bloody pain in the arse noise, bloody nonsense this time in the morning,' he said grouchily. 'People trying to sleep ... Bloody carry on,' he said, clambering back into bed.

'Oh I agree, love, absolutely,' Trudy said sarcastically. 'By the way, how are your shoes this morning?'

Jeremy sat up on his elbows, looking at her uncomprehendingly, before looking down beside the bed at the two shiny black shoes strewn a couple of yards apart from each other on the floor.

'Remember attacking them with the nail scissors last night, do we?' she asked. 'Falling about, hopping around all over the place trying to get them off? It's a wonder you didn't wake the girls.'

Jeremy Ryan lay back flat on the bed, his head on the pillow, 'Urrrrhh fuck'em,' he said morosely.

'I beg your pardon?' Trudy said, astonished.

'The shoes,' he said, half into the pillow, 'the bloody shoes.'

From down the hall Trudy heard a door opening, followed by another: one of the girls getting up early going in to see the other. Now that they finally had separate rooms, they found it fun to pay each other little visits in the mornings.

'I suppose they'll want to go down to that bloody fete today, won't they,' Jeremy mumbled. 'Down where Mouth Almighty bloody Sheep Dundee is off to. Mouthy Aussie sod,' he mumbled.

'He's from New Zealand, actually,' Trudy said.

Jeremy slowly turned his head on the pillow to face her. 'How do you know?' he asked.

'I bumped into him the other day down at that fabric shop on the High Street when I was getting stuff for the spare room,' she said. 'Butch was helping Barbara with her window after that boy had smashed it.'

Jeremy looked confused. 'Butch? Barbara?' he said, holding his hand to his head again. 'What is all this? What, are you neighbourhood watch now, or something, Trude?'

The hangover was clearly kicking in, Trudy could tell, and she delighted in it.

'It doesn't hurt to get to know people when you move to a new place, you know, Jeremy,' she said. 'Especially in a place like this. People actually talk to each other around here, you know. It's not like London, everyone too wrapped up in their own lives to give you the time of day, let alone hold a conversation. If you were to actually spend some time here, you might realise that,' she said, lowering her voice despite the rising anger she felt. She didn't want the children to overhear them rowing.

‘Well, someone’s gotta earn the money, Trude,’ Jeremy retorted superciliously. ‘The mortgage isn’t going to pay itself, is it?’

‘You pig,’ she spat, turning away from him. There was a brief uncomfortable silence.

‘OK, look,’ he said, ‘I’m sorry, I didn’t mean anything by it. I’m just a poppa bear with a bit of a sore head today.’

‘And whose fault’s that?’ Trudy countered. Jeremy offered no resistance.

‘Look, Trude, I know I had a bit too much last night, and I’m sorry for being late in. The train being delayed didn’t exactly help,’ he said. ‘I guess I’m just having a bit of trouble adjusting to the new surroundings, that’s all. I’m not like you, Trude; you’re good at meeting people and making new friends. I can’t do that as easily as you can, y’know?’

Begrudgingly Trudy did understand, to a certain extent. But you could only dine out on that kind of excuse for so long.

‘Listen,’ he said, caressing her exposed shoulder, ‘why don’t you go in and check on the girls? It sounds like they’re up. Just give me another half hour or so to get myself in a bit of a better place, then I’ll come down and make us all breakfast,’ he said. ‘After that we can all go down to the fete together. That’ll be nice, won’t it? Sounds like it might be quite a show this year as well, if what I heard down the pub is to be believed,’ he said, perking up.

‘What do you mean?’ Trudy asked.

‘Oh, something to do with that lad you mentioned. You know, the little nutter that broke all the windows then went mental on the railway. Sounds like they’ve got him set him up in some police dog display. Maybe this place is a bit more interesting than I thought after all,’ he said.

Trudy said nothing. She got out of bed and quietly left the bedroom, closing the door on her husband. She stopped, leaning up against the closed bedroom door, her mind whirring. She thought back to Thursday: when she and Butch had been at the level crossing, and Butch had caught the young lad after he’d leapt the barriers, jumping pretty much straight into Butch’s arms. If he had jumped the other side, he would have got away. Then the police had taken him off, but she hadn’t heard anything about it since. They’d found out from Dan in the signal box what Douglas had done to the vicar's dog, or had tried to do. But she'd not seen Butch since, or anyone else for that matter. She hadn't made it down to the meeting last night either, as Butch had suggested, on account of her husband's own wayward behaviour. Douglas was obviously unhinged, and now they were going to put him in a police dog display? That was a bit sick, she thought. Perhaps Jeremy was mistaken. It wouldn't surprise her. Probably just got sold a line by some drunk down the pub, being the new boy in the village and everything.

Her mind shuddered to a halt.

Some drunk down the pub? So that's where he'd been last night, or for part of it at least. The lying sod, she thought. He'd not only had his Friday drink after work with the city boys, then on the train. But then he'd also stopped in at the pub on the way home. Delayed train, my arse. 'I can't make friends like you can, Trude.' You can after five or six pints, you lying sod, she thought.

Her mind was processing all the information until her thoughts were interrupted by the sound of the level crossing outside: the warning sound of the alarm and the barriers descending. All sounds now harmonising dissonantly with her husband on the other side of the bedroom door, who had once again started to snore.

30

After stepping out into the early morning cool of his garden with his first cup of tea of the day, Terence Russell had gone back inside to get ready. He was a light sleeper and besides, the bed felt too big nowadays without his wife beside him. The early arrival of the butterflies hadn't helped either. Today was the day when all the hard work was going to pay off in front of a rapturous home crowd.

Back in his bedroom, Terence sat at the foot of the double bed in his blue pyjama bottoms and white vest, looking out the window at the luscious green field opposite his home, and the small copse beyond that. He sat in silence, save for the early morning song of chirping birds. It was still a little early to start ringing round. Terence liked to make sure everything was in order with a quick ring around beforehand. He was a stickler for detail. The meet-up at the pub beforehand was usually when the butterflies really started; when Terence would permit himself his usual pint of shandy, firstly to settle the nerves but also to toast their success, though he knew that he would have to keep a keen eye on Colin and Bob's drinking.

Bob could drink continuously all day and you'd hardly notice. Sometimes he even danced with a drink in his hand. His performance, however, would somehow remain miraculously flawless, almost as if it were one of the very last biological programmes running in his ageing, demoralised body.

Colin on the other hand could go from nought to Oliver Reed in about ten seconds flat. Much to Terence's displeasure, drinking came above all else with Colin, and today the football club bar would be an ever present concern.

'It'll be fine,' Terence said out loud, clapping his hands on his thighs, hoping that saying it might somehow make it so. He tried his best to allay his concerns, and to focus his mind on more positive thoughts. The recent spell of exceptional weather had been good for rehearsals, and though he had pushed the boys hard in practice, he knew it had all been worth it. They'd thank him for it in the end.

Terence stood up and padded over to the wardrobe, sliding open the right-hand door of the master bedroom's recessed wardrobe. He took out his pristine white Morris man outfit, laying it down delicately on the bed, like a sleeping child he didn't wish to wake; or a beautiful, frail woman who had been eaten away by cancer.

Terence shook the memory from his mind.

The bright ribbons that he would later attach to his arms and legs were all there with the dazzlingly white shirt and trousers, along with the neatly pressed baldricks that would criss-cross his pristine shirt. At the bottom of the wardrobe was an old ice cream tub containing his bells and pin badges. What a glorious sight it was when it was all put together.

'I love a man in uniform,' Iris used to say to him with a cheeky little wink when he put it all on.

He closed his side of the wardrobe and slid back the left-hand door, revealing the rail of Iris's old clothes that he had been unable to part with; the clothes that by the end of her life had hung limply from her tiny frame. They were all still there, covered in cellophane, neatly pressed and hung up, almost as if she could walk back into his life at any moment and pick one off the rail ready for an evening out or a day down on the coast.

Terence felt a niggle of irritation ripple through him as he thought about the change to the line-up. He couldn't shake the feelings of annoyance he felt towards Sergeant Frisk for imposing the last-minute change to the running order. He was sorry for what had happened, but Frisk knew what today meant to him and his boys. Now he only had about half an hour between playing the accordion for the kids' stick dancing display and getting himself ready for his own performance. It was going to be tight, but he hoped that fortune would be smiling on him and his boys today. Along with Iris.

He closed the wardrobe, focusing again on the uniform lying on the bed. It was still early. Best put the kettle on again and try to relax. Maybe he'd polish the bells and badges just one more time. He held up the uniform in the block of sunlight that streamed through the bedroom's open curtains, the sun's rays highlighting the uniform's immaculate condition.

'Beautiful,' he said.

By the end of the day he would be wondering how he was going to get the bloodstains out of it.

31

'You big fat slob,' Edna Glass hissed at the snoring mass seated in the lounge of their static home on Bargus Close.

Graham Glass was asleep in the single armchair, his feet up on the pouffe. His three chins were buried into his chest, and his bottom lip protruded, making him look like a fat sulking child. The rolls of chin fat merged with his chest to make one indecipherable flabby slope. He was in front of the television, which Edna had turned off at two o'clock this morning after he had, as usual, fallen asleep in front of it following another night drinking and playing darts up the pub. He would probably remain where he was until it was time to go to work later. He was a deep sleeper, and that suited her just fine.

'You just stay out of my way today,' she said. 'And when I get back later, you're not here, right!? Maybe I'll've found someone who can get the job done, with a bit of luck.'

Edna could feel the vibrations of his cacophanous snoring through the thick pile of faded pink carpet beneath her feet. Her husband's enormous beer gut spilled out the bottom of his shirt like a bag of burst gravel. The top and bottom two buttons of his shirt were unbuttoned, leaving it to the remaining three to hold back the considerable mass straining beneath them. His darts case protruded from his breast pocket. The top two buttons of his blue jeans were also undone, the blubber of his vast beer gut spilled over it like flabby lava. She looked at the fat snoring mound, arms folded, assessing her current life situation.

'So you're the man I married, are you?' she said to him. She put her face right up close to the side of his, so she could feel his warmth. 'Aren't I the lucky one,' she said venomously, emphasising each word. 'No wonder that other Welsh tart wouldn't have you. Look at the state of you. Not got the gift of the gab like Bertie had either, have you? You couldn't pull in a brothel,' she said mockingly, standing over him, lighting a cigarette and blowing smoke into his face. 'Anyway, I've got more important things to be getting on with,' she said breezily, smoking her cigarette in double-quick time and crushing it in the ashtray.

Edna turned and headed for the bedroom. She looked at her watch. It was 9.30.

So much to do. She had to open up the village hall in half an hour for Petra Carr, the sanctimonious cow, so she could strut about all day eating cake and drinking tea and discussing jam with all the other busybodies. Then she had to go up to the football club to open up there. That suited her fine. She knew after the meeting last night that the police were using the football club facilities to prepare for their little demonstration. And the changing rooms they would be occupying, where she had begrudgingly let Frisk in yesterday to dump their gear, were mere yards from where she herself was going to be for the best part of the day, doing what she did best, apart from pulling men: pulling pints.

She'd been civilised enough last night with the police. She still hadn't been quite sure exactly if she intended to go through with her plan. But after hearing what the police intended to do with Douglas, spurred on by Bowen and Carr, she decided that she would. It was a long shot, but it was well worth a go. No guts, no glory.

All she needed was a bit of luck, she thought, as she crossed to the second drawer down of her bedside chest of drawers, fumbling its contents. It was her sexy drawer. She had all sorts of kinky stuff in here. Not that her husband was aware of it. This stuff was about as much use to him as it was to Reverend Bowen. No, this was for her and her playmates, only when Graham was at work. Seeing the assorted contents of the drawer reminded her of a party game they used to play at Peter's birthday parties, a life-time ago.

A tray loaded up with lots of little knick-knacks would be covered by a tea towel, which was then whisked off for ten seconds. You had to try to remember all the things that were on it before the tea towel covered it all up again.

From out of the drawer she fished out a frilly pink and white eye mask with the words 'Love is blind' embroidered on the front. She quickly shut the drawer, deciding impulsively to play the game with herself now. She pulled the elasticated strap of the mask over her frizzy mane and covered her eyes. The thought of her drawer's X-rated contents being used like this at a children's party struck her as highly inappropriate, but none the less amusing.

'Bottle of lube,' she recited to the empty room, 'furry pink handcuffs, coconut oil, nipple clamps.' She paused briefly. '7-inch vibrator, 10-inch Darth invader dildo,' she smiled, recollecting the long, black helmeted *Star Wars*-themed sex toy that diagonally dominated the drawer. 'And ...' she said, removing the eye mask and slowly opening the drawer again, 'and ...' she picked it up, feeling the weight of it, hard and heavy.

'And ....'

32

'Ohh shit, sorry, Guv,' PC Binsley said, rather embarrassed, entering the police station to start his 10-6 shift.

'Don't worry, Dennis, I'm sure you've seen worse in the line of duty,' an aggressive and trouserless Sergeant Frisk said, wielding a large black stapler.

'Not quite got the hang of the admin side of things, eh, guv?' Binsley said.

'Very funny, Dennis,' Frisk said, none too impressed. 'It's these bastard things,' he said, holding up his trousers. 'Split them the other day jumping over that sodding barrier chasing arse features in there, and now the washing machine's taken my other pair frigging hostage. Bloody door won't open,' he said, with rising anger.

'Heard from the missus yet, guv?' Binsley asked.

'Nope. Said she'd be in touch sometime. When sometime is exactly is anyone's guess. She's obviously having too much fun with mad Auntie Pam to bother ringing me.'

'Left you to fend for yourself, has she?' Binsley said.

'Something like that, Dennis, yes,' Frisk answered wearily, snapping another three staples into his inside-out trousers. He turned them back the right way, giving them a cautious shake, hoping that his improvised tailoring would hold.

'Sod it, that'll just have to do, won't it,' he said, gingerly putting the trousers back on. 'We need to be getting on anyway. Laurie'll be here in a minute with Gooch, I should think.'

Right on cue, a white Ford Escort police van pulled into the station. Parking up in the small rear car park, Sergeant Laurie Knox, dressed in black combat trousers, hi-tech magnum boots and black polo shirt bearing the crest of the Thames Vally police, entered the police station moments later to greet his fellow officers.

'Morning, chaps!' he said, unbuttoning the last of his polo shirt's three buttons. 'Gonna be another hot one out there today, and I'm not just talking about my flaming hoops,' he said.

'Just glad it's not gonna be me again in all that gear today. Hot as a motherfucker,' Binsley said, loosening his tie. Frisk shot him a glance but did not say anything.

'Good morning, Laurie,' Frisk said. 'Welcome. I trust you and Gooch are both ready and raring for today's fun and games?'

'Oh, absolutely, Sarge,' Knox said. 'Always happy to help a troubled individual see the error of their ways,' he said. 'Rehabilitation, Guv, that's what it's all about.'

'Yeah, well, I hope you're right. That boy is gonna be on thin bloody ice after today,' Frisk said. 'If he steps out of line once more, it'll be the young offenders' institute for him and no bloody mistake. If he's not careful he might even end up with the big boys; he's pushing eighteen, after all. I've warned him about it. A boy like him in prison? I tell you, he wouldn't go flashing his arse around inside, you mark my words. Red rag to a bull. They'd eat him for bloody breakfast!'

'Whereas today he's gonna get eaten for lunch, eh, guv?' Binsley said gleefully, looking at Frisk and then Knox.

'Now now, Dennis,' Knox said, 'let's not be forgetting we'll still be kitting our young volunteer out with all the same gear we have every year,' he said. 'I've got a nice balaclava for our man to wear as well, just to give him that extra authentic Burglar Bill look. Gooch really goes for that sort of thing,' he said. 'Been using it a lot in training.'

'Speaking of which, how is young Gooch?' Frisk asked. 'We were all obviously really sorry about what happened to Beefy,' he said sombrely. 'He was great last year, wasn't he, Dennis?'

'Can still feel him dangling from my arm, Guv.'

'Yeah, he was good, wasn't he,' Knox said reflectively. 'Gooch has been coming on great though, these past few months. I'm so confident in his abilities. I've been able to spend a lot of time with him, what with me being a fully-fledged bachelor now,' Knox said. 'So I've been able to fully dedicate myself to his training.'

'Yeah, can't be easy making the adjustment to single life.'

'It's not that bad, Guv. Good riddance to the adulterous slag, I say,' Knox said.

Frisk was a little disturbed by Knox's sudden change in tone, but he clearly had his reasons. He couldn't imagine what it must feel like for your partner to do something like that to you. It must...

Frisk suddenly felt himself go cold, his blood turning to ice in his veins. A wave of paranoia washed over him. He hadn't even questioned his wife's story about going away. For all he knew, it could be a big lie. He hadn't tried to get hold of her himself, he'd been too stubborn, too busy. 'Will call u' is all the note had said. She could be off with someone else ... with his daughter. So much of his time had been taken up with the antics of Douglas Blouse over the past few days that he'd just taken it all at face value. He tried to compose his thoughts, telling himself that his wife was not capable of doing something like that to him. But Laurie had sewn a seed of paranoia, and it stuck in his mind like gristle between the teeth.

'You OK, guv?' Laurie asked him.

No actually, Laurie, you've made me think my wife is having an affair and now I'm really frigging paranoid about it, he thought to himself.

'Yeah, yeah, fine,' Frisk said, clapping his hands together, returning to the here and now. 'Well, we've got a lot to get done before midday, chaps. Firstly I am going to get a couple of cans of petrol from over the road for your flaming hoops, Laurie,' he said. 'Then I have to meet the elders down at the village hall for eleven. Laurie, I'd like you to come down just after then, if you could, please. I'll help you to set up for the display. It'll give me a good excuse to get away from Hilda and Petra. I've got some of our bits and pieces for the stand in the back of the van already,' he said. 'Usual freebies. Leaflets stickers, badges, that sort of thing. Stuff for the kids, you know. Dennis, I'm afraid you get to stay here and keep an eye on the railway child. Make sure he gets some food before the display as well, please. And a wash if he's feeling adventurous. I'll be back later to pick you both up, then we can go down to the football club together to get ready. I spoke to Edna briefly last night about changing facilities. She wasn't exactly thrilled to speak to me, as you can probably imagine, but we did arrange that we'd be using one of the changing rooms down at the sports club for Mr Blouse to prepare for his star turn, OK?' Frisk checked for agreement from his two officers.

'Absolutely, guv,' Knox said.

'Yes, guv,' Binsley concurred.

'Edna'd better stay out of the way though, guv,' Binsley said defensively. 'You know she still blames me for what happened.'

'And I can't change that, I'm afraid, Dennis,' Frisk said. 'All I can say to you is what I have already said to her ... many times. That it was settled in a court of law and the judge's decision is final, OK? As unfortunate as it all was, that is just how it is. Whether she chooses to accept that or not is both up to her, and entirely out of my control. OK?

'Yes, guv,' Binsley said, looking past Frisk.

'Good, right. Well, I'm off to the garage,' Frisk said, cautiously walking to the door, hoping not to put too much stress on his trousers.

'Bring Gooch in, Laurie, if you want,' Frisk said. 'Introduce him to Douglas; it might be good for them to get to know each other before this afternoon. See if they've got good chemistry. Get him a bowl of water as well. It's gonna be a scorcher.'

'No problem, guv,' Knox said. 'Will do!'

'And Dennis, don't forget what I said. Make sure Douglas gets something to eat. He may be a little nutter, but we still have to feed him, OK? And don't wind him up!'

'Yeah, OK,' Binsley said as Frisk took the van keys off the hook and left the police station.

Grinning, Dennis Binsley walked over to his desk and opened the bottom drawer. He fished around before extracting a can of dog food which he placed on top of his desk.

'What d'you reckon then, Laurie?' he said grinning. 'Half for Gooch, half for Douglas?' They both laughed.

33

Colin Blunsden was scraping at the back door of The Crafty Digit like an anxious dog. The pub was due to open any minute and he was thirsty, very thirsty. He'd been outside since quarter to eleven, sitting on the bench with Bob Dobson in anticipation of that first thirst-quenching drink of the day. The first of many, he hoped. In the meantime he nipped from a small hip flask tucked into his sock. He checked his watch again: 10.58.

'Come on, Pat, we're dying out here!' he yelled at the door.

To his right he heard the sound of a latch being fumbled with, then at last, much to his relief, the serving hatch doors swung open and Pat Wilkes stuck her head out.

'Morning, boys,' she said, looking the expectant drinkers up and down as they ambled towards her. 'My, my, don't you look lovely in your outfits,' she said.

Bob Dobson looked passable, particularly after the treatment Terence had given their uniforms. He was a bit ragged and his shirt was untucked at the back, but he would pass inspection.

The same could not be said for Colin, however, who looked as if he had been startled out of bed by a 3 a.m. fire alarm. His shirt, which over the space of one evening had turned from brilliant white to a stained and crumpled mess, clung apologetically to his sorry frame. The yellow and green Baldricks that criss-crossed it hung limply from him in a sagging X. His top hat was partially flattened, as if it had been accidentally sat on at some point, and the flowers that lined its brim appeared to be either dead or dying. His dull, dented bells had turned the colour of muddy sand after years of neglect, and were sadly lacking in both jingle and jangle. His baggy grass-stained trousers hung loosely on him, a pair of crumpled hankies spewing from the pockets like crinkled tongues. All of this, however, was completely irrelevant to Colin, whose sole purpose at this moment was to drink what he hoped would be his first of many cold lagers.

'Hallebloodyluja!' he cried, in a squawky high-pitched tone. 'Now then, Pat love, how's about a couple of pints for a pair of dying men, eh?' he said. 'And give us two pies and two pasties n'all, will ya,' he said, rubbing his belly, untucking his shirt further. 'Choo 'avin then, Bob?' Colin said, knowing full well what the monosyllabic answer would be.

'Pint,' Dobson said.

'Ding ding! Top bloody answer,' Colin said. 'You win the money, the car and a pint of lager!'

Pat Wilkes had started pouring the drinks before Colin had even begun to speak, such was his predictability.

'Actually, make it four pints, Pat. Boss'll be here in a minute to start bollocking me, won't he,' he said, laughing like a naughty schoolboy.

Pat Wilkes put the first two pints on the counter of the hatch.

Colin took his pint, holding it up to the sun with the reverence of an archaeologist who has just discovered a precious, holy artefact.

'Cheers, Bob!' he said, clinking glasses with his silent friend.

Colin raised the glass to his lips and proceeded to neck his pint, the cold lager spilling from the glass around his mouth and dribbling down his white dress shirt, forming light amber islands on the already grubby frontage. He still had a quarter of a pint to go when a shadow fell upon him.

'As if I shouldn't have guessed, look at the bloody state of you,' Terence Russell said, addressing his alcoholic duo, his boxed accordion slung over his shoulder. Gerry Hayman stood behind him, shaking his head. Under his arm, Hayman held a bound clutch of sticks, as if he had been out collecting firewood.

Terence was the complete opposite to Colin in every way, standing in the sunshine of the beer garden, immaculately turned out in his dazzling whites. His trousers were crisp and pressed, likewise his shirt. His Baldricks were taut across his chest in a tight X. His ribbons were vibrant, and swayed in the summer sun. His pin badges that adorned his shirt glinted, as did the bells that shone a glorious gold, hanging like glistening grapes just below the knees and above the elbows.

'How the hell did you get into such a bloody mess, Colin?' Terence asked, amazed. 'I only gave that lot back to you last night, for crying out loud.'

Gerry continued shaking his head.

Colin's face crumpled as he tried to think fast, something which, in his still relatively sober state, he was just about capable of doing. 'I practised again when I got home, din I,' he said defiantly, hoping his apocryphal tale of extra curricular practice might let him off the hook. 'On me own in the garden. I wanted to try all the gear on n'that, so then I had a drink and another dance in me garden, ready for today, n'it.'

There was at least a half-truth in his story. The bit about the drink, and he did have a dance in the garden, sort of. But it had resulted in him falling about drunk, unable to stand and looking a complete shambles.

'Here're the others, Colin,' Pat Wilkes said, placing another two gleaming pints on the counter.

Terence clocked this and marched over to the serving hatch. 'Oh, perfect, thank you, Pat,' he said sarcastically, taking the two pints from the counter.

Colin looked on in horror as Terence poured half the contents from each pint onto the scorched brown surface of the pub's beer garden before walking to the hatch and placing the half-empty pint glasses back on the counter. Blunsden emitted a feeble high-pitched moan at the sight of perfectly good lager being used to water the baked earth of the beer garden.

'Top them up with lemonade, would you please, Pat,' he said politely. Pat gave him a wry grin and did as she was asked. 'Them two are on the shandies n'all from now on, Pat, please, love,' Terence said, pointing to Colin and Bob, before moving back over to join them. 'Every bloody year,' he said, shaking his head. 'I just can't leave you alone, can I?'

Colin wilted in the heat at the inevitable bollocking. His face crumpled as his eyes looked shiftily towards the bar. 'Iss tradition, ennit,' was all he could manage, snapping back in response at his scornful leader.

'Terence!' Pat said, placing the now-diluted drinks back on the counter.

'Thank you, Pat, love,' he said, walking back over and picking up the two pints, now lighter in colour after the additional lemonade. He handed one to Gerry, keeping the other for himself. 'Thanks for the drink then, Colin,' Terence said, raising the glass.

'Yeah, thanks, Colin,' Gerry echoed, smiling.

'Piss it off, you,' Colin spat. 'Bloody teacher's pet.'

The beer garden was beginning to fill up with more locals keen to take advantage of the earlier opening time, and Terence's words were now a little more camouflaged among the growing chatter.

'OK, gentlemen, how's about we start again?' he said to his dancing quartet. 'I don't want to start on a downer, and I don't mean to get at you, Colin, really,' he said. 'But you know how much today means to me. All I want is for us lot to put on a good show, that's all. I know it might seem like I act like an old headmaster sometimes, but that's only because I want what's best for you boys. What's best for us,' he amended. 'We've worked bloody hard this summer, lads. And today's gonna be the real feather in the cap. Home town show,' he said, clenching his fist. 'So how's about it then, boys? We gonna show 'em what we can do, or what!?'

Blunsden wrinkled his face, miserably contemplating the remaining couple of inches of lager left in his pint glass. Gerry stood behind Terence, nodding, holding his drink as if obediently waiting for permission to take his first sip.

'Here's to it then, boys. Cheers!' Terence said, holding his drink aloft and toasting their success. They clinked glasses, the droplets of condensation on the cold pint glasses glinting in the sunshine. Blunsden swallowed the last mouthful. Bob Dobson stood motionless, half his pint already drained, saying nothing and looking at nothing in particular. Gerry sipped his shandy beside his lead dancer.

'Colin, food's ready,' Pat called.

Blunsden meekly made his way over to the hatch to collect his pastries, seizing the opportunity to take a generous nip from his hip flask behind Terence's back. 'Two pints,' he said, under his breath, as he gingerly took the food from her and placed it on a nearby bench. 'Don't tell Hitler over there.'

A distant noise came from up the causeway, towards the railway. The patrons of The Crafty Digit turned to face it. It sounded as if there was a strange disagreement taking place in a language that no one could understand. With the whisky now muzzying, his head Colin was a little confused. The noise got closer and he soon realised it was in fact the sound of bleating sheep he could hear. Behind them walked a beautiful shepherdess. Her pink dress was dazzling in the sunshine. The matching bonnet on her head was a sumptuous pink crescent which sat like a shimmering hemisphere of silk and lace.

Colin stood rooted to the spot, transfixed and becoming increasingly aroused. His aged, withered penis twitched in his crumpled trousers as a fantasy formed in a mind not yet obliterated by alcohol. Around him other drinkers also noticed the approaching shepherdess. Wolf whistling and yelling filled the air. The black and white sheepdog maintaining order kept a close eye on the flock as they drew nearer to the hollering drinkers.

The whistling and yelling increased, though Colin was oblivious to it now. He was mesmerised. The gentle waves of early-morning booze washed over him as the vision before him moved with seduction and beauty.

'Colin ... Colin,' she called softly ... 'Coliiiiin.'

Blunsden emitted a high-pitched squeak of delight as the imagined words floated through his mind like a summer breeze. Then something changed. The voice Colin heard in his head changed, becoming deeper, more masculine. And there were more of them now.

'Go on, Colin!' the voices now said, no longer in the private surroundings of his own mind, but all around him in the beer garden. Sober realisation returned to the fantasising drunkard as he snapped out of his trance, surrounded by laughing faces, hands covering their mouths while drink spilled from jerking pint glasses that shook with their shared hysteria.

Colin looked around him, confused. They were all laughing, pointing and laughing at the erection that had formed in his crumpled trousers.

34

Tony Gables cupped his hands against the sports club window, looking for signs of life. There weren't any. It was gloomy and dark in the bar. He could just about make out the beer mats on the small round tables dotted about, and tantalisingly he could see the glimmer of sunlight on the row of optics behind the bar. He thought Edna would've been here by now. She should have been. There was now less than an hour to go until the opening ceremony, and he needed to set his gear up. The turntables and the speakers were in the car, and he'd given himself a bit of a headstart by already assembling the gazebo, but he needed to get to the internal power supply and get the extension cables for the juice to power it all. He checked his watch, looking furtively around the green.

Then at last he saw her. She was marching purposefully across the green from the direction of the village hall, her handbag slung over her shoulder. He watched with delight as her breasts bounced inside her low-cut top like two skinheads having a head-butting competition. She strode past the bouncy castle, straight over Jim Leyland's blue judo mats and headed for the football club. She was now just about within earshot of the anxious DJ.

'Edna, what time do you call thi...'

'Piss off, Tony, don't bloody start,' she snapped, cutting him off and walking straight past him. 'I know you need to get ready, and I know I'm late, so just get out of my way and I'll open up.'

Tony gave chase. 'Edna, I don't think you quite understand. I'm a professional DJ, and my public expect a certain standard from me,' he said pompously. 'Every time I perform, my reputation is at stake. If I don't make the right preparations, my head's gonna be a mess and the whole day could be a disaster. I'm a professional, Edna.'

Edna shook her black and grey snowball of hair, unlocking the side door of the club that led into the changing rooms. 'Oh, don't give me that load of old bollocks, Tony,' she said, giving the stubborn door a shove with her meaty shoulder and striding down the cool shady corridor. 'It's not 1980 any more. You're a bloody has-been whose best days are long behind him. You only come down here to show off and try to recapture some of that so-called glory you had back in your so-called prime. It's tragic, Tony, it really is. It's no wonder that Karen's left you. Now get out of my bloody way, will you.'

Tony flinched at Edna's scathing remarks, his ego cut to ribbons. He was too emotionally fragile to take this kind of early-morning character assassination from her. And bringing Karen into it just drew more blood.

'You're still late though,' he said feebly, flirting with danger and following her into the soft gloom of the bar.

'Yeah well, if it wasn't for that fussy cow over in the village hall demanding a total rearrangement of all the tables for her and her cronies to put their silly little pots of jam on, and their longest sodding runner beans, I might have been here a bit sooner, Tony,' she said. 'Petra treats me like I'm her bloody skivvy. And I'm gonna have the bloody police setting up camp in here shortly,' she said, with obvious disdain. 'I'm doing this all on my own, you know, Tony. No help. Understand? Now, I've got a lot on my mind and a lot to be getting on with,' she said, exasperated. 'So what do you need?'

Like a naughty schoolboy, Tony tentatively gave her his list, hoping that she might cool down and cooperate, which eventually she did as she started going about her own tasks in the club.

Tony finally got the extension cables and adapters, before unloading the rest of his equipment from his people carrier in the club car park. The decks, the speakers, the deckchair, his record boxes, including his special box that contained his day's refreshments. Not to mention his obligatory collage board of past glories from his time served at various radio stations, just in case there was anyone within a five-mile radius who didn't know who he was.

His ego rallied, thinking back to his glorious past, and Tony managed to put Edna's verbal tirade behind him, giving her the benefit of the doubt.

It was still early, after all, and he guessed she was stressed out. She certainly looked it.

*

Edna placed her handbag under the bar. Just carrying it around made her feel nervous: as if she was about to go through a metal detector and was waiting for the alarm to go off. With the police soon to be hanging round, she had to be hyper-vigilant. She would be sure to keep her bag nice and safe and out of the way. Until the time came. God willing, until the time came.

She began to polish the long wooden bar. She quickly polished the tables, placing ashtrays on each of them and had a quick run around with the Hoover. What did it matter? she thought. The place would be a tip again by this afternoon anyway. Then she would have the pleasure of tidying it all up again after everybody had gone, when once again it was just her tidying up other people's mess. If things went to plan, as she hoped they would, she might at least have a smile on her face for once.

She looked at the fridges, bursting with bottles of booze; at the beer pumps, charged and ready for action. Thankfully after last night's late-night stocking of the bar and cellar, all the needs of the local power drinkers were taken care of. She glanced out of the window, watching Tony frantically untangling various wires, plugging them into their little holes on the mixing desk, his makeshift DJ booth taking shape.

'I'm a professional after all,' she said, with a smile to the empty bar.

Tony also had a little smile on his face, and was now happily whistling away as he ran to fetch more stuff from his car. She watched him toddle back past the windows a couple of minutes later holding a record box in each hand. She could see the strain in his face as he marched like an inappropriate contestant in the world's strongest man. She felt bad about what she had said to him earlier. He was harmless enough. Just another ego-centric luvvie who needed to be told they were great all the time. Showbiz in the blood and all that crap. A bit sad really.

The French doors that opened out onto the green gave Edna a perfect view of the fete. It would be intermittently obscured by thirsty revellers for most of the afternoon, but she could still keep a watchful eye on the day's proceedings. The cricket pitch where the Morris dancing was due to take place was directly in front of her, with the football pitch just off to the right. This is where the famous police dog display would be happening.

Goose pimples ran up Edna's chunky forearms, resting on the gleaming surface of the well-polished bar. She was thinking about her plan, and she kept her handbag close by.

Her eyes scanned the walls of the club, taking in the trophy cabinet and the framed team photos of Steventon's football and cricket teams past and present. Her eyes landed on one in particular, as they inevitably did when she was in here. It featured a light-haired young boy of fifteen dressed in cricket whites, seated second left from the captain at whose feet stood a gleaming trophy. Her son beamed from the photo. Captured forever young, smiling at her from across the bar. She thought about the police. And what she had to do to make things right.

'Hey!' Gables said, sticking his head through the double doors, startling Edna from her vengeful daydream. 'If you've got time to lean, you've got time to clean,' he said, smiling.

She was about to unleash another verbal tirade on him, but held her tongue. Instead she took a deep breath, trying to calm herself. She needed to remain calm. That was most important.

'Just about done, actually, Tony,' she said with a trace of relief. 'Drink?'

Tony looked surprised. 'Well, Edna, I don't usually this early you know ...' he trailed off as Edna turned to the row of optics behind her and poured a double vodka.

'Piss of Tony,' she said, more playfully this time. 'It'll do you good. Steady your nerves for your big day.'

Tony strode up to the bar like a cowboy entering a saloon in an old western. 'You know I suppose you're right,' he said. 'I'm nearly all set up out there anyway. Just got to do a couple of sound checks and make sure the levels are right.'

Edna poured a second vodka and placed it in front of the DJ, noticing the glint in his eye as he stared at the small glass of clear liquid.

'You know, Edna,' he said, leaning an elbow on the bar and cupping his chin in the palm of his hand, 'while it's still quiet, if you get a minute before the opening ceremony, maybe you could uhhh, y'know...' he said, looking down at his groin before re-establishing eye contact ... 'Give me a hand?'

Edna smiled, leaning forward, her breasts resting on the bar. She raised her glass to the ageing lothario, her face now only a few inches from his own.

Tony leaned in, pouting and breathing the intoxicating mixture of perfume and cigarette smoke, their mouths barely an inch apart.

Edna leaned ever closer. 'Piss off, Tony,' she said softly.

Deflated, Tony raised his own glass, stepping back from the bar. 'Yes, well,' he said, a little ruffled, still with his eyes on Edna's cleavage, 'you can't blame a man for trying,' he said. 'Here's to you, Edna. All the breast ... err, I mean best!'

He blushed, and swallowed the vodka, feeling it trickle down his gullet, warming his belly as it reached his gut. It felt good. He smiled and placed the empty glass back on the bar. 'Well, I best get back to it,' he said. 'Not long to go now.'

Not long indeed, Edna thought as Tony left the bar. Soon they'd all be descending on the place. She savoured the temporary quiet, knowing that in an hour it would be full. She looked down to where she had safely stowed her handbag, her heart beating faster at the sight of it. She would not let it out of her sight.

She looked over again at the team photograph. The last one that Peter was to feature in. The smile of an innocent boy. His life cut short at seventeen by the reckless actions of those employed to protect.

'Don't worry, my lovely boy,' she said, her eyes vacant, almost staring through the photograph. 'Mummy'll make it better.'

Revenge, she thought. It's in the bag.

35

Douglas Blouse was in his cell. He'd finished re-reading the copies of Kerrang and WWF magazine that Sergeant Frisk had relented in getting for him from Kareshi's newsagent to ease the boredom of his incarceration. He had been locked up for over 48 hours now, but soon he'd be free to go. Once he'd done their silly little dog show.

Now he was pacing. He'd marked out an imaginary oche on the floor and in his head was throwing endless 180's. Other than the magazines, it had been the only thing to help him kill the boredom. It was unlikely he'd be having any visitors.

Douglas looked around at the cold sterile confines of the police cell. Two days in here was bad, but two years in a prison cell would be worse. The caravan wasn't much, in fact it was nothing more than an old heap of crap that held nothing but bad memories, but at least you could open the door and go out whenever you wanted to.

He was secretly quite glad that Bowen had agreed to drop the charges against him if he cooperated with their little display. But they'd thrown in a restraining order for good measure: now he couldn't go within fifty feet of her, or her dog. If he did, he faced the possibility of all charges being re-instated and the very real prospect of a young offenders' institute, or worse, prison. Do not pass go. Do not collect £200. Do not flash your arse at a high-speed train on the way. He'd turn eighteen in just under three months, after all. He'd just have to work a little harder on his long game. He could put a window through from fifty feet, easily. And there was plenty of ballast on the railway to practise with.

He pulled down his shorts to inspect the damage that PC Binsley had inflicted on him with his belt. A thick red line ran across his fluffy bum cheeks, like a red road traversing two pink, pimply hills. This was another reason he was pacing. He'd been unable to sit down comfortably since the angry copper had leathered his arse.

From down the corridor he could hear voices. It was the filth – and they were laughing. Maybe after the show he would take their little police dog for a walk.

As if in response to his mental threats, Douglas heard the dog bark, almost as if it could read his mind. Were dogs telepathic? He'd heard they could see ghosts.

'Piss off, dog shit breath,' he said, standing alone in his cell.

The dog barked again, only louder.

Douglas felt a rising anxiety in the pit of his stomach. He continued to pace, trying to put the noise from his mind, hammering the invisible treble twenty. He heard footsteps and hushed voices coming towards his cell. Then silence. It was broken seconds later by three loud thumps on the cell door.

'Open up! ... This is the police! … We have the place surrounded!' the voice shouted.

Startled, Douglas turned to face the door as the envelope-sized flap in the cell door fell open. He could see two eyes staring at him. He could also hear the sound of laughter. Then he saw a mouth, the pursed lips of which began to whistle. It was a tune Douglas knew only too well. One that brought back only bad memories. Binsley was whistling the theme tune to *Bullseye.*

Over the top of it another man spoke: 'Now Douglas, we've already got you for actual bodily harm, trespass, obscene behaviour, and being a general dick head,' the voice said, attempting a poor impression of *Bullseye*'s Lancastrian host, Jim Bowen. 'We'd like you now to consider a gamble. Would you like to gamble all of that for what's hiding behind this door?'

'Yeah, very funny, you pair of twats,' he said, his voice a little on edge.

'It's trio of twats, arse face,' PC Binsley said as the two coppers burst into the cell with the police dog.

Douglas leapt back, standing up against the back wall, slowly sliding down into a crouched position, face to face for the first time with the wild-eyed Alsatian. The maniacal dog's face was just inches from Blouse's own. Douglas could smell its hot, sour breath, and its jaws seemed to move mechanically in perfect synchronicity with the deafening bark that filled the cell and echoed off its walls. Douglas pushed back against the wall in a futile attempt to distance himself from the dog. He winced at the pain from his sore backside as it made contact with the hard stone floor between the bed and the sink.

'Gooch!' Knox snapped at the dog. 'Gooch, come,' he commanded. The lead went slack and Gooch obediently returned to his master's side.

Douglas felt a wave of relief flood over him, but he was still scared. Backs to the wall, quite literally. He tried not to show his emotions. He didn't want to give them the satisfaction of thinking they were getting to him.

'Good morning, Douglas, my name is Sergeant Laurie Knox and this here is my partner Gooch. We're going to be having a bit of fun together later today, aren't we, young man,' Knox said. 'Now the good Reverend has told me a lot about you and your recent activities,' he said. 'You're an animal lover as well, I understand. Starting your own little dog walking enterprise in the village, from what I hear. You walk them,' Knox said, gently rubbing his chin, 'you get them drunk, you feed them pizza. I mean, it doesn't sound too bad to me so far, Douglas,' Knox said. 'But unfortunately you're not quite so keen on returning them, are you? No, see, from what I hear, you display strong resistance when it comes to returning them to their rightful owners, don't you, Douglas? A somewhat violent resistance, some might say,' Knox continued, now crouching down in front of Douglas, his eye line, like Gooch's, now level with his.

'Now Douglas, there are three things in this world that I really can't abide,' Knox said with quiet menace, looking Douglas squarely in the eye. 'One is people endangering the life of a fellow officer – tick, as our temporarily absent Sergeant Frisk could attest to. Two is violence against women – tick again Douglas, and a vicar as well, so extra nutter points for that one. And three,' he said, now eyeball to eyeball with Douglas, 'is cruelty to animals,' he snarled, his white knuckles tightly gripping Gooch's lead. 'So,' he said, getting to his feet and regaining his composure, 'today we are going to redress the balance, because today, my friend, is cruelty to humans day.'

36

The laughter in the beer garden of The Crafty Digit doubled in both volume and intensity as the disoriented Colin Blunsden turned a sharp ninety degrees to face the hysterical onlookers who surrounded him. The point of his erection standing proud and unabated gave his trousers the look of a crumpled circus tent turned on its side. As he pivoted, it made contact with a precariously placed pint glass on the edge of a bench, sending the half-empty vessel hurtling to the arid surface below.

In the car park directly beside the beer garden, Butch Ransom, dressed in the immaculate pink and white silk dress and bonnet that he had been tirelessly working on for the past month, stood behind his sheep, bent over double, laughing, holding his matching pink shepherd's crook in one hand and his stomach with the other. The bleating of his sheep around him merged with the laughter of the crowd, making it sound as if it was not only humans who found the situation amusing.

'Sorry, Col,' Butch said, trying to compose himself, 'but you're just not my type!'

'Pissin piss it off, you ya bleddy mouthy tranny Aussie twat!' Blunsden screamed in a high-pitched squeal of embarrassment. 'This ain't what it looks like, right' he said, 'I got a ...'

'A beer bottle down your trousers?' Butch yelled, sending the congregation back into hysterics. 'It doesn't seem to be going down there, mate. You're not sweet on my sheep as well are you, ya dirty old bastard!'

The embarrassed Morris dancer turned to leave, banging his shin on the bench as he fled. He stumbled, falling to the floor, only just managing to put his hands out in time before he hit the ground. His florally decorated top hat fell to the floor, exposing the smattering of wispy grey hairs that littered his sweaty, wrinkled scalp. He did not stop to pick it up; instead he gingerly got to his feet and staggered towards the pub, limping in part from the whack on his shin, but also from his persistent erection.

A relative quiet was re-established in the beer garden as everyone got their breath back.

'Are we going down there then, boys?' Ransom asked, wiping the tears from his eyes. 'Once young Colin has run his little fella under the cold tap, that is.'

'Little Bo Butch, my, don't you look pretty,' Terence said, smiling. 'Yes, we'll be leaving soon. Just give him a minute to get himself together,' he said, cocking a thumb towards the toilets. 'That's a lovely dress by the way, Butch. I tell you, if I was twenty years younger,' Terence said playfully, giving Butch a saucy wink.

Gerry Hayman stood by Terence's side. He had been joined in the garden by his wife, who had come down to watch her man proudly walk down to the fete with his new-found merry band of brothers. Hayman's wife was proudly fussing over her man: straightening his collar and adjusting his Baldricks, smiling at her husband on his big day, like a mother seeing her child off on his first day of school.

Five minutes later Colin Blunsden re-appeared in the sweltering beer garden, invigorated after necking what was left in his hip flask and draining two pints in quick succession behind Terence's back.

'You all right there, Colin?' Butch said. 'You're looking a bit sheepish, mate,' he said, sending a ripple of laughter through the crowd.

'Come on now, Butch,' Terence said. 'Don't be so *hard on* him.'

Blunsden turned and scowled at his leader, who looked to have surprised even himself with his spontaneous humour.

Butch stepped forward, picking up Colin's black top hat from the dusty ground. 'Sorry, Col,' he said, regaining his composure, 'Just having a bit of fun with ya there, mate. No harm intended,' Butch said, patting the dust and dried grass from Colin's hat. Something came loose from the floral decorations around the hat's crinkled brim and fluttered to the floor. Butch picked it up and smiled. He started laughing as he read aloud what was written on the card.

'In loving memory of our beloved mother,' he said. 'You were always the most beautiful flower in the garden. Forever in our thoughts, love from Mary, John and Kevin. Colin, have you been stealing flowers from the graveyard, mate?' Butch asked.

'Oh Colin, that's bad,' Terence said, shaking his head.

'Gimme that bleddy thing!' Colin squealed, snatching the hat back from Butch. Some more flowers fell to the ground as Colin placed the shabby hat back on his head at an odd angle, folded his arms and began to sway in the sunshine.

'All right, all right, enough of this silliness,' Terence said with authority. 'It's almost half eleven, lads, time we were all off.'

'I'd better be careful around here with the old bill in attendance today,eh' Butch said, looking at his sheep. 'Wouldn't wanna get done for drinking and droving.' There was a collective groan from the beer garden.

'OK then, ladies, gentlemen, dogs and sheep,' Terence said, his accordion now unboxed and sitting proudly strapped across his chest. 'Let us be on our merry way.'

Gerry walked beside him holding the accordion case and the sticks, smiling as they prepared to leave. Colin and Bob shuffled on behind.

Butch gave swift command to Finn, who had been watching the flock like a hawk.

As they were about to cross the road from the pub to the causeway, the sheep became jittery at the sound of a loud rumbling coming from up the causeway. Reverend Bowen roared into view, sitting astride her gleaming trike. Moses sat attentively behind her on the trike's rear bench seat. Drawing level with the pub, she began to slow, before stopping altogether. The trike's engine was now a low rumble as it idled outside the pub, and Reverend Bowen surveyed the scene of jovial drunkenness.

Decked out head to toe in black, except for the white rectangle of her dog collar, Bowen looked formidable in leather trousers, Crossroads motorcycle club waistcoat and chunky black biker boots. She sneered at her wayward flock, disappointed but at the same time pleased, knowing that at least one lost little lamb was today heading for the altar of sacrifice.

She revved the trike, the sheep again becoming jumpy. As the engine died down she bellowed at the bemused onlookers. 'And behold, mine eyes beheld a steel horse!' she said, again revving the trike, 'and the rider that sat on it was death ... and hell followed with her!'

37

In the sticky confines of Steventon village hall, and with midday fast approaching, Petra Carr in her gaudy floral dress and sweaty fringe clinging to her forehead darted from table to table, meticulously inspecting the myriad offerings of jams, cakes and crafts, ensuring everything was of the highest possible standard.

Stall holders checked their cash tins, raffle prizes were being laid out on a table in front of the stage and, despite the heat, tea urns the size of oil drums were brewing gallons of boiling refreshments.

Outside, the village green had become a patchwork of stalls, attractions, displays and food stands. The Barbeque being fired up next to the football club challenged the scent of the freshly cut grass for number one stereotypically delicious summer's day smell, with the rotary club making their own late challenge after cranking up their doughnut maker. The smell of sizzling oil, sticky batter and warm sugar sweetly permeated the air.

Outside the football club, a number of villagers had already begun to congregate in search of their first day's refreshment. The football club bar would not open until after the fete had been officially declared open by the officious Petra Carr at midday, which she would do from Tony Gables' DJ booth where the local disc jockey was now making his final checks.

Having skipped breakfast, Tony was now very hungry. From his position just to the right of the football club, he could smell the barbeque, tantalisingly close, the scent of sizzling burgers wafting towards him like a sensory distress signal. His stomach rumbled, but so far he'd had no time for food. After furiously assembling his equipment, he was now just about happy with his set-up. The heat, however, he was not so happy about. The Hawaiian shirt he had changed into already stuck greedily to his back as he flicked switches and turned nobs. Despite Edna running him close, he'd managed to get everything set up in time. He was a professional after all. He fanned himself with his panama hat, relieved to be up and running. He adjusted the levels of the fader on the mixer positioned between his two Technics turntables. The decks reflected in his mirrored aviator sunglasses looked like two large black pupils. All that remained was to complete the ritual, which he did by blowing the tiny spec of fluff from the two turntable needles. He smiled, reaching for his dummy record box, pouring himself a generous amount of vodka over the glass of icy lemonade that he had recently procured from Edna, leading her on with the fictitious narrative that, other than the little tipple they had shared earlier on, he was to remain sober all day.

The refreshing effect was indescribable as the vodka and lemonade fizzed in his mouth, the ice cubes in the glass still glinting in the sun. He felt the little hit from the vodka, thankful that there was plenty more. He squatted down and flipped the two latches on his dummy record box, opening the lid and placing the vodka bottle back alongside its two companions, a bottle of gin and a bottle of Bacardi. He stared contentedly at the three bottles standing proudly to attention, neatly stowed in their own individual sections, and smiled as he sipped his vodka and lemonade. He was happy with his work.

Butch Ransom had assembled his sheep pen to the rear of the village hall early this morning. The 20 X 12 foot rectangle of glimmering steel now awaited its woolly occupants' arrival. The pen was divided into two sections: one for pre-shorn sheep, the other for post-shorn. His pick-up truck and trailer stood next to it, ready for the ride home. He would not be droving the sheep back home again after his work here was done, that was for sure. Especially as he had offered up his Little Bo Peep dress as a mystery prize in the raffle. Luckily, he had a change of clothes on the pick-up's front seat.

Butch's adopted mother, Barbara Rix, had set up her spinning wheel next to Butch's shearing equipment, procuring wool at source from Butch as part of her sheep to shop demonstration.

It was past Butch's sheep pen that Sergeant Frisk walked with Laurie Knox and Gooch towards the village hall, after jointly setting up the police information stand and also assembling the pieces of apparatus for the police dog display on the football pitch. The poles and seesaws, hoops and netting were strategically spread out, the white markings of the pitch making for excellent navigational reference points for Knox and Gooch to follow.

Groundsman Fred Hillock, who was already aggrieved at the Morris dancers being granted use of the cricket pitch, had not shied from telling Frisk what he thought about the police using the football pitch for their display, especially considering the trio of soon to be flaming hoops they had lined up. Hillock eventually backed off, sensing he was not going to dissuade either the police or their fearsome-looking German Shepherd into altering their position on the matter.

The two policemen had locked their vehicles, parked up just behind the goal line, and stowed away the rest of their belongings in the football club changing room. Frisk waved to the headbanded figure of local judo instructor Jim Leyland, whose young students would also be performing at the fete a little later on. The rectangle of blue judo mats looked like the hazy mirage of a welcome swimming pool.

At the hall Knox diverted away from Frisk, making his way towards Reverend Bowen, who was standing just inside the open double doors of the village hall with Moses. After her spectacularly loud entrance, she had parked her trike up and was now conversing with Petra Carr, whom she broke away from to speak to Laurie Knox. Alone.

Noticing that Petra was now looking as if she desperately needed someone to talk at, Frisk continued on past the doors of the village hall and towards the car park's entrance, keen to get things underway. He was also anxious to get back to the station, to try to phone his wife. He needed to know where Jenny was. And who she was with.

Over the road, Frisk could hear the sound of jangling bells and an accordion floating melodiously beneath the green canopy of the causeway, and the sound of sheep bleating over the top of it all in stark contrast to the accordion's lilting melody. Looking down the causeway's tree-lined tunnel, Frisk watched them approaching.

Nearly time to get this show on the road then, he thought to himself.

39

'I'm tellin ya, Terence, I bleddy twisted the beggar!' Colin Blunsden called out in vain to his lead dancer up ahead. 'Or broke it or sprained it. Either way the bleddy thing's buggered, ennit, Bob, look, that's swelling already,' he said, hopping along on one leg and holding his foot in the air. Bob Dobson looked blankly at Colin's leg and said nothing.'

'You are a sprain, Colin,' Gerry Hayman shouted from over his shoulder. 'A sprain in the backside.'

'Piss it off, you,' Colin said. 'You just stay up there with teacher like a good little boy.'

Terence Russell, absorbed in both his accordion and the occasion, was oblivious to Colin's painful protestations.

Bringing up the rear was Little Bo Ransom and his flock. Under Finn's watchful eye, the sheep were now gaining on the limping Morris dancer, who fell further behind, swallowed up by the sheep who began butting him in his rear end. Attempting to pick up the pace, Colin squealed in pain and distress as he was harried and cajoled by Ransom's jittery flock.

Behind them all, Butch was getting plenty of attention from the amused villagers who lined the road beside the causeway, wolf-whistling their approval of the sheep farmer's provocative cross-dressing.

'These cobbles are a soddin' death trap, iss no wonder I went over on 'em,' Colin moaned, looking like he was now only discussing the matter with the jostling sheep that surrounded him. 'Should pave the bleddy lot. Gonna have a word with bleddy Petrol about this when I see her, you mark my words,' he moaned. 'And keep them bleddy sheep off my arse, Ransom, you Aussie twat!' he wailed.

‘It’s your own fault, Col,’ Butch called out. ‘I think after your little display up at the pub some of ’em might’ve taken a bit of a shine to you,’ he said. ‘I’m just glad you’re not walking behind me, ya randy old bugger.’

Before Colin could respond, Gerry, walking up ahead, called out again from over his shoulder. ‘Perhaps if you minded where you were going, Colin, and weren’t such a drunken nuisance, then you wouldn’t fall over so much, would you?’

‘Piss it off, Hayman, I’m bleddy warning you!’ Colin called out. ‘Bleddy teacher’s pet. You n’ all Ransom, ya big Aussie sod, I’ve had enough of it, I ain’t in the bleddy mood no more.’

‘Ahh, ya hear that, girls?’ Butch said, addressing his sheep, ‘Colin’s not in the mood, he’s got a headache. Well, don’t you listen to the silly man.’

Colin hobbled on, wondering about how many pints of pain relief it was going to take to dull the throbbing pain in his ankle.

Terence and Gerry reached the crossroads first where the causeway met the High Street, waiting for Colin and Bob straggling on behind to catch up. Terence continued playing his accordion, smiling in the sunshine as the crowd of onlookers grew in the village hall car park to greet their arrival.

Gerry stepped out into the road like a lollypop Morris man to halt the traffic, waving his hankies at the patient, if rather bemused drivers, some of whom beeped their horns and whistled as Butch also crossed the road with Finn and his sheep.

The Morris men made their way through the car park and round to the village green, with Colin hobbling on behind them. Terence was gladdened by the sight of his other four Morris men waiting for them in the car park.

‘Looking good, boys,’ Sergeant Frisk said to the assembled dancers. Terence, who continued playing his accordion, gave Frisk a cursory glance, nodding his head in time with the music, his beaming smile wilting slightly at the sight of the policeman.

Petra Carr emerged from the village hall with Reverend Bowen and Moses, strutting onto the green like a visiting dignitary, a pinched smile of self-satisfaction beaming from her pointy-featured face. At her mother’s stern insistence, Daisy had begrudgingly joined her mother for the opening ceremony, walking a little way behind her and looking rather embarrassed by the whole affair.

Reverend Bowen in her familiar black attire and leather Crossroads waistcoat walked with Moses and the Carrs towards the DJ booth and the grinning Tony Gables.

'Right oh, lads,' Terence shouted as the three women approached the DJ booth. 'Tunnel!'

Gerry handed out the sticks he had been carrying to the other six Morris dancers, who obediently lined up in two rows of four in front of Tony's gazebo. Terence, standing in line also but remaining stickless, continued playing the accordion. The dancers held up their sticks, pointing them towards the clear blue sky, lowering them to a peak and crossing them with their opposite man, forming a guard of honour for Petra, who was in her egotistical element. Daisy, Reverend Bowen and Moses also passed through on their way towards the waiting DJ, who held out a microphone.

'Bit warm for all that today, isn't it, Reverend?' Terence said over the sound of the accordion. He gave the passing vicar a smile and a wink as he joyfully carried on playing. The look he received from her sent a chill down his spine, and the red crosses that zigzagged her face became uncomfortably close, causing him to fumble a couple of notes on the accordion.

A large crowd of villagers, young and old, had gathered around the gazebo, much to the delight of Petra, who smiled, as much pleased with herself as with the sight before her. She took the microphone from Tony's outstretched hand and began to speak.

'Good day to you,' she began. 'And how lovely to see you all on such a fine day...'

A few mumbles and cries from the crowd distracted her, she became flustered, fumbling her words, soon noticing with extreme displeasure that the microphone was not in fact turned on. She turned, holding the microphone up to the embarrassed Tony Gables with a look of contempt. Tony darted to his mixing board, hastily twiddling a couple of knobs. After a large hoot of feedback that brought a collective wince from the crowd, the microphone was at last working and she continued.

'Thank you, Tony. As professional as ever, I see,' she said with extreme sarcasm. 'I can't imagine why they all let you go.'

Tony blushed as Petra regained her composure and persevered.

'And thank you to Terence and his band of merry men for that wonderful accompaniment,' she said with the pointed smile of a Mako shark. 'As I was trying to say, thank you all so much for coming today. We hope that today is going to be a very special day indeed, as it is of course every year. We certainly have the weather for it. I think maybe Reverend Bowen here must have had an extra special word with you know who,' Petra said smiling and looking up at the clear blue sky, then turning to the figure in black standing beside her. Bowen did not return her smile.

'We have all the usual fun and games for you to enjoy this year. There's the craft stands in the hall that I will be taking a particular interest in. Not to mention a host of other wonderful demonstrations from some very talented and creative members of our wonderful community.'

A ripple of a cheer ran through the crowd.

'And I know how much we are all especially looking forward to seeing Sergeant Frisk and his colleagues in action later. Crime certainly does not pay around these parts, I can tell you,' she said, putting an arm around her daughter's waist. Daisy squirmed uncomfortably. Beside them Reverend Bowen sneered and bit down on her lower lip.

Petra took a deep breath. 'As I am sure you are all aware, this village has been subjected to some rather disturbing occurrences of late at the hands of ...' she hesitated. 'Well, I don't think I need tell you who, do I,' she said dismissively. 'Some of us have suffered more than others at the hands of this ... this menace who has plagued our lovely village.' She looked again at her daughter and Reverend Bowen. 'Whether you have personally been a victim, or whether you merely know of someone who has, one thing is for certain: this village will not tolerate such wilful disobedience of the law. Nor will we shy away from bringing those responsible to justice!' The microphone squealed with feedback. 'These crimes will not go unpunished!' she said, now looking at Sergeant Frisk and sounding more and more like a hysterical substitute teacher. 'But,' she said, regaining a little of her composure, ' I hope that after today we can all leave here contented, knowing that order has been restored, and that justice has well and truly been served.'

'Hear hear,' came a week smattering of voices in the crowd.

'I would now like to hand you over to Reverend Bowen, who I think would also like to say a few words. Perhaps even bestow a blessing on our little gathering?' she said, smiling at Bowen in hopeful expectation.

Reverend Bowen stepped out of the shade of the gazebo's porch, where she had retreated to during Petra's speech. She held Moses' lead in one hand, and slowly took the microphone from Petra with the other. Petra's hand, if one were to look closely enough, was trembling slightly as she did so.

Decked out head to toe in black and wearing a pair of black wrap-around sunglasses, the midday sun beat down on the formidable figure of Hilda Bowen. Large beads of sweat popped on her forehead, dripping down over the red welts that streaked her face. A hush descended as she began to speak in deliberate, menacing tones.

'For behold! ... The day cometh that shall burn as an oven,' she said, casting her eyes up at the blazing blue sky, as if in prophecy. 'And all the proud, and all that do wickedly, shall be as stubble,' she said, now casting her menacing gaze over the crowd itself, as if in judgement. 'And the day that cometh shall burn them up, saith the Lord! That it shall leave them neither root nor branch!'

There followed a deathly silence as Bowen scanned the crowd.

'For it is written, "Vengeance is mine; saith the Lord. And I will repay."'

The crowd looked on in stunned silence as Reverend Bowen dropped the microphone to the floor. Another hoot of feedback from the PA system broke the silence as Bowen gathered Moses up in her arms and walked towards the football club.

'Amen!' came the solitary response from a grinning Butch Ransom, standing out like a sore thumb in his frilly pink dress and bonnet.

A few others attempted a half-hearted round of applause, but the general sense of bewilderment at Bowen's speech had put paid to that idea.

Petra scuttled over and stooped down to pick up the microphone. She smiled up at the rather perplexed looking crowd, fumbling again to regain her composure.

'Well ... err... thank you, Reverend,' she said, vainly scanning the area for the departed vicar. 'Umm ... I think, as you can gather, the Reverend is still rather upset by everything that has happened... as we all are of course.'

'Whadda load of old bollocks,' Colin said to his mute friend. 'Come on, let's go get a drink in eh, Bob? Me bleddy ankle's killing me.' They slipped away through the crowd, Colin cursing the bells that risked giving away their position to their ever watchful lead dancer.

Others had also begun to drift away from the gazebo, ready to seek entertainment in other areas of the village green.

'Well then,' Petra said to the thinning crowd, 'I suppose it leaves me with little more to say other than I hope you all have a wonderful day, and that I hereby officially declare this year's Steventon village fete ... open!'

PART 3

40

'Jingle bells, jingle bells, jingle all the way,' Edna sang as Colin and Bob jangled their way into the football club bar, looking like a pair of dishevelled fugitives. 'Here you are, lads, there's a Bell's each, that'll put an extra jingle in your step,' she said, placing two single measures of whiskey on the bar. Despite his ankle injury, Colin quickened his pace to reach it.

'On the house, boys,' she said, uncharacteristically cheery. 'Here's to a good show.'

'God bless you, Edna, God bless you, woman,' Colin said as he downed the whisky in one gulp. 'If you see Terence coming in, throw a blanket on us or give us a bleddy signal or something.'

'Pint,' Bob said.

'That's the most sensible thing you've said all day,' Colin said, turning to Bob in mock surprise. 'It's better than Petra's load of old bollocks we 'eard out there anyhow,' he said, slurring his words as the fresh injection of alcohol recharged that already in his system.

Edna obligingly picked out two pint glasses from under the bar, smiling at Bob's monosyllabic request. Her eyes dropped down to her left, to where her handbag sat on a shelf under the bar. She poured the lagers, much to the delight of her first two paying customers. Though they hadn't been the first to enter the bar.

'And as for Hilda!' Colin said, crowing with laughter, 'God alone knows what that was all about. Didn't sound too cheery, mind, did it,' he said, lapping at his pint. 'Wants to lighten up a bit. Think she must have a bit of that postal manic stressness order.'

The two Morris men leant against the bar, sipping their pints, when a shadow fell upon them. Both men stared into the large mirror behind the bar, looking at one another, and for once Colin's facial expression matched that of his friend.

In the mirror, a figure in black had appeared standing directly behind them. It seemed to have materialised out of nowhere, like a black storm cloud. They began turning their heads, first facing each other, then round a full hundred and eighty degrees. Colin emitted a squeak of fright as he registered the red zigzagged abrasions on the face of Reverend Bowen, who in her biker boots towered over the dishevelled drunkards. She was still wearing her black sunglasses.

'Come now, gentlemen,' she said softly, a slight sneer on her face. Moses was down by her side panting in the heat. 'You two should understand as well as anyone what was implied by my reading,' she said, looking down at the slouching drinkers.

The men crumbled in her presence, Colin for once as equally silent as his friend. She slipped between the two Morris men, who retreated to a corner table, and placed her hands on the bar.

'I would like some change for the phone,' she said in a tone of passive neutrality, placing a one pound coin on the bar with a click.

'Looking forward to the show then, Reverend?' Edna asked, making her way over to the till. 'Nice speech.'

Bowen remained silent.

'You seem to be pretty chummy with the police this year,' Edna continued. 'Bit of a romance blooming between you and that dog handler, is there? 'I suppose it's because you both share a common interest, don't you,' she said, scraping out the correct change from the till.

Behind her sunglasses, the vicar's eyes widened.

'A love of dogs,' Edna said. 'That and watching them purposefully attack defenceless members of the public,' she said in a menacing whisper. 'But then again, I suppose the police don't have much regard for the well-being of public safety around here, do they?'

'Enjoy is not exactly the word I would use, Edna,' Bowen said, finally taking off her sunglasses and hooking them onto her dog-collared neckline.

Glass winced at Bowen's injuries, for a fleeting moment feeling sympathy for the woman.

'But,' Bowen continued, 'I shall certainly derive a great deal of satisfaction from seeing that boy atone for his sins,' she said calmly. 'For as you sow, so shall you reap.'

Beside her, Moses barked, as if in agreement.

'Yeah, and you wanna remember that one, Reverend,' Edna said, looking into the vicar's cold expressionless eyes. She'd noticed how Hilda's pupils did not dilate when she removed her sunglasses. It made her blood run cold. Something wasn't right with this woman, but getting into a theological argument with her was not part of the plan.

'Tens and twenties all right?' Edna asked, steely.

'Fine,' Bowen responded, holding out her hand.

'Or would you prefer thirty pieces of silver?' Edna asked

Bowen said nothing. She turned and made her way to the public telephone in the corner like a retreating phantom, the warm change in her cold hand. She took out a small black book from her leather waistcoat pocket, rifling through its lined pages. She found the number she was looking for, lifted the receiver and began to dial.

41

From his position in the police information tent, Sergeant Frisk scanned the green. The fete was getting busier now. He picked out faces, recognising some, if not most of them. They all smiled as they meandered from one attraction to the next: from the lucky dip to the ice cream van; from the tombola to the doughnut van. He sighed, missing his daughter. She loved the doughnuts; and the bouncy castle, although the two rarely made a good combination.

Music pumped out of Tony's gazebo, and Frisk listened with mild amusement as the local celebrity DJ provided an almost constant running commentary. He sounded pretty happy, maybe a little too happy. He hoped Tony was behaving himself.

Frisk's thoughts drifted back to his wife and daughter. He was wanting to get back to the nick to try to contact Jenny at her sister's; then he would call Jenny's mum and dad to try and speak to his daughter. He should have done it already, he knew that now, but he'd been too busy. Wasn't he always? 'Will call u' the post-it note had said, and like an idiot he had settled for it, waiting for her call. The call that so far hadn't come. He tried to quash his growing paranoia, but lack of information bred speculation, and Frisk was a naturally suspicious person. It went with the territory.

'You OK, guv?'

The voice floated in one ear and out the other, not registering at any point in between.

'Sarge?' Laurie Knox said, as something shattered at the smash-a-plate stand nearby.

'Sorry, Laurie,' he said, looking at the dog handler, 'miles away. Just thinking about later, that's all,' he lied.

The two policemen stood in the shade of the police information tent, Gooch by Knox's side a constant source of interest to passers-by.

Knox had parked his specialist K9 police van up next to the information stand, which was now crowded with mums, dads and enthusiastic children, fascinated to look inside the van and see where and how Gooch travelled to police incidents. Some had their photo taken in the driver's seat, some in the back in the kennel itself, where the protective clothing was. The children took it in turns at putting on the padded bite sleeves, gleefully whacking each other with their black, over-sized spongy arms.

'Listen, Laurie,' Frisk said, 'I'm going to have to go back to the nick shortly to pick up Dennis and Douglas. Will you and Gooch be all right looking after things here while I'm gone?'

'Absolutely, guv,' Knox replied enthusiastically. 'Gooch and I are having a great time, aren't we, boy?' he said, rubbing the dog's sleek black and gold coat.

'Good. I just hope Dennis hasn't been winding Douglas up too much,' Frisk said, concerned. 'You know what he's like sometimes.'

'Yeah, Dennis can get a little bit carried away, can't he, guv,' Knox said.

'You can bring all that gear over when we come back later,' Frisk said, pointing to the bite sleeves currently on the arms of a couple of nearby kids.

'Absolutely, sarge,' Knox replied.

'OK. I've got a key for the changing rooms. I'm going to drive him back down here and get him in there straight away. I'd rather not draw too much attention to it. The hoops are all soaked and I've locked the petrol cans in the changing room with our other bits. I'll be back at about one o'clock with them; then we can all run through the final details of the display together, OK?'

'Sounds good,' Knox said, reaching into the back of the van for a 2-litre bottle of water and refilling Gooch's bowl. The dog lapped it up as more villagers surrounded the information tent requesting photos and asking questions. Frisk excused himself and walked the short distance back to his transit van in the sports club car park.

'Hear that, boy?' Knox said quietly into Gooch's ear,' Alan's popping back to fetch your dinner.'

‘So to start with, we gotta get the first of our lucky little bleeters outta the pen,’ Butch said, dragging the first sheep out. He pulled down on the nearby chain to activate the hand piece, as if he was flushing a toilet, the shears buzzing into life before Butch began the process of shearing the first sheep.

‘So we start on the belly,’ he said, beginning to buzz away at the compliant sheep, removing thick woolly strips from the animal’s underbelly. Butch held it firmly in his grasp, the sheep passive in his grip. ‘Then we head around the crutch and the back end,’ he said to titters of laughter from the audience. The children were gathered around him, seated in a semi-circle, their parents and other casual onlookers standing behind them. ‘Course we gotta be extra careful around there, don’t we,’ he said, looking up from the sheep and smiling at a female member of the audience. ‘Then it’s down the first hind leg,’ he said, the shears gliding smoothly down the animal, ‘up around the tail, up the underline and onto the back of the head and onto the neck,’ Butch said, his work appearing effortless as he removed the wool from around the sheep’s face, ‘an area particularly sensitive to potential damage,’ he said cautiously. ‘Round the back of the head, then we drop down onto the front leg before we run the full length of the sheep.’

A fluffy pile of wool now littered the area in front of Butch. Large drops of sweat dripped from his nose as he buzzed through the last strokes. ‘Then it’s over the back bone, back up to the other side of the face, before we head down to the last front shoulder, down the flank and out the last hind leg,’ he said with satisfaction as the last of the wool was removed.

He pulled the hand piece once again and the shears ceased buzzing. The whole process had taken butch less than a minute. He cajoled the sheep through the gate and into the empty side of the pen, shutting the gate behind the newly shorn sheep. The ratio now 8 to 1 in favour of unshorn sheep.

The crowd enthusiastically applauded the efforts of the sweating shearer, who wiped his dripping face with the hemline of his white vest, exposing a wall of rigid abdominal muscles. A short collective gasp came from some of the ladies in the audience. Butch heard it, and decided he would take it off by the third sheep.

'So!' he said, clapping his hands together. 'Looks like I need some help clearing all this mess up, don't I?' Butch said looking bemused at the small woolly mountain in front of him. 'What I need is all this taken over to young Barbara there and put in a nice neat pile.'

The kids didn't need asking twice as they leapt to their feet and set about collecting up all the shorn wool from where Butch had been shearing. The first children to it grabbed handfuls of wool and deposited it in front of Barbara's craft stand. Those not so quick off the mark only managed a couple of wispy tufts, much to their disappointment. They needn't be upset. There would be plenty more where that came from as Butch buzzed his way through his flock over the course of the afternoon.

*

Trudy and Jeremy Ryan contentedly watched their two girls watching Butch. Trudy quite enjoyed watching Butch also, though she kept that piece of information to herself. The atmosphere between the two parents was in stark contrast to the day's sweltering temperature, remaining frosty at best.

'Come on, Trude, how long are you going to keep this up for?' Jeremy enquired, trying not to sound desperate. Comprehensively busted for his late-night drinking antics, Jeremy had been well and truly in the doghouse since he surfaced from his little lie-in this morning.

'Look, Jeremy,' Trudy said sharply, looking straight ahead of her, tilting her head slightly towards her husband's. 'It's not me I care about. You can mess me around all you like, you usually do. But when you make promises to your children,' she said with rising anger, 'you keep those bloody promises,' she said, hoping her expletive had not been audible to the other parents or surrounding children.

Jeremy continued to grovel. 'Trudy, I'm sorry, really I am. What can I say? You know how much you and the girls mean to me,' he said, trying but failing to establish eye contact with his wife.

'I stopped off for one last drink at The Fruitbowl after a long, tiring day at work, and I guess I just got chatting. I mean, you did say that it would be good to get to know some of the locals, after all,' he said hopefully.

'Yes,' Trudy said, her voice measured, 'but not when your children are sat up at home waiting for you to come and read them a story for just one night this week. I guess you find the company up at the pub more interesting though, don't you.'

Jeremy Ryan paused. 'Well, it was quite interesting actually.'

Trudy turned to face him at last, but it was not a look that inspired confidence. Still, Jeremy persevered.

'I got talking to a guy called Graham. Graham Glass, his name was. Big fat fella. Anyway, he's quite the talker after a drink, and he's pretty good on the dartboard as well.'

'I'm very pleased for him,' Trudy said.

'Anyway, here's the funny bit. This Graham bloke, he was telling me he went on *Bullseye* a few years ago now, can't remember when he said exactly, late eighties or something. He was the one answering the questions out of the pair. You know, one throws, the other answers questions. He was an OK darts player, but not as good as this other fella he went on there with. Well, it turns out the fella he was on there with was wossername's dad,' Jeremy said, with failing memory. 'Bertie someone, I think he said it was.'

Trudy tried to recall where she'd heard the name Bertie before. She couldn't place it.

'Ohh, what was the surname, it's on the bloody tip of my tongue. You know, Trude,' Jeremy said, 'the lad who went bat shit on the railway, the one they're stitching up later, smashed all the windows.'

Blouse. Trudy thought. Bertie Blouse, Douglas Blouse's father. Jeremy now had her full attention, though she still feigned casual disinterest, trying to maintain her act of hostility.

'Some drunk spinning you a yarn in a pub? So what's new?' she said. 'And what else did this drunken mystic gameshow contestant have to say for himself?'

'Well, Graham – fat fella up the pub, he's Edna's husband, Edna Glass, she's that big made-up old tart behind the bar in the football club.'

'Jeremy,' Trudy tutted, displeased with her husband's terminology.

'Well anyway, she does a few other odd jobs about the place, and she's also a dinner lady up at the school. Anyway Graham and Edna had a young son who died a couple of years ago around here. Car crash. Anyway, Graham went on there with this Bertie, Bertie ... BLOUSE!' Ryan said, with enthusiastic recall. 'Bertie Blouse, that's it. Well this Bertie Blouse fella did a bit better than he expected and ended up running off with one of the other contestants. Oh, where was she from? God, my memory's crap today.'

'I wonder why,' Trudy said sarcastically, but with marginally less hostility. Jeremy smiled.

'Bruh, bruh ... Bruh something ... Bristol? Brighton? Bromsgrove? ... He fumbled for the name. 'Bridgend!' he shouted, like he'd just won a house on bingo. 'That's it, bloody Bridgend, I remember now because the Swansea train I get from Paddington stops there. That's it, she was a Welsh bird ... err, lady' he said, correcting himself. 'Well, Graham and Bertie did pretty well on the show. Got a load of cash, but this couple of Welsh ladies were pretty tidy n'all and they pipped them to it by about twenty quid and went through to bully's prize board. You remember, Trude? All that "IIIIN ONE" business,' Jeremy shouted, doing his best Tony Green impression. 'Well, these ladies, they bag all but one of the prizes. Bike, watches, nest of tables, you know all that kinda crap they have on there. So when it comes to the gamble, they give it the old, "Well, Jim, we've had a lovely day and we done really well,"' Jeremy said, putting on his best Welsh accent, '"But we're going to let someone else have ago."'

Trudy managed a smile at his attempted accent.

'So ... out come Graham and Bertie, them being the ones with the second highest amount of cash. Bertie comes out, puts the money straight down on Jim's little table, no mucking about. "We're gonna have a gamble, Jim," he says before Jim Bowen can even get a word in.'

Trudy was now engrossed, living the story with him.

'So up steps Graham, and he gets bloody bed and breakfast doesn't he, twenty-six. He claims he had sweaty fingers because of the lights in the studio. Well that left Bertie needing 75 or more for the star prize. So Bertie steps up to the oche, and with zero fuss he hits treble twenty, single twenty. Bang. Doesn't even need his last dart. Jim Bowen goes mental, leading the lads over to where Bully's star prize is hiding, and up comes the screen thing, and there's this caravan being wheeled out.'

Trudy made the connection instantly. 'The caravan on their driveway,' she said.

'Got it iiiiiiin one,' Jeremy said in Tony Greenesque confirmation. 'Graham took the money, I mean he already lives in a souped up caravan as it is, plus he wanted to invest it in his video pirating sideline he's got going on. By the way, don't tell anyone about that, it's meant to be all very hush hush,' he said. 'So Bertie took the caravan. Unfortunately, by the time the nice people at Granada dropped the thing off, he'd had it away to Bridgend with this Welsh woman, leaving the kid and his mum to enjoy the delights of the caravan without him. Of course Graham told me the other Welsh lady was hot for him the same way her mate was for Bertie, but Graham said he was far too committed to his family to do the dirty on them,' Jeremy said, raising his eyebrows. 'Says she still calls him, asking him when he's coming to the valleys. Course the boys at the pub all cried bullshit at that one, and I'm inclined to believe them.'

And Douglas has been stewing in that caravan ever since, Trudy thought.

'So now Blouse junior is in the shit, it would seem,' Jeremy said, standing up straight and rocking back on his heels.

Trudy beside him was silent, her mind processing everything she had just heard. She looked over at her own children, now busily scurrying to collect more wool, increasing the size of the fluffy white mountain beside Barbara Rix's stand.

She turned as a shadow seemed to pass over her. It wasn't from the clouds that were now beginning to appear off in the distance. It was Reverend Bowen passing by with her dog. Trudy felt a chill, despite the sticky heat, but couldn't help emitting a small laugh as the vicar continued on her way, wondering if Hilda Bowen was any relation to Jim.

43

Terence Russell's smile was reflected in the faces of all the children happily dancing to the proud accordionist's tune. They numbered half a dozen and they were doing him proud. The sextet of youngsters in their striped trousers and matching sashes, two in red, two in yellow and two in green, flawlessly ran through the routine that Terence had choreographed for them, and had been rehearsing with them every Wednesday afternoon for the past six weeks down at the school hall. He'd even smuggled them in crisps and fizzy drinks as a morale-boosting treat for the break in afternoon rehearsals, which they had been excused from normal lessons to take part in. Another bonus for any child. Terence knew that a happy team was a loyal team, and now, here, at just gone half past twelve on this beautiful summer's day, they looked a happy little team indeed.

It had been a real pleasure to teach the youngsters the stick-dancing routine, and Terence's smile was fixed to his face as they pulled it off with aplomb in front of their proud parents watching on among the sizable crowd of onlookers. The wooden clack of half a dozen sticks being hit in unison by the grinning children, set against the soft lilt of Terence's accordion, was the perfect soundtrack to this summer's afternoon, and though a few clouds had begun to build up in the distance, it could not diminish the spirit with which the youngsters went about their work.

In the distance, outside the football club, he could see a couple of his boys, their white outfits bright in the sunshine. What were they drinking? He couldn't see. He couldn't see Bob or Colin amongst them either, not knowing whether that was a good or a bad thing. It worried him what they might be up to. With them on the loose at a place like this, he knew he would have to find them pretty sharpish after he had finished here. He put it out of his mind for now, needing to concentrate on the job at hand.

The children were following his music, and though the routine had been simplified to cater for their inexperience, he had to remain focused. He'd find the boys later anyway. You didn't need to be Sherlock Holmes to track down the likes of Bob Dobson and Colin Blunsden.

Gerry Hayman, loyal as ever, watched from the crowd in support of his gaffer. He stood with his wife, clapping along with the rest of the audience as the children made their turns and hops and banged their sticks. What a treat they had been to teach. He only wished he could say the same of his own dancers. He wished he could somehow instil in them the same kind of innocent enthusiasm and joy of entertainment that these kids displayed. It was hard to believe that Bob and Colin were ever this young.

Terence wished he could be their age again. He would have a whole lifetime with Iris ahead of him: all those joyous years, her face being the last thing he would see at night and the first thing he would see in the morning. She made him feel young and alive. He hoped she could see him now, wherever she was; hoped she would be looking down on him when he was dancing. She'd always loved watching him dance. He'd never danced here without her.

Terence fumbled a few notes on his accordion, a ripple of embarrassment running through him at his basic error. It seemed to have gone unnoticed by the crowd, and the children carried on as if nothing had happened. His nerves were beginning to show, he knew it. He had to remain professional. Concentrate. Focus.

All around him the clapping continued as the children danced, and for now, Terence tried to put all other thoughts out of his mind. He smiled as the children danced, and thought that other than the face of his beloved wife, there was no sight lovelier in all the world than watching smiling children dance.

44

'Tony Gables willing and able, and I'm not telling fables when I say I'm sending sounds through the cables and out through the tables.'

Despite his early drinking, Tony still managed to deliver the well-rehearsed rapid-fire dialogue he'd been so fond of during his professional days. He put another glistening black 12" record onto the turntable. It was the *Wham Rap*. He sank back into his deckchair as the music played, looking out at the passing crowds, contented with his work. He had been in full flow since the opening ceremony nearly an hour ago and was feeling enlivened by a few drinks, enthused by the reactions of the crowd, and pumped by the sound of the music. Yep, he felt pretty good as he reclined in his deckchair, fanning himself with his panama hat as George Michael sang about someone's fiancé.

And then he saw her.

Karen. Kaz. His former partner whom he was currently undergoing a trial separation from. She was coming his way. And she was not alone. Jesus, was she not alone.

Tony hastily stood up, flustered by her sudden appearance. He banged his knee against the table, causing the record to scratch and skip, the noise magnified over the PA system. Embarrassed, he instinctively fumbled at the needle before placing it back as close to the beginning of the track as he could, much to the amusement of the passing villagers and drinkers over at the sports club who cheered and raised their glasses at him.

Tony picked up the microphone. 'Sorry about that folks,' he said in his slick radio announcer's voice, turning the music down a little. 'Someone's left their skipping rope in my DJ booth and I want it out!' he said with a chuckle. 'Now how about I put that down for a minute and let George carry on doing his thing! What d'you say we keep the music going and the good vibes flowing.'

He turned the music back up and placed the microphone between the turntables, leaning over the decks to check his equipment. As he did so, the sun was eclipsed. He looked up, expecting to see cloud cover, but was faced with the sight of Karen arm in arm with one of the biggest men he had ever seen. He almost blocked out the whole front of the gazebo. The man was as big as a garage door. Karen, smiling softly, held onto the giant man's anaconda arm.

'Hi, Tony,' she said pleasantly, 'how are you doing?'

She was in a short powder blue summer dress and white flipflops, and looked years younger than the 47 he knew her to be.

Well, I WAS doing just fine.

'Me? Oh yeah, I'm fine, Kaz, just fine, thanks. Having a ball!'

'I'm glad to hear that,' she replied. 'It looks like everyone's having a great time too,' she said, looking around the green. 'Tony, I'd like you to meet Darren,' she said, officially introducing the mountain beside her, who not looking a day over thirty despite his size, obviously had a thing for older women.

'Pleased to meet you, Tony,' the mountain said in a northern accent, shaking Tony's hand and nearly crushing it. 'Karen's told me a lot about you,' he said, smiling and still crushing.

I bet she has, and all bad I'll wager, he thought, wincing from the pain in his hand as Darren finally relinquished his grip. Why did muscle freaks always have to emphasise how tough they are, Tony thought as he flexed and stretched his hand under the table.

'All good, I hope, Darren,' he said, smiling tentatively.

The mountain smiled also, but did not reply. 'Babe, I'm just going to get a mineral water, you want anything?'

'I'll have the same, thanks,' she replied.

Mineral water? Get a proper drink down you, you big ponce! Tony thought as the mountain swathed a path the size of a dual carriageway through the crowd.

'Anyway, Tony, I just wanted to say hello. I didn't want you to see me here with Darren and for it to be awkward, or for you to think that we were avoiding you. That's the last thing I would want,' she said, smiling sweetly.

We? Tony thought. *You do the thinking for both of you, do you? Can't hardly say I'm surprised with a meat head like that in tow.*

'Hey, I feel exactly the same,' he lied. 'It's fine, honestly, and I wish you both all the very best for the future, I really do.'

'That's nice of you to say so, Tony,' she said. 'You know I care about you a great deal. I know things didn't work out between us,' she said, leaving no doubt in Tony's mind that the 'trial' separation they were supposedly still undergoing was now simply a separation, 'but I just want you to know that you are a very special person. We had some great times, and that's what I'll remember.'

Tony said nothing in response, he couldn't. He just smiled, smiled as his heart split in two.

'Anyway, I'd better go and see where Darren has got to with those drinks. Maybe we could have one with you later,' she said. 'I mean, if you're not too busy?'

I'm never too busy for you, Kaz, my darling.

'Yeah, gonna be a bit in demand with things here for a while yet,' he said, trying to sound casual, 'but maybe stop by when things are winding down later on, if you're still around. Have to be a lemonade though,' he said holding up his glass. 'I'm on the soft drinks. New regime. Gotta keep it professional on a day like today,' he said, trying to impress her with his disingenuous sobriety.

'I'm glad to hear that, Tony. Maybe see you a bit later then,' she said, walking off into the sun in search of her mountain. Tony's smiling face crumbled into a mask of despair as she turned her back.

'Later?' he said mournfully to himself, reaching for the bottle of vodka. 'Why wait?'

45

'Why is he called Gooch?' Sophie Ryan asked, her head tilted to one side looking at the sleek German Shepherd. Her face was scrunched up in an inquisitive squint as she shielded her eyes from the glare of the sun.

The two daughters of Trudy and Jeremy Ryan, along with their parents, had made their way over to the police information tent where Laurie and Gooch were still positioned. From the DJ tent Tony Gables continued to pump out the music. The *Wham Rap* had finished, and Trudy recognised the song that was now playing. Funnily enough it was The Police.

'Well,' Laurie Knox said, 'Gooch and I really like cricket. Do you like cricket?' he asked the young girl.

'No,' Sophie replied, 'it's boring. Daddy watches it when he drinks beer, don't you, daddy?' she said turning to her father.

Jeremy Ryan had little defence against the simple accusation. He smiled at his daughter and ruffled her hair playfully. 'Sometimes,' he said, smiling.

'Well, I really like cricket,' Knox said in his very best talking-to-children voice. 'And Gooch here is named after a favourite cricketer of mine. A man called Graham Gooch. I had another dog, whose name was Beefy. That was the nickname of another cricketer, but unfortunately Beefy has since passed away.'

Passed away? That was a good one, he thought. *More like knifed by a piece of human excrement.*

'Gooch here is his replacement,' he said.

'How old is he?' Sophie asked.

'Gooch is just coming up to 18 months. Still quite young for a police dog, but he's been a fast learner.'

'Does he go to school with other dogs?' Amy Ryan asked, standing just behind her older sister, a little more cautiously.

Laurie laughed at the amusing naivety of the question. 'Actually no,' he said, 'Gooch has what you would call home schooling, and I'm his teacher! Aren't I, boy?' he said, rubbing Gooch's sleek backline. 'We do a lot of work together at the police training facility as well, which I suppose you could say is a bit like a school for dogs. We have a lot more equipment and things for him to play with there.'

'Does he bite?' Sophie asked briskly.

Knox recalled their private training sessions: Gooch tearing into mannequins; chomping down on his old cricket bat; his snarling white teeth splintering the wood as his jaw salivated. He recalled with pride the transformation the dog underwent when given the magic word. All done in secret, far from the prying eyes of his superiors and fellow officers.

'Well yes, sometimes he does bite,' Knox said. 'There are a lot of bad people around and it's Gooch's job to catch them. He's very quick, and if the bad person doesn't stop, then Gooch will sometimes have to bite them to make them stop. He's trained to go for their arm, which is why we use the padded sleeve in training and in displays like the one we're doing later, so's not to hurt them too much. Usually he just latches onto their sleeve, and the worst he does is rip their jumper,' Knox said with a cheerful smile. 'The bad person soon gives up, then I call Gooch back. We always give the bad person a chance to give themselves up before Gooch is called into action, and they usually do.'

Knox leaned a little closer to the girls, who were listening intently. 'They are often quite scared too. Gooch can be quite scary when he's working,' Knox said, looking at Gooch and rubbing the dog's head.

Trudy Ryan, listening in, stood behind her girls, looking into the eyes of the German Shepherd which appeared to be ever so slightly crossed. She didn't like the way the dog handler had looked at his animal at that last comment. It was fleeting, almost imperceptible, but there was definitely something there, something a little sinister. She was sure she wasn't imagining it.

'I don't think he looks scary,' Sophie said. 'He looks like a sweet dog. Mummy,' she said, turning to Trudy, 'when can we get a dog like Gooch?'

Trudy had told the girls they would consider getting a dog once they had settled into their new home. It would be nice for them to have something to fuss over, and she would enjoy having some company around the home in her husband's absence and when the children were at school. Plus the surrounding countryside was perfect for walks with the girls, and there was so much in the area to explore. Maybe even Jeremy would join them, if he wasn't too busy. Yes, they would consider getting a dog. But she was damned if it was going to be anything like this boss-eyed creature. It gave her the creeps. She had always been a sensitive person, in the sense that she could pick up on the emotions and energies of others. She was what was often termed an empath, and she could pick up on these same kinds of energies and emotions in animals.

It finally registered in her mind what Sting was singing about over at the DJ tent. People often laughed at Trudy for paying too much attention to what to them were nothing more than odd coincidences. But Trudy firmly believed in recognising the messages and following the signs the universe gave you. The Police song that was playing was 'Don't stand so close to me'.

'Sophie, come back from there,' Trudy said, suddenly uncomfortable with her daughter's proximity to the dog, which was beginning to emit a low growl. She reached out to put a hand on her daughter's shoulder.

'He's a cute little boy, aren't you?' Sophie said, going to stroke the animal.

Amy behind her gently pulled on her sister's T-shirt, trying to stop her getting any closer. Gooch growled again as Sophie's hand moved to the top of the dog's head. Gooch barked and his jaws snapped, thankfully biting down on nothing but air. Sophie withdrew her hand in immediate, panicked surprise.

'Gooch! Come!' Knox snapped, yanking on the dog's lead.

He attempted to laugh it off, patting his dog on the head. 'You're all right, aren't you, boy?' he said. 'That's just Gooch's way of saying hello, isn't it?' Knox said, mollifying his dog. 'Plus he's probably getting a bit hungry standing so near to that barbeque. I know I am,' he said, smiling, trying to allay any concerns.

'Mummy, is Gooch going to kill someone?' Amy Ryan asked.

The directness of her daughter's question startled her.

'No, darling,' she said stroking Amy's long, blonde hair, 'of course not.'

'Gooch is gonna have a great time showing off to you all later,' Knox said, cutting in over Trudy's parental concern. 'He's really looking forward to it, aren't you, boy? He's got all that fun stuff over there to play on,' he said, gesturing towards the apparatus assembled on the football pitch. 'Then Gooch is going to show you how fast he can run. Gooch is really fast!' Knox said, stroking Gooch proudly, looking at the girls. 'He's going to chase a naughty man who has done some very bad things,' Knox said, looking at Trudy. 'Gooch here is just going to give him a little nip, like I told you about, just so the naughty man knows not to do it again,' he said. 'Don't worry. I've trained him well.'

*

Over at the DJ tent, the music had temporarily ceased and Tony Gables was now talking in what sounded like a poor attempt at a Chinese accent, announcing a judo display that was soon to be taking place. His semi-racist ramblings were soon being drowned out by a distant rumbling. People looked to the skies, at first believing it to be thunder.

The rumbling sound was dwarfed by the tearing cacophony of Reverend Bowen starting her trike in the village hall car park. Butch's sheep in the nearby pen became skittish at the noise, some of them nearly jumping out of their newly-shorn skins. Reverend Bowen sat astride her trike, slowly revving the machine. Moses in the rear passenger seat was accustomed to the noise.

The rumbling thunder drew nearer and got a lot louder, overpowering the sound of Hilda's one engine as the six bikes and three trikes of the Crossroads Motorcycle Club came riding in to view.

Bowen gave one final ear-splitting rev of her mighty engine, the noise so loud that one small child standing a little closer than perhaps he should have burst into tears. She pulled up to the entrance of the car park as the other motorcyclists coming from her right slowed down, drawing level and allowing her to exit the car park. She did so, taking an immediate left down Milton Lane, running parallel with the causeway and the fete, leading the convoy of roaring steel towards the sports club car park.

46

'I'm telling you, Douglas, Laurie's forgotten his kit. You're just going to have to do the display in your pants,' PC Binsley said, 'like you probably did in PE lessons.' Binsley had been unrelenting in his antagonising of Douglas.

'And Gooch is trained to go for clothing first, so he'll tear those little skidded pants off you in no time. And your gay little Mr Tickle socks. You'll be starkers in front of the whole village, with that famous little arse of yours on public display, proud as punch with a nice set of teeth marks to add to your three little dots and the stripe I put across you.'

'If I didn't have these handcuffs on, I would've sparked you clean out by now,' Douglas said casually to the sneering policeman.

Binsley had been winding up Douglas on and off for most of the morning. He had been the sole occupant at the police station, since Frisk and Knox left this morning to attend to their duties, and Douglas was beginning to lose his patience with the smug, piss-taking copper.

They were standing round the back of the police station, by the back doors of the Ford Transit police van that Sergeant Frisk had driven back a short while ago, waiting for him to come back out. Despite Douglas knowing that what Binsley had been saying almost incessantly for most of the morning was total bullshit, he was still anxious as the reality of the situation really began to dawn on him. That dog looked like it meant business.

He tried to put the thought from his mind, turning his attention back to the lesser of two evils, that being the continual bullshit of PC Binsley, who was now saying something about prison.

'Gonna have to watch your step around here after this as well, aren't you, Dougie boy?' he said, perching his left foot on the Transit van's back bumper and spitting on the ground just a couple of inches from Douglas's foot. 'You go near Hilda and she's gonna rain down hell on you now that she's got that restraining order against you. All charges reinstated, like that!' Binsley said, snapping his fingers in Douglas's face. 'You'd be banged up quicker than you could say holy shit,' he said. 'Still, I think you'd like prison. There're lots of nice people there who just love to see new, young exhibitionists like yourself, flashing their pretty little arses about, the way you do. I'm sure you'd have no problems making new friends. More than you ever did around here, that's for sure. Maybe the Bumstead twins would come in and visit you?' Binsley said, wagging his index finger and smiling. 'I can just see you now, lying on your bunk, a picture of Mandy and Donna in their peekaboo butcher's aprons blu-tacked to the cell wall. Those big nipples of theirs hanging out all over the place. Bigger nips than any burgers their dad sells, eh, Douglas?' He lowered his voice and leant in to Blouse's ear. 'I know you think no one knows about your little love-in with those two heifers back at bully's star prize, Douglas, but, well, what can I say? It's a small village, isn't it? Still, if you can't land the likes of Daisy Carr, I suppose someone like you has to take what he can get, eh, Douglas?' he said, grinning a big shit-eating grin.

Douglas said nothing at first, trying to keep his cool, just staring at the concrete beneath his feet and the handcuffs in front of him.

'How do you know they've got big nipples?' he finally said cheekily to the sneering copper.

'Shut it,' Binsley said, shutting him down immediately. Douglas was just beginning to find his voice though.

'Where's your bum chum boss then, Dennis?' he asked. 'Taking his time, isn't he? At this rate you might have to drive us down there,' he said, smiling. 'Don't fancy our chances of getting there in one piece much with you behind the wheel though. No dodgy overtakes, eh, Dennis? You never know what's coming the other way, do you?'

'I said shut it!' Binsley reiterated.

'Your first chase and you do something like that. Got a bit excited with your new green card, did you?' Douglas said, referring to the special card any police officer has to hold to allow them to engage in high-speed pursuits.

'Only kids as well, weren't they? Younger than I am now. What kind of a copper are you when you can't even catch a couple of twats in a stolen Vauxhall Nova?'

Binsley's blood boiled but was overtaken by his mind as it span back to the night of the pursuit. That dark, wet night, gripping the wheel white-knuckled as the police car tried to keep pace with the stolen Nova. The dangerous overtakes he was forced to perform on the rain-lashed roads as the police car gave chase. The massive droplets lashing on the windscreen obscuring his visibility, the wipers clacking away at full pelt. Then the headlights coming out of nowhere from the opposite direction. Peter Glass's Ford Fiesta coming towards them, unable to stop in time, smashing into the stolen Nova as it went for what was to be its final overtake. Binsley watching in horror as the two cars crumpled into one giant mess of tangled steel. He himself only just managing to skid to a halt in time, side on and just inches from the wreckage.

'You killed Peter, Dennis,' Douglas said matter of factly to the vacant-eyed Binsley. 'Edna told mum and me all about it. And all for the sake of a shitty old Nova.'

'Yeah? And where the fuck is mum these days, eh, Douglas!?' Binsley said, reaching down to his waistband and removing his truncheon with a swift, coordinated grace, before slamming it hard across Douglas's stomach.

'Dennis!'

Sargeant Frisk had emerged from the police station just in time to witness his constable slam the truncheon into Douglas's gut. Douglas bent over double, gasping for air.

'What the bloody hell do you think you're doing, Dennis?'

'He's been chopsing off at me again, sarge! Saying stuff about the crash. I had to shut him up,' Binsley said.

'He's right, sarge, it was my fault, I was out of order,' Douglas said, straightening up, trying to get his breath back. 'I should NOVA little love's a bit sensitive about the accident by now,' he said, bursting into a spluttering laugh.

Binsley retracted his arm once more in readiness for another blow. Douglas's laughter had turned into a coughing fit as the residual damage of Binsley's aggression took its toll. Frisk caught his arm just in time.

'Stop it, Dennis!' Frisk shouted. 'That's an order.'

'All right, all right!' Binsley said, retreating, slowly putting his truncheon back in its leather holder before turning his attention back on Douglas in another verbal tirade.

'Mum's probably gone down to Wales looking for Bertie, eh, Douglas? Gone to find daddy? "Bertie, I can't take it any more, our son is just too much of a retard, can I stay with you and that Welsh tart you're nobbing now?"'

'That will do, I said, Dennis!' Frisk said sternly. 'I won't tell you again. Give it a bloody rest, the pair of you!'

'"I'll do all the cleaning and washing and scrubbing and all those other little povvy jobs I did around the village for fuck-all money before you had the good sense to abandon me and our retarded son,"' Binsley said in the best female voice he could manage.

'Dennis, I said that will do!' Frisk barked, standing eye to eye in front of his constable.

'Sorry, guv,' Binsley said, looking a little shaken and taken aback by Frisk's directness.

'Sorry, guv,' Douglas repeated in a syrupy, sycophantic voice towards the flustered constable, making kissing noises.

In the distance they could hear the rumbling of engines, followed by the jarring sound of one single engine firing into life. They all turned their heads towards the noise.

'It sounds like the good Reverend might have invited a few of her friends down to witness your big day, Douglas,' Frisk said.

Douglas looked indifferent. 'More God squad. Scareeeeey,' he said sarcastically.

'OK, you two, get in the van,' Frisk said, opening the back doors. 'And no mucking around, OK? We've only got to go two hundred yards. Do you think you can leave each other alone for that short length of time?'

'Dennis is the one with the short length around here, from what I've heard,' Blouse said, sneering at Binsley.

Frisk stood by the open rear doors. 'IN!' he said.

The pair clambered aboard. Frisk slammed the double doors with satisfactory force, relieved that the pair were, for the time being at least, out of sight. Frisk climbed into the driver's seat, started the engine and put his seat belt on.

Between the driver's seat and the passenger seat, level with the headrests, was a small metal shutter that allowed communication between those in the front with those in the back. Thankfully it could only be opened from the driver's cab. Though the two rear passengers were at last appearing to do as he'd asked, Frisk kept it shut. It would not be long before they were at it again, and more of their sniping bullshit was the last thing he needed to hear right now.

Where the bloody hell was she? he thought, his mind helplessly returning to the whereabouts of his wife and child.

Still no answer at her sister's, or at her mum and dad's. It was now really beginning to bother him. The contagious paranoia that he'd picked up from Laurie Knox had receded slightly while he'd been busying himself over the past hour. Now, unable to reach his wife, it washed over him like an incoming tide, and he was drowning in doubt, fear and suspicion. He could add another emotion to the list as well: anger.

Frisk turned right down Milton Lane, heading back from whence he'd come towards the sports club car park.

'What the fffff ...' he said, leaning forward into the windscreen. He slid the communication shutter open, immediately hearing the bickering that must have ceased for all of about ten seconds.

'Looks like we've got company, Dennis,' Frisk shouted over his shoulder as the Transit van slowed to a halt in front of the motorcycle road block. They were lined up in a four three two one formation, their bikes and trikes blocking the police van's access to the car park. Reverend Bowen was at the front of the blockade. On top of everything, Frisk did not need an argument with these holy rollers, so instead he wound down his window, opting for diplomacy.

'If I say my prayers and promise to be a good boy for the rest of my life, will you all please move your vehicles out of the way?'

The gleaming blockade of polished motorcycles remained motionless. The faces of those astride them expressionless.

'Or do I have to charge you all with obstruction of justice?' Frisk said, raising his eyebrows, his tone becoming a tad more serious.

'You have our sacrificial lamb, I trust, sergeant?' Reverend Bowen said, breaking the silence.

Your what? he thought.

'Myself and my brothers and sisters are all keen to make a peace offering today,' she said. 'A sacrifice to a God who has become increasingly angered by the wayward actions of his flock. He must be appeased, sergeant. Bring forth the lamb and let us offer him unto the Lord, so that peace may be restored.'

What was this? Frisk thought. He knew that Bowen had been through a lot, but this was all getting to be a bit dramatic. And why was she talking like that? It all sounded a bit too hellfire and brimstone for his liking.

Though Reverend Bowen was wearing her black sunglasses, Frisk could feel her eyes boring into his. He could almost see those two flaming points of light burning behind those black lenses. Each rider sat astride their vehicle in silence, eyeing the police van.

Though he didn't like it, something inside Frisk's mind said he should just get on with it, get it out of the way. With any luck, like the reverend said, they might all then get a bit of peace around here.

'If you mean Douglas, Reverend, he's in the back. Everything is under control and everything is going as planned, so if you and your friends could just move out the way and allow us to do our job?'

Bowen smiled, though there was no warmth to it. 'We respect your position of authority, sergeant, but our power flows from a much higher source,' Bowen said. 'We have been called to this place and we request of you that, cometh the hour, we are to lead the sacrificial procession. Grant this unto us and we shall not obstruct you any further.'

Frisk bristled at her continual demands: Hilda declaring some kind of God-given right to constantly intervene. Well, fine, if that's what they wanted, sod it, why not? Let the Bible-bashers have their little ride along.

Frisk agreed and the Crossroads bikers were true to their word, allowing Frisk to enter the car park before filing in behind him, ensuring there was no chance of him reneging on their deal. The motorcycle engines ceased and the collective sounds of the fete could once again be heard.

Frisk opened up the back doors, allowing Binsley and the handcuffed Douglas to emerge. Binsley tutted, looking at Blouse.

'I wouldn't want to be in your shoes, Douglas,' he said, shaking his head. 'Looks like you've well and truly pissed off the wrong crowd this time.'

Douglas remained silent. His wrists wriggled in the warm handcuffs.

Laurie Knox, making his way over from the information tent with Gooch, paused briefly to converse with Reverend Bowen, who was, along with her Crossroads biker pals, striding out onto the green. He put his hand on her shoulder, saying something indecipherable. He smiled at her, then made his way over to join his fellow officers and their volunteer.

'Look who's come back to see you, Douglas,' Binsley said, smirking, acknowledging the presence of the police dog.

'Right then, gentlemen,' Frisk said, unlocking the door to the changing rooms, 'let's get young Douglas here into his Burglar Bill outfit. Laurie, if you could get the sleeve and the other bits, please.'

'Yes, guv. It's been very popular with the kids today. Think they're looking forward to seeing it in action,' he said, smirking at Douglas. 'I'll just grab it from the van.'

'OK you lot, in there,' Frisk said, nodding to the door that led to the changing rooms. 'We're in number one, first on the left.' They all filed in.

'And don't worry,' Binsley said to Douglas, walking handcuffed in front of him. 'If you shit yourself later, they've got showers.'

47

Colin Blunsden watched in drunken confusion as a group of four identical leather-clad bikers, all wearing dog collars and silver crucifixes, entered the bar. He was sat slumped at the same corner table he and Bob had selected earlier in the day, his still throbbing ankle wresting on a small bar stool. Bob looked on, still and silent as usual.

'What the ffffsssssallllliss'en,' Colin slurred as the bikers approached a perplexed-looking Edna Glass at the bar, requesting four glasses of water.

'Ice and lemon?' she asked.

'No,' came the curt response.

Edna poured them their drinks from the tap and placed them on the bar in front of them. The bikers made the sign of the cross at the glasses before exiting the sports club with a collective look of disdain for its inhabitants. Outside, one biker kicked a nearly full pint of lager over on the patio as they strode past the benches and onto the green. Terence Russell and Gerry Hayman were coming in the opposite direction towards the club, and Terence was not happy.

'If Alan hadn't changed that bloody running order, we'd've had plenty of time, Gerry, plenty of time.'

'Plenty of time, chief,' Gerry echoed.

'Instead, I've got to run around looking for every other bugger as bloody usual.'

Terence was relieved to see at least four of his dancers outside the sports club. One of the dancers, looking a little hostile, held up an empty pint glass. Terence gave them a tense smile as he and Gerry entered the sports club. Two were missing, and there were no prizes for guessing where they were.

His fears were confirmed when through the smoke and the bodies in the bar he saw Colin and Bob over at a gloomy corner table. Four empty pint glasses, two half-empty pint glasses and a packet of dry roasted peanuts scattered across the table lay in front of them.

'I should have known I couldn't trust you two to be left alone,' Terence said. 'You do realise that we are due to perform in less than fifteen minutes?'

'Just the same old story, isn't it, chief,' Gerry said, shaking his head in mutual disappointment.

Colin looked up, his face flushed red from the alcohol. 'We'll be all right, Terence!' he said boisterously. 'Don't get your knickers in a twist, we're just getting loosened up, ent we, Bob?' he said, turning to his mute drinking accomplice, who stared blankly back at him, then at Terence and Gerry.

'There you are, you heard it straight from the 'orse's mouth,' Colin said, bursting into a wheezy laugh which turned into a hacking cough.

Terence was neither impressed nor convinced, but with show time fast approaching, he had to take them in the condition he found them. 'Well, come on then!' he cried, grabbing Colin by the arm.

'Hey ey ey!' Blunsden squealed, as if he was being sexually assaulted. 'Getchorr bleddy hands off me!' he said, flapping at Terence's intrusive fussing.

They shuffled out of the bar as a quartet, joining the others outside. They were finally all together. Terence's optimism strengthened slightly as he gave his usual pre-show team talk, hoping that he could infuse in them some of that energy that he always tried to generate in himself before a show. He persevered, like the leader he was. Like the leader he always had to be, giving his team talk, but the words fell flat the moment they left his mouth. He didn't know whether it was them or whether it was him. And what was worse was, for the first time in his life, he felt as if he didn't care. He felt weak and lost and he missed his wife terribly. He looked around the fete at the sea of faces. He saw one of the schoolchildren from their earlier performance. She smiled and gave him a wave. It was the spark he needed: it was show time, and this was their moment. Despite his apprehensions, Terence Russell went out there knowing that he would give it everything. Trying his best, as always. He always tried his absolute best.

It was safe to say that Tony Gables had had a few, and was now, despite the shade of his gazebo, starting to feel the heat. He was hot and feeling increasingly tired. Tired, emotional and drunk.

He'd done quite well to keep himself together as long as he did after seeing Karen. Initially buoyed by a feeling of emotional resilience, Tony had celebrated his fleeting victory over delusion by keeping the music going and the hard stuff flowing. He was now on the Bacardi, the Coca Cola mixer injecting some much-needed caffeine and sugar into his ailing system. It failed, however, to overpower the encroaching nihilism that was now enveloping him after he'd stupidly played 'Careless Whisper' by George Michael.

A lot of villagers had been, and still were, passing by his gazebo, chatting affably and making requests that he could not fulfil. He had to be really careful not to sound as drunk as he now knew he was, which was easier said than done.

He'd taken a break from spinning records; not only because the public were increasingly losing interest, but also because the intense heat had started warping his vinyl and making the songs sound strangely out of tune. Fortunately he had brought his CD player along with him; unfortunately he hadn't brought his CDs. The only ones he had on him were what he'd found in the glove compartment of his people carrier, and this selection would not do his credibility amongst his listeners any good whatsoever. So it was with reluctance that Tony now put on 'Native America plays the hits of the Eagles'. The pan-pipe music was suggested as a relaxation technique by a friend after Tony had disclosed he was experiencing difficulty relaxing and getting to sleep. He had bought the CDs from a busking Native American in full Navaho clothing: two CDs for £10, the other being 'Native America plays the hits of Fleetwood Mac'.

Most of his records had been placed back into their record boxes. Some records had suffered more than others, as the increasingly inebriated and emotionally fragile DJ stuffed the albums back into the boxes with scant regard for the well-being for their flimsy card sleeves. He was now reclining in his deckchair as the CD softly played the pan-pipes version of 'Hotel California'.

Over the top of the virtuoso pan pipes, Tony's ears picked up on another kind of music off in the distance, their sounds overlapping in a dissonant dovetail. It sounded like folk music. He could detect the raspy sound of someone scraping away at a violin. Tony hated the violin. He hated folk music. He leant over his turntables and squinted into the sunshine and out onto the main arena. He could see members of the public happily clapping along to something. It was slow and rather turgid, not his kind of music at all, and he could hear bells. Terence Russell came prancing out onto the village green with his band of merry men following on behind him, moving with a little less enthusiasm than their leader, it had to be said. One of them was limping, but Tony could not make out which one. In his inebriated state, he could not pin down exactly how many of them there were either, as the blurred men in white multiplied in front of his bleary, drunken eyes.

Terence looked over towards him, making a furious chopping motion with his hand over his throat, like he was signalling an execution. Tony could not work out what this meant. Was it code for something? He leant out of his booth a little further, trying to ascertain what it was that Terence wanted.

'Turn the bloody pan pipes off, Tony!' a voice called from somewhere, and through his blurred memory he remembered the assurances he had given to Terence earlier in the day that he would turn off his music when the Morris dancing started; which he at last did, receiving a sarcastic round of applause for his troubles.

Tony slumped back into his deckchair. On his way down, he caught a glimpse of something huge; or someone huge. It was the mountain, the mountain that Karen had been with earlier when she had come over to unintentionally ruin his day. Here she was again, only this time she had climbed that mountain. He was holding her up on his massive right shoulder, the way a lumberjack might carry a log through the woods. Tony peered over his turntables. He did not want her to see him, but he wanted to see her. More than that, he wanted to be with her again. He could see her shimmering blonde hair swaying in the sun. She was smiling, in a way he hadn't seen her do in a long, long time.

Tony did the opposite and burst into tears.

49

Terence stood proudly, shoulder to shoulder with his boys, ready to do battle once more. The Morris men faced each other in two rows of three, with two musicians standing by holding their instruments, one with fingers poised on the white imitation ivory keys of the accordion, the other with violin planted firmly under his chin, bow poised ready to scrape the first notes from its quartet of strings. The nerves in Terence's stomach had subsided from a spin cycle to a gentle wash. He was focused now on the performance, glad that the moment had finally arrived.

A substantial crowd had gathered around the square wicket of the cricket pitch, which groundsman Fred Hillock had begrudgingly allowed the men to dance on. Usually this sacred patch of earth was roped off to all but those in cricket whites; today an exception was made for the men in Morris whites.

In Terence's capacity as lead dancer, it was down to him to guide his boys, to literally lead them through the dances using prompts and calls, most of which were undetectable to all but the initiated. The buck stopped with him, as it always did. He could see a lot of familiar faces in the crowd, and that made him feel good. The most important one that was missing, however, made him feel sad.

'All right then, Gerry?' Terence asked in hushed tones from the corner of his mouth to his rookie dancer standing opposite him.

Gerry was looking decidedly nervous, a small smile playing on his lips as he gripped his hankies with whitening knuckles. Hayman's wife looked on from the front row of the audience, wearing a beaming smile of pride. Terence half expected to see Iris looking on at him in the same way.

Colin Blunsden, though swaying and on occasion wincing still from the pain in his ankle, looked about as ready as he would ever be. He'd done a pretty good job in the bar, acting as his own anaesthetist, and he smiled boozily at his opposite man, Bob Dobson, who stared back blankly at him, a white hankie in each hand. The group was completed by Steve and Mike, Terence's other boys. They were solid, experienced dancers. Terence knew he needn't worry about them.

The dark thunder clouds that had been steadily building up in the east now looked as if they might eventually pose a real threat, but for now the sun still shone and the Morris men sweated in the sticky afternoon heat.

Bob Dobson dropped his hankies and started untucking his shirt, then unbuttoning it, as if performing some kind of catatonic strip tease. Alarmed, Terence called across to him, 'Bob ... Bob! Not today. Not now. Shirts on.'

Dobson, it seemed, as in dress rehearsal, was in the mood for another topless dance.

Terence regained his focus. 'My lords, ladies and gentlemen!' he boomed, back in the zone. All murmuring from the crowd ceased. 'Queen Mary's favour,' he said, proudly introducing the first dance.

The accordion struck up in time with the violin, as simultaneously each Morris man took his first step and began to dance, hankies flailing, bells jangling and colourful ribbons swaying with the music. 'Queen Mary's favour' was a straightforward, routine dance Terence had deliberately chosen to ease his boys in, intending to allay any early nerves they might have, and get them nicely warmed up.

Colin hobbled in pain as he put pressure on his injured ankle, but the robotic Dobson helped lead him through the moves with smooth assurance. Dobson's blank features were in stark contrast to those of Terence who was grinning, always surprised at the silent, expressionless man's ability to perform, come show time.

Gerry Hayman missed a couple of steps, and at one point dropped his hankie; he also bumped into Terence, much to the irritation of his lead dancer who, despite his annoyance, managed to keep his frustrations in check, safely guiding the embarrassed Hayman through the little pocket of turbulence. Fortunately these minor slip-ups went mostly unnoticed by the smiling crowd, who cheerily clapped along in time with the otherwise competent first dance.

As the accordion and violin held their last refrain, the dancers reassembled into their original positions, breathing a little heavier but back in line, relieved to have the first dance out of the way. The audience clapped appreciatively.

Colin was wheezing hard, and beads of perspiration formed on his wrinkled brow. He bent over, his hands on his knees, hacking up phlegm. His shabby top hat tumbled from his head as he went into a coughing fit. He fired out a ball of phlegm, hitting the brim of his hat with a soft thud, splattering against a dead flower and detaching some of the dry petals that now stuck to the hat, glued by the sticky green globule glistening in the sun.

Terence loudly tutted his disapproval, while some members of the audience shook their heads. He thought for one horrifying moment that Colin was going to be sick, maybe on his hat. Fortunately his fears were ungrounded as the dishevelled dancer straightened up, re-attaching his head gear and trying to regain a little composure.

'Fuuuuck meee, thass a bastard,' Colin said. Mums and dads frowned in the audience, tutting and placing their hands over their children's ears.

Bob Dobson raised a full pint of lager to his lips, swallowing half of the amber liquid in two greedy gulps. Terence had absolutely no idea where it had come from. Bob placed the half-empty pint glass down next to him in readiness for the next dance.

'How do you do, sir?' was a lot trickier, containing far more turns, pivots and pirouettes than the previous number. There was more complexity to the dancing, and the men had to be in complete unison with their opposite man, as well as all the other dancers, having to shuffle carefully amongst each other before meeting in the middle to shake hands with their opposite man and ask the question that gave the dance its name.

Terence's stomach was cranking back up to spin cycle as he introduced the song, and the instruments struck up once again.

He looked over at Gerry, and didn't have to be psychic to work out what was going on in the man's mind. He looked like a kid going in for an exam they hadn't revised for, who desperately wanted to dash off to check the textbook. The nervous smile attempting to mask his anxiety was still present, and it was at that point that Terence knew that the dance was going to go wrong; and go wrong badly.

He was soon proved right: Gerry was in total disarray from the word go, making a string of obvious errors, completely out of time with the music and completely out of step with the other dancers. He smiled nervously, looking around at the others, desperately trying to follow their steps. His red face and nervous smile only served to embarrass and infuriate his lead dancer, who could do little now to help him. In the audience, Gerry's wife put a hand over her nervous smile.

'Come on, Gerry, bloody get it together, man,' Terence snapped as he began to hear the first titters of laughter coming from the audience.

Colin Blunsden, only just about meandering in time with the other dancers, again began to cough his lungs up in rasping, hacking bursts. Sensing danger, Terence slowed the dance down, giving an innocuous signal to the musicians. Colin's retching cough, however, was merely a decoy for what was happening elsewhere in his anatomy, for it was not long after spitting out another mini green meteorite that Colin, following a particularly loud and rather wet-sounding fart, very publicly followed through.

The first two rows of spectators drew back in disgust as a brown stain began to show through his crumpled trousers. He clawed and wiped ineffectively at his dirty backside with his hankie, before throwing it disconsolately to the floor. Miraculously he stumbled back into formation, the release of his bowels appearing to literally give him a second wind, and for all of about five seconds he actually managed to remember his place.

Terence and the rest of the dancers struggled on, trying their best to get the dance back on track without him. Their faces wrinkled in disgust as the shit-stained Morris man ambled shambolically among them. Above the sound of the audience's laughter and revulsion, Terence, humiliated and furious, detected a new distraction coming from over by the football club. It started at first with a loud, jarring scraping noise; then a woman's voice, soft and low to start with, before getting fully cranked up.

It soon became apparent that despite Terence's earlier request, the music was coming from the tower speakers of Tony Gables' PA system. It was still only a solitary female voice singing softly, but Terence recognised the words. Tony was playing 'I will always love you', though he didn't recognise this particular version. He'd always preferred the original Dolly Parton one, him and Iris both. It was one of their favourites to dance to after Terence had put away all his bells and ribbons and hankies; after he had put his outfit in the wash, when he and the boys had all gone their separate ways and the chat and the laughter and the bravado had ceased, and it was just him and Iris, dancing together in the living room to the soft crackling sounds of their favourite songs.

Terence hadn't realised he was standing motionless, processing all of this information amidst the laughter of the crowd that surrounded him. Laughing at him.

After all the time and effort he had put in, all the faith he had placed in his men, and for what? To watch them get drunk and publicly foul themselves. To sabotage his dancing with their incompetence. Or to simply walk off the job, as Bob Dobson was now doing, heading back towards the football club with his empty pint glass in his hand.

Terence looked at Colin, who fell down flat on his backside, his brown splattered trousers plapping to the ground like a baby with a full nappy. Gerry's embarrassed, apologetic face muttered something indecipherable as he nervously fiddled with his handkerchiefs.

And that song continued to play. Tony had now started to sing along, his atrocious attempts at karaoke sounding as bad as the warped and out of tune song itself.

And all around Terence, the laughter continued. He couldn't take any more. He was being publicly tortured with his grief, and all anyone could do was laugh at him. The day had descended into a total shambles. The dance was over. It was all over, and Terence had had enough. He threw his hankies to the floor, rolled up his sleeves and jingle-jangled his way towards the DJ booth.

50

Tony Gables, drunk and struggling to focus, rifled furiously through his record collection, recklessly tossing out discs that were of no use to him. He had to tell her. He needed her to know how he felt. He had to find that record. He took a massive slug of warm gin and madly continued the search.

Over at the cricket pitch, the music had stopped. A smattering of applause and someone coughing replaced the scratchy scraping sound of the violin and the accordion which, no matter what it played, always sounded to Tony like the theme tune to *'Allo, 'Allo*. From her position on top of the mountain, Karen was also applauding.

Bingo! Found it. He scrabbled towards his decks, his drunken double vision confusing him as to which turntable to put the record on.

Over on the cricket pitch the music had begun again.

Tony hastily switched the signal back to his decks, pulling the warm 7" single from its card sleeve and fumbling it onto the turntable, dragging the needle across its gleaming black surface to the record's outer groove. Whitney spoke out over the PA system, her a capella voice soft in the stillness of the summer's day. Tony swayed to the sound.

A few heads turned in his direction, but the majority, including Karen sitting on the mountain, continued watching the dancing. He turned up the volume as the musical accompaniment joined in with Houston's soulful voice. He could no longer hear the music of the Morris men, only the words of the song taken from the soundtrack of what proved to be the last film he and Karen saw together as a couple.

She turned towards him now, one hand shading her eyes from the sun as she looked over at him from atop her boyfriend's enormous shoulder. Tony picked up the microphone and began to sing. He mumbled most of the verse, picking out the odd correct word about bittersweet memories, before ploughing into the chorus that gave the song its name.

He watched as Karen climbed down off her man, the smooth lilt of the saxophone solo kicked in, playing slightly out of tune. Tony persevered, singing about life treating you kind. Soon she would come to him. Soon they would embrace. He screamed about wishing joy and happiness, and did not register the figure in white barging past his former lover, moving inexorably towards him. The PA system squealed with feedback as Tony wailed. All over the green, people put their fingers in their ears, wanting the racket to end. They didn't have long to wait.

Terence stormed towards the gazebo as Tony sang softly about wishing you luuhhh -uhh- uhhuuhhve.

The song paused. There was a second or two of total silence. Tony closed his eyes, gently swaying and puckering his lips, waiting for the song to kick back in and for Karen to sensuously plant one on his kisser.

The thump of the drum heralding the key change and the song's final bombastic chorus hit, and with perfect synchronicity Terence Russell's crunching fist smashed into the nose of the swooning DJ. An arc of blood spurted skywards, spraying Terence's pristine outfit with dark red blood. Whitney sang on as Terence tried to wrestle with the drunken DJ, grabbing him fiercely by his Hawaiian shirt and shaking him madly. The vast quantity of alcohol in Tony's system sloshed in disturbance, and something unpleasant began heading north from the DJ's stomach.

Terence grabbed Tony by his hair, slamming his head down onto his right-hand turntable. Whitney, still playing on the left deck, continued to sing, though not for long as Tony emitted a mammoth stream of chunky orange vomit onto the black 7" single. It splattered over the record and the song ceased. For a short time the needle managed to plough through the thick mess that covered the turntable, until it finally came to a halt as the record deck stopped revolving.

The blood poured from Tony's squashed nose onto the circle of vomit that had now begun to cook in the heat. Terence relinquished his grip on Tony, who through watering eyes watched the dazzling brightness of the summer's day morph into the dark black void of oblivion as he fell back into his deckchair and finally passed out.

51

'Ohh Douglas, you look absolutely lovely,' PC Binsley said in the most overblown, camp tone he could muster. 'Everyone's going to love you, I just know it!' he said, removing his black peaked hat, clasping it over his chest and pirouetting theatrically. His voice reverberated off the cool walls of the sports club changing room and down through the tunnel of showers. Binsley's blue short-sleeved shirt was unbuttoned, and his black tie was loose and slightly askew.

'Dennis,' Sergeant Frisk said in a cautionary tone, from beside the changing room door which he'd left open to allow as much air into the humid changing room as possible. From outside he could hear all the hustle and bustle of the fete. The collective sounds of the Morris men and their instruments drifted in, accompanied by the clapping of the audience.

Douglas Blouse, however, was far from cool. After being dressed up like a terrorist version of a Debenham's mannequin, he now stood before all three policemen and Gooch, ready for inspection. The black boiler-suit he wore was zipped up from his waist to his chin. His eyes were the only things visible beneath the black ski mask that covered his head. His handcuffed arms out in front of him were disproportionately large after being adorned with the protective bite sleeves, and a pair of black combat boots that were two sizes too big for him completed the outfit. His own clothes were hanging on a peg next to him.

'You think Gooch is gonna take a shine to our Douglas looking like that then, Laurie?' Binsley asked the dog handler, who was seated with Gooch a few yards from where Douglas was standing. Two petrol cans were stowed underneath him.

'Absolutely,' Knox replied. 'Gooch loves that paramilitary kind of look, don't you, boy?' he said, stroking the German Shepherd between the ears.

Gooch, seated beside his master, lapped at a bowl of water, his jowls glistening as strings of drool fell from the sides of his mouth. The dog remained calm, passive almost, unnerving Douglas who watched the dog with unease through the ski mask's oval eye hole.

'You look like you're going for a job interview with the IRA, Douglas,' Knox said.

Binsley laughed, his smile morphing slowly into a sneer. 'If only mummy and daddy were here to see you on your big day,' he said, lowering his head, his bottom lip protruding in mock sadness.

Douglas, whose hands had been recuffed out in front of him after his wardrobe change, growled, lowered his head and bent over, turning himself into a human battering ram to charge at the smirking constable, knocking him sideways with his shoulder as he drove blind into the startled policeman.

'OI oi oi, pack it in!' Sergeant Frisk shouted, turning towards the boiler-suited battering ram.

Douglas could not get up enough speed or momentum for a second charge, and Frisk managed to grab hold of him, wrestling with him and trying to sit him back down. A series of popping sounds came from Frisk's trousers, and moments later he felt a cool draught against the bare skin of his inner thigh.

'Ohh, bloody brilliant,' he said, pulling staples free of the re-torn fabric. He raised his head, fixing his eyes on PC Binsley. 'Stop bloody winding him up, Dennis!' he said. 'It's all you've done all bloody day. Any more and it might just be you going out there with Gooch after all. No more, understood?'

'But sarge, he ...' Binsley attempted.

'Understood!?' Frisk shouted. Gooch looked up, taking an interest in proceedings for the first time.

'And straighten that bloody tie,' Frisk ordered.

'Yes, guv,' Binsley said meekly, lowering his head and doing as he was told.

'Yes, guv,' Douglas said, imitating Binlsey. 'Sorry, guv. Three ball bags full, guv.'

'And as for you,' Frisk said, turning his attention to Douglas and pulling the black ski mask from off his head. 'Sit down, shut up, and bloody behave yourself,' he said fiercely, looking straight into Douglas's eyes.

Douglas did as he was told, grateful for the cool air on his exposed face, spitting bits of fluff and hair from his mouth. He raised his cuffed hands to wipe at the irritating coarse fibres left behind by the ski mask that had been itching his sweaty head. The padded arms made it hard to reach. 'Shitty fucking thing,' he said.

The music of the Morris dancers out on the green could once again be heard in the merciful quiet that had descended on the changing room.

'Just remember, Douglas,' Frisk said probing around the hole in his trousers, 'one wrong move after today and I swear to you, I will not hesitate for one split second to have charges reinstated against you. Do you understand?' Douglas gave two piggy grunts in response.

Enraged, Frisk charged over to Douglas and clenched his jaw in his hand. The tip of Douglas's tongue protruded from his mouth. 'I asked you a question,' Frisk growled.

With fear and surprise clearly evident in his eyes, Douglas nodded silently in agreement, as a string of dribble fell from his mouth onto Frisk's hand.

'Good,' Frisk said, wiping the dribble on Blouse's padded arm and retaking his position by the door.

From outside he could hear music: the Morris dancers, but also something else. Checking his watch, he ascertained that the Morris dancers still had about ten minutes to go. He could still hear them, but their music sounded oddly disjointed; and now there was that other music playing loudly over the top of it, drowning it out. Someone had also begun doing karaoke to it, badly. The song played on for a couple more minutes before abruptly coming to an end. This was followed by screams and shouting. Sensing that perhaps all was not well and following his copper's nose for trouble, Frisk decided to go out there and take a closer look.

'Stay here for a minute, you two,' he said looking at Binsley and Knox. 'Keep an eye on him. I'll be back in a minute. No pissing about.'

'Yes, guv,' Binsley responded as Frisk vacated the changing room.

52

It was fair to say that over the years Edna Glass had seen her village at its best, but also at its worst; and as she stood among the crowd of onlookers watching a blood-splattered Tony Gables throw up on his turntables, at the hands of the demented Terence Russell throttling the hapless DJ, she thought she could confidently place this moment among the village's low points.

She turned away from the fight, looking towards the car park: two police vehicles, but not a single copper in sight when you needed one. Typical. She would have to go and fetch Frisk herself, she supposed. Someone was going to have to break up this melee. It certainly didn't look as if any of the locals, standing around gawping in amusement at the eruption of spontaneous violence, were going to do anything about it, particularly when a man the size of a garden shed strode in to join the action. Terence was wild-eyed: she had never seen him like this before and someone was going to have to...

Edna suddenly froze. Her handbag. For the first time today she had left it unattended. Jesus, she hoped no one had discovered it and gone rummaging through it. It struck her as unlikely, but being away from the bar and knowing the type of people that operated around here on days such as this, it wouldn't surprise her if one of them took it upon themselves to start pouring their own drinks. She turned quickly on her heels, away from the violence and the enthusiastic whoops and cheers of amusement, and dashed back towards the bar.

Thankfully, the bar was as good as empty: only Bob Dobson sat in the corner nursing a pint. Everyone else, it seemed, was out on the green rubber-necking at Bob's leader engaging in hand-to-hand combat. She raised the wooden counter like a mini-drawbridge, allowing it to slam down behind her. Startled by the noise, Bob briefly looked up before focusing back on his pint. Much to her relief, her bag was still there, exactly where she'd left it. She picked it up, feeling the extra weight of its additional contents. She reached inside just to make double sure, feeling the now warm, hard surface, breathing a huge sigh of relief. She knew she must somehow get to Douglas, but right now she needed to go and get Frisk to see to the trouble over at the gazebo.

She made her way from the bar, out through the back passage leading to the changing rooms. She opened the door onto the corridor, handbag safely tucked under her arm, and was greeted by the sight of Sergeant Frisk's blue-shirted back exiting the building.

'Bloody hell,' she grumbled to the empty corridor, about to turn and head back to the bar.

She was startled by the rapid-fire sound of a dog barking from down the corridor. It was coming from the changing room that Frisk had just vacated. Though the door was closed, the barking was still loud enough to make her jump and very nearly drop her handbag. Then the barking ceased, replaced by the sound of muffled, murmuring voices, then by laughter.

She edged towards the changing room, the murmurings becoming louder as she got closer. She couldn't work out what was being said exactly, but from the tone of voice she knew that it wasn't good. She turned back towards the bar, her mind racing and agitated, but then stopped in her tracks, struck suddenly by a thought. In the cool of the corridor she quickly assessed its plausibility. Following her instincts, she tiptoed up the corridor towards changing room number four, the room furthest from the police. She slowly turned the handle and entered, praying for a slice of good fortune as she gently closed the door behind her.

53

'All right, all right, break it up, come on, clear a path here!' Sergeant Frisk shouted as he waded through the five-deep semicircle of excited onlookers surrounding Tony's gazebo.

As he got nearer, he could see Terence Russell, bells jangling and ribbons flailing, attempting to clamber over the turntables. Tony, apparently unconscious and totally defenceless, was splayed out in his deckchair bleeding heavily from the nose.

Thankfully, Terence was caught before he could make it over the audio barricade, and was now being restrained by a mountain of a man, whose muscular arms were wrapped around Terence's waist in a firm bear hug. The Morris dancer's own blood-spattered arms scrambled at the turntable, trying to breach its defences to get at the incapacitated DJ.

'Terence!' Frisk shouted, drawing level with the two men. Terence lashed out at the giant man, who held fast to the elderly dancer squirming in his arms.

'He was going mad, officer,' the giant man said. 'Over there,' he said pointing towards the cricket pitch. 'They cocked up the Morris dancing and then he went mad; punched Tony in the face and then smacked his head on the record player. The old boy's snapped.'

'You big, bloody, tell-tale sod!' Terence shouted, struggling in the big man's arms.

'Terence, get a grip of yourself, for God's sake. What the hell has got into you?' Frisk said.

Terence turned his gaze towards Sergeant Frisk, who was at this moment extremely grateful for the huge man's intervention. Frisk did not like the look in Terence's eyes one bit. He thought for a moment that he was going to try to take a swing at him.

'This is all your fault, Alan!' he shouted, still squirming. The bells on his legs jangled as he kicked and struggled. 'You screwed us, Alan. You screwed us all! Top billing, me and my boys, I told you. But you had to go and interfere, didn't you. Now this clown here's put the cherry on top of the bloody cake,' he said, unable to point in the bear hug, but nodding his head towards the still unconscious DJ, who, still slumped in his deckchair, was now being attended to by his ex-girlfriend.

'Wake up, you bloody useless tosser!' Terence yelled.

Nearby parents once again covered their children's ears.

'All right, folks, nothing more to see here, please go find your fun somewhere else,' Frisk said, trying to disperse the crowd. 'Big police dog display coming up shortly, should be about ten, fifteen minutes,' he said, as the crowd at last began to thin out.

'Terence, for crying out loud, calm down,' Frisk said, quietly but firmly. 'Sorry, mate, I didn't catch your name?' he continued, turning to the giant man restraining Terence.

'I'm Darren, Karen's boyfriend,' he said, nodding towards Gables and his unlikely nurse in the gazebo. 'Didn't like to see the old boy hurt. Karen said Tony's been a bit of a liability lately, but he doesn't deserve the abuse this old boy's dishing out.'

'Ohh, sod off, Arnold bloody Schwarzetosser,' Terence said.

'OK,' Frisk said calmly, 'now if I ask Darren here to let you go, are you going to behave yourself, Terence?' he asked. 'What say you come with me for a minute and cool off, and we can have a little chat.'

Terence's rapid, shallow breathing was beginning to slow. He agreed, and Darren released the Morris dancer into the policeman's care. Frisk grabbed Terence by the arm, firmly leading him away from the gazebo.

'Big dog display?' Terence said with an air of disdain. 'You've got a bloody nerve. Should've been me and my boys closing the show today. Not that bloody arse-flashing hooligan you got in there! Rewarding ...'

'... bad behaviour, yeah, I remember, Terence,' Frisk said. 'After that little performance, you're lucky I'm not running *you* down the station to cool off for the rest of the afternoon. You'd better hope that Tony doesn't decide to press charges against you. I mean, how many people saw what you just did, eh?'

'He won't bloody remember,' Terence said, casually and confidently.

'Regardless, Terence, I've got enough on my plate at the moment without you going rogue and taking matters into you own hands,' Frisk said. 'I've got Hilda and her gang of Bible-bashing bikers baying for blood. I've got Petra lurking around every corner. I've got Douglas sodding Blouse sat in there, and now you.' He omitted the part about his wife and child going AWOL for the weekend, which despite everything else was still top of his list of concerns.

Turning into the car park, Frisk was greeted by the sight of the Crossroads motorcycle club who had all returned to their respective vehicles, staring intently astride their machines as Frisk led Terence towards the side door of the sports club. Laurie Knox, who had vacated the changing room with Gooch, was now chatting with Reverend Bowen.

'Terence,' Frisk said, softening his grip and coming to a stop by the door. 'I know you're upset, and I know how much performing means to you, and I suppose I am a little bit to blame. But it's not like I was given much choice about the line-up change,' he said quietly, nodding towards Bowen and her biker pals blocking his vehicles in. 'I suppose I can see why you might've wanted to let off a bit of steam,' he said, relenting a little. 'Listen, I think I know how I can maybe make it up to you,' Frisk said, with a conspiratorial nod towards the changing rooms. Terence's brow creased in curiosity as Frisk relinquished his grip on the Morris dancer's blood-stained arm and popped his head round the door of the changing room.

'Cuff his leg to that bench a minute, Dennis, and come out here. I want a little chat,' he said. 'Slight change of plan.'

54

Edna Glass's heart was beating hard and fast as she stood in the cool confines of the changing room. It was beating so loud in her ears that for an irrational moment she thought the sound might give her away. The changing rooms smelt of dry mud and shower gel. Silently she walked between the benches towards the showers, hearing the voices from the far end echoing off the tiles in the communal shower area.

She stepped onto the dark terracotta tiles of the empty shower area, clutching her handbag under her arm, her heart still pounding. She tiptoed towards the voices, walking as tentatively as if she had stumbled onto a minefield, as if every step she took could potentially be her last. She heard laughing now: childish laughter, like two ten-year-olds looking at their first porno mag. Douglas was in there with them, she knew that. But he wasn't laughing.

They were berating him, teasing him. In between that and the bursts of laughter, she could hear the faint sound of the dog panting. She was close now.

She was startled by the sound of a door opening. 'Gotta go, rabbit, with the Rev,' she heard one of them say.

In a sudden state of panic and for fear of being discovered, Edna ducked out of the showers and into changing room number two. Now just one wall separated her from Douglas and the police.

'It's not looking good, is it, Douglas?' she heard someone say. Dennis Binsley. The man responsible for her son's death. She recognised his smarmy little voice, she'd listened to it enough when he was giving evidence at the inquest. Binsley was laughing like a child. Well, she'd give him something to laugh about.

She sat on the bench, her heart thumping in her chest, trying to compose her thoughts and wondering what to do. That decision was made for her when she heard the door open again, and a voice, Frisk this time, asked to see Binsley outside.

'Now you stay here and be a good boy, Douglas,' she heard Binsley say. 'We're just going to have a little chat, then when I come back we can all go out there and watch Gooch have some fun with you. I'm just gonna pop this on you so you don't go wandering off anywhere, OK?'

She heard the sound of jangling metal and the ratcheting sound of handcuffs closing. A sound she knew well. Then the door shut again. Leaving Douglas alone? She couldn't be one hundred per cent sure. But there was only one way to find out.

Tentatively, she stepped back into the empty showers. Changing room number one was now just inches away. She took a deep breath, remembering why she was doing this. She stuck her head round the corner of the shower block. Douglas sat alone, dressed head to toe in black, with big black Michelin-man-like arms that were handcuffed out in front of him. He stared back at her with wild-eyed surprise. His face was pale, and she could now see that it was his leg that was cuffed to the bench. Before he had the chance to say anything, she placed a podgy index finger vertically over her glistening red lips, praying that her luck would hold.

55

'See you up there then, Terence,' Sergeant Frisk said with a nod to the lead Morris man, who gave a thin smile in return. Terence had been joined by an anxious-looking Gerry Hayman. The policemen, along with Gooch and the two Morris men, were standing outside the door to the sports club changing rooms.

'Dennis,' Frisk said, 'once we park up, I want you to make yourself scarce while Terence and his boys do their thing, OK? Take a little wander round. Maybe pay a visit to our drunken friend over in the gazebo, make sure he doesn't go pulling any more stunts.'

'Yes, guv,' Binsley said, 'no problem.'

'You're running late!' Petra Carr squawked, happening upon Frisk's conference like a headmistress discovering a group of school boys smoking behind the bike sheds. 'My goodness, as if we haven't had enough problems today. And as for the antics of you and your gaggle of reprobates,' she said, pointing a skinny finger of accusation at Terence, 'you should jolly well be ashamed of yourselves. Fred Hillock is furious at what that animal did on his cricket pitch. I can tell you now, Terence, there'll be no place for you here next year, that's for certain.'

Terence took a step towards her, and Frisk quickly grabbed him by the arm. 'It's all in hand, Petra,' he said, holding on to Terence. He looked at his watch: ten past two. She was right, they were late, but he wasn't going to give her the satisfaction of getting in a flap over it.

'Well, I should jolly well hope it is all in hand,' she said, having the final word as always.

'I believe our time is at hand, sergeant,' Reverend Bowen said from astride her trike.

Out of the frying pan and into the fire, Frisk thought, turning from the parish councillor to the vicar.

Reverend Bowen and the other members of the Crossroads motorcycle club were also eager to get things underway. Moses stuck his head out from behind the leather-clad vicar, also taking an interest in proceedings.

'OK, boys, let's get this show on the road, shall we?' Frisk said to Knox and Binsley. 'You all know what you've got to do, so let's get on with it. Dennis, go and get Douglas, would you, please.'

'With pleasure, guv,' Binsley said, grinning and ducking swiftly back into the changing room.

He emerged moments later with Douglas, who appeared unphased in his big padded bite sleeves. His ski mask was stuffed into the top pocket of his black boiler-suit, like the terrorist version of a hankie in a dinner jacket. He looked straight into the eyes of Reverend Bowen and smiled.

'Forgive us our trespassers, eh, Reverend?' he said, smirking. 'As we forgive those who trespass against us.'

Bowen removed her sunglasses, not saying a word but returning Douglas's gaze, holding it steady. She looked over at Laurie Knox, down at Gooch, then back to Knox. The dog handler discreetly drew his index finger across his neck.

Everybody stood for a moment in total silence, watching the stand-off. Petra, who was still present, for once did not say anything. The three policemen looked on, some looking at Blouse, some at Bowen. The Crossroads bikers all looked at Douglas. After what seemed like an eternity, the silence was finally broken by Reverend Bowen.

'Let he who is without sin cast the first stone,' she said.

'Ooooh, like it, Reverend,' Douglas said, smiling, 'like it.'

'Thy wheel be done,' Bowen said.

The words echoed all around her, spoken in response by the other members of her group.

'I think his outfit is missing something, gentlemen,' Bowen said, nodding at the ski mask protruding from the boiler-suit pocket.

Sycophantically, and with obvious glee, PC Binsley removed it, pulling it down over Douglas's head, at first putting it on the wrong way round. He adjusted it, and Douglas's eyes stared out from the oval eye hole, not straying from Reverend Bowen's, who steadily returned his gaze.

'In case you get cold,' Binsley said, patting Douglas on the head. 'There's a good boy.'

'OK, you lot, let's go,' Frisk said.

Gooch hopped up into the rear kennel section of Laurie Knox's van. Laurie shut the doors on him and got in the front. Sergeant Frisk climbed in the front cab of the police Transit van as Binsley and Douglas clambered into the back, Binsley slamming the double doors shut behind them.

Police officers pride themselves on their powers of observation, possessing a keen eye for detail in an almost forensic pursuit of truth and justice. Combined with the famous copper's nose, it makes their instincts almost second to none. But on this day, all three police officers failed to notice that Douglas Blouse's hands were now cuffed *behin*d his back.

They also failed to notice that he now had a little something up his big padded sleeve.

56

The car park exploded with the sound of ten motorcycles simultaneously firing into life. All over the village green, heads turned in the direction of the car park, looks of excitement and anticipation spread across their faces. The ten vehicles of the Crossroads Motorcycle Club, led by Reverend Bowen, pulled out of the car park, turning right down Milton Lane and heading for the High Street. The two police vehicles followed on behind. For a bit of added drama, Frisk switched the siren on, with Knox following suit. Such was the monstrous roar of the motorcycle outriders that the sirens were barely audible to the villagers watching the impressive spectacle.

At the top of Milton Lane they all turned right, the cavalcade of vehicles wailing and thundering parallel to the green. A quartet of men dressed in white could be seen making their way towards the top of the football field, one of them looking as if he was carrying a bundle of firewood.

Out front, Reverend Bowen, leading the procession, aggressively revved her trike as she approached the housing development where her new vicarage would be located. She turned right, away from the estate, leading them onto the green itself, revving furiously, much to the delight of the large crowd that smiled and cheered as the vehicles roared closer.

In the front cab of the police Transit van, Sergeant Frisk, enjoying the spectacle, took the Transit for a once around the display area, taking in the atmosphere and looking at all the excited faces of those watching. Sergeant Knox followed on behind him.

The leather-clad Crossroads motorcyclists peeled away from the police van and threaded their way through the grounds of the fete itself and the crowd, and headed back towards the main car park. Reverend Bowen was the only one to park up at the top of the football pitch next to the police vehicles, which had just completed their lap of honour.

Bowen dismounted, her black wrap-around sunglasses reflecting the sunshine that was now close to being extinguished by the growing towers of cloud that had been steadily building. Beads of sweat popped on her forehead and dropped down her face, snaking their way over the red marks left by the bamboo cane. She made her way towards the main body of the crowd at the edge of the display area to meet up with her fellow bikers who were heading back up from the village hall car park.

Reverend Bowen's all-black attire was in contrast to the white outfits of the four Morris dancers she passed on her way. Terence Russell walked towards Sergeant Frisk with the still-drunk Colin Blunsden, whose earlier accident continued to show through his trousers in a jagged brown patch. Bob Dobson walked beside them with a pint in his hand. Gerry Hayman, looking decidedly uneasy, also walked with them. Under his arm, Terence held the bundle of short sticks that the schoolchildren had used in their earlier display.

Away to the right, Laurie Knox had freed Gooch from the back of the van and was waving to the crowd as man and dog ran out onto the football pitch, much to the delight of the cheering crowd. The row of three black hoops stood ominously amongst the other pieces of apparatus.

'Well, Alan,' Terence said, dropping the bundle of sticks to the ground with a clatter, picking up four and handing one to each of his men, keeping one for himself. 'You screwed me once,' he said, stretching and holding either end of the stick above his head like a dangling trapeze artist. He lowered his arms and began patting one end of the wooden stick into the palm of his hand. 'Let's hope you aren't gonna screw me again.'

57

Butch Ransom and Barbara Rix both held Callipo ice lollies as they made their way towards the football pitch, along with almost everyone else in attendance. Begrudgingly Butch had put his vest back on, now that the working part of his day was over. His toned legs were still on display, thanks to his Daisy Dukes shorts, and his faded All Blacks shirt was tied around his waist. Finn trotted along beside him.

'I think I've gone bloody deaf, thanks to that lot,' Barbara said, irritably wiggling a finger in her ear and nodding towards the collection of bikes in the village hall car park.

'What did you say, Barb?' Butch said.

'I said I think I've gone deaf!' she said, raising her voice.

'Huh?'

'I SAID! I THINK I'VE ...' she stopped mid-sentence, smiled and whacked Butch on his sweaty arm.

The shorn conscripts of Butch's earlier demonstration were now lazing in the shade of the village hall, looking ten years younger after their respective haircuts. A fluffy white mountain of fleece was piled up between the pen and Barbara's spinning wheel.

As they neared the football pitch, Butch picked out a familiar face in the crowd between the halfway line and the eighteen-yard box. He crept up behind her, raised his ice lolly and pressed it against the back of her neck. Trudy Ryan span round in surprise.

'Stick a voddy in there and we're away, eh, Trude?' Butch exclaimed.

'Butch,' she said, looking marginally flustered by the sheep farmer's impersonal display of public interaction. Jeremy Ryan, standing close by with their two daughters, didn't look too impressed either at the sight of the smiling, muscular Kiwi.

'Daddy, daddy, look, it's the shepherd man,' cried the older of the two Ryan daughters, before noticing Finn and, along with her younger sister, immediately fussing over him.

'Ohh yes, it's sheep Dundee from this morning,' Jeremy said sarcastically. 'Nice to see you again.'

'Not much of an early bird then, mate?' Butch said, grinning at the dour Jeremy Ryan. 'I can get by on as little as three hours' sleep a night,' he said, winking at Trudy, who looked a little embarrassed at Butch's innuendo. 'Always something to do, eh, Barb?'

'No rest for the wicked, Butch,' she said. 'Lovely to see you again, dear,' Barbara said to Trudy. 'How's the spare room coming along?'

'Oh fine, thank you, Barbara, just fine. In fact I might need to pop back in for a few more bits and pieces next week. It's taken on a bit of a life of its own. Getting a bit carried away with it all.'

'Any time dear, any time. You're always very welcome.'

'You're all right for wool after today though, eh, Barb?' Butch said. 'Make a few hats and scarves out of the little pile I took off 'em today. That's winter sorted, eh?'

Jeremy looked distinctly left out as Trudy chatted amiably with Butch and Barbara, and his girls played with Finn nearby. His hangover had returned with a vengeance. The burger he'd had twenty minutes ago had not helped, and the humid temperature made him feel tired and irritable. He looked towards the football pitch, noticing a few men dressed in white walking towards the police van.

'How long till we see this little shit get what's coming to him then?' Jeremy said.

'Jeremy!' Trudy snapped. 'Watch your language.'

'Shouldn't be long now, I don't suppose,' Butch said, standing up on his tiptoes, surveying the display area.

Right on cue, a cheer went up from the crowd as Laurie Knox appeared from behind his van, the German Shepherd by his side following his master's command as he led the dog around the football pitch, parading him to the excited onlookers who waved and cheered.

'This is all a bit sick, don't you think?' Trudy said, shaking her head.

'Daddy, daddy, I want to see.' Jeremy obligingly lifted his eldest daughter onto his shoulders. His head span with the exertion of it, and for a brief moment he thought he was going to faint. He rode it out and thankfully both he and his daughter maintained their upright position.

'I've said it before, Trudy, the kid needs teaching a lesson,' Butch said. 'Why bother the courts when you can sort the problem out amongst yourselves? Anyway he's gonna have all the gear on. It's not like he's getting fed to the lions. They just wanna put the wind up him.'

'I wish they did have bloody lions,' Jeremy grumbled, before becoming more animated. 'People like him get away with too much these days. I don't want my kids growing up in a place where nutters like him are running around causing merry hell. Personally, I think it's a good idea.'

Trudy, looking embarrassed at her husband's sadism, quietly shook her head.

On the football pitch, the police dog had completed its circuit and was now starting to tackle the first of the obstacles. On the opposite side of the pitch, another police officer walked down the touch line in the direction of the sports club. At the far end of the football pitch, the police Transit van began gently rocking.

58

'All right, boys, all right. Jesus, take it easy,' Frisk said for the second time to the Morris dancers in the back of the van. 'You could've at least taken your bloody bells off! Bloody noise.'

In the back of the van, under the meagre yellow glow cast by the interior light, Terence Russell, Bob Dobson and Colin Blunsden, with sticks in hand, jingled and jangled as they each rained down blow after blow on the boiler-suited Blouse, who flinched and winced under the attack, handcuffed and defenceless. The smell of stale body odour combined with the whiff of excrement coming from Colin's trousers turned the van into a stifling, smelly sweat box. Gerry Hayman, standing by the rear doors of the van, watched on, looking extremely uncomfortable.

'Not me, ya twat!' Colin shouted as Bob hit him twice on the shoulder. Colin pointed at the two glazed-over eyes peering out from the ski mask. 'Him!'

Dobson did as he was told, hitting Blouse on the leg with his stick.

'Teach you to put my shed all to bollocks, won't it, you bleddy bastard vandal,' Colin crowed with sadistic delight. 'And smashing all my bleddy gnomes!'

Sergeant Frisk kept a watchful eye out as the Morris men let off some steam. On the football pitch, Laurie Knox ran with Gooch, waving to the crowd.

In the van, Terence's mind boiled over with anger and frustration, as all his repressed emotions came rushing to the surface. Every blow he inflicted was another frustration exploding in his mind.

Whack! ... All that hard work for nothing…

Whack! ... Bloody rookie dancers mucking everything up.

Whack! ... Bloody unprofessional.

Whack! ... Bloody Tony.

Whack! ... Laughing stock of the whole village.

Whack! ... Everybody pointing and laughing at the stupid old man with his silly bells and hankies prancing about.

Whack! ... Iris.

Terence held his stick in mid-air, ready to inflict another blow, but the stick would not come down. He froze, looking at his arm, feeling like it didn't belong to him, like someone else was operating it. What was he doing? And what would she think of him if she could see him now?

Tears began to well in Terence's eyes, and for the first time that day he felt utterly ashamed of himself. Shame that if Iris was watching down on him from a world beyond this one, how appalled she would be by his actions. What had he become?

He broke down and began to sob.

'Woss up with ya, Terence, ya big sissy?' Colin said, crowing with laughter and jabbing his stick into the midriff of the slumped, boiler-suited torso.

Terence dropped his stick with a clatter and turned around, making his way towards the square of daylight at the rear of the van.

Gerry, who had not inflicted a single blow, helped Terence step down from the van and out into the sunshine as tears streamed down his lead dancer's face. He tentatively put an arm around him. 'It's OK, chief,' he said, comforting his friend and leading him away from the van. Terence's shoulders shook with each hitching sob. 'It's OK, you're all right, chief. Come on, let's go.'

59

Gooch scampered up the incline of the seesaw. It tilted under his weight as he ran down the other side, before he snaked his way through a set of posts. Laurie Knox was talking constantly to the dog, on occasion discreetly removing a small biscuit from his pocket, rewarding the dog for his obedience.

Gooch negotiated his way through a black plastic tunnel about ten feet long, appearing at the other end to the sound of rapturous applause from the delighted audience, who watched on as the dog flawlessly negotiated the obstacle course.

Knox called Gooch to him on the goal line nearest to the sports club. A small metal pole protruded from the ground next to where he stood; attached to it was a length of chain with a small clip which he fixed to Gooch's collar. He gave the dog another biscuit, commanded him to wait and walked to the first of the three black hoops that ran from the edge of the eighteen-yard box and up to the halfway line.

Beside the first hoop was a small torch soaked in petrol; it was about ten inches long, with a round head that resembled a microphone. Knox picked it up, and from his pocket removed a silver Zippo cigarette lighter which his adulterous ex-wife had given him on their anniversary. Their initials and wedding date were engraved on one side. He clicked it open and thumbed the wheel, holding the flame to the torch's bulbous end and setting it alight. The crowd gasped.

Knox moved towards the first hoop, holding the flaming torch to the bottom of the ring. Instantly flames snaked up both sides, meeting at the top as the hoop became engulfed by fire. The crowd cheered and Knox applied the same treatment to the other two. The three hoops now all burned steadily as Knox returned to the goal line where Gooch was still obediently crouched, calmly watching on like a statuesque canine goalkeeper.

At the other end of the football pitch, a dark figure emerged from behind the police Transit van, being held by Sergeant Frisk. The crowd gave a big pantomime boo as they collectively registered the appearance of the ski-masked captive being led onto the pitch. The individual looked unsteady and was clearly having some trouble standing.

The noise of the crowd's disapproval increased as the figure was marched ever closer to the flaming hoop nearest the halfway line, the hoop furthest from Gooch, who continued to wait patiently at the other end.

Sergeant Frisk could feel the heat emanating from the flaming hoops as they drew closer. His eyes watered at their sheer intensity.

Douglas's groans and grunts grew louder as he too appeared to be registering his surroundings. Frisk struggled to hold him upright as he led him onto the football pitch.

The noise of the crowd swelled as Frisk dipped into his pocket, fishing out the keys that would unlock the handcuffs from his padded arms. Frisk felt Blouse's weight slump to one side, and for a moment thought he was going to fall to the ground. He righted him again, and thankfully Douglas stood up straight again under his own power.

At the other end, Laurie Knox knelt on one knee beside Gooch. Through the shimmering heat of the flaming hoops, Frisk saw his fellow officer lean in to the dog, appearing to say something into the animal's ear. The dog was immediately up on all fours, barking like a dog possessed. Knox held onto the lead for dear life as he struggled with the animal's instantaneous frenzy.

Undetectable to Sergeant Frisk or the crowd were the secret code words that Knox had just spoken to the dog.

'GOOCH ... USE THE GOOGLY.'

Frisk stared through the flaming hoops towards the dog, hearing the animal's relentless rapid-fire barking. He suddenly had a very bad feeling. Something in him said that he should abandon the whole thing, right here and now. Call the whole thing off. But he didn't.

The noise. The intensity of the crowd. The events of the past few days. It had all been leading to this moment, and he knew he couldn't go back now, even if he had wanted to.

Ironically it was at that moment that he caught sight of Reverend Bowen standing among the crowd with a sadistic smile on her face.

Frisk fumbled with the small, warm keys to the handcuffs, and after ignoring another short burst of muffled remonstration coming from underneath the black ski mask, he unlocked the handcuffs.

At the other end, Knox unclipped the dog.

61

The speed of the dog took the crowd entirely by surprise, as Gooch wasted no time in putting distance between himself and his handler, leaping gracefully through the first flaming hoop to gasps and applause from the spellbound crowd. Gooch's legs and body merged into one furious blur of teeth and fur as he sped away like an Exocet missile, relentless in his pursuit.

Laurie Knox stood up, shielding his eyes from the glare of the flames, watching Gooch with pride as he leapt through the second hoop, zeroing in on his target, his dog diminishing in the distance as he headed for the third flaming hoop.

Standing on the eighteen-yard line at the other end of the football pitch, the dazed figure in black staggered, struggling to remove his ski mask. The black padded bite sleeves he wore had slipped down over his now uncuffed hands, but he was unable to get any purchase on the stifling piece of knitwear.

Though he was still dazed and his limited field of vision blurred, he could see that something was coming, even through the heat haze of the fire and the pain of his injuries. It looked like a moving mirage, only this mirage was far too real, too solid, and coming straight at him. His legs buckled with both pain and fear as the dog made its approach. The cheering and the clapping of the crowd washed around in his ears, like being submerged in and out of water. He was on his way down when the dog hit. His battered legs soon gave way from a mixture of the pain of the beating he had sustained, and the abject terror of what he was now facing.

The dog cleared the last six feet in mid-air as it leapt from the ground and slammed into him. The crowd gasped as all four paws collided with the falling prisoner, who toppled backwards on impact. The dog's back legs pressed against his thighs, and the two front paws hit his chest, knocking him flat on his back.

Ignoring the protective bite sleeves being held up in futile protestation, Gooch pushed his thrashing head between them, his salivating jaws sinking into flesh as he clamped down on the victim's collar bone. The crowd cheered, still ignorant of the crazed dog's intent. Their wild exultations matched the frenzy with which Gooch set about his target.

The cheering and the applause gradually decreased, and a collective unease fell upon the crowd, who at last sensed that something might be wrong. It spread like a telepathic contagion as the abnormal brutality of the attack became all too apparent. They watched as Gooch shredded the collar and chest area of the boiler-suit, teeth snarling as flesh was torn from bone, and flailing arms beat helplessly at the maniacal dog.

Laurie Knox stood motionless at the other end of the pitch, watching on in growing panic and increasing horror at this thing he had unleashed. He had never seen an animal he had trained behave like this. But then again he had never trained any other animal the way he had trained Gooch.

Knox began edging towards the attack zone, trotting with trepidation past the flaming hoops, the intense heat of the flames now beginning to dissipate. He quickened his pace as the sounds from the crowd turned from excitement to concern, and from concern to horror.

Next to the police Transit van, Sergeant Frisk was stunned by what he was watching. His mouth hung open with incomprehension, and his stomach turned with revulsion. He could hear muffled sounds coming from under the ski mask. It was like someone screaming at the top of their lungs, but doing so into a pillow.

Hearing the noise and sensing the abject fear coming from his victim, Gooch quickly turned his attention to the ski mask, retracting his head from the upper torso, opening his jaws wide and clamping down either side of the head. Strands of black wool hung from the animal's teeth as it quickly shredded the ski mask and raked at the flesh beneath it. The mask's tattered oval-shaped eye hole had been widened in no time, the eyes, nose and hairline now visible; then the ravaged, bloody face.

'Jesus Christ, Dennis,' Frisk said. His voice a mixture of terror and incomprehension as the lacerated and panic-stricken features of Police Constable Dennis Binsley were barbarically revealed by the frenzied Alsatian. The ski mask had been torn completely from his head. Gooch shook it violently from side to side like a rag doll.

Something protruded from Binsley's mouth. Frisk could not tell what it was from where he was standing and, despite his obligation to his fellow officer and to public safety, he did not want to get any closer to find out, fear keeping him rooted to the spot at a distance of about twenty feet.

How in the hell is that, Dennis? he thought. And where in God's name then is Douglas?

Gooch honed in on the small protrusion that hung limply from Binsley's mouth, his jaws biting down, lacerating Binsley's bottom lip in the process. Gooch retracted, and for a moment Frisk thought he was going to be sick as the thing unravelled from Binsley's mouth like a macabre conjuring trick.

Laurie Knox had drawn level with the attack, a mix of horror and disbelief flooding his system as he too realised the identity of Gooch's victim.

Stepping backwards, Gooch pulled the last of the black tie free from Dennis Binsley's blood-stained mouth, and the young PC gasped as oxygen flowed through him. His chest heaved with the huge intake of breath. Discarding the tie, Gooch prepared to attack once more.

'GOOOCH, OWZAAAAT!' Knox cried at the frenzied animal in a high-pitched tone. He repeated it, over and over, decreasing in volume each time as the dog responded to his assigned code word, ceasing his attack just as quickly as he had started it.

Dennis Binsley, his upper torso shredded, his neck and face lacerated from Gooch's sustained attack, continued to scream Gooch's de-activation code word, giving the longest, loudest and most blood-curdling appeal the village green had ever heard. He continued to scream it long after Gooch had been safely led away.

'Jesus Christ!' Jeremy Ryan exclaimed, with scant regard for the proximity of either his or anyone else's children. Three heads on leather-clad torsos turned simultaneously at his blasphemous outcry. Hilda Bowen and two of her Bible-bashing bikers looked at Jeremy with more disdain for his choice of words than they did for the poor man being viciously mauled just yards away from where they were standing. Reverend Bowen raised an eyebrow, then gave the man a disturbing smirk.

Trudy did nothing to reprimand her husband either, she was too stunned. She couldn't comprehend whether this was real or not. She had told her children that it was all just part of the display, trying to convince herself as much as her two girls, who at first seemed to believe her. That was up until the point when the dog's jaws snapped shut across the man's face.

'That I did not expect,' Butch said, standing next to them. His brows arched in horrified surprise.

Barbara Rix beside him groaned at the ferocity with which the animal had attacked, clasping Butch's bicep for reassurance and hiding her face behind his sweaty shoulder as the thing that looked like a long black tongue was pulled from the man's mouth.

'Bloody hell, that's not Douglas,' Butch exclaimed. 'That's bloody Dennis Binsley!' he said, squinting his eyes in the sun as Laurie Knox ran to the aid of his fellow officer.

Trudy Ryan covered Amy's eyes, feeling the moistness of her youngest daughter's tears behind her hand as she began to sob.

From her vantage point on top of her father's shoulders, Sophie Ryan had a perfect view of what was unfolding on the football pitch, and despite the chaos around her, high above the grown-ups and the other children, she had a strange feeling of security.

The same could not be said for the rest of the villagers, who began to feel genuine panic at what the dog might do if it were to turn its frenzied attention on them. As one, they began to back away from the gory scene enacted on the football pitch, like a slowly retreating human tide. It was only the sight of Laurie Knox stepping in to help that averted a contagious panic from taking hold. Their fears were swiftly allayed by the dog handler, who called to his animal with firm authority, asserting control over it. The crowd breathed a collective sigh of relief as the dog's lead was safely clipped back onto its collar, and Sergeant Knox was able to get the dog back to the safety of his van.

Sergeant Frisk knelt beside his pale and panic-stricken constable as blood flowed from the various puncture wounds and lacerations that adorned his neck, face and upper torso. Frisk did his best to reassure him, promising him that help would soon be with him.

Though Binsley's screams finally began to fade, Frisk knew that this could be an even more dangerous time for his stricken constable, as the potential for Binsley going into shock became a very real possibility. The man needed urgent medical attention. Frisk ran to the Transit van to radio for an ambulance. The whereabouts of Douglas Blouse was now the second most urgent point of order on his mind, after his young constable's well-being.

In the meantime, two luminously dressed members of the Saint John's ambulance team appeared from among the crowd, shuffling over to where PC Binsley lay. Frisk looked over at them from the van, radio in hand, thinking of the futility of the care these two part-time paramedics could provide. But it was better than nothing, he supposed.

Douglas Blouse watched the mauling of PC Binsley from under the shade of the horse chestnuts on the causeway, just to the right of the sports club. He had a great view straight down the football pitch of the ensuing carnage that, if all had gone the way they had hoped, would have had him as the star of the show, rolling around on the floor, helplessly trying to defend himself against that bat-shit crazy dog that Knox had trained. The dog handler had openly gloated to him and Binsley about it in the changing rooms after Frisk had left. Well, their little plan had backfired. Them and that sadistic bitch Bowen, whom he had no doubt would have been in on it all along.

At his feet stood the two petrol cans he had retrieved from the changing rooms moments ago, where he had also changed out of the police uniform he had forced Dennis Binsley to swap with him in the back of the van. Binsley's face had been a peach as he'd laid out the two choices available to the once smug, but now totally flummoxed constable, watching with glee as the blood drained from his face in the back of the gloomy van. It was quite simple: A) Stay here and get blown up by the pipe bomb I'm holding behind my back, or B) Go out there and take your chances with the dog. Not so smug now are we, cuntstable?

He hadn't really wanted to light the pipe bomb. In fairness he didn't even know if it would go off. It had been ages ago that he and Peter had made the improvised explosive from part of the Ford Orion's exhaust pipe. But Binsley knew that Douglas was suitably unhinged enough, given his history. So when Douglas had shown Binsley the fuse protruding from the bite sleeve and Edna's cigarette lighter in his other hand, the decision was quickly made; the sound of the thundering motorbikes and sirens affording the perfect cover for the switch to go undetected.

Good old Edna, Douglas thought. Christ, did she just arrive in time: those big boobs of hers, that he used to fantasise about when she'd babysat for him, appearing out of nowhere in the showers. He looked fondly down at them as she fiddled with his handcuffed leg, before slipping him the pipe bomb she herself had confiscated from him and Peter nearly two years ago.

He could not work out what those Morris dancers were doing, waiting for them holding those sticks, when they pulled up. Frankly, he didn't care. He cracked the handcuffed PC Binsley on the jaw for all the verbal abuse he'd given him over the past few days, and once more for Peter, and then got the hell out of there almost as soon as the van had come to a stop. He'd pulled Binsley's black peaked cap down over his face and had it away on his toes. Frisk had told him to put his tie back on as he'd left. Not much chance of that after he'd stuffed it into Binsley's smarmy mouth.

From the far end of the football pitch, Douglas could hear screaming. The discovery would soon be made and his whereabouts would once again be brought into question. Then they would be after him again, for sure. He pulled his Mr Tickle socks up as far as the limp elastic in them would allow, and strode confidently down the causeway, passing the bouncy castle on his right and approaching Butch Ransom's sheep pen a little further on. The two petrol cans banged lightly against his legs, and the pipe bomb bulged out of the back pocket of his cut-off denims. After the stifling heat of the black overalls and ski mask, he was glad to be wearing his own clothes again. In his other back pocket was the rectangular outline of a darts case, and he still had Edna's cigarette lighter on him in his front pocket.

As he drew nearer to the sheep pen, Douglas could see that the sheep, despite the carnage happening elsewhere, were surprisingly relaxed, dozing in the shade of the trees and the village hall. The remnants of their once-fluffy white fleeces were piled up a short distance away. Douglas continued on, round the side of the village hall.

It was quiet down this end of the green and in the hall. Everyone it seemed was up at the football pitch rubber-necking at PC Binsley's misfortune. Douglas still walked cautiously though, round into the car park, taking in the rather impressive sight of the gleaming row of bikes and trikes that belonged to Bowen's Crossroads God-squad biker club.

Despite everything, he felt a little like the sheep dozing round the corner – surprisingly calm. He was a lot like them. Except around here he had always been the black sheep. The little boy who lived down the lane. Bowen had intended him as the sacrificial lamb. What they didn't realise was that he was really the big bad wolf. And what was it that the big bad wolf had so enthusiastically pursued in that old story his mum used to read to him before bed time?

He looked beyond the row of bikes, past the judo mats and stalls and towards the gawping onlookers now surrounding the display area. Through a break in the crowd he could make out the panic-stricken face of Sergeant Frisk urging the onlookers to give him and his stricken constable some space. That sadistic dog handler Laurie Knox was walking back over from his van towards his fellow officers.

Frisk, Knox and Binsley, Blouse thought. The three little pigs.

64

'Ambulance is on its way, Dennis, you just take it easy, mate,' Frisk urged, kneeling beside his ashen-faced constable.

He had elevated Binsley's legs, remembering from his first-aid training that it was an effective way to deal with victims of shock, designed to send blood from the legs, down the body and back towards the brain. For his other numerous wounds, he was about as useful as the two Saint John's ambulance attendees. One fumbled with a bandage while the other bit into a packet of plasters.

'What the hell happened, Dennis?' Frisk whispered to Binsley, not wishing to be overheard. 'Where's Douglas?'

'Guh..hu .. hu .. huv,' Binsley stuttered, 'he's got a ff .. ffuh ... fuckin ...puh puh ... pipe bomb,' he blurted out, blood spraying from his lacerated lips.

The flecks of blood sprinkled Frisk's cheek as he knelt close to Binsley, his head just inches away as he leaned in.

'Dennis,' he whispered, 'did you just say a pipe bomb?'

Binsley nodded grimly as Frisk's mind began to assemble at least some of the pieces.

'He tri ... icked me,' Binsley said. 'In the ba .. aack of the van. Had it behind his ba .. ah .. ack,' he stuttered. 'Was going to blow us all uh .. hu ...hup... fuckin.. fuckin up!'

Beneath his blue shirt, Frisk's heart pounded. 'OK, Dennis, OK, take it easy, mate, save your strength,' he said, trying to calm his trembling officer. He'd heard enough to know that they were clearly in the shit here.

Behind him, Laurie Knox had returned from locking Gooch away in the back of the van. Frisk stood up, leaving the two so-called medics to attend to Binsley while they waited for the real paramedics to arrive. He took Knox to one side.

'Laurie, what the bloody hell happened? What on earth got into that dog of yours?'

Knox had two clear choices. Lie, or tell the truth. If he lied well, he might at least be able to keep his job. If he told the truth, it would be curtains. Whatever he said, he knew that Gooch was as good as dead, so he chose to lie.

'Guv, honestly, I don't know what got into him,' he said, doing his best to sound genuinely confused. He *was* confused about one thing. About why it was Dennis lying there, but not about Gooch's behaviour. 'Or what made him attack like that. Maybe it was the crowd, or the fire, I honestly don't know. He's been great all through training, I've never seen him like that,' Knox said, almost managing to convince himself.

'Some dogs just go mean, Laurie,' Frisk said, shaking his head. 'They get that look in their eye and they're gone. Sometimes I guess you just don't see it coming.'

Knox nodded his head in silent agreement.

'Maybe you're right,' Frisk continued, 'maybe it was the atmosphere, the crowd, the fire. Whatever, the fact is that Douglas is now on the loose somewhere, armed with a frigging pipe bomb.'

'Bloody hell, guv, did you say he's got a pipe bomb?'

'Yep,' he said. 'That's how he got Dennis to swap with him. Said he was gonna blow the van up.'

Frisk shook his head, struggling to take it all in. He thought this must be karma, after allowing official police procedure to be distorted and corrupted; the rule book being replaced by a mob mentality of vigilante-style retribution. He could have done it all by the book, but it had all got so out of hand, as personal vendettas had subverted official procedure. And this was the result of it all. The question now was, other than where the hell Douglas was, how much did he know? And what was he now capable of?

Frisk thought quickly. 'Right, Laurie,' he said, his mind whirring into action, 'if you get asked about this, you say Douglas Blouse was never involved, right? Wall of silence. As far as anyone outside this place knows, this was a police dog display carried out by law enforcement professionals that has gone tragically wrong.'

Law enforcement professionals? Frisk baulked at how ridiculous that sounded now. 'As a consequence, we will be launching a full internal investigation into what happened, and will be taking all appropriate action against the animal in question, right?'

Knox nodded. He didn't need it spelling out to him.

'What we need to do now is find Douglas,' Frisk said, as his attention turned to the sound of bleating sheep over by the village hall. Looking across the green, he could see Butch Ransom's shaven flock running loose, the metal gate of their pen hanging open as the sheep darted haphazardly around the fete.

'BUTCH!' Frisk yelled over to the Kiwi, who was standing a short distance away, watching what was happening on the football pitch with the other villagers.

'Bloody hell!' Butch exclaimed, turning round towards the pen. 'Finn, come!' he snapped, his dog sparking into life as they set off in pursuit of his escaped animals.

Then came more noise, this time from the village hall car park. A familiar roar: it was the sound of a motorbike thundering into life. With any luck the Crossroads biker lot had seen enough for one day and were now beating a welcome retreat. The last thing Frisk needed right now was more aggravation from Bowen and her bossy Christian posse. He looked around him, doing a quick head count, realising with growing confusion that every member of the leather-clad biker group, including Reverend Bowen herself, whose own vehicle was still parked up alongside his own van, was still amongst the crowd that surrounded him.

So who the hell was that then?

65

I love it when a plan comes together, Edna thought, polishing glasses behind the bar in the deserted sports club. Only the inevitable drinking tag team of Bob Dobson and Colin Blunsden, who Edna had had to send outside due to Blunsden's lack of personal hygiene, had bought drinks in the last fifteen minutes. Everyone else was outside watching the display.

Edna continued polishing glasses with a damp tea towel, the image playing over in her mind of her son lying on his belly in front of the television set, chin resting in his cupped hands watching enthralled as Colonel Hannibal Smith and his boys set about another mission. The A-team, preventing injustice, protecting the innocent and helping the helpless. Just as she had luckily been able to do. Perhaps it was divine intervention. If it was, it was from a God who clearly thought her actions far more deserving of his cooperation than he did the likes of Hilda Bowen and her cronies.

She was pleased to see Douglas back in the changing rooms, and was glad she had been able to help. When she first saw the uniform, she thought for a moment it was Binsley coming back, possibly to arrest her after Douglas had mucked it all up. Binsley and Douglas were roughly the same height, and in the hat and uniform they were pretty hard to tell apart. But it was Douglas. He had made his miraculous escape. She'd let him back in to get his clothes, and didn't offer any resistance when Douglas's eyes alighted enthusiastically on the petrol cans stowed under the benches.

'There's a little extra something for you in the back pocket of your shorts as well, Douglas,' she'd said to him. Douglas patted down his cut-offs, finding the darts she had confiscated from her slumbering husband early this morning. 'Maybe they'll come in handy,' she said. She'd forgotten to get her lighter back off him though, so she lit her cigarette from a box of matches from behind the bar, where she'd since returned to her duties. After watching

Douglas head for the causeway, it was as if she was proudly releasing him back into the wild. The pipe bomb she had originally confiscated from him and Peter many moons ago bulged in his back pocket.

She'd thought about using the boys' pipe bomb before herself. Maybe blowing up the police station after Peter's accident; throwing it through a window. She'd also thought on more than one occasion about rolling it under Graham's armchair as he snored in front of the telly. She could have just dropped it into his lap as the fat drunk snored in blissful ignorance.

She collected some glasses and placed them on the bar, hearing screams from over at the display. Her mind turned to Douglas's mother Alice, her dinner lady partner in crime; Alice's timid but gentle nature. All the kids loved Alice.

'What's for lunch, Mrs Blouse?' they would ask to the open kitchen window. 'Wait and see,' she would always say, poking her head out. 'My favourite!' the kids would answer back, before running off to attend to the more important task of being young and full of fun.

Douglas had had little to say about his mother's whereabouts when he'd quickly changed out of PC Binsley's uniform and back into his own clothes.

'She's gone. Don't know where,' is all he'd said. When she'd pushed him on the subject, he'd just shrugged and shook his head, staring blankly at her. Lost.

Edna thought it was hardly surprising that Douglas had gone completely off the rails – and on them – in his mother's absence. Alice was his guardian, sole protector; and likewise, in the absence of his father, he was hers. Edna knew that despite how difficult Douglas could be, his wilful and erratic behaviour, Douglas doted on his mum, was fiercely protective of her, and loved her very much.

Leaning on the bar, Edna sighed, her head resting in her hand. Amongst all the hustle and bustle on the football pitch, she heard the distant sound of a bike firing into life, and watched as heads turned in its direction. She walked over to the French doors, looking out onto the green, surprised to see a sheep suddenly run past.

The noise of the engine got louder, as did the sound of screaming villagers, and Edna could see now what it was. It was a trike, and it was heading across the green. Riderless, at least in the conventional sense. She could see something slumped on the front seat, but it didn't look like a person. The trike was heading towards the display area, swathing a path through the crowds. Edna gasped, smiling as she watched it thunder towards the police.

People scattered, fleeing in panic, screaming as they dispersed. Shortly after this, Edna knew that she would not be seeing the pipe bomb again.

The dull silver tube stuffed down the sheep's throat rattled imperceptibly against its crooked, discoloured front teeth. The fuse burned down in the mouth of the sheep as it sat limply astride the trike. The sheep bobbed along as the vehicle hurtled across the village green. Three 22-gram unicorn darts protruded from its skull. Blood trickled down from the stab wounds in thin red rivulets.

Douglas had, in neutralising the sheep, found the perfect use for Edna's darts. Now it sat astride the trike, heading straight as an arrow across the village green from the car park. It had already driven over Jim Leyland's judo mats, thundering across the blue rectangle of the instructor's open-air dojo.

The villagers were scattering, fleeing from its path as it drove headlong towards the football pitch; towards the police and the vehicles beyond them.

In a very public display of absolute faith, one member of the Crossroads motorcycle club stood in front of the oncoming vehicle. 'In the name of the Lord, I command thee, tool of Satan ...' The holy biker did not get a chance to finish his sentence, his words cut short as he leapt out of the way in a near-death dodge that would have made Douglas proud.

On the football pitch, Sergeant Frisk's eyes widened in growing horror at the sight of the oncoming vehicle, and their proximity to it.

The two members of the Saint John's ambulance crew who had been attending to PC Binsley both scrambled to their feet. 'Sod this,' the elderly male member of the duo mumbled to his female colleague, as they both beat a hasty retreat.

'Jesus, Laurie, grab his feet, I'll take his arms,' Frisk shouted with total urgency to Knox, who did as he was told, grabbing the legs of Dennis Binsley, who groaned in pain as the two men rushed to save him from the runaway, riderless vehicle. Only Frisk could see now that it wasn't riderless. There was a bloody sheep sat on it. A bloody BLOODY sheep, he re-appraised, noticing the things sticking out of its head and the blood coming from the wounds. And there was something in its mouth.

OH SHIT.

Frisk only caught a glimpse of the pipe bomb sticking out of the sheep's mouth as the trike and the sheep thundered past them, missing them by a matter of inches. He saw the sparkling of the fuse and the glinting brass barrels of what he now recognised as darts in the sheep's head as the arrows caught the sun, and the trike careered on towards the line of vehicles that lay beyond them. His own Transit van, Reverend Bowen's trike and Laurie Knox's van were all parked together in a staggered formation a short distance behind them. It was a one in three chance of which one the trike would hit. The trike zoned in on Laurie Knox's Ford Escort van: the van he had brought Gooch down in earlier; the van he had put Gooch back IN a short time ago.

The trike exploded as it crumpled into the bonnet of the van, the two vehicles merging in a tangled fireball. The sheep was thrown from the front seat and sent flying through the air, thumping against the windscreen of the van and exploding on impact as the fuse burnt down and the pipe bomb detonated.

Gooch, unseen in the rear kennel section of the van, miraculously survived the first impact and began barking furiously, only to be silenced seconds later as the police van's petrol tank caught and exploded, destroying what was left of the vehicle.

The three beleaguered policemen watched on in stunned silence, unable to believe what they were seeing. Knox and Frisk both knelt beside PC Binsley, as all around them people either screamed in horror or simply stood rooted to the spot, stunned by what they were seeing.

Frisk had always thought it an exaggeration when he heard the term 'destroyed' used in relation to a dangerous animal having to be put down. In this case, it seemed like a massive understatement.

Laurie Knox looked on as the flames consumed his van's crumpled, metallic carcass, and the animal he had trained being cremated within it. Plumes of black smoke spiralled into the darkening skies, and the smell of burning flesh began to fill the nostrils of those who lingered nearby.

Knox looked at the lacerated face of PC Binsley, a human parody of the mangled wreck burning behind them. The guilt in Knox's eyes was clear. This had really happened, and he had contributed to it. He looked around him, surveying the damage, hearing the screams and watching the flames. He looked into the eyes of Sergeant Frisk, kneeling beside him, who in turn stared down at PC Binsley, and in their eyes the same look of guilt was just as clear.

67

'I've just had an update on the barbeque situation, folks,' Tony Gables said over his PA system, holding a damp cloth to his broken and bloody nose. Re-energised by the two black coffees Karen had forced down him, but merry from the alcohol still in his system, he had sobered up enough to recommence his jovial waffling. 'I've been reliably informed that there is now plenty of roast lamb to go round and lots of hot dogs.'

'Not bloody funny, Tone!' a sweating Butch Ransom shouted while herding three of his escaped sheep back into the pen with Finn.

'It looked for a while there as if we might've been having roast pork belly and crackling, but I'm afraid that's been scrubbed for now,' he said, bursting into laughter and looking over at the ambulance making its way onto the football pitch.

'As you can see by all the flaming wreckage, injured police officers and the growing presence of emergency service vehicles, the annual police dog display has been a massive success,' he said, looking over and waving to a bedraggled Sergeant Frisk, currently watching PC Binsley being lifted onto a stretcher. Frisk looked up from his stricken constable, giving the DJ an icy stare across the no-man's land of the fete. Tony just giggled.

*

'You're going to be OK now, Dennis,' Frisk said as Binsley was elevated onto the trolley. Frisk was resisting calling for extra police units to attend, hoping to contain the situation as much as possible. He wasn't hesitant, however, in calling for other sectors of the emergency services, radioing for the fire brigade from his police Transit van parked yards from the burning shell that was once Laurie Knox's van. He'd also called for a second ambulance to attend. With everything that had happened, he couldn't be sure yet if there had been any more injuries, or whether there would be more to come. It was better to be safe than sorry. Right now, though, fully engaged in damage limitation, he felt pretty sorry, and far from safe.

The rambling nonsense coming from Tony Gables' gazebo was not helping his state of mind much either, but Frisk had more important things to worry about. As much as he would love to take his truncheon to whatever equipment the burbling DJ had not already vomited on, he felt his efforts were best applied elsewhere. Like here. And in finding Douglas.

Many villagers had remained on the green, milling about in grim curiosity around the burning van and the ambulance.

'Laurie, keep those people back!' Frisk shouted at a bewildered-looking Laurie Knox, lingering by his burning van.

Two fire engines with sirens wailing made their way onto the field, their presence drawing the attention of even more villagers. They parked a short distance from the mangled wreckage, their crews immediately scrambling to unravel their hoses and begin their attempts at quelling the blaze.

Just as one fire was being brought under control, another seemed to be breaking out over by the village hall car park. Frisk paused from his efforts at coordinating the emergency services and seeing off the ambulance that carried away PC Binsley, and looked over to the village hall, perplexed at what he saw. A wall of fire dissected the green, cutting it off from the car park beyond. Among the villagers who had turned their attention towards the fresh blaze were the members of the Crossroads Motorcycle Club, who, including Reverend Bowen, now marched defiantly towards the flames.

Reverend Bowen's trike was still parked up next to the police vehicles on the football pitch; the rest of their bikes lay beyond the wall of fire. As did Douglas.

He stood behind the rippling flames, his outline shimmering fuzzily in the heat. The wolf in sheeps clothing. His upper torso and head were covered in a tatty blanket of grubby white fleece, and he stared through the flames, grinning at Reverend Bowen and her Christian cronies. He began to whistle the melodious lilt of 'Who's afraid of the big bad wolf', the tune drifting softly across the fire.

From among their number, Reverend Bowen stepped forward from the rest of her crew, approaching the flames with Moses tucked under her arm.

'Hot, isn't it, Reverend?' Douglas shouted. 'Especially for a fluffy little lost lamb like me, eh?'

A single petrol can sat on the tarmac beside him.

Bowen stared at Douglas with intensity but said nothing.

Douglas turned his mouth down and frowned in an expression of insincere sadness. 'I'm a poor little sheep,' he said, in mocking, sorrowful tones from under his fleece, 'with no place to sleep ... Please open the door and let me in,' he said, mimicking the pitiful, insincere tones of the big bad wolf in sheep's clothing from the old cartoon.

Bowen stood motionless, staring intently for what seemed like an eternity, before Blouse's abrupt bellowing broke the silence.

'I'll huff!...' he shouted at her through the flames, 'and I'll puff!...', picking up the petrol can and raising it above his head, 'AND I'LL BURRRRRRN YOUR CHURCH DOWN!!!'

Petra Carr stumbled around the carnage of the village fete, looking like the bedraggled survivor of an air disaster. It was fair to say that this year's festivities had not quite turned out how she'd planned. After the mauling of PC Binsley and the explosion of the runaway trike, Petra had run away herself, to the unlikely confines of the sports club bar. One reason was simply to hide, hoping her absence might somehow psychologically exonerate her from any wrongdoing; the other reason was to down a couple of stiff sherries.

Edna Glass smiled, surprised to see the upstanding pillar of the local community panic-stricken and demanding booze. Edna gave her a double, on the house.

Petra emerged from the bar, blinking back into the sunlight, stumbling and trying to focus. She'd had another large sherry before she left.

Flickering orange flames caught her eye off to her left; she realised through blurred vision that a new fire had broken out over by the village hall. She could also see, other than the crowds still gathered around the carnage on the football pitch, just how deserted the green had become. Stalls stood unattended. No one was bouncing on the bouncy castle. The rotary club doughnut-making van was unmanned. The only noise was the clattering of the sheep pen over by the hall as Butch Ransom shut in some of his sheep.

Amongst the gawping villagers on the football pitch, the tangled wreckage of what were once a police van and a trike sat like an ancient smouldering skeleton of some long-dead animal. The fire brigade had brought the blaze under control. Frisk's van and Hilda's trike were still parked up near by, she observed. She could see the owners of the two vehicles walking towards each other across the green: Frisk from the football pitch, Bowen from the fire by the hall.

Taking in the desolation of all that stood before her, Petra reached out to the thinning crowd in a pitiful attempt at salvaging what little remained of the day.

'Please, don't go,' she said to one family, her eyes wide and pleading. 'There's plenty more fun to be had, children ... Don't go ... We haven't even done the raffle yet. There's a video recorder for first prize ... A video recorder!' she said, growing increasingly desperate, 'I'll let you win.... I'LL LET YOU WIN! Ohh, please don't go, children,' she said, stooping down to the eyeline of a fleeing child being firmly led away by her frowning parents. 'What about the lucky dip?'

'Leave us alone,' the mother of the child said, as they walked briskly away from her.

She turned to another family: a mum and dad and two girls. 'Hey there, how about we go and have some lovely cake, hmmm? Doesn't that sound nice? Won't that be wonderful?' she said, now with tears in her eyes.

The family beat a hasty retreat, leaving Petra all alone in the centre of the green. She watched, her eyes moist, as the two young girls holding hands with their parents disappeared from view. The older-looking one of the pair reminded her of how Daisy looked at tha ...

MY GOD, Daisy!

A surge of panic like a bolt of lightning ran head to toe through her as she realised how long it had been since she last saw her daughter. So dedicated had she been to her official duties, that she had quickly lost sight of her daughter, whom she had not seen, she now realised, since just after the opening ceremony.

Her heart raced, the effects of the alcohol leaving her almost immediately as abject fear sobered up the trembling parish councillor on the spot. With that lunatic Blouse on the loose, who knew what might have happened to her? It was his perverted behaviour towards Dasiy in that grotty garden shed that had landed him in hot water to start with. Not to mention all the other unpleasantness. Perhaps he had taken her hostage as an act of revenge, she thought with growing horror. Seizing his opportunity to act out whatever disgusting fantasies he had towards her sweet, innocent daughter. She had to find her, and to do that she needed Alan Frisk.

Thankfully she still had him in sight: he was with Hilda, the pair now walking towards their respective vehicles at the top of the football pitch. Petra broke out into an uncoordinated, mumsy run across the no-man's land of the village green. Her arms flailed limply out in front of her, and her hands shook from side to side, giving her the look of a gangly T-Rex marionette. In a high-pitched, ear-piercing tone, she screamed across the green, 'ALAAAAAAAAAAAAAAAAAN!'

69

'Where is he, Hilda?' Frisk asked urgently. 'It was him, wasn't it? Over by the fire. It was Douglas?'

Frisk and Bowen were standing face to face in the middle of the green. Bowen had been walking back to her trike, away from the fire, Frisk towards it.

'Yes, it was bloody well him, Alan,' she said frantically, 'and the little lunatic is going to burn my church down. He's got a can of petrol, for God's sake.'

'OK, calm down, Hilda,' Frisk said, 'we'll find him. If he was still on foot, we've got a good chance of catching up to him before he gets anywhere near the church, if that's where he intends to go.'

'Well of course it is, Alan,' she said. 'Where else is he going to go after everything that we...'

She trailed off, and Frisk sensed that Bowen knew a lot more about what had happened today than she was letting on. All those clandestine chats he'd seen her having with Laurie Knox – and Frisk had very strong suspicions about him too. Since the dog show and the runaway trike, Frisk had seen Knox mumbling to himself, pacing by the wreckage of his van and shaking his head.

Frisk lowered his voice, and his head, staring intently at the vicar. 'What happened here today, Hilda?' he said. 'Who is Laurie Knox to you?'

Her mouth began slowly and silently to open and close, like a goldfish, as if searching for the right words, a look of helplessness spreading across her face. For a moment Frisk thought that Bowen was at last going to unburden herself to him, in what would be an ironic act of confession. She was completely silent, almost as if she'd gone into a trance. When she snapped out of it, some moments later, she narrowed her eyes, looking directly into

Frisk's own. Her face had clouded over once again, as if whatever force had been in control over her was once again re-establishing its dominance within her fractured psyche, overpowering any impulse to admit to her sins.

Suddenly she broke out into a wild-eyed grimace: 'Oh for God's sake, Alan, we haven't got time to be messing about. Get out of my way, will you!' she said, swiping Frisk aside and marching towards her trike. Frisk followed on behind her.

A high-pitched scream that Sergeant Frisk vaguely recognised as his name pierced the air and his ear drums. He turned in its direction, to see the clumsy form of Petra Carr running towards him, like a praying mantis in a flowery dress.

Reverend Bowen did not pause to find out what the parish councillor wanted, but continued marching towards her trike.

Petra grabbed hold of Frisk's arm, stopping him in his tracks. Panting breathlessly she said, 'I can't find Daisy, Alan. I can't find my beautiful girl!'

Christ, Frisk thought, was he ever going to be rid of these two?

'He's got her, Alan!' she wailed. 'He's got her, oh I just know he has,' she said, beginning to sob. Frisk could smell booze on her.

'All right, Petra, all right,' he said, trying to placate the panic-stricken woman. 'Hilda's just seen Douglas. He started the fire over by the hall, and as far as I can tell he was on his own. I think it's extremely unlikely that Daisy is going to be anywhere near him.'

'But what if he wasn't on his own, Alan?' she said, looking up into his eyes, no longer sobbing but still clearly frightened. 'How can you be sure? What if Hilda was mistaken and he's taken Daisy hostage?'

'Highly unlikely,' Frisk said, 'But if you are that worried, then come with me, I'm going to look for Douglas right now. Hilda is under the impression that he's heading for the church. I'm going to drive up there now. If it will make you feel better, then come with me in the van and we can look for Daisy and Douglas together. But right now, finding Douglas is my number one priority.'

Not wishing to enliven Petra's hysterics any further, Frisk strategically chose to withhold the fact that Blouse was last seen carrying a can of petrol.

Another ambulance was now pulling onto the green. This was the extra one that Frisk had called for earlier.

'Laurie!' he shouted at the dog handler. Knox was still wandering around the burnt-out wreckage of his van, muttering. Frisk could not make out whether he was talking to himself, the fire fighters nearby, or the charred remains of the dog interred within the van's black and mangled husk. 'Laurie, I want you to get checked out by the paramedics,' he said, staring into Knox's expressionless face.

Reverend Bowen placed Moses on the bench seat of her trike before straddling the front seat.

'I'm sorry, Reverend! God forgive me!' Knox began to wail, throwing himself at the bike-booted feet of the leather-clad vicar. 'God have mercy on our souls, Jesus, what have we done?'

'Pull yourself together, Laurie, for crying out loud,' Bowen said, kicking him away from her like he was a randy dog trying to hump her leg. She gunned the trike's engine.

Frisk walked briskly over to the ambulance, giving instructions to the two paramedics and pointing towards the crumpled figure of Laurie Knox, who lay prostrate at the feet of the vicar.

Petra Carr ran the last few yards towards the passenger door of the Ford Transit police van. 'Alan, quick, hurry hurry, please hurry!' she shouted.

Frisk dashed over from the ambulance, fumbling in his pocket for the keys to the van. His pocket lining protruded from the hole in his trousers like a small black glove puppet trying to escape from his groin. He extracted the keys and jumped into the van, firing the engine into life. He turned the van away from the green and headed back the way they had come, towards the main road.

Reverend Bowen, taking the more direct route, wheel-span a gouge in the ground with her meaty tyres before tearing across the green, careering through the receding wall of flames at the other end.

70

Douglas Blouse felt safe beneath the causeway's towering trees. From the darkened sky above them, rain had started to fall. Douglas began to hear the first pitter patter sounds above him as the droplets began to land on the trees' outstretched leaves.

The causeway stretched out before him like a long cobbled snake, providing him with good all-round visibility. To his right, he could see across the allotments and beyond; down to his left, the road that ran parallel; in front and behind him, the view was clear. The petrol can banged up against his bare leg as he quickened his pace, and the shorn tatty fleece that covered his head and upper body began to shake loose, leaving a trail of white wool behind him.

His mind was still racing with everything that had happened: the trike roaring across the green; the crash; the explosion. He just hoped that someone in the audience had a video camera pointed at it. Jeremy Beadle would have been more than happy to hand over £250 for that clip. He thought about Peter. After all, it was thanks to him that he had been able to pull it off.

Peter had always said he'd teach Douglas how to drive one day. That now would never happen. Peter may not have lived to teach him how to drive, but he had taught him how to hotwire the Ford Orion that sat on Douglas's driveway; a skill that had come in handy when it came to getting the trike going.

Peter and he had never been able to find the keys for the Ford Orion, or for the crook lock attached to the steering wheel and clutch pedal, so in homage to one of their favourite TV shows *Finders Keepers*, they had looked high and low for both sets of keys, tearing Douglas's caravan apart in the process. Peter pretended to be Neil Buchanan, describing the object, before Douglas, in an impressive display of wanton abandonment and total disregard for the caravan and its contents, would set about trashing the place in search of the elusive keys. They never found them.

It hadn't stopped them breaking into the Orion with a coat hanger and hot wiring it, though: sitting in the front seats and revving it on the driveway, listening to Iron Maiden cassettes on the car stereo and annoying the neighbours.

Douglas was jerked out of his reminiscing by the sound of something else being revved up behind him, and instantly he knew it would be Reverend Bowen coming after him. Let her try, he thought. God was on his side now.

Douglas heard the sound of bleating sheep down to his left, and recalled lumping the dead sheep with the three darts in its head onto the trike's front seat, before he had sent it off on its way with a mouth full of trouble. There's the sacrifice you so badly wanted, Reverend. There's your lamb to the slaughter.

The many sheep that were now running along the road parallel to the causeway were in much better condition than the one he had put to work earlier. They were sprightly, and travelling in his direction. Douglas stepped out of the tunnel of trees and down the causeway's cobbled steps and onto the path as fat drops of rain fell from an increasingly leaden sky. Opposite him, the beer garden of The Crafty Digit was quiet, and the road ahead was empty. Unlike behind him.

Douglas did not let up on the pace. Petrol can still in hand, he glanced round at the five sheep that followed on behind him, heading up the road towards the railway, perhaps mistaking him for one of their own as he, like they had themselves earlier in the day, continued to shed his fleece. What was left became damp and mottled and stuck to his upper torso. He broke into a gentle jog, cautious of the sound of the trike that he sensed was getting closer, much closer, the sound of a police siren now accompanying it. He could see the blue lights flashing on the roof and the van's bright headlights, alternating on full beam. They were after him. But he hadn't far to go.

The rain began to fall more heavily, the humid air felt oppressive, and off in the distance Douglas detected the sound of rumbling thunder. A storm was brewing. He looked behind him, watching the vehicles coming after him in hot pursuit. The sirens wailed, the trike roared, and the blue lights flashed. Yep. A storm was definitely brewing.

71

Petra Carr was wrong about Daisy being kidnapped by Douglas. But if she was looking for her daughter, she was at least heading in the right direction. Sitting nervously beside Sergeant Frisk in the front of the police van, Petra chewed her nails as they motored along beside the causeway.

The Crafty Digit pub came into view just up ahead. Their out-rider Reverend Bowen was a little way out in front, rounding the bend by the pub and temporarily disappearing from view. Following her, Frisk rounded the same right-hander before turning a sharp left to continue running parallel with the causeway, which was now on his left. Beside him, Petra Carr held onto the dashboard with one hand and the grab handle above her head with the other, swaying in the van as they negotiated the two sharp turns. As they turned, they could see that Reverend Bowen's progress had been halted by a tightly bunched group of sheep.

'What the ffff....' Frisk said, trailing off. He stuck his head out the window as fat drops of rain fell on his head. The bleating of the sheep up ahead was barely audible over the combined noise of his siren and Reverend Bowen's idling engine. 'Well, that explains where they got to then, Butch will be relieved', Frisk said, wishing that the flock could have found another part of the village in which to congregate. The sheep were skittish and meandering in a tight bunch just beyond the vicar's front wheel. Beyond her, Frisk could see Douglas heading towards the railway, his progress unhampered by the barriers that stood vertical either side of the road.

'There he is, Alan,' Petra exclaimed. 'There he jolly well is. After him!' Petra returned to her old dictatorial self, the sight of Douglas, not with a captive Daisy slung over his shoulder kicking her legs, obviously of huge relief to her.

Sergeant Frisk, however, was stuck behind Reverend Bowen, who in turn was still stuck behind the sheep.

'Alan, look, he's got a bloody petrol can. Get aft....'

'Well, it's a little bit tricky at the moment, isn't it, Petra, for crying out loud!' Frisk said, finally losing his patience. 'Did Butch ever teach you how to herd sheep? Because if he did, now would be a good time for you to go out there and demonstrate those skills.' Petra Carr shrank in her seat. 'Well, there's no need to shout, Alan,' she said meekly.

Sergeant Frisk raised his hand, bringing the flat of his palm firmly down on the Ford logo in the centre of the steering wheel. The blare of the horn dissonantly accompanied the wailing siren.

In front of them, Reverend Bowen gave a monstrous rev of her trike and lunged at the herd of sheep like a speedway rider making a false start against the tapes.

Not wishing to be outdone, the sky emitted a loud clap of thunder, followed moments later by a flash of brilliant white lightning that illuminated the darkened sky.

The cacophonous combination of sounds startled the sheep into action as they made a collective dash towards the railway line. Towards Douglas, who was already there.

72

Daisy Carr had had the hots for Dan Fowler ever since the twenty-three-year-old had started manning the signal box a little under two years ago. At that time she had just turned sixteen, was headstrong and heading for her A levels. By then she had also become interested in boys. Not boys her own age, who she looked upon as immature and intellectually inferior. But older boys like Dan. He was funny, handsome, a little aloof, and a bit nerdy, but in a good way. He loved to read, whiling away the hours sitting in the signal box in his comfy chair with his nose in a book: usually Shaun Hutson or James Herbert. He was also a heavy smoker of marijuana.

Dan's one and only vice had caused him some professional misconduct problems in the past, and he had received regular visits from Sergeant Frisk as a result. Dan had tried to clean his act up when it came to smoking on the job, and in the main he was vigilant not to indulge while on duty. Until his relapse today, that was.

Daisy had got away from the tedium of the fete as soon as her mother had finished giving her self-congratulatory speech at the opening ceremony, knowing that her mother, along with the rest of the village, would have much more important things to concern themselves with. So she had ascended the flight of wooden steps to the cosy but humid confines of Dan's signal box.

The pair had spent their time talking, smoking and eating. The munchies from the joints they had smoked quickly kicked in, meaning that Daisy was sent on a mission to the shop to get more supplies in.

They had fooled around a little, kissing and cuddling, and Dan had got as far as feeling a bit of tit but no further. Daisy, by no means inexperienced when it came to boys, was still a little hesitant to let Dan's wandering hands venture any further south. Dan, though a little disappointed, was respectful of her wishes, and so had put his idle hands to use in other areas: namely, rolling another reefer the size of a marker pen.

Now In a temporary state of ganja-induced paralysis, the pair lay side by side, completely motionless on the thin Afghan rug that took up most of the signal box's floor space. Barely able to think, let alone move, it was only the sound of a roaring engine in the distance that caused Dan to stir. That and the sirens. Paranoia surged through the very stoned signal man, who sat bolt upright next to the comatose Daisy.

'Shit, it's the fucking old bill,' he said, looking around the cloudy confines of the signal box, making a mental inventory of all his smoking paraphernalia. 'Shit, shit, shit,' he repeated manically to himself. Beside him, Daisy began to stir. He grabbed all his smoking gear and shoved it recklessly into a nearby drawer, scrabbling about the signal box, looking around to make sure he hadn't missed anything incriminating.

Then his heart froze. Above him he saw the blinking light of the train location indicator panel: the lights that told you whereabouts on the line approaching services were and, as a consequence, when it would be necessary to lower the barriers. He'd been fine so far at operating the barriers, up until that last reefer. Now the blinking light was dangerously close to the level crossing, and under normal circumstances, the barriers should have been lowered by now.

'Oh Jesus, oh fuck,' he said.

Hearing the panic, Daisy sat up on her elbows. 'Dan, what's going on, what's the matter?' she asked woozily.

'Frigging train coming, Daisy, that's what's the matter,' he said through the clearing mind fog of his dope haze.

'Oh my God,' she said, trying to clear her own head.

Dan dashed across the signal box to the panel of buttons, locating the one that lowered the barriers. Looking up at the indicator panel, he knew it was not going to be long before the train came hurtling through. Approaching from the west, it was now under a mile away, and at the speed it was going the HST could cover that ground in no time at all.

Looking west through the rain, he could now see the distant lights of the approaching train and hear the rumbling sound of thunder from the clouds above. He looked down onto the level crossing, pausing momentarily in disbelief, not knowing if what he was seeing was real or whether it was some kind of a drug-induced hallucination.

It was the unmistakable figure of Douglas Blouse, standing motionless on the railway line with his denim shorts around his ankles, looking towards the causeway in the direction of the church. Dan could just see a portion of his bare arse hanging out the back of his semi-pulled-down underwear. Old habits die hard, he thought. The expression on Blouse's face was one of utter sadness. His bottom lip protruded and it looked as though he might be crying.

Hoping it wasn't too late, Dan pounded the button that sounded the warning sirens and activated the red warning lights. After they had made their precursory wail, the barriers would descend. On the line, Douglas remained completely still, appearing not even to notice the barriers or the alarm.

Through the pattering sound of the rain on the windows, Dan could now hear the train approaching. The flashing light on the indicator panel above him confirmed his fears.

Outside, the sound of the revving engine and the wailing police sirens drew closer. He could see them now. But there was something else. Jesus, this had to be a dream surely, Dan thought.

Sheep: bleating hysterically and running headlong towards the descending barriers of the level crossing.

'Daisy, are you seeing this?' he said. Beside him, Daisy was looking out of the signal box in a mixture of panic and incomprehension.

'Jesus, that's Douglas,' she said, seeing him for the first time, standing motionless on the railway line as the HST thundered towards him.

'And who's that woman over there?' Dan asked, following the direction of Douglas's gaze.

73

For Douglas Blouse, old habits did indeed die hard. He couldn't resist it. Just as Gooch had been programmed to kill, Douglas was programmed to flash his bare arse at trains.

After cresting the incline to the level crossing, Douglas stood panting on the railway line, looking first east towards the bridge, then the long straight, seemingly endless rails that headed west, where off in the distance, two pinpricks of light were just visible through the gloom.

He looked up at the barriers, confused as to why they had not already descended. He placed the petrol can down by the edge of the railway line out of harm's way, before putting himself directly in it. He could see that Reverend Bowen was still a little way down the causeway, with the police, blue lights flashing and siren wailing, not too far behind. In front of Bowen were the sheep, impeding her progress.

He began the familiar ritual, popping the button of his cut-off denim shorts. He bent over, sliding down his shorts and his boxers to expose the pale full moon and began to slap. The rain pattered down on him and his heart beat faster as the lights of the upside-down train grew bigger and brighter, but he felt no sense of elation, only an empty desolation. A despair the like of which he had never known consumed him as his mind played out the prospect of a long, lonely future that stretched out ahead of him like the railway line he was standing on. Still viewing the train from upside down, he ceased slapping, and for the first time since *the first time*, he thought he might just stand his ground on this one.

'Careful, Mr Bump,' the soft voice said. Her voice reverberated in his mind and time seemed to stand still. Douglas stood upright, turning towards her, completely oblivious now of the HST bearing down on him. His unbuttoned denim shorts were shrugged softly to the ground, but his frontal modesty was maintained by his boxer shorts that held their position. A pale crescent of moon was still peeping out from between his T-shirt and boxer shorts.

Though the day had turned dark and the rain persisted, the clouds had begun to break, allowing the sun to shine through in places. In a ray of crepuscular light that penetrated the leaden sky stood the figure of Alice Blouse, standing in the opening of the green tunnel of horse chestnuts on the opposite side of the causeway. Her lustrous auburn hair billowed around her shoulders, shimmering in the slanting sunshine, and there was a hint of rouge on her prominent cheek bones that was offset by the purity of her porcelain skin.

She was holding something out to her son, who looked on, mesmerised by her presence. She held up the light grey woolly jumper by its sleeves, its neckline just beneath her smiling face. The familiar blue and white image of Douglas's favourite accident-prone Mr Man character adorned its front.

Alice had a serene, tender smile on her face, as she stared lovingly at her son. Impervious to the rain that continued to fall, both she and the jumper remained bone dry, as if she was in a protective bubble.

Douglas could not move, and could not speak, feeling only a sense of overwhelming love and loss as he looked into the sumptuous brown of his mothers twinkling eyes. Her youthful complexion bore no resemblance to the tired and anxious woman of thirty-six that she was forever destined to be: the woman who had given him all the love and support that she possibly could, in spite of the detrimental physical and emotional toll it had taken on her own body and mind.

Memories washed over Douglas, like the rain that fell from the sky: things that he had not thought of in years, beautiful but simple images that had been eroded over the years, blotted out by the confusing anger and hardened resentment that had grown inside him since his father had left them to fend for themselves nearly six years ago.

He remembered Sunday nights after bath time when she would clean his ears; the feeling of the cotton bud as it probed and prodded, tickling his inner ear, his giggling head resting on her lap.

He remembered baking with her, and could almost taste the sweet cake mixture on the whisk beaters that she always allowed him to lick clean; twisting and turning his tongue around the metallic utensils, trying to get at every last scrap of left-over mixture.

Most of all he remembered the jumpers: the warm, soft jumpers she knitted for him in the autumn and winter months; that feeling of warmth and comfort he felt when he put one on, a feeling second only to that of slipping into bed under freshly washed sheets in clean-on pyjamas, when she would tickle his feet under the duvet. 'Good night, Mr Tickle,' she would say, turning out the light after they had both caught their breath.

If Douglas's life was a stick of rock, the tender and sentimental childhood memories its sweet flavour and vibrant colour, then his troubled teenage years would be the hard, blank centre, and the word that ran through it from end to end was regret: regret for all he had put his mother through whilst lost in his private world of rage and confusion; a world of bullies on busses; a world where teasing was the only attention ever paid to you by snooty girls way out of your league; a world where your only friend could be listening to music with you in the car one day and be dead the next, snatched away without prior warning; a world where so-called grown-ups merely looked on with contempt as you tried your best not to drown in the pain of it all.

He'd thought he had wanted to kill himself the first time he had trespassed on the railway line, until when it came down to it, he had jumped out the way at the very last second. Then again the next time. And the next time. The feeling he felt every time he did so became an antidote to the trauma he was having to deal with on an almost daily basis: an unparallelled rush that dulled the pain of a life made increasingly difficult, in a world he had trouble understanding.

But through it all she had been there: selfless, loyal and loving. If only he'd been able to see it. Well, he saw it now, and he was thankful to her for it, even if he knew it was far too late. Only somehow it felt like it wasn't too late. In that eternal moment where everything seemed to stand still, and all sounds appeared to cease, it felt as though maybe it wasn't too late. The unspoken, almost telepathic exchange that passed between the two of them as they simply looked at each other in silence was overwhelming. He could feel her strength, and he could feel her love, and as the tears flowed he could say only one word: 'Mum.'

74

Reverend Bowen continued to rev her trike hard behind the five sheep now charging headlong towards the level crossing. She could see Douglas standing on the railway line, upright and motionless. His bare backside hanging out from his half-mast shorts was in full colour, as if it had undergone a technological upgrade from the black and white image that had come smashing through her stained glass window two days ago. The lights on the crossing were flashing red, and the barriers were now coming down.

'Jesus wept,' she hissed.

The sheep were not stopping, nor indeed were they even slowing for the barriers. They were just mindlessly running towards them.

The mindless herd she thought, thinking of her own dwindling flock as the five animals carried on inexorably towards the railway, totally unconcerned for their own safety as they crested the incline, just yards from the metallic barriers that shimmied and shook as they came down.

Douglas, on the railway line, was still standing motionless. Beyond him a slanting beam of sunlight descended from the heavens, skewering the canopy of trees on the other side. She could see now that this is where Douglas's attention was focused.

Reverend Bowen also saw the fleeting figure of Alice Blouse, standing beyond her son in the piercing beam of sunlight. She only caught a brief glimpse, but the moment seemed like an eternity. The woman she saw looked nothing like the timid, nervous woman she had known in recent years. She looked younger, fresher, more youthful, beautiful, as on the day she had married her to Bertie.

Reverend Bowen did not divert her gaze from the smiling, serene woman, despite the sound of hissing rails and the blaring horn of the approaching train. She simply stared with calm, astounded focus as the bleating sheep finally made it to the barriers.

75

'Oh my God,' Sergeant Frisk said in disbelief, watching in horror as the train came through.

In the cab of the Transit van, both he and Petra sat, unable to speak as the red, white and black livery of the Intercity 125 stormed into view from the right. The deafening sound of its horn filled the air as it hammered over the level crossing. From somewhere he thought he heard a girl scream. Even over the police siren, the revving trike and the noise of the train, he thought he heard it.

There was a burst of red as something exploded against the front of the train. Reverend Bowen, just in front of the police van at the barriers, did not turn away, even as the blood of whatever had just been hit sprayed against her face.

'Jesus, the barriers didn't come down in time,' Frisk said in total astonishment. 'Where's Douglas? Shit, that train just hit something. Douglas was standing right there on the line. What the bloody hell happened?'

Petra looked on in stunned silence.

'How many sheep do you see, Petra?' he asked her.

'Huh?'

'I think some might have got onto the line,' he said, reaching for the radio. 'Fuck's sake, what happened to Douglas? He was standing right there.'

Whatever had happened had happened far too fast for either Frisk or Petra to be able to judge with any degree of accuracy. His view was partially obscured by Reverend Bowen astride her trike, and what he now counted as three remaining sheep, milling around in front of the fallen barrier. All he knew was that *something* had been hit. There was enough blood to know that. Frisk hammered the steering wheel before radioing for another ambulance. 'Jesus,' he said, unbuckling his seatbelt and replacing the radio. 'What the hell have we done?'

76

After bumping into Douglas and knocking him out the way of the train, the first sheep to make it under the descending barrier went helplessly beneath it. Its back legs got stuck in the recess between the rails and the concrete of the crossing. The animal's suicidal dash was rewarded with instant death beneath the steel bogies that instantaneously smeared it across the tracks.

There was even less left of the second kamikaze sheep, who in an admirable attempt to leap the first, had jumped onto the back of the stuck sheep, ascending to the perfect height to be completely obliterated by the apex front of the enormous power car, the sheep exploding like a blood-filled water balloon as the high speed train hit it head on.

Fearing for sure that he was going to hit the person standing motionless on the tracks, the driver did what he was trained to do in such situations: he looked away before the moment of impact. Travelling at such a speed, it would take up to two kilometres of track to be able to stop in time, leaving the driver utterly helpless to do anything to alter the fate of whoever stood in its path, be it human, or in this case, and much to the driver's eventual relief, animal. All you could do was look away and hope that the memories of such an incident did not return to haunt you later on in your dreams.

The blood-splattered train did eventually stop, coming to a halt just over a mile away, where the driver composed himself sufficiently to radio the accident into central control, halting all other services due in the area. As he called in the details of the accident, his voice faltering, the phone trembling in his hands, he said the two words all drivers dread: 'One under.'

As he ended the call, the driver was as white as a sheet. Or a sheep.

It was a mixture of the large quantity of weed she had smoked, combined with the sight of Douglas Blouse's feet being severed just above the ankles, that made Daisy Carr lose her lunch over the edge of the signal box's steps. Douglas's feet, still in their Mr Tickle socks and trainers, now sat between the rails, the stumps peeping out from under his crumpled denim shorts. Dan and Daisy had both watched, completely helpless as the two sheep had scuttled under the descending barriers before bundling into Douglas. They saved his life, but could not prevent his feet from being cut clean away. The scream Daisy emitted when the train came through was still ringing in Dan Fowler's ears.

The barriers had come down in time to prevent the trike now idling in front of the barriers from getting onto the line as well. Astride it, Reverend Bowen had a strange, almost serene look on her blood-splattered face. She dismounted and scrambled over the barriers, just as she had two days ago, making her way onto the tracks and towards the prone figure of Douglas Blouse, lying in the channel between the two sets of rails.

Behind Bowen's trike, and to Dan's growing concern, was the police Transit van, the doors of which had just been flung open. The siren had ceased its wailing, but atop the van roof the blue lights continued to flash.

Sergeant Frisk emerged from the driver's side. From the passenger side, Petra Carr got out. Behind Dan, Daisy, ashen-faced, saw her mum before carefully descending the signal box's steps and for once running towards her.

78

Butch Ransom maintained a brisk pace as he walked the cobbled path of the causeway heading towards The Crafty Digit, Finn as ever by his side. They were sheltered from the falling rain that gave the trees an intoxicatingly fresh smell. He had left the trio of sheep he'd managed to round up back in the pen on the green.

Following in the direction taken by Bowen and the police van, Butch made his way towards the pub with the Ryan family who, following on closely behind Butch, just wanted to reach the safety of their home and try to think of a way to explain to their children what had happened today.

Trudy's pace was swift, but not swift enough to keep pace with Butch. Behind them, Jeremy Ryan held the soft, clammy hands of his two daughters, walking either side of him.

As Butch reached The Crafty Digit, standing in the rain and the broken sunshine of the beer garden, he heard the voice of landlady Pat Wilkes coming from the serving hatch, and she sounded pretty shaken.

'They all went up there, Butch,' she said, pointing towards the railway. 'Your sheep n'all. Went running up towards the railway line. I think Douglas might've been leading the charge. I saw him from the window. I almost took him for one of them, the way he looked, covered in all that wool. Hilda and the police were behind him. Train was blaring his horn something rotten. If you ask me, Butch, something bad's happened up there,' she said with grim finality.

Trudy Ryan reached the pub just in time to catch the last disturbing sentence of Pat Wilkes' update. She turned to her husband and daughters, who were now catching up to her.

'Darlings,' she said softly, pushing a lock of wet hair from her face, 'why don't you go inside the pub with daddy and have a drink and some crisps,

OK? Stay out of the rain while I go up with Butch and make sure that everything is OK.'

She stared at her husband with a wide-eyed look of hoped-for cooperation.

Still confused but encouraged by their mother's suggestion, the girls grabbed an arm each of their father and smiled, looking up expectantly at him.

'Or I might be able to find some pizza for you girls, if you'd like,' Pat said smiling, cottoning on to the necessary act of bribery taking place.

Jeremy and Trudy exchanged a brief glance of understanding.

'Come on then, girls, let's get out of this rain, come and show me what you want,' Jeremy said as he led his girls towards the pub.

'Save a piece for me!' Trudy called, trying to feign enthusiasm before setting off towards the railway line with Butch.

'Jesus, Butch, what else is going to happen today?' she said. 'I thought this was meant to be a quiet village.'

'Guess you just picked a good time to move here, Trude, eh?' Butch said, nervously grinning.

They could see the warning lights of the level crossing flashing, and the barriers were down. In front of them stood Reverend Bowen's riderless trike and the police van behind it.

Butch could hear the familiar sound of sheep, and counted three milling around by the barriers. He did a quick calculation. He'd had nine this morning. Three more were back in the pen and one had been lost on the trike. He was still two sheep short. He quickly snapped an order at Finn, the dog immediately reacting to his master's instructions and heading off the sheep, ensuring that another getaway was not possible.

As they approached the railway line with the rain now easing off and the sun beginning to reassert itself, they could see the visibly trembling figure of Daisy Carr being held in a tight embrace by her mother at the barrier. Daisy's head was jerking up and down, her sobbing audible from some distance. Her mother stroked her daughter's hair and whispered something in her ear.

It was only as Butch reached the barrier himself that the full bloody extent of the accident became apparent. He peered over grimly at the slick, crimson railway, and the splattered mess dotted with fluffy white tufts that he presumed were once his sheep.

He saw Douglas between the rails being cradled by Reverend Bowen; saw his trainers and shorts on the railway, wondering why he had taken them off. They were crumpled between the rails, the shorts sitting on top of the shoes, but they had ...

'Oh, Jesus Christ,' Butch said, raising a hand to his mouth and looking at Douglas's bloody stumps. Underneath those crumpled denim shorts were Douglas's trainers. The trainers that still contained his feet. Butch noted with grim humour that one of Douglas's severed legs was now slightly longer than the other, just as his shorts had been when he caught him at this exact spot two days ago.

A soft whimpering sound coming from his right indicated that Trudy had also correctly identified the same thing.

On the railway, Reverend Bowen was muttering something to the stricken Blouse, looking down at him and cradling him in her arms. Ransom could see the faraway look in Douglas's eyes.

Trudy Ryan began to weep, watching the vicar cradling the helpless, bleeding boy in her arms, the tears flowing freely as she did so.

79

Reverend Bowen held the trembling form of Douglas Blouse in her arms, doing her best to keep his eyes trained on her and not to where his feet used to be. As well as the obvious injuries to his legs, blood was seeping from a wound in the back of his head where he must have hit the concrete after being knocked clear of the train.

The figure of Alice Blouse had dematerialised right in front of her eyes as the train passed out of view, but she knew what it was she had been shown. She had snatched a glimpse of the life eternal: a mystery for so long hidden to her, a snapshot into the world beyond worlds, and part of her would never be the same again.

A heady cocktail of sorrow and compassion, the like of which Bowen had never known, flowed from her open heart, which was once again beating to the gentle rhythm of unconditional love. All her old feelings of shallow malice and petty bitterness, her anger and injustices, had all been washed away. A weight that she could physically feel had been lifted from her shoulders, and the irony of her leather waistcoat was not lost on her. She had been at a crossroads in her life for some time, lost and bewildered, but only now did she realise just how lost she had become. Maybe now she could begin again to find her way.

She looked down at Douglas's trembling form: the blood-stained boy in his boxer shorts and cut-off T-shirt, streaked with blood and matted with patches of tatty damp fleece that stuck to his quivering body, dripping in the gentle rain that diluted the blood that pumped from his stumps. She looked into his eyes, fixing her gaze firmly on his, and only now did she understand the look of utter loss and pain that those eyes conveyed. They were soft and unfocused, but in the silence of that shared gaze, there was both forgiveness and understanding.

A little smile formed on Bowen's lips as the rain trickled down her face, mixing with her tears as she began to speak.

'What do you think?' she said, almost choking on the words that struggled to make it past the lump in her throat. 'If a man owns one hundred sheep, and one of them wanders away, will he not leave the ninety-nine on the hills and go to look for the one that wandered off?' The old familiar words came easily to her now. 'And if he finds it, truly I tell you, he is happier about that one sheep than about the other ninety-nine who did not wander off. In the same way, your father in heaven is not willing that any of these little ones should perish.'

Reverend Bowen stroked Douglas's forehead with a tenderness that had been so alien to her. Her tears flowed steadily once again, tasting salty on her smiling lips.

Douglas half-opened his mouth, as if to try and speak. Bowen put a gentle finger to his lips and a very brief smile formed on Douglas's face. He looked peaceful in the arms of Reverend Bowen, as he finally lost consciousness.

The ambulance arrived within two minutes of Sergeant Frisk's radio call. It was the second of the two ambulances he had summoned while on the green earlier. It had still been down there when the call came through for it to make its way up to the railway line, and Frisk was extremely grateful for its proximity. It was this that saved Douglas's life.

Dan Fowler raised the barriers to let the ambulance onto the line, trying to remain as composed and professional as he could. It wasn't easy after what he had done; or had not done, and he knew he would have to answer for his own part in today's events.

Petra Carr took Daisy home and into the loving arms of her father, who was only now being filled in on the extraordinary day that he had missed out on. Robert Carr was stunned, enjoying an uncharacteristic moment of peace and quiet from his wife, who in an abnormal display of affection silently hugged him as tenderly as she did their daughter.

The Ryan girls consumed three cans of Coke, two packets of Quavers and a slice of pizza each before they were all finally reunited, then took their time to walk the long way home via the Stocks Lane crossing; the crossing that wasn't awash with blood.

The sun was back out and the storm clouds that had hung so heavily over the village had cleared away to the east. The heat remained imposing, but after the storm the air felt so much fresher. The summer fragrances smelt good in the nose of Reverend Bowen, who had watched the ambulance take Douglas to the hospital. She hoped, and for the first time in a long time prayed, that he would be OK. She would take a ride up in the sunshine to the hospital later to see him. God knows, she needed it.

The railway line was still closed off, and the barriers remained down. If people wanted to cross, they would have to use the Stocks Lane crossing until Sergeant Frisk gave the OK. Thankfully for Frisk, the area would not be sealed off and treated as a crime scene, but rather for what it was: the scene of a terrible accident. Accordingly, it just needed to be cleaned up and returned as quickly as possible to its original state, so that it could be re-opened to the rail traffic temporarily disrupted by what had happened. For now though, the slick red blood that had pumped from Douglas's severed legs cast a glossy sheen over the level crossing, the blood diluted by the rain that had fallen so suddenly.

Breathing the sweet summer air deeply into her lungs, and with her leather waistcoat slung over her shoulder, Reverend Bowen leant against the barriers of the deserted level crossing. Dan Fowler was up in the signal box on the phone. Sergeant Frisk, on her advice, had gone to attend to business elsewhere in the village.

She realised suddenly that Moses had been sat the whole time, as quiet as a mouse, on the rear seat of her trike: a spectator to all the events that had taken place here. She called him over to her, the small King Charles spaniel quickly scampering down from his elevated position on the leather bench seat, and trotting towards the smiling vicar.

Mild panic rippled through her as Moses walked straight past her, scampering through the barrier's metal wires and onto the railway line towards the slick sheen of glistening blood that covered part of the crossing. She watched in amazement as a strip of bone-dry concrete opened up before him like a runway, and Moses crossed dry-pawed to the opposite side, settling down in the exact spot where just a short while ago the figure of Alice Blouse had been standing in the sunshine holding the Mr Bump jumper.

Sergeant Frisk had been to the Blouse household several times over the past few days, banging on the front door of the quiet, seemingly deserted bungalow on Pugsden Lane, looking for Alice Blouse. This afternoon, though, following the rather cryptic information given him by Reverend Bowen shortly after Douglas had been taken to hospital, he was taking a different approach.

He shoulder-barged the back door, gaining entry by force, and was immediately struck by the faint but sickly sweet smell that every police officer knows and dreads. The smell was made worse by the summer heat.

The house had been in complete darkness day and night since the time Douglas had begun his violent spree around the village, and now, as he vainly flicked light switches on and off, Frisk was beginning to understand why.

Frisk walked down the silent hallway towards the master bedroom. The door was standing slightly ajar and Frisk could see that the room was in darkness, looking like the entrance to a cave. He hesitated before softly pushing the door open. In the eerie dark he could make out the shape of a person lying in the bed. The curtains were fully closed and the room was in near darkness save for the light now coming in through the bedroom doorway. The sweet and sickly smell was stronger in the hot and stuffy confines of the bedroom, and so Frisk walked over to the bay window, opening a window to allow in some fresh air. He also opened the curtains just enough to shed some light on the woman lying peacefully and serene under her duvet. Alice Blouse looked just as if she was sleeping, only Frisk knew that she wasn't. Alice was dead, and in the light of day he could see now that her left eye was slightly open.

Gently pulling back the duvet, he could see that she was fully clothed, wearing blue jeans and a faded Boomtown Rats T-shirt. Her auburn hair hanging loosely over her thin shoulders and upper arms. It was clear she had not died in her bed. She had been placed there.

'She's tired, and she's gone. I don't know where.'

Poor bastard, Frisk thought, feeling for the second time that day a deep sympathy for Douglas.

Frisk gave Alice a cursory examination, holding one cold, clammy hand up to the daylight streaming in through the open curtains, and feeling for a pulse he knew would not be there. He noticed a scorched, blackened discolouration to her right hand. He gently placed it back on her chest before trying the light switches in the bedroom. Nothing happened.

A box of Propranolol tablets sat on top of a small bedside table. It was an anti-anxiety drug he had once been prescribed himself. The box looked new and there were only three pills popped from the two blister packs within.

Frisk noticed a pair of framed photographs standing at opposite ends of a dressing table by the bedroom's bay window, and opened the curtains a touch more to allow himself to see a little better. He recognised the first one instantly as a young, fresh-faced Douglas, grinning in his school uniform; probably his first one taken at secondary school. The other photo was of a good-looking young man, probably in his early twenties with black, spiky hair. Frisk had a feeling he might be a pop star. Possibly Scottish.

Not wishing to disturb the scene any more than necessary, he closed the curtains, pulled the duvet back up to Alice's chin and exited the room, leaving her in peace.

Standing in the hallway, Frisk saw a tangled coil of extension cables leading from the kitchen towards the front door. He followed them to where, beneath some free newspapers and unopened post, a six-socketed extension head unit sat on the doormat, its multiple plug sockets black and singed. He followed the cables back to the kitchen, to a pair of overloaded sockets. A grubby black halo of soot surrounded them. He gave a heavy hearted sigh, thinking of Alice's burnt and blackened hand as his mind at last began to put the final missing pieces of the tragic jigsaw puzzle of the past few days together.

Frisk reached for the small radio attached to his shoulder, about to call in his grim discovery, when a loud crackling male voice came from it, making him jump in the eerie silence of the not quite deserted bungalow.

'Control to Sergeant Frisk, over,' came the voice.

'Sergeant Frisk to control, receiving, go ahead, over.'

'Message from your wife, sir, received at the station. She said she'd like you to call her at home when you get this message, over.'

He stood motionless, holding the radio to his mouth, and was silent for a second or two as relief washed over him. Standing in the Blouses' kitchen, Frisk smiled, realising almost immediately that he didn't even care what Jenny had to say by means of an explanation. He'd come to realise just how much he needed her, and how much he loved her, and he was glad that she and Katie had not been around to see what had happened at the fete. He was not proud of his part in it all; he was just thankful that his daughter had been spared the psychological scars of witnessing the infliction of his young constable's very real ones.

He radioed back, assuring control he would phone her as soon as he got back to the station. He then relayed the details of his present location.

Frisk needed some air. He stepped back out into the glorious late afternoon sunshine, standing on the path of the Blouses' front garden. The smell of rain was still sweet and fresh in the air.

He looked over at the shabby caravan that sat forlornly on the driveway next to the Ford Orion. Frisk thought of the three little pinpricks on Douglas's bum: Orion's belt. He couldn't help but have a little laugh at that. He looked again at the caravan, the Marauder 500. Bully's star prize. He thought about what the dilapidated caravan represented in the unfortunate young life of Douglas Blouse.

Frisk thought about his wife and child, wanting nothing more than for them to enjoy a happy, stable family life together.

Through the hole in his trousers a soft breeze fluttered against the exposed flesh of his inner thigh. He smiled, standing in the sunshine, thinking that he might even ask his wife to teach him how to sew.

Epilogue

Like every other passenger aboard the 14.08 Swansea to London Paddington service, the man sitting towards the rear of the train in coach F, seat 34, now sat quietly, staring out the window and awaiting further instruction. There had been no meaningful update other than essentially 'we are still stuck' following the initial announcements just over an hour ago of an 'incident'. It was this 'incident' that had forced the train to come to a shuddering halt only a mile or so outside of Didcot Parkway, where the passenger, to his frustration, wanted to get off.

'Bloody typical issenit,' he muttered to himself in his pseudo Welsh accent.

Despite telling himself he would not drink, and that it would be advisable to keep a clear head given the explaining he knew he would have to do, two empty cans of McEwan's Export sat on the drop-down table in front of him. The delay and the nerves of exactly what he was going to say to them had put paid to the idea of facing them completely sober, and he had taken refuge in the red and black cans. He couldn't shake his concern either that the 'incident', it seemed, had happened just as they were passing through his old village, fuelling his anxiety. Now, as he sat looking out at the familiar landmark of Didcot power station, he even considered making the duo of cans into a trio.

Just as he rose to make his way back to the buffet car, the train jerked forward, causing him to put his hand out and steady himself on the seat in front. Slowly the train began to move again. Two minutes later it pulled into Didcot Parkway.

Walking down the centre aisle of the carriage, holding the black and red sports bag that contained his meagre belongings, he made his way towards the train door. An hour and fifteen minutes late, the train had finally come to a stop at his intended destination.

The man pulled down the door's sliding window, gripped the metal handle on the outside of the Intercity 125 and swung the door open.

In the warm, late afternoon sunshine, Bertie Blouse stepped from the train and onto the platform.

DOUGLAS BLOUSE WILL RETURN
in
"THE FEET OF DOUGLAS BLOUSE"

Acknowledgements

Thank you to everyone who has helped, encouraged and endured me over the past two and a half years.

Special thanks go to Jason Cripps for helping with the cover design and layout. To Neil Frame for the photos. To Cherry Mosteshar for her editing skills (we got there in the end!) And to Nigel Mitchell and his team at Biddles Books.

Lastly, thank you to the people of Steventon. Past, present and future. Here's to you all! … COME ON STIVVY!!!